TYRTLE ISLAND

BOO AND THE BULLKATS

DENNY B. MOORE

TYRTLE ISLAND

BOO AND THE BULLKATS

Tyrtle Island: Boo and the Bullkats

BY

DENNY B. MOORE

Cover Art & Illustrations by Alfredo Rodriguez

tyrtle

Tyrtle Island: Boo and the Bullkats

Published by

TYRTLE ISLAND
Press

Burlington, WA

www.tyrtleisland.com

Kindle ISBN: 978-1-7364579-4-8
ePub ISBN: 978-1-7364579-3-1
Paperback ISBN: 978-1-7364579-1-7
Hardcover ISBN: 978-1-7364579-2-4

Foreword

My son was very young when he first told me about his dream. He was always full of life, laughter, and imagination. It was his imagination that was the spark that brought this amazing story to life.

Like a roaring fire, some dreams begin with just a tiny spark!

"...stand still, and consider the wondrous works of God,"
Job 37:14

Acknowledgments

Most achievements in life can only be accomplished through the encouragement and kind support from family and friends. These special people somehow find the time in their busy schedules to lend a helping hand by sharing their special gifts and suggesting words of literary and creative wisdom.

The spark for this story began long ago and slowly came to life after many years of thought and more than a few conversations in my head, and occasionally with other people. The simple truth is that this story would not exist without the creative and skillful contributions of so many people.

I would like to begin by thanking my wife, Tammy, for her unending patience. Your husband, children and grandchildren know that you are a precious gem indeed.

Proofreading was a much bigger challenge than anticipated. Randy and Lisa, thank you for enduring all the long conversations and debates on the phone.

Thanks so very much to Freddie, Toni, and Aiden for being the first to read this story. Your positive contributions and creative criticism were a tremendous help in making this story come to life.

Like many talents in life, being a brilliant artist is a gift from our Creator. Thanks to Alfredo Rodriguez for sharing his gift and making the characters and creatures of Tyrtle Island come alive through his amazing illustrations.

I would love to thank all my grandchildren for the joy they bring to life and especially Natia and Mathis for making your family laugh and for allowing me to share some of that humor in this story.

Table of Contents

Tyrtle Island: Modern Day Map 7

Chapter One: Kats Caves 9

Tyrtle Island: Dream Map 21

Chapter Two: Best Day Ever.......................................23

Chapter Three: Professor Katnip's Warning 31

Chapter Four: Honey Bees and H-Bees 44

Chapter Five: Do You Believe?...................................53

Chapter Six: An Unexpected Find 61

Chapter Seven: Belly Bird Battle................................70

Chapter Eight: Pee-Wee Poppers and Big-Toed Buggers 82

Chapter Nine: Rainbows to the Rainforest 94

Chapter Ten: Holy Smoking Cat-Roll 107

Chapter Eleven: Walkabout Wilderness........................130

Chapter Twelve: Hidden Paradise 149

Chapter Thirteen: Blast from the Past..........................171

Chapter Fourteen: The Ride of Your Life!.....................199

Chapter Fifteen: Zooming and Ziplines 225

Chapter Sixteen: Up in Smoke 238

Chapter Seventeen: Hidden Secrets 249

Chapter Eighteen: Recoil Oil 257

Chapter Nineteen: Tyrtle Tunnel 271

Chapter Twenty: The Journey Home.............................293

Tyrtle Island: Land Descriptions *303*

Tyrtle Island: Characters..*304*

Tyrtle Island: Creatures *306*

Tyrtle Island: Places and Points of Interest *311*

Tyrtle Island: Plants and Food..*314*

Tyrtle Island: Words and Phrases..*316*

tyrtle

TYRTLE ISLAND: MODERN DAY MAP

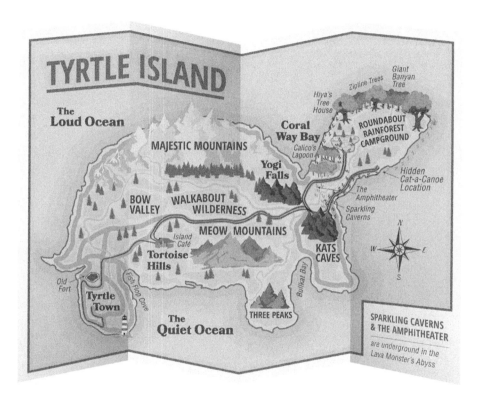

turtle

CHAPTER ONE: KATS CAVES

Jᴇssᴇ Qᴜɪɴɴ ᴛᴏᴏᴋ ᴏɴᴇ ғᴏᴏᴛ out of the salty blue water and carefully watched where he placed his toes on the edge of the black lava rocks surrounding the cove.

"Just another day in paradise," he thought out loud, his eyes slowly taking in the breathtaking surroundings.

Paradise was not just a cliché Jesse used to describe his island. Tyrtle Island really was a paradise full of turquoise-blue lagoons, lush green rainforests, and enchanted waterfalls. This wonderland is surrounded by colorful coral reefs, golden sandy beaches and of course, sea turtles. All this magic added up to one thing in Jesse's mind: one big adventure.

Sunday was Jesse's favorite day of the week. He always felt restless the night before as his heart raced with excitement, anticipating the next day's big adventure with Uncle Tinman. Jesse's cat and best furry friend named Boo always accompanied him and his uncle on their adventures. Tinman, as Jesse called him, was the quintessential cool uncle. Jesse thought of him as a kind of real-life superhero. Well, a superhero who also happened to have a few mortal flaws.

In the short fifteen years of Jesse's delightful life he had learned many valuable life lessons from Tinman. Jesse jokingly referred to them as "Tinman's Tips." Tinman would often say: "Always remember that life is one big adventure and it's up to you to choose how you're going to live it." Tinman was also fond of sharing some of his opinions, such as "Believe me, canned ham is actually good for you." Jesse loved his uncle but didn't necessarily agree with all of his tips or opinions, for that matter.

Tyrtle Island provided a never-ending playground full of adventures just waiting for Jesse and Tinman to experience. Today's big adventure was no exception.

"I'm growing old over here," said Tinman, waiting near the opening of Kats Caves. "Remember we have to get in and out of there before the tide comes back in."

Jesse's eyes carefully followed the shoreline, looking around at the giant lava rocks lined up like ancient warriors ready to defend their island. The rugged black rocks quietly slipped down under the sparkling emerald waters and into the unending ocean. He spotted a green sea turtle with a magnificent weathered green and gold-flaked shell propelling itself effortlessly through the water.

"Keep calm and Tyrtle on," said Jesse, reciting the island mantra quietly under his breath.

He always felt something special inside when he saw one of his favorite creatures. Sea turtles were definitely at the top of his list.

Jesse loved turtles and loved the fact that he actually lived on an island named Tyrtle Island. Tyrtles, as the Islanders affectionately call themselves, describe their island as a playground full of every awe-inspiring wonder ever created by God. When the inhabitants of Tyrtle Island first reached these golden beaches, they encountered hundreds of sea turtles paddling around the island. The turtle symbolized "the spirit of love in motion" for the Islanders. They wanted to emulate that same spirit so they have referred to themselves as Tyrtles ever since. The Islanders know that the word Tyrtle is not beautiful because of how it sounds, it's beautiful because of what it means.

Jesse was caught up in his daydream and hypnotized by the beauty of the island surrounding him. Tinman was growing impatient, knowing they had to get moving soon. He opened the cooler, grabbed the biggest, stinkiest fish by the tail, and sent it sailing over the sand in Jesse's direction.

"Jesse, look out!" shouted Tinman, laughing as the big slippery fish grazed Jesse's cheek.

"That's just great. Boo, you're my witness. Tinman just tried to take me out with a big, stinky fish," exclaimed Jesse, wiping his face off.

"I had to snap you out of your daydream," said Tinman. "Boo's over here with me. Put that smelly fish in the cooler and give Boo a belly rub. Let's get going."

You can never have enough belly rubs, thought Boo, hopping over the rocks toward Jesse.

Through the years Jesse and Tinman had been fishing at just about every honey hole around the island. Tyrtle Island is surrounded by magical colorful reefs swarming with big fish, little fish, beautiful fish, ugly fish and, best of all, the rainbow fish.

"There are plenty of fish in the ocean," as one old saying goes, but the Islanders, including Jesse and Tinman, didn't eat the rainbow fish. The rainbow of colors represented by the colorful fish also represented the spirit of Tyrtle Island.

"There you are, big guy," said Jesse, reaching down to catch Boo as his big cat jumped into his arms. "I think you've been hangin' around some bad company." Jesse ran his fingers along Boo's long, soft, tiger-like tail and over his big orange paws.

"I might smell a little like fish, but I'm not so bad. Am I, Boo?" said Tinman. "I think he kind of likes being around me."

Don't flatter yourself, thought Boo. *It's mostly the fish smell.*

"I think it's because you smell like fish," replied Jesse, smiling at Boo.

Great minds think alike. I love fish, thought Boo, running his tongue around his mouth.

"Maybe it's more about the free food he gets when he's around me," said Tinman, sniffing his shirt.

Jesse and Boo were inseparable. Cats are generally seen as curious creatures, and Boo was no exception; however, he did have a couple of very unusual cat characteristics. Most felines have a tendency to roam around freely and show a distinct distaste for water. Boo always stayed in the same place where Jesse left him and, most of the time, didn't mind getting wet. Despite these unusual cat characteristics, Jesse never took Boo into the caves with them. He wasn't about to take a chance on Boo getting lost in the unending maze of tunnels in Kats Caves.

"I hate to keep repeating myself," said Tinman, "but if we don't hurry up and get in that cave, we might not get back out."

Chapter One

Jesse gave Boo's big white belly another quick rub and slammed the door to Tinman's Jeep, shutting Boo safely inside. He swiftly followed his uncle across the sand and rocks toward the opening of the cave.

Boo's wild blue eyes watched Jesse as he walked sure-footed toward the opening of that crazy-looking cave and thought to himself, *All I know is that I was meant to be his cat.* He quickly got comfortable, settling in for a short catnap on the shady seat of the Jeep. He loved the feeling of the cool island breeze brushing up against his fur.

The golden sand led Jesse and Tinman to the entrance of one of the many small openings dotted along the shoreline which, together, were known as Kats Caves. Jesse and Tinman could feel the jagged rocks under their shoes as they climbed past the black rocks that looked like rotten teeth surrounding the mouth of the cave. The cave crabs swiftly danced their way deeper into the darkness and disappeared as Jesse and Tinman quickly stepped into the mouth of the cave. Their shadows faded into the cavern walls as they stepped over the small bits of debris left behind by others who had previously dared to enter the lava monster's mouth.

Jesse and Tinman were no strangers to Kats Caves. The trailblazers had spent many hours exploring the never-ending underground passageways that wormed their way under Tyrtle Island.

Jesse imagined Kats Caves as a living lava monster whose throat led the way to a belly full of steaming, erupting fluids, and whose body sprawled into the unknown darkness. The limbs of the monster crept slowly into a plethora of dark tunnels and underwater channels. The blood-like fluids echoed through the small caverns as it dripped out of the bleeding, fissure-like veins. The endless maze of lava tubes snaked their way through the mountains and deeper into the earth, eventually disappearing into a black abyss.

Jesse threw his arms up, almost tripping over an empty can of ham. "Ouch! I hate canned ham!" He accidentally kicked the can toward the wall of the cave and stopped for a few seconds, listening to the clanking of the can falling deep into the cavern.

"Canned ham? Where? I love canned ham," joked Tinman, licking his lips and pretending to look around on the ground for another can of his favorite snack.

Jesse looked at Tinman in the dim light and said pointedly, "I hope that wasn't your can."

"You know better than that," said Tinman.

Jesse and Tinman headed deeper into the cave as the lights mounted on their foreheads exposed the wet black walls that reminded Jesse of burnt flesh. Not that he had actually ever seen burnt flesh, but he imagined that it might look something like these cave walls. The unsettling sounds and the earthy smell of the caves and caverns were familiar to Jesse and his uncle. This part of the underground island maze would most likely bring no surprises. Although the adventure that Tinman had planned for today would take them deeper than they had ever been into the unknown depths of Tyrtle Island.

On the way through the tunnels and caverns they encountered the usual critters such as bats, rats, and stray cats. None of these animals made them feel uneasy since they had bravely entered the mouth of the lava monster many times before. Jesse did take notice of one very odd-looking feral cat that was carrying around a shell-shaped cover which it looked like the poor creature was using for his home.

"That's a first," said Jesse. "I've never seen a cat do that before."

Tinman slid his swimming goggles over his eyes. "Ready to get a little wet?"

"Don't forget to turn your light back on before you get in the water," said Jesse jokingly, knowing he was the one who usually forgot.

"I've been crawling through these caves since before you were crawling in diapers," said Tinman. "Come to think of it, I'm pretty sure I actually changed your diapers."

"On that note…" said Jesse, stepping into the murky water and disappearing quietly into the tunnel.

Not surprisingly, Jesse forgot to turn on his light. Tinman was right behind him with his light shining brightly through the tunnel. It was a quick and easy swim through the watery passage into the next cavern.

This cavern was one of Jesse's favorites. There were a few old animal bones lying around on the cavern floor that Jesse imagined were dinosaur fossils. There were also incredibly huge stalagmite daggers sticking up all across the cavern floor and stalactites hanging down from the black rocks above. The natural formations looked just like huge, dangling spider legs.

The two cave explorers swam through several more water-filled tunnels and decided to take a short break before venturing into unknown territory. Tinman had been to this part of the caves before but had never ventured any deeper into the next caverns and tunnels.

Tinman sat down to enjoy a quick snack in the dim light flickering off the cavern walls. Jesse glanced over in disgust at Tinman's choice of snack, which resembled some kind of unrecognizable canned meat.

"Not canned ham," said Jesse, repulsed.

Jesse walked past and wandered around the cavern, disappearing around the corner into the darkness.

Tinman heard Jesse yell from a distance but couldn't quite make out the echoing words. He licked his fingers and ambled over toward where the voice came out of the darkness.

Just as he rounded the corner, Jesse yelled at the top of his lungs into Tinman's ear, "What's down this big hole?"

"Probably nothing!" shouted Tinman, plugging his ear with his finger and shaking his head.

Jesse picked up a rather large lava rock and tossed it into the big black hole. Leaning over the hole, they both listened quietly, waiting to hear any type of sound coming back up out of the darkness. Finally, after a few seconds, they heard the faint sound of the rock hitting the bottom of the abyss.

"See?... Nothing. Just another one of many deep, deep holes," said Tinman, confidently raising his hands up in the air.

Convinced, they both turned to walk away, but Tinman hesitated and turned his ear back toward the hole. He could hear what sounded like a faint windstorm gathering deep down inside the hole.

Whoosh! Whoosh! The faint sound in the distance quickly grew louder, faster, and closer. Whoosh! Whoosh! Whoosh! After a few more seconds, the sound became almost deafening.

Tinman and Jesse backed away from the open hole and retreated quickly to the other side of the cavern. With their arms stretched out in front of them, they braced themselves from crashing into the jagged wall. Turning around frantically, they were astounded by the creature that came flying out of the hole with its giant wings, spread wide, and its big red eyes, heading directly toward them.

"It's a dragon!" screamed Tinman in a high-pitched voice.

Tinman's mouth and eyes stretched wide-open, in awe of what flew right in front of them. Jesse's eyes followed the flying creature's every move. The expression on his face was somewhere between amazement and terror.

Jesse caught a glimpse of Tinman's wide-eyed stare as the unidentified flying creature smoothly flapped its powerful wings and sailed right past them. The creature's wings seemed to move in slow motion right before their eyes. Before they could close their mouths, the creature flew out through the tunnel into the next dark cavern. The thunderous sound of the flapping wings faded just as quickly as the creature disappeared into the darkness.

"Unbelievable!" shouted Tinman, slapping Jesse on the back. "That was incredible. Was that a dragon?"

"I'm pretty sure that was a really, really big owl," said Jesse, grinning.

Tinman unbuttoned the top of his shirt, took his water bottle out, and splashed some water on his face.

"You don't think that was a dragon?" asked Tinman, wiping the water off his forehead.

"Nope," replied Jesse with a big grin. "I hope that's not the new tunnel you're planning on exploring." Jesse pointed toward the hole in the ground. "Because I don't really want to be down there when that dragon decides to come back home."

Tinman smiled at Jesse. "Come on, you have to admit it: you thought it was a dragon at first too."

"Nope, never thought that," said Jesse, smirking.

Tinman and Jesse gathered their gear. Tinman walked over to the dark corner where the owl had flown out of the hole.

"I thought you said that wasn't the hole," said Jesse curiously.

Tinman waved at him. "It's not. Just follow me."

They stepped cautiously, looking into the owl's hole as they passed by, and walked deeper into the cavern.

"Watch your head on the stalactites in this area. The passageway gets pretty narrow, and the ceiling closes in on you," said Tinman, running his fingers along the low, rocky ceiling.

Jesse could see the end of the wall with his headlamp. "It's a dead end."

"Look up a few feet on the cavern wall," said Tinman. "This is as far as I've ever explored in this part of the caves."

After looking at each other without saying a word, they stepped carefully up onto the lava rocks. They pulled themselves up just far enough that they could get their lights shining through the mysterious cavern opening above. They stood there for a few more minutes in silence, trying to focus on the enormous cavern that opened up before them. The headlamps and flashlights were growing dimmer, and they couldn't quite tell where the cavern walls stopped and started in the darkness.

"What was that? I just thought I saw something," whispered Jesse. "Turn the light off."

They were engulfed in total blackness and complete silence except for the sound of their own breathing and the faint sound of water dripping off in the distance. Jesse imagined they were trapped inside the monster's throat, and the sound they heard was really the sound of blood dripping out of the lava monster's veins. An eerie feeling engulfed both of them as they stared into the utter darkness.

"You see it?" whispered Jesse. "Tinman, you there?"

"I see all the sparkles and glitter around the cavern if that's what you're asking," muttered Tinman.

"What? No, the things glowing over by the wall," said Jesse, his voice wobbling as he pointed across the cavern in the dark.

A pair of creepy yellow eyes glowed from out of the darkness across the cavern. Jesse and Tinman stared at the dead-still eyes for a few more seconds. The creature began to move slowly in their direction.

Jesse quickly flicked on his headlamp. The creature's cat eyes were the color of rotting yellow squash, and bone-white horns protruded from each pointed ear. The cat crept slowly away from the cavern wall and, like a ghost, floated closer to them. Its face disfigured with scars and patches of bare skin exposed on its mangy body. The creature moved as if the fleshly bones were disjointed. The cat's long black tail flicked back and forth like a whip through the air. Jesse and Tinman heard the scraping of its sharp claws against the rock. They could feel the eerie rumbling sound, from deep within the creature's bowels, penetrate the air when it exited through the cat's tiny sharp teeth and echoed around the cavern walls.

"A bullkat," whispered Tinman. "Quietly, turn, jump, and run as fast as you can for the water."

Without saying another word and with their hearts thumping out of their chests, they both turned and leaped down off the cavern ledge. They landed with their feet sliding out from under them and skidded along the wet sandy floor. Ducking their heads, they both sprinted like they were running for a touchdown, barely missing the sharp, pointed tips of the stalactites hanging down from the ceiling. Their hands scraped along the rough, cold lava walls as they made a beeline straight for the water tunnel.

"Dragon's hole!" shouted Tinman, warning Jesse as he ran past the owl's hole.

Tinman knew they had to make it to the water to escape. Odds were that, like most cats, bullkats didn't much care for the water. He also knew bullkats didn't like the sunlight, but the two of them still had to make it out of the darkness of the cave and into the sunlight on the beach.

They could hear the scraping of the bullkat's deadly claws against the rocks. The terrifying rumbling of the bullkat's growling pierced their ears as he quickly closed in behind them.

Tinman leaped into the water, creating a huge splash as he performed a perfect belly flop, with Jesse a heartbeat behind him. Jesse hesitated for a fraction of a second to keep from jumping on Tinman's back. It seemed like an eternity. That split-second decision was just enough time to allow the bullkat's claw to scrape the back of his heel just before he hit the water. In an instant, they both ducked under the water and disappeared into the safety of the dark tunnel.

Seconds later, and out of breath, they exploded out from under the murky water. Their adrenaline was pumping as they jumped and swam through the system of caverns and tunnels at Olympic speed, without uttering a single word.

The tide was nearly at the cave opening as they stumbled into the sunlight, exhausted and out of breath. Their hearts raced, pumping blood through their bodies. They both wanted to jump out of their skin, feeling the rush of having just escaped the close call with the bullkat unharmed. Tinman and Jesse just smiled at each other as they tried to calm down and catch their breath.

Jesse finally broke the silence, saying, "Keep calm and Tyrtle on."

"You can say that again," said Tinman, leaning over with his hands on his thighs, breathing heavily.

After catching his breath, Jesse walked over to the Jeep where he had left Boo earlier that morning. He saw that his big orange cat with black and brown stripes was still sitting in the seat where he had left him.

"I just love this cat," said Jesse, picking Boo up out of the seat. "You are amazing."

Boo slowly winked at Jesse and purred loudly as he rubbed his head against Jesse's cheek.

"Speaking of cats, we gotta go back in there," said Tinman, looking over at Jesse.

"Seriously?" asked Jesse, wiping the sweat off his worried face.

"Seriously. I left a half-eaten can of ham in there," laughed Tinman, pointing toward the cave.

"Pretty sure your can of ham is safe. Bullkats won't even touch that stuff," said Jesse. "You go ahead. I think I'll wait here with Boo."

He brought Boo close to his chest and rubbed his forehead along the top of Boo's soft furry head.

"Got scared by the big old owl, did ya?" said Tinman. "I still think it would've been so cool if it had actually been a dragon."

"A dragon… he really thought it was a dragon," said Jesse, looking at Boo and chuckling quietly to himself.

Dragons sound scary, thought Boo. *I think I'll stick with fish.*

From the windward side of the island Jesse and Tinman drove back home to Tyrtle Town through the lush green mountainsides of Bow Valley. The fresh island air and long winding road provided the perfect atmosphere for both of them to unwind in a daydreaming state of mind. They were mesmerized by the glimpses of golden beaches and enchanted rainforest-covered mountains along the way. Neither one of them was ready to talk about the bullkat encounter. Jesse didn't mention to Tinman that the bullkat brushed his heel with its claw. He didn't want to worry his uncle. He didn't even want to think about the possibility of Tinman reconsidering taking him on future adventures because they were a little risky. It had been a very long time since Tinman had encountered a bullkat. In fact, he didn't give them much thought anymore because he believed the dangerous creatures to be extinct. It was a wake-up call for both of them and the beginning of a great adventure.

Jesse arrived home, and his mom greeted him as usual at the back screen door.

"What fun adventure did Tinman take you on today?" she asked, giving him a big hug and a kiss on the forehead.

"Nothing too exciting," said Jesse. "We went on another hike through the caves and saw some funny-looking cats."

Jesse limped past his mom, through the kitchen, and into his bedroom.

"Why are you limping?" she asked, following him into his room.

"It's nothing," said Jesse, expressionless. "I just scraped my heel."

"Make sure to put ointment on it," said his mom. "Don't need it gettin' infected."

Jesse lay back on his bed, and for reasons unknown to him, he started thinking about that goofy-looking feral cat that was carrying his shell-shaped house on his back. He chuckled to himself and smiled thinking about that strange cat.

He went to bed that night without telling his mom everything that happened in the caves. He didn't want to worry her about the bullkats, at least not yet. Jesse crawled into bed exhausted, with Boo curled up in his usual spot at the foot of the bed.

"Bullkats," he mumbled, just before he closed his eyes and drifted off to sleep.

Chapter One

Boo slowly moved up along the blanket covering Jesse's body. He crept up to Jesse's face, stopping just short of touching him nose to nose. Boo looked hypnotized as he stared right through Jesse's closed eyes.

Jesse's mind slowly wandered into a deep sleep, and he began to dream. An image of hot, flowing lava flashed through his mind. His body began to sweat. His imagination had ventured past the ordinary world of dreams. Jesse's mind had traveled into the imaginative world of island dreams.

TYRTLE ISLAND: DREAM MAP

tyrtle

CHAPTER TWO: BEST DAY EVER

Jesse was amazed when he opened his big blue eyes and found himself looking into an exotic new world. His mind had passed through the island dream tunnel, and amazingly, he began to see everything before him through the eyes of a cat. Not just any ordinary cat, though—he was looking through the eyes of Boo.

"Boo!" shouted Roxy Roo. "Boo! Look out behind you!"

Her beautiful chocolate-brown feline body came to an abrupt halt on top of the wall with her long fluffy tail pointing straight up behind her.

"Come on, Roxy Roo. I know that trick," said Boo confidently.

He didn't even break his stride. Boo continued at a rapid pace, placing his big orange paws one in front of the other.

Roxy Roo grinned at the big tiger-like cat walking a few feet in front of her through the darkness.

Boo turned around, calmly looking at her with his big eyes and tilting his head to one side.

"Quit mousin' around. We're in a hurry," said Boo with a roguish smile.

Boo's ears faced forward as he relaxed his long whiskers, looking into Roxy Roo's pretty face. Silently they tiptoed into the night, prowling along the top of the wall through the shadows of the giant trees that rose high above Tyrtle Island. The glow from their eyes could be seen from the old speckled walls of the Pouncing Place just a short distance away.

The feline friends picked up their pace and began to move swiftly, like two panthers, keeping a watchful eye as the stones weaved a path through the center of Treetop Woods. Roxy Roo moved along quietly, staying a few steps behind Boo. Her pace began to slow as her big brown eyes caught the movement of a shadow stretching into the night along the wall.

"Boo, w-watch—" yelled Roxy Roo, stopping dead in her tracks.

Before she could get the words out of her mouth and beyond her whiskers, she watched as Boo was knocked off the wall and up into the air by a big gray furball.

Boo's body flipped up into the air, and his long orange tail followed obediently behind him. Instinctively, he performed a complete flip in the air and landed perfectly with all four of his big paws on the ground and his body spread out like a parachute. The black and brown stripes on his fur puffed up and claws flared out as he started to charge at the unknown attacker.

Ready to pounce on his opponent, Boo came to a sliding halt. To his surprise, it was Roxy Roo and Chops that he saw rolling from side to side between the bushes. He instinctively stood there, frozen in a defensive position, watching his friends lying on their backs. They were holding their bellies and meowing uncontrollably.

"I should have known," said Boo, trying to act cool and calm.

Breathing heavily, he trotted closer to them with his tail extended straight out.

Chops laughed hysterically for a few more minutes and was unable to speak. He finally calmed down and managed to spit the words out of his mouth.

"You—" Chops held his paws over his stomach to keep from laughing. "You should have seen the look on your face," he finally blurted out. "You'd thunk you saw a bullkat."

Chops continued his loud, riveting laugh. He fully enjoyed the experience when he was able to pull off any kind of prank on Boo.

"It's not thunk, it's think, and that's one thing you always have a hard time doing," said Boo, smirking and doing his best to hold back his laughter.

Roxy Roo and Chops were still wheezing from laughter while Boo smiled and continued to declare to his friends, "Besides, we all know that if we actually saw a bullkat, you would be the first one to tuck your tail—fat little stubby thing that it is—and run like a big bulldog was chasing you. You know the only thing that we would see would be your fat, furry, feline behind running away in the distance."

Chops smiled at Boo and blurted out, "Ouch! That hurt!"

Boo tried to act serious for a minute and calmly walked closer toward his best friends with his tail straight up in the air, trying his best not to smile.

"It's all fun and games until some fat cat pokes an eye out," said Boo, pointing over at Chops with his claw extended out from his paw.

"Hey, careful who you're callin' a fat cat," said Roxy Roo.

Boo, Roxy Roo, and Chops were all born Meow cats in Treetop Woods on Tyrtle Island. They had always been best friends and dreamed of one day going on a big island adventure. They were ready for something more exciting than running up and down the catwalks and the tall walls inside their home. Up to this point in their short lives, their biggest adventure had been catching delicious fish at Fish Flop Cove. Little did they know that tonight would be the beginning of their first adventure together and of many more big adventures to come.

Unexpectedly, an unknown figure walked out of the dark from along the wall, startling the three friends. Boo didn't recognize the strange-looking tall cat. From out of the shadows, the dark figure slowly moved closer to them.

"Bones… is that you?" asked Roxy Roo nervously. "What a surprise… running into you here so late at night."

Roxy Roo's heart started beating faster and her ears flattened as the cat continued to approach Boo without saying a word. He slowly stretched out his boney gray paw with claws extended out. The sinister-looking cat took his other paw and tipped his black hat as he leaned his lanky body forward toward Boo. They could smell the foul smoke that floated through the air like a fog from the cat-roll sticking out from the side of Bones' crooked mouth.

"Can I help you … with something?" asked Boo reluctantly, extending his paw. "Do you need—"

Bones snapped back his paw in a flash, startling Boo. Boo yanked his paw back quickly and scraped it over one of Bones' long yellow claws. Boo glared at Bones. He had the feeling that the alarming cat had intentionally tried to frighten him.

"Good evening, my dear sweet pets," said Bones in a dead tone of voice.

Roxy Roo scowled at him, but she tried not to sound rattled and asked, "Do you need help with something?"

"It's a very dark evening, isn't it, Boo? Going somewhere tonight in hopes of seeing Professor Katnip?" asked Bones in his monotone voice.

The shifty-eyed cat glanced at the three Meow cats staring back at him.

Boo was hoping to lighten the uneasy conversation and half-jokingly said, "Well, not really. Looks like we got a full moon up there tonight."

Roxy Roo and Chops erupted into forced nervous laughter that quickly faded to silence. There was a sense of uneasiness, and they felt like they could cut through the air with a claw.

Boo paused for a moment, feeling the tension rising. He decided to get right to the point, saying, "How do you know my name and why do you care where we're going?"

"Oh, I know some things. Don't you worry about how," said Bones, grinning.

They all watched as his tongue slipped in and out of his mouth while he switched his cat-roll from one side of his black lips to the other.

"I have to go now, but we have plans for you... Boo," said Bones strangely.

Bones turned like a ghost floating through the air and quietly disappeared back into the darkness. Only the foul scent from the smoke of his cat-roll rising up from the ground lingered in the air.

"Okey-dokey, somebody pull my whiskers. That was just a wee bit weird. Just in case you guys missed it," said Chops. "Think happy thoughts, get a belly free of knots!" he sarcastically sang out.

Boo and Roxy Roo chuckled at Chops, who was always good for a laugh, especially in serious situations. Their smiling faces turned to worried looks as they turned around and faced each other.

"How do you know that... shall I say... really strange cat?" asked Boo, looking at Roxy Roo.

"He's one of the, and I quote, 'good old cats,'" said Roxy Roo. "One of the Meow cat elders told me about him. I really don't know him at all; I just know his name. Who could forget a name like Bones? I also know that some of the elders don't like him very much. It has something to do with what happened between the Meow cats and bullkats a long time ago. That's about all I know."

"Well, we also know one more thing about Bones," said Chops, looking down at the smoking cat-roll with a big, orchestrated grin on his face. "He's a really big litterbug."

The three of them grinned and tried to shake off the awkward encounter. Jumping back up on the wall, they continued toward the gathering place of the Meow cats known as the Pouncing Place.

In the days of old, when the first cats arrived on Tyrtle Island, the felines made their home on the southwest side of the island. That part of the island was filled with magnificent trees, so they decided to call the place they settled Treetop Woods. At the northernmost end of Treetop Woods was a special gathering place called the Pouncing Place. This natural island stronghold was a protective place where all the Meow cats could come together for celebrations and in times of trouble. The colossal natural walls were created out of black and red lava rock that formed a protective circle around the center. The natural castle-like structure had two lava-rock walls that led back to Treetop Woods. The only way a cat could gain entry into the protective structure was to crawl through one of the small openings along the wall. The openings provided just enough space for a normal-sized Meow cat to squeeze through.

Tyrtle Island is home to many extraordinary creatures and is also home to what might be described as some relatively ordinary creatures. The Meow cats would fall into the category of an ordinary island creature, although Meow cats are not necessarily what one would describe as a domesticated cat. Meow cats have very large, strong, and agile bodies. Most Meow cats are very quick with their reflexes and have large paws with retractable claws. They have large heads with big and bright-colored eyes. There is nothing magical about Meow cats. Although they are extraordinary in that they are very creative, most are exceptionally good-natured, and they all love an adventure. Perhaps one of the most unusual traits among Meow cats is that they really don't mind getting wet.

Boo, Roxy Roo, and Chops stopped just short of the wall that surrounded the Pouncing Place. It was already dark, and the protective wall was only illuminated by the light of the full moon.

Chops, who was larger than a normal-sized Meow cat, was contemplating just how he was going to jump up through the narrow opening. This was always a challenge for Chops. Although he acted as if it was the first time he ever had trouble getting his big body through the little opening.

"What do you guys think?" said Chops, jumping up.

"About what?" asked Roxy Roo, playing along.

They knew Chops was just trying to distract them with some small talk.

"Do you know if the rumors about the bullkats are true?" asked Chops, jumping up and down with a slight quiver in his voice.

"I don't know," sighed Boo, looking at Roxy Roo and then back at Chops. "We need to have a talk with Professor Katnip about the bullkats as soon as he gets back from his trip."

Boo was interrupted by Chops, who let out a long, loud grunt. He jumped up again, attempting to get through the opening. They watched patiently as he huffed and puffed, trying to squeeze his thick body through the little opening. Chops' unmatched strength was still not enough for him to pull his white-striped belly through the small hole. It had more to do with his inclination to be a little clumsy and overreact in stressful situations than with a lack of feline strength.

Chops always went first because Boo and Roxy Roo knew that eventually he would need a little help. That help usually came in the form of a big push from behind.

Cats always do what they want to do, when they want to do it, always. Chops was no exception.

Roxy Roo asked Chops playfully, "Need an extra paw?"

"I got it!" snapped Chops, trying to sound confident. "Why do you two always ask me if I need help?"

"We don't actually have to answer that question, do we?" replied Boo.

Chops always insisted he didn't need any help. He pulled and pushed with all his might to force his big furry belly through the hole, trying to prove to his friends he could do it by himself.

Boo and Roxy Roo had been through this a hundred times before and knew he always needed a little help from his friends. They silently gave him a couple of hard pushes. Chops squished through the opening and shot out the other side, making a big thud on the ground below.

Quickly Roxy Roo and Boo leaped up and slipped through the opening and jumped down onto the black and red lava-rock floor.

Chops, still gasping and trying to catch his breath, said, "What took you guys so long?"

Boo rolled his eyes as he looked over at Chops and then looked back at Roxy Roo, who was smiling broadly. He slightly raised his long tail up in the air and turned around a couple times before finding a comfortable place to lie down on the rocks next to the wall. Roxy Roo loved Boo's wild looks, which could be described as a Bengal tiger cub with big blue eyes. His big claws and muscular orange body with its black and brown stripes had always intimidated the other Meow cats. Boo was not a magical cat, but he did have a knack for being able to get out of most any dangerous situation.

Roxy Roo looked at Boo's face, surrounded by his black and white checkered scarf. Boo stared at the wall without blinking for a few minutes. He was in deep thought, and his expression took on a more serious look as his whiskers and ears stood straight out.

"Do you know when Professor Katnip will be back?" said Roxy Roo, like she could read his mind.

Roxy Roo knew her friend very well and, like most good friends, could tell when he was worried. Boo was thinking about when the professor might return, and he was also worried about the return of the bullkats.

Boo thought about what the Meow cat elders had told him about the feared bullkats.

I wonder why nobody has ever mentioned that creepy cat Bones to me. No reason to worry my friends right now, thought Boo. *Yeah, I'll wait for Professor Katnip and see what he's found out.*

Chapter Two

Boo and his friends always tried to end the day with good thoughts.

"Keep calm and Tyrtle on!" sang out Boo, trying to comfort his best friends.

Roxy Roo and Chops knew their friend was an extra special cat.

Roxy Roo and Chops moved closer together, gazing up at the full moon and bright stars shining above them. Chops and Roxy Roo had grown up together, and her cocoa-colored eyes and gentle spirit had always comforted him even though she would occasionally act as though she was the queen cat.

Chops curled up next to her as his eyelids grew heavy thinking about their fishing adventure tomorrow at Fish Flop Cove. Any kind of fish was tempting to Meow cats, but the rainbow-colored fish at the cove were likened to a type of catnip and were simply irresistible.

Chops yawned and let one slip out as he stretched his large back legs and paws. Roxy Roo and Boo looked at each other and laughed out loud. Chops was not the least bit embarrassed because he was completely comfortable with his friends.

Chops cracked a half-smile just before closing his eyes. He was right at home with his friends as he snuggled against their soft fur and slipped into a long catnap, purring away.

"Best day ever," said Boo, slowly winking at Roxy Roo.

turtle

CHAPTER THREE: PROFESSOR KATNIP'S WARNING

Roxy Roo slowly opened her soft eyes, squinting just as the sun was peeking through one of the entryways into the Pouncing Place.

"Chops, get off of me!" shouted Roxy Roo sleepily.

She tried to push his big furry leg off of her, but Chops didn't move a muscle.

"Chops, wake uuup!" she whined, trying to wiggle loose.

Boo got up and gave his big buddy a healthy shove, knocking him off of Roxy Roo.

Chops was startled out of his sleep. He slowly raised his head and said, "Hey, what's the big idea? Can't you see I'm sleeping here?"

"You were squishing me," said Roxy Roo, stretching out her legs and curling her back. "Come on, you guys. I'm hungry. Let's get down to the cove before all the fish are gone."

Chops smiled, and his ears stood at attention. He pointed his tail up in the air as he looked into her furry face and said, "Last one there has to go fish."

The cat race was on, but everyone knew who would be the last one there. It was the perfect island day for fishing. The sun was partially hidden behind the marshmallow clouds floating along through the tropical sky. The sun's rays were already at work warming the shallow waters of Fish Flop Cove. Today was the perfect temperature, and everyone knew the fish would be jumping for joy.

Out jumped the cats, bracing their falls with their padded paws. The felines landed perfectly on the lava rocks outside the fortress stronghold. Boo cautiously scanned up and down the river's edge before running swiftly over the stone bridge that crossed the Rainbow River. He paused briefly to give Chops a chance to catch up. One by one the cats jumped up on the crooked rock wall leading them in the opposite direction from the Pouncing Place. Boo glanced around just before jumping off the wall and stepped quietly through the thick cattail bushes swaying gently in the island breeze.

Fish Flop Cove was hidden by rainbow eucalyptus and mangrove trees. The giant green leaves of the taro plants blanketed the ground around the cove. Boo and his friends were well aware of the risk they were taking every time they went to their favorite fishing hole, but the fish found in the cove were simply irresistible.

Creeping up to the crumbling wooden fence surrounding the cove, Boo's eyes dilated slightly as he carefully looked around, checking for any signs of danger. Something moving in the bushes caught his eye. His sense of smell prompted him to stop just short of the fence, and he stared directly ahead. His ears stood straight up and forward, but he couldn't hear or see anything unusual coming from that direction. They passed through the fence, and all three hesitated as they approached the cove.

"Hold on, something doesn't smell right," whispered Boo, perching up on his strong hind legs.

Boo soft-pawed his way closer to the water as Roxy Roo and Chops slowly retreated back to the fence. Chops' stomach growled loudly as he stood there on all fours, intently watching Boo move closer to the water.

"Was that your belly?" asked Roxy Roo, looking at Chops.

Chops gave her a half-starved, pitiful look. "I'm hungry. My belly is telling me it's time for a delicious fish snack."

"Don't do it, Chops," said Roxy Roo, trying to hold him back by yanking on his tail.

Cats always do what they want to do when they want to do it, always. Chops was hungry, and he wasn't waiting any longer. Danger or no danger, his stomach was telling him it was time to eat, and the delicious fish were a made-to-order dish.

Chops quickly but quietly crept up to the edge of the dark blue water in an area just beneath a wooden pier that had fallen halfway into the water. He peered into the water, which was dotted with a palette full of colorful water lilies. He stared for a few seconds, seeing nothing but the reflection of his big green eyes looking right back at him. In a flash, a big, colorful fish popped up out of the dark water and flipped its tail, smacking him right across the face. Chops fell over backwards, disappointed as the fish escaped back below the water.

Boo laughed, looking at Roxy Roo, and walked toward Chops. "That's the best illustration of why they call this place Fish Flop Cove that I've ever seen."

They had all but forgotten about the possibility of any danger. The three friends stood at the water's edge and watched with wet whiskers as the rainbow fish steadily sacrificed themselves by flopping right into their willing paws. It was nothing new for Boo to share his food with Chops. In some respects, Chops was almost like having a little brother. He didn't mind sharing since Chops' feline reflexes were on the slower side, especially when it came to catching fish.

After feeding Chops a couple dozen fish, Boo exchanged perplexed glances with Roxy Roo.

"Good grief, you're not full yet?" Boo asked Chops earnestly.

"Do I look full?" said Chops, a bit of rainbow fish dangling out of his mouth.

Boo and Roxy Roo looked at Chops' big belly. They smiled at each other and shouted, "Yes!"

All three of them finally filled their bellies with the colorful fish and sat down next to the edge of the cove, ready for a short catnap.

Chops ran his tongue back and forth over his whiskers. "When it comes to fabulous fillets, rainbow fish are pawsitively purrfect," said Chops. "I have to admit those were the best fish I've ever tasted."

"I'm pretty sure I've heard you say something similar to that every time you eat fish," said Boo.

"Yeah, well… that's probably true," said Chops, smacking loudly.

Chops' eyes were feeling heavy as he rubbed his full belly.

After a short catnap, Chops slowly opened his lazy eyes, trying to focus them through the sunlight reflecting off the water. He raised his head and wiped his paw over his eyes. He saw his friends taking a dip in the cool water of the cove. Most cats' dislike of water is widely accepted as fact, but most Meow cats actually delight in getting wet. Boo and Roxy Roo were no exceptions, but when the Creator was handing out that unique Meow cat trait, he must have overlooked Chops. As far as Chops was concerned, cats should only participate in swimming as a spectator sport.

Boo looked across the cove and saw that Chops was finally awake from his catnap. He knew that his buddy didn't like the idea of being left alone at the edge of the water. Boo watched as Chops nervously kept turning his furry body from one side to the other, scanning the area beyond the fence. Boo glanced around and thought he saw something moving slowly through the bushes toward Chops.

Almost at the same time, Boo and Roxy Roo yelled, "Chops, look out! Look behind you!"

Chops turned around with his mouth and eyes wide open. To his surprise he found the funniest-looking creature he had ever seen staring right back at him. Chops was so startled that before he could react, he lost his balance and stumbled, falling face first right into the prickly little creature's back.

Chops slowly bellowed out a loud, painful scream. The scream was followed by what sounded like a long yodel. He then jumped back and, using his tail like a loaded spring, he bounced all over the grassy shore with silver needles sticking out of his fluffy fat cheeks.

The little silver-backed prickly creature jumped backwards into the cattail bushes with only his pudgy pink nose sticking out between the stalks.

Boo and Roxy Roo scrambled as quickly as they could to get out of the water. They ran up to where Chops was screaming and hopping around on his tail. They laughed hysterically as Chops continued to hop around. At the same time, they were frantically trying to pull the needles out of his cheeks as they bounced up and down in rhythm with his body.

"Purr, purr," said Roxy Roo, a Meow cat smile mixed with a look of concern on her face. "Chops, quit hopping around and hold still!"

Chops unconsciously ignored her and continued hopping around. He bellowed out screams until Boo finally was able to tackle him to the ground.

"Chops! Good grief! Hold still!" yelled Boo, trying to hold him down on the ground.

Roxy Roo squeezed between Chops and Boo. She was amazed and very concerned when she realized how many needles were sticking out of Chops' puffy cheeks. For a few minutes they had all but forgotten about the curious creature that was the cause of Chops' pain. Boo and Roxy Roo looked back over toward the bushes to see what the little creature was doing. The little guy had crept out of the bushes with his silver needles on his back still sticking straight up. It was as though the pinpointed daggers were ready to strike again.

The little creature seemed to be amused as he watched the three friends continue to wrestle on the ground.

Boo and Roxy Roo were finally able to get Chops to stop moving around.

"My face is—" groaned Chops, irritated and drawing in a big breath of air. "Ouch, feels like I fell against a cactus."

He let out another shriek, with his eyes popping out in front of his face. "Where is that funny-lookin' little whatever it is?"

Chops continued to let out long, painful moans as Roxy Roo carefully removed the rest of the needles one by one from his aching body.

Boo looked back again in the direction of the little creature. The silver-backed bundle of needles with the pudgy, round pink nose was now standing right behind them.

"What's wrong with you?" Boo asked accusingly. "Why did you stick a bunch of needles in our friend's face?"

Realizing how close they were to the unknown creature, they all stepped cautiously backwards.

"All right, hold onto your bubbles," said the little creature in a very proper and bold tone of voice. "Now, just you wait a minute. Your rather large friend fell directly into me. As for me, it was just instinct. Which can be described as a certain pattern of behavior in response to certain stimuli."

Boo had a weird look on his face as he glanced in the direction of Roxy Roo. He then quickly focused his attention back on the curiously-speaking creature.

"In this case, it was your friend's face falling on me," he said. "When that happens… I can't deny it… you are sure to receive a face full of quills."

Before continuing his speech, the silver-backed creature stood silent for a couple of minutes, intrigued by the three Meow cats looking mystified.

"In addition, I would like to inform you that those little pointy things are not called needles," he said matter-of-factly. "I certainly did not intend to hurt him. To be quite frank, I got scared, and my amazingly-designed body just reacted. There it is. That is the whole, indisputable truth."

He finally finished his long explanation, sounding a little out of breath and relieved.

"Unbelievable… wow… very, very descriptive," said Boo, shaking his head and looking at his friends. "Who are you and more importantly, what are you? A prickly, pink-nosed walking dictionary with what appears to be a tin plate on your tail."

They all three stood there in cool amazement, looking over the creature's features.

"Why don't we try and start again? What's your name?" Roxy Roo asked in a friendly tone. "I'm Roxy Roo."

Before he could answer, Chops interrupted in a painful, purring laugh, "I'll bet it's something like Pinhead or Pincushion."

The little creature leaned toward Chops and proclaimed proudly and loudly, "My name is Silver!" He pointed his curved claw over his shoulder to the silver needles now lying flat on his back and running all the way down to his tin-tipped tail.

Silver started to speak again but was rudely interrupted by Chops. "What are you? Because you're lookin' pretty strange. I know. You remind me of a prickly doormat with four little stubby legs."

Chops panted and laughed loudly and then once more let out a loud, painful groan.

Silver smiled confidently and said, "Well, I assure you that you will not be able to wipe your big hairy paws on me. Not unless you would like more of the same. I'm a porky porcupine."

"I would say you are more like a prickly porcupine. But hey, what do I know," said Chops. "I'm only speaking from experience."

They all looked inquisitively at the big pink nose protruding from the front of Silver's face and the two long, orange-colored front teeth sticking out of his mouth.

"Well, we're all very pleased to make your acquaintance," said Roxy Roo, looking directly at Boo and Chops. "I would like to apologize for my very good friend. Chops is very sorry for falling into your… umm… backside and startling you… and using up some of your beautiful silver quills. Aren't you, Chops?"

Chops was still lying on the ground with his mouth wide open. His face had a look of disbelief as he tried to prepare an answer for Roxy Roo.

"Uhh… sorry, I got nothin'," said Chops.

"Good, it's all settled then. Everyone forgives everyone," said Roxy Roo.

She purposely ignored Chops' response, trying to put an end to the situation.

"I just love a happy ending," said Chops, mumbling under his breath.

"We'd better be heading back to the Pouncing Place," said Boo. "Silver, you're welcome to join us if you promise not to needle us again along the way."

Boo smiled at Silver as he helped Chops get back on his paws again. Chops was a little wobbly and having a difficult time gaining his balance. He seemed disoriented as they brushed the sand and leaves off his gray fur coat. His friends turned him around and pointed him in the direction of the trail leading back to the Pouncing Place.

"Now that I think about it, he could be very helpful with all those doggone needles if we run into trouble heading back to the Pee Pee," Chops whispered painfully to Roxy Roo.

Pee Pee was Chops' silly nickname for the Pouncing Place.

Silver smiled with a sigh of relief, saying, "I shall go with you."

Boo led the way, walking back uphill toward the Pouncing Place. Silver's tin-tipped tail kept clinking on the rocks along the way, and Chops seemed to be getting very annoyed at the repetitive sound.

"How come you have a piece of tin covering the tip of your tail?" asked Boo inquisitively.

"He probably bit his own tail," muttered Chops, still feeling a little agitated about the whole needle incident.

Silver didn't answer right away. There was silence in the air for a few minutes. Boo, having just met him, didn't want to press him too hard for an answer.

"Silver, it's OK if you don't want to tell us now," said Roxy Roo.

As they continued to walk along the rocky trail, a couple more minutes passed in silence before Silver started to tell his tin-tail story.

"Our home was ferociously attacked," said Silver solemnly, looking far off in the distance. "A few years back I was rummaging through Walkabout Wilderness near the area known as Kats Caves. I was looking for the secret plants that would keep them away. I wasn't home when they attacked. I never found them. I will never stop looking."

Boo and Roxy Roo waited patiently for Silver to continue his unfinished tragic story. Chops just couldn't wait.

"Umm, not sure if you're aware, but you may have left out a few details in your story," said Chops, wondering when Silver was going to fill in the holes.

Boo pulled Chops' tail, and at the same time Roxy Roo glared at him. They all walked in silence the rest of the way toward the Pouncing Place.

Boo looked back at his two old friends and his new-found friend Silver as they arrived back at the openings in the old protective wall. Performing their usual friendly duty, Boo and Roxy Roo helped Chops up into the hole and pushed him through to the other side. Boo and Roxy Roo jumped up and squeezed through the hole, following Chops down the natural rocky staircase.

"Where's Silver?" asked Chops.

Boo and Roxy Roo turned around and went back up the stairs. Boo stuck his head through the hole and looked down at Silver, who was still standing at the bottom of the wall looking up at him.

Boo pulled his head back out of the hole and shouted, "He's just standing there!"

"I don't think porcupines are very good jumpers!" shouted Roxy Roo. "I think you might have to give him a boost."

"You want me to give him a boost? How do you want me to do that without getting a paw full of needles from the prickly little creature?" asked Boo.

"Not sure if you're aware, but porky porcupines do have very good hearing," said Silver, looking upward with his mouth wide open and his two orange teeth hanging out. "My quills, NOT needles, only stick out when I feel threatened."

Boo looked down at Silver from the opening and shouted, "Oh, OK, got it!" He turned around, looking at Roxy Roo and Chops, and whispered, "I'll be right back and hopefully without any needles stuck in my paws."

After a short delay, Silver jumped down from the hole in the wall with Boo following right behind him wearing a big grin.

"Look, no needles," said Boo triumphantly, waving his paws.

Chatter could be heard across the ground from all the cats and other island creatures standing together on the other side of the Pouncing Place. Boo quickly walked over to where everyone was gathered around. His three friends curiously followed after him.

"Professor," said Boo, looking puzzled and pushing his way through the other creatures, "what's going on?"

Just before Professor Katnip was about to speak he was interrupted by a loud commotion. The crowd of Meow cats and other creatures moved apart, clearing a path for the Meow cats coming through. It was three Meow cat elders named Harry, Harriet, and Henry, and all three were sporting long, colorful scarves tied around their necks that matched their colorful eyes. Harry and Henry wore colorful tall hats that had holes allowing their pointy ears to poke out the sides. The senior cats squeezed through the crowd one by one. They pushed the other cats aside until each of them found a prominent place standing next to Professor Katnip. All three raised their paws in the air, motioning for the crowd of creatures to calm down.

"Professor… you may proceed," said Harry, waving his paw slowly through the air.

Boo noticed that one of the professor's legs and paws was badly hurt and wrapped up in bandages.

"Well," said Professor Katnip very cautiously, "I was returning from my trip to Walkabout Wilderness. I was on an expedition to find some plants to use in my… umm… secret catnip formulas."

When the crowd of creatures that were gathered around heard the professor use the words "secret" and "catnip" together in the same sentence, they instantly stopped talking. Their ears pointed straight up, listening closely to Professor Katnip's every word.

Roxy Roo glanced over at Boo and could see that he was becoming very uneasy along with the rest of the cats huddled around Professor Katnip and the elders.

The professor had a painful expression on his face as he continued to tell his story.

"I found a new source for the plants," he said, pausing and looking around at the curious faces of the creatures looking back at him.

Professor Katnip made sure to choose his words carefully. He did not want to give away any clues as to where he found the rare catnip plants. Every island creature knew these plants were the most valuable commodity on Tyrtle Island.

"I was very careful, but somehow they found me," said Professor Katnip, cringing as he looked down at his injured leg.

Boo interrupted, "Professor, what do you mean? Who found you?"

Professor Katnip paused for a moment, breathing heavily, and then continued. "He told me to turn back and go along the marsh."

"Who?" asked Boo, looking confused.

The crowd stared intently at Professor Katnip's weary gray eyes that were full of sorrow.

"Professor Potamus is gone," said the professor, pointing to the blanket covering an old wooden cart in back of him.

There was an uneasiness in all the cats' eyes as they continued to watch Professor Katnip.

"They are vile creatures!" cried out Professor Katnip.

Roxy Roo and Chops looked at Boo nervously.

"Those evil creatures must be stopped before any other cats are hurt," said Professor Katnip.

As if it was meant to be a war cry, the professor then yowled loudly and repeatedly.

Chops waited patiently for the professor to stop his chanting and then blurted out, "What exactly are you talkin' about?"

"Bullkats!" he shouted. "They attacked Professor Potamus and me as we were returning from our trip."

The professor paused to lift the cover off the old wooden cart, exposing the dead feline body of Professor Potamus.

The sight of Professor Potamus' lifeless body caused the cats to tremble and meow loudly. The crowd of creatures rumbled like the Rainbow River.

The three Meow cat elders raised their paws in the air once again and motioned for the creatures to calm down.

"Professor Potamus is dead," said the professor solemnly. "He fell and hit his head on a rock near the creek as we were running to escape from those evil creatures. I barely managed to escape with my life. I was only able to get away by jumping in the marsh, but not before they were successful in tearing my leg apart. They finally retreated because I left the plants behind that we had gathered. I knew the scent of the plants would only keep them away for a short amount of time. That's when I went back and found Professor Potamus' dead body."

There was an eerie silence as Professor Katnip finished his story. All the cats stared at the professor almost as if they were hoping there was more to his gory story.

"I've never really believed that bullkats existed," said Chops wearily and louder than he realized. "I've never seen a bullkat. I've never smelled a bullkat, and I've never been attacked by a bullkat. I've never—"

"Chops! That's quite enough!" cried out Professor Katnip, growing impatient listening to Chops run off at the mouth.

Silver whispered to Boo and Roxy Roo in his dignified tone, "I don't like to speak down upon anyone, but in the short time I have known Chops it seems to me that he could use a little more of the professor's catnip."

"No, that's one thing Chops definitely doesn't need," said Boo.

Chapter Three

Boo's heart began to beat faster. He looked around at all the worried cat ears pointing straight back and the confused expressions on his friends' faces. His eyes stopped and focused on Roxy Roo for a few seconds. She was listening to the other cats that had gathered in the crowd chattering amongst one another. He knew the bullkats must be found and stopped before any other Meow cats or creatures on the island were hurt. They would need a plan and would need to put it together quickly. Boo understood that the professor was in no shape to travel anywhere. If Boo and his friends were going to stop the bullkats, he knew they would need to get some expert advice from the professor.

"That will be all for now," said Harriet. "The professor must get some rest now."

"We will meet back here in a few days," said Henry. "If the professor is feeling better."

"A few days?" said Boo, annoyed. "We don't have a few days."

The cat crowd started to disperse, and Professor Katnip began hobbling away from the crowd.

"Professor Katnip," Boo called out, following behind him. "Professor Katnip, please hold on a minute."

The professor kept limping along, seemingly not hearing Boo's voice.

"Professor, I know your leg is hurting," said Boo. "We're all upset about Professor Potamus, but I was hoping I could ask you a couple questions."

"See me in the morning," said the professor hastily.

Boo looked confused as he smiled respectfully and said, "But you don't even know what I want."

"I know exactly what you want, and I said I'll have it ready for you in the morning," said the professor, extremely agitated.

Boo stood there watching as the professor awkwardly walked away. He wondered why the professor was acting so strangely but assumed his unusual and aggressive behavior was due to the pain from his leg. Boo knew that two of the professor's life passions consumed his world. He loved to teach the island creatures about the incredible plants and herbs growing throughout Tyrtle Island. Furthermore, it was no secret to the Islanders that his secret catnip recipes were his first passion and by far the most important thing to him. One might say that he was totally consumed with his secret catnip recipes and would do almost anything to protect them. Boo understood that the plants used to make the various catnip recipes were by far the most valuable commodity on the island. He also realized that the study of catnip was the professor's life work, and he was not just going to hand over any part of his secrets to just anyone. In Boo's mind, finding the source of the professor's secret plants was a matter of life and death. The bullkats had to be stopped before any other creatures were hurt or possibly killed. The very survival of the Meow family of cats might depend on it.

Boo turned around and, to his surprise, the Pouncing Place was completely empty except for his friends, who were standing right behind him.

"What happened? Like magic, everyone vanished," said Boo, feeling disheartened.

A feeling began to swell up inside of him. He asked himself why he was waiting for some other Meow cat to take action. He knew they were just wasting time if all they did was talk about doing something instead of actually doing something to stop the bullkats.

"We have to save Tyrtle Island from the bullkats. Are you guys in?" said Boo, looking seriously at his friends.

"We got this!" they all shouted together, gathering around for the island handshake.

The island handshake was a special tradition on Tyrtle Island for all creatures. Well, for those creatures that had arms, legs, and elbows anyway. It was similar to making the sign for friendship with your index finger but demonstrated in a much bigger way.

They all formed the island handshake by locking their legs together and singing out loud, "Keep calm and Tyrtle on!"

tyrtle

CHAPTER FOUR: HONEY BEES AND H-BEES

The slamming of the screen door jolted Jesse out of his island dream. The sound of the door was usually followed by the sweet voice of his mom yelling at the top of her lungs that it was time for him to get out of bed. He lay still for a few more minutes under his blankets, wrestling with all the thoughts floating around in his head.

"This dream feels so real," he thought. "As real as life itself."

Somehow, he was fully aware that he was actually Boo in his dream.

"Was I dreaming or was I actually there?"

He was hoping to stay in bed a few more minutes trying to recall all the vivid details of his dream.

Removing the covers from over his head, he half-opened his eyes and raised his head slightly, glancing at the foot of his bed. Boo was lying curled up in his usual spot just as he always was.

His mind went back to wondering about the dream. Jesse thought about how amazingly strange it is to see the world through a cat's eyes, especially in a dream. Pondering the reason, he asked himself, "Why would I be seeing everything in this dream through the eyes of Boo?"

"There's gotta be a good reason," he whispered.

Jesse had been so excited the day he found Boo at the local animal shelter. He knew right away that the little tiger-looking kitten was the one for him. When he first brought the little rascal home, the kitten loved to play peek-a-boo with Jesse. The animated cat would strike the funniest pose. Boo assumed an exaggerated attack position, pretending he was ready to strike at any second. Playing with Jesse, the courageous kitten would jump out from whatever he was hiding behind just like he was saying, "Boo!" And that's how Boo got his name.

Every day, Boo would accompany Jesse to school and then home again, riding shotgun in the wooden box at the front of Jesse's bicycle. They were inseparable, and both of them made an effort to make the most out of every moment they had together. Jesse, like most people, would dream often, but he knew there was something very unusual about this particular dream.

Boo began to stir, stretching out his legs, paws, and claws while still half asleep at the foot of the bed. Jesse could feel Boo moving around and pressing his claws against his feet. The feeling of the sharp claws poking at his feet reminded him of Boo talking to his friends about bullkats in the dream.

"Bullkats," he said, sighing heavily. "Not again."

He reached down and pulled his furry friend closer to his pillow.

"What kind of trouble have you gotten us into this time?" he asked Boo, rubbing Boo's white belly.

Boo was an unusual cat in that he didn't mind being hugged, rubbed, and snuggled to death. Jesse knew that putting a little extra effort into a belly rub was always appreciated by Boo. He pressed his sandy blond hair against the soft orange and brown stripes of Boo's thick fur and drifted back to sleep, hoping to pick up his dream right where he had left it.

"Jesse!" yelled his mom from the kitchen. "Jesse Quinn!" she yelled again, ratcheting up the volume a bit.

There was that sweet-sounding voice he was anticipating a few minutes before. Jesse knew that if his mom said his first and last name together, then she was in no mood to dilly-dally around. He reluctantly crawled out of bed like a snake and stumbled into the kitchen. He flopped into one of the dining-room chairs with Boo trailing behind him.

"Jesse, Mr. Jack said Boo was in his garden again diggin' up the plants," said his mom, setting a hot plate of her famous island hummingbird pancakes down in front of him. "I asked you to keep Boo out of there."

"Come on, Boo, you know better," said Jesse, teasing him. "Sure, we know that you can't resist catnip plants, but all work and no play make Mr. Jack a dull boy."

"Jesse, watch your mouth," she said, trying not to laugh recalling that line from the movie.

Jesse bowed his head to thank God for his food as his mom shouted out from the kitchen, "And don't forget to give thanks!"

The screen door slammed just as Mr. Jack, wearing his old coveralls, rushed into the dining room holding a small hand shovel and axe covered with red clay in one hand and pointing directly at Boo with the other hand. Boo quickly jumped up from the floor onto Jesse's lap.

"Good morning, Mr. Jack. Please... come on in," said Jesse's mom. "Would you like some pancakes?"

"Good morning, Kay," said Mr. Jack. "Quite frankly, I'm in no mood for pancakes, so I will get right to the point."

Jesse turned back around and focused on his stack of pancakes again, which seemed to infuriate Mr. Jack.

"I've tried to be polite... I really have... have I asked nicely, yes, I have, but if you don't keep that stinkin' cat out of my garden then I will have to—" Mr. Jack was quiet for a few seconds, trying to keep his composure and think of the right words. "Well, little boy, I'll just have to do what's necessary."

Jesse's mom looked furiously at Mr. Jack but held her tongue.

Mr. Jack turned around and stormed out of the house. The screen door slammed again behind him as he punished the ground stomping away through the yard.

Jesse's mom watched Mr. Jack disappear down the street. "I'm just not sure what to think of old Mr. Jack. He seems so... I don't know... so much more stressed out these days."

"You know what I think?" said Jesse. "That's one really well-made screen door." He smiled at his mom and at the same time snuck a pancake under the table for Boo.

His mom reminded him, "It's a school day. You don't want to be late. Professor Katnip said that if you're late one more time, it would be hard times for you."

"Yeah, I know… meaning pulling weeds in his garden," said Jesse. "Professor Katnip and Mr. Jack are two peas in a pod. Well, at least when it comes to gardening and playing with their precious plants."

Jesse gave his mom a quick hug and headed out to school. He left earlier than usual because he knew he had to do something to fix the uneasy situation with Mr. Jack. He didn't have the answer but thought he would talk to Professor Katnip before science class started. He was sure that the professor would offer up some kind of suggestion. After all, his name was Professor Katnip, and plants, especially catnip plants, were the most important thing in his life, or so it seemed to Jesse.

Jesse put Boo in the wooden box and rode his bike down the road past Mr. Jack's house. He glanced over at the garden as he passed the old house. All of a sudden, his stomach felt like a boiling pot of lava, as though he had just eaten some Brussels sprouts. He hated that feeling, but for some reason it made him start to pedal faster. He could feel deep down in his gut that something was just not right about Mr. Jack.

"Could he really be that upset about Boo in his garden?" thought Jesse, rolling down the bumpy road.

He knew something didn't add up, but what exactly that something was, he just didn't know.

The school was a mile or so down the road from Jesse's house. When Jesse arrived at the back of the school, he dropped Boo off in his usual place up in the giant banyan tree. His unusual cat waited patiently for him by snoozing the day away until the school day was over, and Jesse came to get him. Jesse could see that there were already a few students lined up at the science lab waiting to talk to Professor Katnip. He was one of the kids' favorite teachers at Jesse's school and on the entire island. However, he was without a doubt the teacher that dressed the weirdest. Red suspenders and a red bow tie seemed to be the style of choice for Professor Katnip on most any given day.

The kids in the class were clamoring for the professor's attention and asking so many questions at once that the professor raised his hand in the air, calling for them to quiet down.

"Honey Bee, what's your question?" he asked patiently, pointing his finger at her.

Honey Bee was Jesse's best human friend. She was also a favorite of most of the teachers, which is why it was no surprise to all the kids in the lab that Professor Katnip picked her to go first.

"Why doesn't an H-Bee sting you?" asked Honey Bee promptly.

Honey Bee already knew the answer. She knew almost everything there was to know about bees. She just asked because she loved talking about insects and especially pollinators.

Her family made local island honey and had raised bees on the island for many generations. Her parents loved honey and bees so much that they couldn't imagine any name for their beloved daughter other than Honey Bee. Some of her aunties called her Bee, and she even had an uncle that called her H-Bee just for the purpose of poking fun at her.

Professor Katnip walked up to the chalkboard and wrote the word "H-bee" before beginning his explanation.

"H-bees look very similar to honey bees, although they do have a beautiful H-shaped marking on their backs. However, H-bees are not really a bee at all. They're actually a drone fly," he instructed, pointing his finger and straightening his bow tie. "A more direct answer to your question is that, unlike honey bees, H-bees have no stinger."

Professor Katnip's lab erupted with sounds of disgust at the very thought of catching a dirty fly. After all, flies are pesky, and they do get a lot of bad press.

Professor Katnip raised his hand in the air again, signaling the class to quiet down.

"I understand flies are thought of by most people as icky insects, along with maggots and so forth," said Professor Katnip. "Here are a couple more incredible fly facts. Did you know flies can taste with their feet and have no teeth? And that is why they live on a liquid diet."

Jesse and Honey Bee smiled while most of the other kids laughed and repeated their sounds of disgust just hearing the word "maggot" come out of the professor's mouth.

"Don't be too hard on flies. Just like bees, flies are actually important pollinators to many plants. Some flies, like H-bees, are not even garbage lovers," said Professor Katnip pointedly. "Does anyone else have a question?" he asked, glancing around the room.

Jesse raised his hand. The room quickly filled with chatter as the professor signaled for quiet once again.

"Why do bees get married?" asked Jesse with a big grin, flipping his long blond bangs out of his face.

Professor Katnip looked over at Jesse, who was still wearing a big grin across his face. The professor glanced around the room at his students, who were now quiet and looking at each other curiously, but nobody was anxious to answer Jesse's question. The awkward silence permeated the classroom, and after several seconds went by, Jesse was prompted to answer his own question.

"Because they found their honey!" he blurted out, slightly embarrassed.

Honey Bee, along with the rest of the class, saw Jesse gazing at her as he gave the answer.

Honey Bee knew that the joke was a little bit on the corny side, but she didn't mind. She knew that joke was specifically meant for her. She had never experienced such a warm feeling which filled her heart and encompassed her whole body.

"Any other questions—or jokes, for that matter?" asked Professor Katnip, clearing his throat.

"I do have one other question," replied Jesse. "What kind of plant will keep Boo out of Mr. Jack's garden?"

Everyone knew Boo, and they also knew scary old Mr. Jack. Jesse was not the only person in town who was uneasy around Mr. Jack or who had expressed some concerns with him.

"Get with me after school today," said Professor Katnip hurriedly. "That's it for this morning. Have a bee-utiful day."

"Have a bee-utiful day" was the professor's standard tag line, but not directly answering a question was a little out of the ordinary for him. Jesse knew that, whatever the professor's answer was, he didn't want everyone to hear it.

The day went by slowly for Jesse. He was anxious to hear what Professor Katnip had to tell him. The last bell rang out, signaling the end of the school day. Jesse darted in and out of the open-air hallways to the back of the school where Professor Katnip's science lab was located. He dashed past the hazy lab windows on his way to pick up Boo, who was waiting up in the banyan tree out back behind the lab. He glanced into the lab window without stopping and noticed that the room looked empty. Without breaking his stride, he leaped over the broken table out behind the lab, landing sure-footed on the grass. He slowed down to a trot and walked across the field over to the giant banyan tree where Boo was meowing and looking at him anxiously. Boo jumped into his arms, and Jesse could feel Boo's purr motor running. Jesse hurried back to the lab, anxious to hear what the professor had to say. To his disappointment, he found the doors were locked. He peered through the small, smudged-up window on the door, and there was no sign of the professor inside. He lay down on the old wooden lab bench to the side of the door with Boo lying across his chest.

After a short period of time, the warmth of the sun and the island breeze began to make his eyes feel heavy.

"Good grief, where are you, Professor?" he thought aloud, just before drifting off to sleep.

Honey Bee walked past the lab and saw Jesse resting on the old bench. She crept up quietly and gently tickled the inside of his ear with her long brown hair.

She started to giggle and then whispered into his other ear, "Bzzzz, bzzzz."

Jesse flew off the bench, flapping his arms frantically, just like an elephant flapping its ears in fear when it hears the buzzing of a bee. He turned around after regaining his balance to see that Honey Bee was holding Boo in one arm and holding her side with the other, aching from laughter.

"Jesse, wow... you should see the look on your face," she said. "That was the bee's knees."

"I don't know why your parents named you Honey Bee. Sometimes you're not sweet like honey at all. They should've named you Bumble Bee because you just keep on stinging again and again," said Jesse, annoyed.

His intent was to be quick-witted, but Jesse wished he could retract his words right after he said them.

"I'm sorry, Honey Bee. That sounded a little on the mean side," said Jesse, looking at her apologetically.

"Snips and snails and puppy-dogs' tails," Honey Bee sang out loudly.

"What?" asked Jesse, looking confused.

"I nearly almost wet myself," she confessed.

Honey Bee wasn't that upset even if that comment might have come across as borderline mean. After all, that attempt at a witty comeback was all about bees, and she had always known Jesse to have a kind and gentle spirit.

"Did you talk to Professor Katnip? What did he say?" asked Honey Bee.

"I waited for him after school, but he never showed," said Jesse. "I fell asleep on the bench waiting for him."

Honey Bee smiled and started to giggle again when her mind replayed the scene of Jesse flapping his arms all over again.

"Did you see the note folded into the doorjamb?" asked Honey Bee, trying to be serious.

Jesse walked over to the steel doors and sighed as he pulled the folded note out and read:

"Meet me at my house Saturday evening at 6:15. Don't be late."

"What's with this cat-and-mouse game the professor is playing?" said Jesse. "All I asked him was how to keep Boo out of Mr. Jack's garden. Seems like an easy enough question to me. Especially since the professor is a plant expert. Why all the secrecy?"

"I don't know. He's been missin' class a lot lately. I gotta go, Jesse," said Honey Bee. "See you tomorrow at the park."

Jesse stuck the note in his pocket and pedaled back home with Boo in his box. The bike ride back home seemed like a blur to Jesse. The more he thought about Professor Katnip's curious behavior, the more curious he became. He just couldn't figure out why the professor seemed reluctant to answer his simple question. He saw Mr. Jack's house ahead of him, and his stomach began to have the same rumbling feeling again as he passed by.

Jesse struggled getting to sleep that night. He felt like his mind was about to explode thinking about bullkats, Mr. Jack, and now the professor. His mom always reminded him to try and think about something good when he felt overwhelmed with worry. Honey Bee quickly came to his mind, and he was whisked off to sleep.

Professor Katnip was not at school the rest of that week. Jesse knew that was very odd. For Jesse, Saturday evening couldn't arrive soon enough.

tyrtle

CHAPTER FIVE: DO YOU BELIEVE?

"Hoo hoo hoo hoo! Hoo hoo hoo hoo!" Jesse's alarm clock sounded repeatedly as he lay in bed trying to ignore it. He rubbed his eyes and looked down at his feet where Boo was normally found curled up in the morning. A few seconds later, he sat up in bed, surprised that Boo was not there. He scratched his head and wondered where his best furry friend might be. Feeling somewhat anxious, he was hoping that Boo was not outside messing around in Mr. Jack's garden.

"Boo! Boooo!" yelled out Jesse, his voice cracking. "Where is that cat?" he said, slumping back down into his pillow.

He lay there for a few more minutes thinking about how quickly the night went by and wondering why he didn't dream. He opened his eyes, and when he turned his head to the side, Boo was sitting there staring right at him.

"Hey, what's the big idea, sneaking up on me like that?" he said, grabbing Boo and pulling him closer to give him a big hug.

Cats cannot live on belly rubs and warm hugs alone, but don't worry, your mom already fed me, Boo thought, staring at Jesse.

Jesse suddenly remembered that today was Saturday. He jumped out of bed and got dressed in a hurry as the scent of sweet-smelling cinnamon rolls lingered in the air. He danced through the kitchen, grabbing one of the hot rolls that his mom had just taken out of the oven.

"Going to the park as soon as I finish my paper route!" he yelled just as the back screen door slammed shut.

He could faintly hear his mom respond with what sounded like a reluctant "Alright. Be back—"

He ran through the backyard with Boo pouncing along right behind him. He quickly grabbed his bicycle, put Boo in the wooden box, and pedaled as fast as he could to the newspaper office.

"There you are. Good morning, Jesse. Lots of inserts today," said Mr. Smitty, smiling enthusiastically. "Looks like Boo is having a good morning. Everything good, Jesse?"

Jesse didn't answer Mr. Smitty right away because he was trying not to breathe in the repulsive paper-ink smell too deeply as he entered the room full of wooden tables and piles of newspapers. The smell was an odor that he never really got used to.

"Yeah, I got a little problem with Boo," said Jesse. "I'm just trying to figure out how to keep him out of Mr. Jack's garden. He's pretty upset about it."

"Who? Boo or Mr. Jack?" joked Mr. Smitty, laughing loudly.

Jesse laughed under his breath and set Boo down on the dusty table covered with newspapers.

"I know he's a tough customer, but be patient with old Mr. Jack," said Mr. Smitty, setting down a box of donuts on the table next to Boo. "His wife died about a year ago. He's having a rough go of it."

Mr. Smitty had worked at the newspaper loading docks for most of his life, or so it seemed to Jesse. He always seemed to notice the same two things about Mr. Smitty. He was always wearing the same old weathered Pittsburgh Pirates cap, and he had newspaper ink stains permanently tattooed on all ten fingertips. Jesse watched Mr. Smitty in amazement as he picked up a glazed donut, took a big bite out of it, and then set it back down on the dusty wooden table with ink-smudged fingerprints left behind on the donut glaze.

Jesse looked at Boo apologetically. "Sorry, no donuts for you, big guy," he said, closing the lid of the box.

If only they made them fish-flavored, thought Boo.

The newspaper folding machines clicked and clacked all over the room as Jesse walked back to a dusty machine that was not being used at the moment.

One of the old-timers pushed his way past, heading toward the front door of the room. With a big smile on his face, he said, "Where's your car, Jesse? You might need one today."

Jesse grinned, but he was not amused. Turning sixteen years old could not come fast enough for Jesse Quinn. In his mind, being old enough to drive around and explore Tyrtle Island anytime he wanted was the ultimate ticket to freedom.

"Oh, man, I don't believe it," he whined under his breath.

He took a long look at the stack of advertising inserts that he would have to stuff in the newspapers before folding and loading them all on his bike.

Jesse looked Boo right in the eyes, saying, "Today is going to be the best day."

Jesse made fast work of adding all the inserts and running the newspapers through the folding machines. He pedaled his bicycle through the nearby neighborhood and apartment buildings, throwing his papers on each doorstep with precision. It was always a cause for celebration when he managed to hit the umbrella lady's aluminum screen door right smack in the middle. He couldn't even see the second-story door up over the railing at the back of the porch, but he had hit that door so many times he could tell by the sound if he had hit his target.

"Strike!" yelled Jesse, hearing the rattling of the door.

The elderly lady always scurried out of her apartment a few seconds after hearing the crash against the screen door. He couldn't really hear what she was yelling at him as he continued to pedal down the sidewalk, but he knew it had something to do with him not getting a tip this month. Jesse smiled, knowing that she never tipped him anyway. He finished the rest of his paper route in a jiffy and headed over to the old fort to meet his friends.

Jesse pedaled down the wooded dirt trail toward the walls of the old fort. He was riding along next to the old coquina walls, and for a split-second he was distracted as he swatted at a bug that flew into his face.

"Not in my face, bee!" cried out Jesse, trying to keep his bike from wobbling.

He tried slowing down by swinging his legs to one side of the bike and skidding his feet on the ground.

CRASH! FA-THUD! FA-THUD! Suddenly Jesse and his best friend Honey Bee collided with each other and landed flat on their backs in the middle of the dirt trail.

"Hey, Jesse," groaned Honey Bee, pulling herself up off the ground.

She glanced over at Jesse with a slightly aggravated look mixed with a slight smile. She was always happy to see Jesse even if it meant running right into him.

"Sorry, Honey Bee. I think a bee… you know… a flying insect, hit me in the face. Umm, you have some dirt on your cheek," he said, pointing at her cheek.

"Umm, yes. I know that a bee is a flying insect," she said, giggling.

He reached out to try and wipe the dirt off her cheek but only managed to smear it around while somehow adding a little bicycle grease to her forehead.

Honey Bee reached down to pet Boo's thick orange fur coat. She ran her fingers down along his back all the way to the tip of his tail. They both knew where they were heading because they had been down this trail many times before. Jesse wanted to tell his friend all about his amazing dream, but he knew it sounded crazy and he just wasn't sure if now was the right time.

"Any word from the professor?" asked Honey Bee.

"No. Remember we have to meet him tonight," he said, hopping on his bike.

Jesse rode in circles around Honey Bee as they went past the old fort and into the park. Honey Bee waved when she saw their friend Caleb on the other side of the park. He was sitting all by himself on the old log that had been lying under the big rain tree for as long as anyone could remember. Honey Bee waved again to Caleb as they crossed the sandy green field toward the other side of the park. Caleb didn't wave back, which was unusual because he was usually such a good-natured and funny friend.

"Wonder what's up with Caleb?" Jesse asked Honey Bee, making their way across the field.

"Hi ya, Caleb!" shouted Jesse.

"Everything OK, Caleb?" asked Honey Bee almost simultaneously with her gentle voice.

Caleb lifted his head without making eye contact with his friends and didn't answer their questions. Jesse and Honey Bee sat down next to their friend. They wanted to question Caleb a little deeper but knew he was upset about something and thought it was best to give him some time. They knew Caleb would talk when he was ready.

It started to sprinkle, and Jesse wiped the light raindrops that dotted his face. He stood up and started to walk in the direction of the covered picnic tables. Honey Bee started to follow and looked back at Caleb, but he was not moving. He was still slouched on the old dead log with his head hanging low.

Honey Bee went back and gave Caleb a big hug and smiled, saying, "Let's get out of the rain. I don't want to mess up my hair."

Caleb had known Honey Bee long enough to know that she wasn't the least bit fussy about getting her hair wet. He looked up at her and managed a little smile as he slid himself forward, dropping off the log.

They followed Jesse to the picnic tables, which were only a short distance from the ocean. They could hear the crashing of the waves on the sandy shore and smell the scent of seaweed in the ocean breeze as they all three sat on the table in silence for a few minutes.

Caleb broke the awkward silence by asking, "Have you guys ever seen a bullkat?"

The three friends stared at one another for a few seconds with confused looks on their faces. It was as if Caleb had asked the question in an unknown language.

"I never have," said Honey Bee, frowning. "A few months ago I was walking through the neighborhood, passing by Nurse Shirley's house. She told me that one night she was out in her vegetable garden very late, and she was almost attacked by some scary cats with glowing eyes and white horns."

"She was picking vegetables after dark?" said Jesse. "That's a little odd."

Honey Bee sighed heavily. "Jesse," she said, feeling a little agitated at being interrupted, "that makes me think that whatever kind of cat it was might not be... well... an ordinary cat."

Honey Bee, you of all people should know that there's no such creature as an ordinary cat, Boo thought, sitting up tall on the top of the picnic table and looking out at the ocean.

"How bad was she hurt?" asked Caleb, wincing.

"Her legs were clawed up pretty bad," said Honey Bee, flinching. "She said she tried to beat them off with a pitchfork and just barely made it back inside the house. She also said that when she stabbed them with the pitchfork, they made the most awful screeching sound she had ever heard."

Jesse pumped his fist and shouted, "Go, Nurse Shirley!"

Honey Bee looked at Caleb curiously. "Why? Do you think you saw one?"

Caleb turned and looked at his friends with wide eyes and his mouth hanging open. He didn't need to give them an answer. His face said it all as he sat there nodding his head up and down. Jesse thought about it but didn't think now was the right time to tell his friends about the bullkat encounter in Kats Caves.

"Are you sure?" asked Honey Bee.

"Sounds just about right... scary glowing eyes and ugly white horns," said Caleb, holding his fingers up by his ears and pointing them upwards.

Honey Bee loved to sing, and she seemed to always have a quick little song in her heart. She thought now would be a good time to lighten up the conversation and help take Caleb's mind off the bullkats.

She smiled as she sang out a quick little tune with her amazingly sweet voice:

"I have a song in my heart, a smile on my face.
Friends sweeter than honey and been saved by grace.
A home on my island, Tyrtle love to start.
No need to worry, because we have a song in our heart."

As Honey Bee sang, Caleb could feel the love of their friendship fill the air. Her songs never failed to put a smile back on her friends' faces. Honey

Bee had something else planned that she knew would take Caleb's mind off of the bullkats for a little while longer.

"Let's go have some fun," said Honey Bee, reaching into her bag.

She stood up and jumped off the picnic table, then handed Jesse and Caleb a little bag of island jelly beans from her family's Island Café.

"A few jellies in your bellies always makes the day a little less smelly," Honey Bee sang out.

Jesse and Caleb grinned from ear to ear at her silly-sounding rhyme. They followed her along the seashore path through the mushy marshmallow trail. The trail's end led to the old marshmallow lighthouse. The landmark lighthouse was built out of large white marshmallow-looking stones and looked exactly like its name. The path along the way was overgrown with a rainbow of lilac bushes and lavender plants. Some of the lilac bushes had grown so big over the years that they were actually more like lilac trees and had become strong enough that Honey Bee could actually climb right through them.

"Let's make a beeline. Hurry up, you guys!" shouted Honey Bee, carrying Boo and looking back at Jesse and Caleb lagging behind.

As the three friends ran into the thick of the lilac trees, they could hear buzzing all around them. Honey Bee slowed down for just a second, pausing to hand Jesse and Caleb a few pieces of bright yellow thread.

"You guys be careful and tie the thread very, very gently," she said, cautioning them.

She watched Jesse and Caleb make funny faces at each other.

"I saw that," said Honey Bee.

She knew from previous encounters that some of her friends had a tendency to be a little rough and clumsy. What they were about to do was very delicate and required a little gentleness. Honey Bee knew the perfect spot to perform the procedure. Jesse and Caleb followed her through the tunnel of trees and into an opening between colorful bushes growing atop a low hill. The buzzing had gotten noticeably louder as the three friends quietly approached the bushes. Honey Bee, without hesitating, spotted an H-bee among the honey bees on one of the blossoms and captured the amazing insect in her gentle hands.

Chapter Five

"Jesse, please be careful," she said nervously.

She held the H-bee softly as Jesse tied a thin yellow thread around it, being careful not to touch the H-bee's delicate wings. She released it back into the air, and all three friends watched in amazement as the H-bee quickly went back to work, buzzing around the bushes with a long yellow tail trailing behind it.

Caleb looked mesmerized as his eyes carefully followed the H-bee's every move, and he whispered excitedly, "It's like having a mini-flying kite."

The minutes quickly turned into hours, and the three friends started to feel relaxed from the strong fragrance of the hundreds of jasmine and lavender plants growing all around them. Caleb lay down and began snoring like a congested tiger.

Jesse looked at Honey Bee and then back at Caleb, saying, "Why not? Catnap sounds just about right."

Boo looked at Jesse as if he understood him purr-fectly and snuggled up between Jesse and Honey Bee.

turtle

CHAPTER SIX: AN UNEXPECTED FIND

THE SOUND OF THE CRACKLING thunder startled Jesse out of his sleep. He opened his eyes just in time to witness a flash of spider lightning skipping across the sky from cloud to cloud. The powerful light show was followed by a long, low rumble of thunder. Big raindrops slowly began to fall on the lilac and lavender leaves, causing the bushes and trees to rock back and forth like a playground seesaw. Honey Bee and Caleb quickly got up and followed Jesse, who was taking cover under the large arching branch of an old rain tree. Jesse knew that Boo didn't mind getting a little wet, but he did his best to keep Boo dry by tucking him under his shirt. Caleb laughed watching Jesse try to cover up the big cat by stuffing him under his shirt. Boo's head would pop out of the top of Jesse's stretched-out shirt, and then when he pulled the shirt back up over Boo's head, the cat's long orange tail would hang out the bottom of the shirt.

"Sorry, Boo, I think that's as good as it's gonna get," said Jesse, with parts of Boo hanging out both ends of his shirt.

Caleb carefully examined Boo from head to tail. "What are you feeding Boo these days? He looks more and more like a baby tiger cub every day."

Jesse smiled, glancing back and forth at both Roxy Roo and Caleb. "Yep, he's a biggin'."

Boo wasn't sure whether to take that comment as a paw-some compliment or purr-haps as an insult. Either way, he still thought that he was as close as you can get to being the purr-fect cat.

"Hey, my Uncle Tinman lives just down the road from here," said Jesse. "I think we've spent enough time catching raindrops. Let's stop by Tinman's house until the thunder and lightning have passed."

Chapter Six

Jesse and his friends sat in Tinman's living room after dinner talking about Boo, bees, and bullkats.

Caleb watched Tinman in the kitchen cleaning up the dishes. He was curious how Jesse's uncle got the name "Tinman." "Why is your uncle's name 'Tinman'? Is that his real name? Were his parents just really big fans of the movie?" asked Caleb in rapid fire.

"I love that movie," said Honey Bee. "Remember this? 'I'm melting, melting. Ohhhhh, what a world, what a world.'"

Caleb smiled, singing out loudly, "If you only had a brain!"

"Why don't you ask him yourself?" said Jesse, his eyebrows raised and his finger pointing as Tinman entered the living room.

"What secrets do you guys want to try and dig outta me this time?" asked Tinman.

"Sir, I—" said Caleb, hesitating.

"I bet you wanna know why everyone calls me 'Tinman,'" he said, preparing to sit down in his favorite armchair. "The short version of the story is: when I was a boy, I had to wear leg braces. The real story of why I got the nickname and how it stuck over the years is a little longer, but it might be a little more interesting. Do you want to hear it?"

Caleb just looked at Tinman in a hypnotic state, slowly nodding his head up and down.

"I was a young boy... I guess a little younger than Jesse is now," said Tinman. "I was hobbling around with those cursed leg braces, and because of those clunky things, I didn't have a lot of friends. Truth be told, most of the kids didn't want to hang around with me because I couldn't play sports and run around like everyone else. I would spend most days out in the woods catching H-bees... I never grew tired of catching H-bees. Most days that I didn't have to go to school, I would stay out there all day and barely make it back home before it started getting dark."

Tinman stopped speaking and just stared straight ahead for a few minutes. Jesse waved his hand through the air, trying to get his attention again.

"Uncle Tinman," said Jesse.

Tinman stood up out of his chair and started to pace around the room before continuing his story.

"Where was I? Oh, yes, one day I didn't start back home until after it was dark," he said. "I remember that night very well… It was a full moon that night, but because of the cloud coverage there wasn't much light. Looking up through the trees I could see the bright full moon peek through the clouds as they floated along in the night sky. I started walking back home slowly along Marshmallow Trail. I had been in the woods hundreds of times before that night. I can still remember that, somehow, I had this eerie feeling that this night was going to be different."

Tinman paused again as Jesse and his friends began to lean forward toward him.

"The one thing I could never forget—never could get out of my mind—were those hideous yellow eyes. When I felt that strange sensation, I looked up and saw those eyes glowing through the bushes above the trail," said Tinman, with his eyebrows slanted upwards.

Caleb's shoulders quivered as he scooted a little closer to Honey Bee.

Glancing over at Caleb, Jesse shook his head and started to laugh.

"What?" said Caleb defensively.

"At first I thought they were just feral cats with creepy-looking eyes," said Tinman, chuckling under his breath. "They moved differently, though… I watched them through the bushes… It was like their bones seemed as if they were disjointed and almost floating through the air."

Tinman's voice was silent again for a few seconds. His face looked repulsed, like he was reliving that night. Everyone in the room could feel their blood pumping through every vein in their bodies and their hearts thumping out of their chests. Jesse, Honey Bee, and Caleb all moved a little closer together on the couch. Even Boo jumped off the chair and into Jesse's lap, startling him.

"Ahhh!" shrieked Caleb, jumping back on the couch.

Jesse gave Caleb a quick whack on the shoulder and started to laugh.

Caleb reached around Honey Bee's shoulders and gave him a whack back.

"I saw you jump too," said Caleb.

"Jesse and Caleb!" snapped Honey Bee, rolling her eyes.

Tinman was amused, watching all the commotion on the couch. He grinned at the wide-eyed stares looking back at him before he continued to say, "Something glowing was sticking out from the sides of their horrible little heads, but I couldn't tell what it was until they got closer to me. Without warning they leaped down off the hill above me, and I scrambled to get away and fell over backwards. It wasn't until they started gnawing and clawing at my legs that I was able to see the long, pointed, glowing horns sticking out from inside of their ears. I tried to fight them off, but there were too many of them. Amazingly, those cursed leg braces were a blessing that night, and that is what kept them from doing any real damage to my legs. But as crazy as it sounds, that wasn't even the scariest part. It was the sound they made... it's the most indescribable, hideous sound I've ever heard."

Tinman stopped speaking and ran his hands down along his legs and then back up again. His face cringed like he was feeling the pain of that nightmare all over again.

"I had been collecting plants for my garden," said Tinman, changing his voice to a lighter tone.

"Wait, hold on a minute!" snapped Caleb. "You just went from 'most indescribable, hideous sound' to 'collecting plants for my garden.'"

Jesse and Honey Bee laughed at the really serious look on Caleb's face.

"That's why... I said... it was indescribable," said Tinman.

"Can he do that?" said Caleb, frowning.

Tinman scratched his head and looked directly over at Boo. "Where was I?"

Boo jumped backwards and landed up on the back of the couch, acting like he understood exactly what Tinman was asking him.

"Oh, yeah, thanks, Boo," said Tinman. "When they attacked my legs, I fell backwards on the ground. The backpack I was wearing fell off, and some of the plants I'd collected fell out on the ground. All of a sudden... they disappeared... they vanished as quickly as they attacked. I'm not sure why. At first, I thought it was a miracle. I looked around in the dark for some other predator... for some reason why they might've run off. Then I realized that a bunch of the colorful plants had fallen out of my backpack. I thought it might've had something to do with the plants but never really gave it much thought after that. I haven't found any more of those plants since that day, nor have I seen any bullkats since that day. Well, up until a couple days ago."

The disappointed expression on Caleb's face changed to a frightened look.

"I'm not sure of the real name for those miracle plants," said Tinman. "Like I said, I haven't seen them since, but when I tell this story, I affectionately call them scaredy-cat plants... and everyone has called me 'Tinman' ever since."

Boo and Honey Bee smiled, but Caleb still had that same frightened look on his face from earlier in the day.

"Tinman, I think we have a problem," announced Jesse. "Caleb, tell Tinman what you saw and where you saw it."

Caleb hesitated a few seconds, fiddling with his fingers while he gathered his thoughts, and finally said, "I was riding my bike down by Fish Flop Cove one day after school last week."

"Please don't tell me you saw a bullkat at Fish Flop Cove," Tinman interrupted.

Tinman didn't need an answer from Caleb. He could tell just by the look on his face.

"Are you sure? How do you know it was a bullkat?" asked Tinman.

"I was hoping it was just a really ugly-looking cat," said Caleb. "I wasn't sure until you finished your story. Now I'm positive. You know, glowing yellow eyes and horns coming out of its ears. Pretty sure it wasn't the Easter Bunny."

Caleb was hoping a joke would help him muster up some courage. After all, courage is stronger than fear.

"How many?" asked Tinman, hoping the answer was only one.

"Just one... I think. Well, I can't be sure... That's all I saw. Let me put it this way: I didn't hang around at the cove to see if I could find any more," declared Caleb, raising his voice.

"Jesse and I got chased by one in Kats Caves," said Tinman. "We didn't say anything because we didn't want to worry anyone. Those creepy creatures have been around on the island since the beginning. Tyrtle Island archeologists have dug up bullkat bones going back thousands of years. I really believed they were no more, gone, extinct for many years now. Before being chased in Kats Caves, I hadn't seen or heard of a bullkat sighting since that day everyone started calling me Tinman."

"Let's see, we got chased by a bullkat, Caleb saw a bullkat, and Nurse Shirley was attacked. I've heard there are other Islanders that have seen strange-looking cats and even been attacked," said Jesse emphatically. "I think we can start to worry a little now."

They all sat quiet for the next few minutes. In the middle of all the bullkat talk, Jesse and Honey Bee almost forgot they had to meet with Professor Katnip that same night.

"Hey, we gotta go. It's a couple minutes after six," said Jesse, looking at his watch. "Professor Katnip, remember?"

"Make sure you tell him about all the bullkat sightings. We have to figure out why there seems to be so many around the island now and how we're going to stop them. I'm not sure, but Professor Katnip will know or should at least have an idea of what we can do," said Tinman confidently.

"What do you mean by that?" asked Caleb, feeling an unsettling knot developing in his stomach. "Doesn't the island have a wildlife department or something for catching bullkats?"

"I wish," said Tinman, waving his hand as everyone headed out the door.

Jesse and Honey Bee hopped on their bikes and arrived at Professor Katnip's farm a few minutes later. Boo jumped out of the wooden box and looked over toward the professor's garden.

Yummy, irresistible catnip, thought Boo, sniffing the air.

Jesse and Honey Bee could see the rows of greenhouses lined up as they walked up the professor's gravel driveway and knocked on his bright red front door.

Professor Katnip was known throughout the island for growing all sorts of plants and herbs. He was especially known for his special catnip recipes, and for that reason he was one of Boo's favorite Islanders.

Leaving Jesse in the doorway, Honey Bee walked to the side of the porch and looked around toward the backyard where all the greenhouses were lined up.

"Jesse, somebody just ran out of one of the greenhouses!" exclaimed Honey Bee.

They both leaped off the porch and bolted toward the greenhouse.

"Professor!" Jesse called out, pointing at the greenhouse. "Make sure he's OK!"

Jesse darted past the greenhouse and into the thick trees at the back of the property with Boo trailing closely behind him.

Through the open louvered-glass windows of the greenhouse Honey Bee could see the professor leaning over some plants and holding a handkerchief against his head.

"Professor, are you OK?" hollered Honey Bee, rushing through the door. "Come and sit down over here," she said, helping him over to an old wooden bench.

"Just like a successful science experiment, you showed up right on time," quipped Professor Katnip.

"Lost 'em in the jungle," said Jesse, breathing heavily as he burst through the greenhouse door. "Who was it?"

"I was tending to my plants and next thing you know, lights out," said Professor Katnip painfully.

Jesse and Honey Bee helped Professor Katnip back to the house and nursed his head with a bag of frozen vegetables.

"Professor, we really need your help," pleaded Jesse.

"Slow down, Jesse, my boy," said Professor Katnip as he walked through the kitchen door holding the bag of vegetables against his head.

"Professor, the bullkats are back," blurted out Honey Bee. "Jesse and Tinman were chased by one inside Kats Caves, and Caleb was terrified by one of those awful creatures over by the lighthouse."

"I see," said Professor Katnip calmly. "Yes, unfortunately it seems that our problem is getting a little bigger than just keeping Boo out of Mr. Jack's garden. I have a theory, and if it's proven true, then we are about to run into a hornet's nest."

Professor Katnip never missed an opportunity to use a scientific term in the middle of a sentence, especially when it involved plants or flying insects.

"Go home and get some rest. We all need to meet as early as possible tomorrow morning and take a trip to the Roundabout Rainforest. Oh, by the way, we're going to need Tinman. He knows the rainforest very well, and without a doubt, we need his expertise."

Jesse and Honey Bee walked outside and noticed that Boo was looking at them both inquisitively from the edge of the porch.

I know... I'm just a cat, thought Boo, jumping off the porch. *I hope they follow me.*

Jesse knew by the look on Boo's face that he was trying to tell them something. Boo darted past the garden with Jesse and Honey Bee following right behind him. They ran past the greenhouse and along the trail that led them to the edge of the jungle. Boo stopped just short of the palm trees and pointed back and forth with his big orange paw at some kind of colorful dried-up plant that was lying in the middle of the trail. Boo didn't touch it, though. He just backed away, staring at Jesse. Honey Bee and Jesse had learned a lot about catnip plants and other rare island herbs from Professor Katnip.

"You recognize this plant?" asked Jesse, looking puzzled.

Honey Bee shook her head back and forth. "I think Boo does, though."

Jesse and Honey Bee could almost read each other's minds and knew that Boo's incredible feline sense of smell was warning them about the unknown plant.

"I don't want to bother the professor any more tonight," said Jesse, looking around for something that he could use to pick up the potentially toxic plant.

He saw an old burlap bag, grabbed it, then carefully scooped up the unknown plant with a piece of bamboo.

"We'll show it to him in the morning," said Jesse, stepping backwards and stumbling over Boo, almost tripping himself.

Good thing cats aren't that clumsy, thought Boo, springing back out of the way.

That night in bed, Jesse's mind and imagination were flooded with the day's adventure and the mysterious events unfolding on the island. Boo was resting at the foot of the bed. Jesse stared at the moonlight filtering through the wooden shutters into his room for a few more minutes, thinking about the bullkats, and then quickly fell asleep. An image of hot, flowing lava flashed through his mind. His body began to sweat, consuming his imagination, while his mind traveled back into the imaginative world of island dreams.

tyrtle

CHAPTER SEVEN: BELLY BIRD BATTLE

Jesse opened his eyes and found himself in that same magical place. He was looking vicariously through Boo's blue cat eyes, and this time he was staring at a big red door.

Bright and early the next morning, Boo, Roxy Roo, and Chops were standing in front of the stairs leading up to the entryway of Professor Katnip's big treehouse.

Professor Katnip lived in the middle of Treetop Woods in a treehouse built inside one of the hundreds of giant trees towering above the southwest side of Tyrtle Island. Now, this was not just any ordinary treehouse built in any ordinary tree. Treehouses in Treetop Woods were incredibly gigantic and full of intricate platforms and artistic spiraling catwalks. They were constructed with beautiful floor-to-ceiling scratching posts and most any cat comforts and feline features that a Meow cat could possibly want, including walkways that connected to custom kitty boxes.

Professor Katnip's treehouse was without a doubt the grandest of any treehouse in the woods. Surprisingly, Chops was the first one up the rocky stairs, and he pulled on the rope hanging to the side of the giant red door. A deep-toned bell sound came from inside the treehouse, and then, as if by magic, the door opened. A hollowed-out tree trunk appeared before them. The three friends stepped inside, and automagically they were slowly lifted up high above the ground. The lifting log stopped abruptly at the first floor of the professor's treehouse. The three Meow cats stepped cautiously inside and grinned as they were greeted with the aroma of various catnip scents that permeated the air.

"Stop lollygagging around and come on in," called out a voice from within the huge hollowed-out home.

The wide-open room was full of wooden tables, shelves, and contraptions of every shape and size imaginable. The professor's laboratory was covered with a maze of bamboo pipes and smoking tubes that wormed their way in and out of intricate bamboo workshops. The artful bamboo workshops were covered by an intricately-designed bamboo dome. Below the domes were flames that burned brightly under boiling pots and gurgling kettles filled with various laboratory concoctions, many of which were bubbling over the sides.

Each workshop was equipped to make a specific blend of one of the professor's catnip recipes or a special brew of his herbal catnip teas. Two of the most popular amongst the Meow cats are Purple-sea Tea and Big-paw Katnip. The table tops and chairs were covered with open books and scrolls propped open. Wood, stone, and unusual island artifacts were lying around in what appeared to be no particular order.

The professor was standing at the back of the vast room next to one of his huge wooden lab tables. He was hovering over a big red kettle and appeared to be closely watching some kind of experiment that was about to boil over.

"Quickly!" Professor Katnip waved his paw in the air, signaling for one of them to come over and help him.

Roxy Roo didn't hesitate and raced over to assist the professor in the center of the noisy and chaotic laboratory.

It appeared to Roxy Roo, watching closely, that the professor was waiting for the exact right moment to add some dried herbs to one of his boiling brews.

Professor Katnip handed Roxy Roo a small bowl of herbs that he was holding.

"Add this slowly to the kettle when I say when," he said.

He took two wooden paddles and stirred the mixture in the kettle very carefully in one particular direction. He repeated the process until the smoke billowed into the air in a perfect circular pattern. The professor watched the smoke spiral up into the open room and, without any warning, shouted, "Quickly! Now!"

After pouring the herbal mixture into the kettle, Roxy Roo stepped back lickety-split. She watched as the kettle began to shake violently, exploding high up into the room in a puff of smoke, like a volcano releasing its steam. The explosion shocked all the Meow cats, and then, in the next instant, the smoke was sucked back down into the kettle. The smoking extravaganza amazed all the Meow cats.

Chops scooted closer to Boo whispering, "He never said 'when.' He said 'now,' not 'when.'"

Boo didn't say a word. He just smiled at his funny friend and continued thinking about the spectacle they had just witnessed.

"Purr-fect," said the professor. "Yes, that will do."

Professor Katnip motioned for them to follow him to the center of the treehouse. As usual, he was wearing his signature red bow tie around his neck, which was partially covered by his exceptionally long, curly gray cat hair.

Stopping in the middle of the room, they looked up at the maze of catwalks that spiraled up and around the multi-colored bark-covered walls. The walls were covered with smoking laboratories and various kinds of plants and trees growing everywhere as high up as they could see.

Professor Katnip looked directly at Boo and handed him a large catpack.

"Guard this with your life, because all of our lives depend on it," he pronounced loudly and sternly. "Do exactly as I have written… exactly… Do not let this information fall into the wrong hands."

With that, Professor Katnip turned and walked away into the next room and closed the door behind him.

"That's it? 'All of our lives depend on it' and that's it?" said Chops wildly, throwing his paws up in the air and then scratching his furry head. "What's inside the catpack?"

Boo walked back outside through the big red front door, and Roxy Roo followed him gracefully down the stairs. Boo looked up just in time to see

Chops slinky down the stairs nose first and perform a beautiful face-plant on the bottom step.

Boo laughed as he watched Chops slither down the steps. "There he goes again. Tryin' to plow his way to the middle of the island," said Boo jokingly.

Boo opened the catpack and peeked down inside the leather bag. He reached his paw inside and pulled out a copper-colored scroll tied with a leathery cord. He put the scroll into Roxy Roo's gentle paws. She carefully untied the leather cord and slowly opened the scroll.

Roxy Roo read from the scroll:

"DO NOT TOUCH THE PLANT! Go to the Roundabout Rainforest and find the RAINBOW PLANTS. The plants MUST look exactly like the one lying in the leather pouch. Make sure a PORKY PORCUPINE cuts the plants as they have protective paws. This plant can be lethal to Meow cats and harmful to other creatures. Cut ONLY the plants that are flowering and place them in the backpack. Take as much of the flowering plant as you can fit into the backpack. DO NOT TOUCH THE PLANT!"

As if he didn't hear a single word that Boo had just read, Chops reached down slowly with one claw extended.

SLAP! Boo quickly knocked Chops' paw out of the way. "Did you just take a catnap for the last five minutes?" shouted Boo, losing his temper. "Don't touch the plant!"

Chops raised his paw up to his nose like he was hoping to get a whiff from the scent of the plant and then cried out softly, "Ouuuch."

Boo didn't say anything. He shot him a sideways glance and just shook his head.

"Anything else in the catpack?" asked Roxy Roo, glancing at Chops.

Boo reached his paw back into the catpack, searching for a few moments. "Nope, just this red claw cap," said Boo, holding it up for them to see. "Must be the professor's red cap to match his red bow tie. I know that sometimes he wears these caps to keep from damaging the delicate catnip plants."

Chops smiled, holding his paw up off the ground. "He's one stylin' old cat."

"I wonder what kind of potent potion he had in that kettle," said Roxy Roo, sounding perplexed. "I will say this, though, it had the most pleasant catnip aroma. It was intoxicating."

Boo's face lit up with a big cat grin. "So good that even a bullkat might drink it?"

"I hope that volcanic eruption wasn't one of his catnip tea recipes that we've all been drinking," said Chops, holding his paw up to his mouth as if he were sipping a cup of catnip tea.

Boo flipped his black and white checkered scarf back over his shoulder, accidentally slapping Chops across the face with the tassels.

"Chops, looks like we're going to need your prickly little friend," said Boo.

"Hi ho, Silver!" Roxy Roo and Chops sang out together, almost like they had rehearsed it.

"Silver told me last night that we would be able to find him at the Meow House Inn," said Roxy Roo.

Chops' face lit up all of a sudden, and he ran his tongue around the outside of his mouth. "Ooooh, I just love those little mint-'n-fish-flavored cookies they have. You know the ones? They're shaped like little mice. I like to eat the tail first and then one leg at a time and then—"

Roxy Roo gave him a disgusted look. "Chops! Would you please stop it!" she shouted, interrupting him.

"I think Silver knows more about bullkats than we're aware," said Boo. "I also think he's very anxious to help us because of what happened to his family."

Following the path back through the center of Treetop Woods, they walked across Cattail Crossing. Cattail Crossing was a natural architectural marvel. The crossing was formed with two arching branches, each the size of a massive tree trunk, that crisscrossed over one another and provided a natural covered catwalk. The catwalk crossed over the Rainbow River, which ran through the center of Treetop Woods. The incredible catwalk also provided a path to the three tree towers which, together, are known to all the Meow cats as the Meow House Inn.

Chops made a quick stop along the way at one of the many public cat scratching posts throughout Treetop Woods.

"Puuurrrr, Puuuurrrrr," sighed Chops, his face grinning from ear to ear.

Roxy Roo and Boo turned around, hearing the loud purring sound, and found Chops enjoying himself rubbing his back and shoulders against the scratching post.

Chops purred and stretched out his claws. "Oh, this is sooo paw-some. This really is the cat's meow," he said.

"Not now, Chops. Come on," said Boo, yanking his friend away from the post by his short gray tail.

The three cats strolled through the turtle-shaped cutout in the trunk of the tree that was the entryway into the Meow House Inn. The sweet aroma of the herbal teas swirled through the air and instantly ignited their feline senses. Their faces beamed as they strolled into the entrance hall of the inn.

Boo looked around at the beautiful surroundings that were furnished with magnificent long wooden and stone tables. Each table itself was an ornamental work of art. The tables had carvings depicting intricate scenes from the nine lands of Tyrtle Island. Each elaborate scene was displayed in a beautiful array of tropical colors. The hanging gardens of bright and beautiful flowers, leafy green plants, and streaming vines wove a tapestry of color inside and outside the palatial walls of the Meow House Inn.

Boo knew the Inn like it was his own home, and he quickly spotted Silver sitting next to an open window on the far side of the cat-yard. Silver appeared to be sipping on a cup of catnip tea and chewing on some sort of flavored bark. The tea was most likely one of Professor Katnip's magical blends. The professor had the most popular catnip teas in the woods. In fact, catnip tea and other herbal blends were the most sought-after treats on Tyrtle Island. Other than the blends that Professor Katnip created, there were only a few other small tomcat and mollycat shops in Treetop Woods that made herbal tea blends. Professor Katnip was known as "The King of Catnip" and was by far one of the wealthiest creatures on Tyrtle Island.

Chapter Seven

The Inn was bustling with a clowder of cats and other wonderful and strange creatures from every walk of life across the island. There were cats, porcupines, bulldogs, and big-toed buggers of all shapes and sizes enjoying their own particular tasty treats. They could be heard slurping and sipping on their preferred choice of catnip and other delicious herbal teas.

Boo's intent was to greet Silver inconspicuously. He knew the adventure they were about to take had to be conducted with the utmost secrecy. Chops, on the other paw, had a different idea.

"Say hello to my little prickly friend!" Chops sang out loudly in his best operatic voice as they all three approached Silver.

Roxy Roo attempted to quickly cover Chops' mouth with her paw, but it was too late. Every creature in the courtyard had heard his boisterous singing and was now looking curiously over in their direction.

"Seriously," said Boo, letting out a big sigh.

They all gathered around, sitting on top of the stone table as cats and creatures will sometimes do. Boo sat next to Silver and glanced around to see who was looking in their direction.

Chops raised his upper lip, making a stinky face, and held his paw over his nose when he saw the bark hanging out of Silver's two front teeth. "Ew! That looks like… well… that looks awful. That just can't be your favorite thing to eat," he said, crinkling his nose.

Silver ignored Chops and continued to chomp on the bark, spitting pieces out of his mouth as he began to speak. "On your way across the room did any of you happen to see a rather odd and tall and, might I add, creepy-looking cat sitting a few tables over in the corner?"

"I saw that cat. His name is Bones," replied Boo. "He's sitting with Harry, Harriet, and Henry."

"He creeped us out one night when he abruptly stopped us as we were walking to the Pouncing Place. He's more trouble than a cat o' nine tails," said Roxy Roo quietly.

"I think he's following us," said Boo. "In fact, I know he's following us. I wonder what the elders are talking to him about."

"OK, let's not panic," said Silver, talking to himself as much as to the others sitting on the table.

"We have to crawl out of here quietly, without being noticed," said Boo. "Quickly, follow me. I know a back way out."

Chops glanced over at Silver's unfinished cup of catnip tea and quickly gulped it down. He cringed as he got a taste of the tree-bark backwash that was left in the bottom of the cup.

Boo picked up the catpack and, with his friends trailing behind him, they all walked in single file out of the room. They exited through a set of double doors that Boo knew would lead to the library. He recalled that the library had a passageway through the tree that led to the outside of the Meow House Inn. Boo glanced over his shoulder as he entered the library, and Bones was nowhere to be seen.

Silver was in awe seeing the seemingly endless books and scrolls made out of leather, wood, and bark. The books and scrolls were stacked up, one upon another, and spiraled upwards toward the ceiling. The shelves, walls, and ceiling were decorated with the colorful bark from exotic trees growing all around the island. Silver paused for a second, gazing up at the beautiful tree-bark lining the ceiling above him. He wished that he had more time to look around and nibble a little bit on this splendid room. After all, bark was one of his favorite foods, and he had actually never seen a room completely full of it. He understood they were in a hurry, so he followed everyone as they scurried through the room and into the tunnel leading to the outside of the Inn.

"To the Walkabout Wilderness and beyond!" shouted Chops as they pushed open the heavy wooden tunnel door and stepped out into the sunshine filtering through the tall trees.

"Oh, kitty litter. I forgot my scarf," said Chops, looking longingly over at the one hanging around Boo's neck.

"Chops, watch your language," said Roxy Roo.

"Too bad. You'll have to do without it," said Boo.

"But you have yours on," said Chops, whining.

"That's because I remembered to put mine on this morning," snapped Boo.

Roxy Roo looked at Boo, and he knew what that look meant. He handed over his scarf to Chops without saying another word.

Chapter Seven

"Stylin' on the island," Chops said with a big grin, wrapping the scarf around his thick neck.

"I don't mean to sound alarming, but I suspect this adventure won't be a cat-and-mouse game," said Silver. "I've traveled beyond the Rainbow River. I have walked in a land absent of friendly smiles, void of the warmth of loved ones, and without the comforts of home." He wanted to warn his friends as gently as he could while trying not to alarm them.

"No catnip tea and scratching posts?" asked Chops jokingly. "Well, as long as I have fish."

Silver wanted them to understand that on this adventure they would be without the familiar comforts and protection that Treetop Woods provided them. The porcupine had seen things and experienced hardships that he hoped his friends would never have to face. He was worried for his traveling companions.

Boo, Roxy Roo, and Chops had never ventured much farther than the Pouncing Place. In fact, up to this point in their lives, the only big adventure they had ever taken together was going fishing at Fish Flop Cove. The reward of the delicious fish far outweighed the small risk taken in going there. The craziest thing that had ever happened to them, outside of getting slapped in the face with a delicious fish, was on the day that Chops literally ran right into Silver.

Up until now, there had been no reason to travel beyond that point. Beyond The Land of To Fiddle About, the island was full of many wonderful places and many curious and dangerous creatures, including the feared bullkats.

Quietly walking along the rocky edge of the Rainbow River's swiftly moving water, the rainforest-covered Majestic Mountains could be seen behind the clouds off in the distance. Trotting past the outskirts of Treetop Woods they reached the old gathering place. Boo jumped up through one of the openings to see if any creatures were inside. The Pouncing Place appeared to be empty, and they all decided to keep pressing on, maintaining a purposeful pace. Silver wanted to make it past the river's fork and across the river into Bow Valley before the sun had set behind the mountains.

"I think I need a cat snack," said Chops, sitting down next to the crystal-clear river and watching a few fish swim by.

Boo and Roxy Roo knew Chops' definition of the word "snack" was more like a big meal for most cats.

"Alright, I'll get some for you," said Boo, reading Chops' mind.

Fishing came easy for Boo with his big, powerful claws and quick cat reflexes.

Boo exchanged glances with Roxy Roo as they watched Chops devour one fish after another.

"You're not full yet?" asked Boo.

"Do I look full?" Chops replied with his pat answer.

"You know, you really are eating a lot of fish," Silver informed Chops.

"What? This is just a snack," said Chops, slobbering.

Silver was fully aware that this wide-open area of the island could be very dangerous, so he kept a watchful eye on the horizon. He peered into the sky and then watched Chops gobble down a few more fish. He was fascinated by Chops' amazing appetite. All porky porcupines have poor eyesight, so Silver was surprised when he actually spotted a large group of birds flying in their direction coming from the Majestic Mountains. He was fairly certain that he had encountered these very birds before and started to run for cover.

"Here they come!" cried out Silver. "Hurry, take cover!"

Boo and Roxy Roo looked up in the sky and ran toward the pile of big boulders, following Silver as they watched the flock of birds flying toward them.

From the cover of the rocks, they all looked back at Chops, who was still eating and had a big fish hanging out of his mouth. Without saying a word they read each other's minds and shouted out together, "Throw the fish!"

All at once, hundreds of belly birds swooped down like a plague upon them. Now, belly birds, at first glance, appear to be harmless with their cute little round faces and brightly-colored feathers. They're fat in the belly and have a leathery skin padding on their white underbelly that can be used as a landing pad since they have no legs and no feet. Rarely do they land on their bellies, but when they do, all they are able to do was wobble back and forth until they flap their tiny wings fast enough to be able to take off again. Appearances can be deceiving, as the old saying goes. Though belly birds appear friendly, they are very angry, carnivorous little birds. The unfriendly birds have very sharp beaks, which at this moment was unfortunate for Chops. The little birds aggressively went after what was left of his delicious Rainbow Fish dangling from his mouth.

Silver, Boo, and Roxy Roo watched from the safety of the rocks as Chops battled the little birds. Chops was not going to give up his last fish without a good old catfight.

"Chops, let 'em have it!" yelled Boo again as they watched Chops in a tug-of-war with the belly birds. "I mean the fish! Give 'em the fish!"

Cats always do what they want to do when they want to do it, always.

"No way this cat is giving up his snack to a bunch of goofy-looking birds with no legs and feet," cried out Chops, using his big paw to swat at the tiny, vicious birds. "Not in all nine of my lives. Ouch! Ouch! Ouch! OK, that really hurt," he said as the cute little belly birds continued pecking at his furry body.

"Oh, good grief," said Silver dramatically. "Hi ho, Silver to the rescue, again!" he sang out in a heroic voice as he plucked and fired a couple of his quills like tiny spears at the cute little nasty birds.

Boo and Roxy Roo quickly loaded their slings with small pebbles, and after a few swirls through the air, they released the tiny rocks, hitting the birds with deadly accuracy. The pebbles flew silently, striking the vicious little birds on their plump bellies, leaving them disoriented and wobbling around on the ground.

The legless birds flew off with chunks of Chops' fish dangling out of their yellow beaks and disappeared toward the mountains as quickly as they had arrived.

"I showed them who's at the top of this food chain," said Chops, looking around at the bits of his yummy fish scattered on top of the rocks.

Silver rolled his prickly eyebrows and said, "Without a doubt."

"No more snack stops until we stop to rest for the night," said Roxy Roo.

Chops picked himself up off the ground and picked the tiny leftover bits of fish off his gray fur with his pointy claws.

As if in protest of Roxy Roo's snack ruling, Chops grumpily slid his paw sideways along the ground and caught the tip of his paw on one of the many jagged rocks. "Ouch!" he cried out, jumping around.

"Feel better now?" asked Boo sarcastically. "Don't get a cattitude."

turtle

CHAPTER EIGHT: PEE-WEE POPPERS AND BIG-TOED BUGGERS

THE SUN WAS DIRECTLY ABOVE them as the band of friends continued their trek through The Land of To Fiddle About. They walked along talking about their families and nibbling on smoked fish, despite what Roxy Roo had just said about no more cat snacks.

The Land of To Fiddle About is a wide-open delightful place full of rainbow wobbler catnip plants, some sparse fiddle-wood trees, and a painter's palette full of exotic plants and flowers. The breathtaking landscape gave way to rolling hills cascading down to the ocean cliffs below that offered very little protection from various creatures such as belly birds, big-toed buggers, and bullkats. This land was a wonderfully dangerous place for Meow cats who found themselves fiddling about in the intoxicating air, filled with the tempting scent of wobbling catnip plants. When any Meow cat lingered too long, which was usually the case, they would find themselves rolling, pawing, and nibbling on the exhilarating herbs. It's for this reason that this place is called The Land of To Fiddle About.

Silver anticipated that his friends might just be a little tempted to stop and sample the plants, so he decided to caution them.

"I know what effect wobbling catnip has on cats, so absolutely no nibbling or dawdling along the way. This is a dangerous place to take a cat-nap," Silver warned his feline friends, standing on his hind legs and looking out over the animated landscape.

"Silver's right. Absolutely no dawdling," replied Boo as all the cats stood looking at one another with whiskers sticking straight out.

"The flowers look like a fantasy, and the scent is so unbelievable," exclaimed Roxy Roo, taking in a deep breath and then sighing.

Chops looked over at all his friends and said, "Yeah, OK, no dawdling."

The waving long-stemmed plants with multicolored flowers were given the name of wobblers with the help of little green geckos called *poppers*.

The pee-wee poppers popped up and down from flower to flower and caused the lively flowers at the end of the long stem to wobble back and forth. The poppers held on tightly with their sticky feet, busily sipping the sweet nectar from the center of the flowers. The flowers seemed to have the same stimulating effect on the little green poppers as they do on the Meow cats.

"Wow, look at all those little green creatures hopping around like crazed frogs from flower to flower," exclaimed Chops, his eyes bouncing around, following the poppers from stem to stem.

Boo knew Chops well enough to know exactly what he was thinking. "Don't do it, Chops!" shouted Boo.

Cats always do what they want to do, when they want to do it, always.

Chops jumped right in the middle of the bobbing flowers, and little green poppers went flying all over the place. Immersing himself in the intoxicating plants, Chops smothered his long whiskers and fat cheeks as Silver watched in disbelief at the way the plants completely overwhelmed him.

"This is unbelievable! Look at the crazy effect these plants have on Chops!" Silver cried out, amazed. He turned around, looking for Boo and Roxy Roo, and to his astonishment they were rolling around like crazy cats through the plants and sliding head-first on their backs down the hillside.

Silver watched his friends frolicking in the catmint, and the porcupine could not help but smile at them. He felt slightly grudging because he could not experience that same sensation. Then something from deep within him caused Silver to react in a way that was very unusual for him. He jumped into the middle of the plants and flowers, rolling around for a few minutes, imitating his friends. The porcupine somehow hoped that he could enjoy the moment just as much as the cats.

Chapter Eight

He stopped after a few minutes and thought to himself, "Guess you have to be a cat."

Silver continued to keep watch as his friends got their fill of the intoxicating plants. They all lay leisurely among the smashed plants and flowers, fiddling about and singing songs as the effects of the plants slowly faded away.

"Some say you shouldn't fiddle about
For us we say we have no doubt
Catmint, maybe just a hint
There's nothing wrong with a short timeout

Beautiful flowers you hear about
Plants that cause you to lay about
Catnip, maybe just a bit
Then you can continue your walkabout

The Rainbow River is just below
The view is majestic, so take it slow
Bow Valley is waiting just beyond
The rainbows are sure to steal the show

Tyrtle Island is our home
The ocean we have no need to roam
The ancients found us paradise
Love in motion is on the throne

So take up your bow and arrows
Follow your paws to where the trail goes
Walkabout Wilderness is just beyond
Of this we are sure we know."

Silver tried to keep them singing as long as he could so they wouldn't fall asleep. He finally managed to get them standing on all four paws, and slowly they moved away from the potent plants and fragrant flowers.

Roxy Roo was quiet as she listened to the cat tales told by Boo and tall tales told by Chops. They all placed one paw slowly in front of the other and continued to follow the trail through The Land of To Fiddle About.

She hoped that Silver would eventually tell them all about his family. She couldn't help but wonder what happened to them that fearful day the bullkats attacked their home in the Land of Wig Waggle. Silver was quiet as Boo and Chops continued to ramble on about their great adventures, which, up to this point, meant fishing at Fish Flop Cove.

"Silver, forgive my prying," said Roxy Roo, interrupting another one of Chops' tall tales. "If you don't mind sharing with us, I would like to hear about your family."

There were several minutes of silence with only the faint sounds of Silver's claws scratching along on the rocky ground and the clinking of his tin-tipped tail.

Silver finally broke his silence. "Some days I wake up and it seems like it was so long ago and other days it seems like it was only yesterday. We have a saying in the Land of Wig Waggle: 'May your prickle be as strong and numerous as the quills on your back.'"

A prickle is the word used to describe a family of porky porcupines and porcupines on Tyrtle Island who all live together in the Land of Wig Waggle.

"My porky-mate is so clever, and she has the fullest collection of beautiful brown quills that I have ever laid my eyes upon," said Silver gleefully. "Ah, my little porky ones, what terrific climbers they are. They balance so gracefully in the trees it's as if they had been trained by the most acrobatic monkeys in the rainforest. We had the best tree in the best bushy wetlands. We had the best home on the island… the Land of Wig Waggle. It was perfect. Up until the night the bullkats came and destroyed it all. The porkies were all scattered about. Well, all those that survived that terrifying night."

Silver slowed for a few moments and then stopped in the middle of the trail. His plump tail clinked, plopping on the ground.

Chops was so engrossed in Silver's story that he was not paying attention when Silver came to an abrupt stop. He stepped on Silver's prickly tail and then his belly thumped up against Silver's back.

"Ouch!" cried out Chops, jumping. "You did it again!"

"I certainly did nothing of the kind," replied Silver. "Are you going to start that again?"

Chops looked down at his paw and belly, and suddenly realized that this time he had no quills sticking out of him.

"One of you should be in the front and one of you in the back," said Roxy Roo, chuckling and pointing her paw in each direction.

"Chops, you in the back. Silver in the front... since he's our best defense," commanded Boo.

"I have to believe that my prickle is safe somewhere on our island," said Silver, walking to the front of the line. "I only wish I had been there that night. I know one day I will find them again."

"I'm not so sure. Not many creatures survive a bullkat attack," said Chops, thinking out loud, then instantly wishing he could take it back.

Boo smacked Chops on his thick gray head as he walked past him.

"I have faith that your family is safe," said Roxy Roo, looking back at Chops and shaking her head.

One by one they rounded the gigantic rocks known as Buggers Boulders, and the long, glimmering river flowing down from the mountains came into view. They started winding their way down the switchbacks along the hillside to the Rainbow River's crossing point. Silver had crossed the Rainbow River before, and he knew it could be an adventure all by itself. You see, on Tyrtle Island, big-toed buggers were responsible for bringing creatures across the rivers. The level of excitement on any particular crossing was dependent on whether there was a good big-toed bugger or a bad big-toed bugger navigating the river raft. One could never tell if the big-toed bugger was good or bad until one arrived at the raft and was able to look the big-toed bugger right in the eyes.

Big-toed buggers are large in size, covered in stinky, matted hair, and of course have two very big toes on each foot with two large claws. They have very large, long noses and little tiny eyes popping out of their coconut-shaped heads, which make a very good explanation for their exceptionally great sense of smell and very bad eyesight. Coincidentally, their own stinky, moldy smell does not seem to bother them at all.

It's very difficult to approach a big-toed bugger from the southwest side of the island since there was usually an onshore wind blowing in the direction of Rainbow River. A gallivanter's chances grew increasingly better when traveling through Bow Valley, unless, of course, the unlucky traveler happened to be passing through on a day with an offshore wind. A big-toed bugger's claws might also become a problem if you happen to encounter a bad big-toed bugger on the raft. In the event travelers encountered a bad big-toed bugger, their chances of avoiding being clawed were fairly good, since big-toed buggers can only move extremely slowly except when they're in the water.

The friends bounced down the very last switchback and then pounced down onto the sandy shore where a large wooden raft lay gently bobbing at the river's edge. The raft's navigator, a giant big-toed bugger, could be seen sitting at the stern next to the rudder handle.

Reaching the edge of the trail, Chops stopped, gawking and gaping. "What… in the world… is that thing?"

"What is that awful sour smell?" asked Roxy Roo, covering her brown nose with her paw.

"Are you asking about the large raft or the large creature on the raft?" said Silver, looking at Chops.

"I'm sure he's asking about the large creature on the large raft," said Boo, staring in amazement.

"That, my cat friends, is what is known as a big-toed bugger," said Silver. "What I don't know is if this big-toed bugger is a good big-toed bugger or a bad big-toed bugger. But no cause for worry. I got this."

"I got this! I got this!" cried Chops. "Are you serious? Did you happen to see the size of that thing?"

"I know how to handle this creature," said Silver confidently. "Chops, follow me closely. Not too closely, though."

Porky porcupines are not known to be the best jumpers. Silver had to make sure that he timed his jump with the rhythm of the raft. The large wooden structure slowly bobbed up and down, bouncing up against the river's edge while the rocks whittled away at the raft's wooden side.

Boo, Roxy Roo, and Chops stood patiently on the shore, anticipating Silver's jump. Their eyes moved back and forth with the rhythm of Silver's prickly body and the raft's movement. Honestly, this jump was not much of an effort for a Meow cat, but for a porky porcupine it was tantamount to an Olympic endeavor.

"Are you sure about this?" said Chops, dancing along with the rhythm of the porcupine and raft. "You got this?"

The anticipation of Silver's jump seemed to take forever. Chops couldn't wait any longer and decided to take the matter into his own paws by giving Silver a helpful shove at the absolutely wrong time. Chops' scarf snagged one of Silver's quills, and they both went tumbling head first into the river.

"Chops, nooooo!" screamed out Roxy Roo.

It was too late. Silver and Chops were already tumbling through the water, and they quickly disappeared under the bouncing raft.

Contrary to being poor jumpers, porky porcupines are known to be very strong swimmers. Cats are also very good swimmers. Unfortunately, so are big-toed buggers, who happen to move much faster in the water than they do on dry land—or in a raft, for that matter.

Roxy Roo and Boo jumped effortlessly onto the raft, trying to get a better view of their wet friends in the water. Boo had been watching the big-toed bugger, who had slowly clawed his way to the side of the raft while everyone else was preoccupied watching and waiting for Silver to jump up on the raft. The big-toed bugger was now in the water and heading toward Silver and Chops as they were still floundering in the water a short distance downstream. Reaching the shore, Silver and Chops tried to regain their balance. They climbed up and over the jagged rocks and through the slimy plants, struggling to reach the river bank.

Fortunately for Silver and Chops, big-toed buggers are herbivores, but it's the claws that one needs to worry about if you happen to encounter a bad big-toed bugger. Especially one who happens to be having a bad day.

Once a day, every day, this particular good or bad big-toed bugger would slowly move his hairy body across to the side of his raft and methodically use his large sharp claws to lower himself into the water. He would make his way rather swiftly with the downstream current over to the lush green plants along the shore, which is where Silver and Chops happened to be standing. This feeding ritual was unknown to the big-toed bugger's captive audience.

"Out of the water! Get out of the water!" screamed Boo. "The bugger is right behind you!"

Chops and Silver screamed out together in high-pitched voices as the big-toed bugger stretched out one large, sharp claw. Slowly the hairy creature slapped it down into the water, right in front of their faces. Silver and Chops stood motionless and in shock as the bugger slowly pulled his claw back out of the water with a handful of plucked plants, roots and all.

Boo and Roxy Roo were captivated as they stood on the raft. Chops' facial expression went from a look of terror to a look of disgust as he covered his nose with his wet scarf.

"Somebody needs a large bar of lavender soap," said Chops as he finally jumped up on the shore.

"This did not go exactly how I envisioned it," yelled Silver from the riverbank, picking wet moss and plants off his body. "Chops, I can't thank you enough for your help."

"I'm guessing this one is a good big-toed bugger?" said Boo.

They all sat quietly in the corner of the raft, waiting for the big-toed bugger to finish eating his plants, and then watched painfully as the poor creature slowly found his way back to buggering the rudder.

"Must be an exciting life, living on a raft that never moves up and down the river," said Chops as the big-toed bugger started to slowly move the raft across to the other side.

The raft was guided across the river by a large rope that was threaded through a set of iron rings attached to the raft's wooden platform and anchored to the opposite shore.

"How do we pay him?" asked Chops, looking curiously at Silver.

"Pay the bugger nothing," said Silver. "Good or bad, all big-toed buggers work for free with no expectation of any kind of payment."

Chapter Eight

"Wow, lives on a raft that goes nowhere, eats slimy plants, and works for free," said Chops enthusiastically. "Sign me up!"

Eventually the raft bumped into the Bow Valley side of the Rainbow River. One at a time, the four travelers jumped onto the moss-covered, wet shore. Silver went last to make sure he had some help if he didn't quite make the jump, which, to everyone's delight, he did.

"I think I know a good place to rest for the night," said Silver. "Follow me."

"For some reason, I don't get a warm furry feeling of confidence when you say things like that," said Chops.

"Silver knows the valley better than any of us," said Boo. "We only know what we've been told about it. Silver has actually walked through the valley."

"Well, actually, no. Truthfully, I have never really been through Bow Valley," confessed Silver. "I was given directions by Professor Katnip. He assured me that this particular spot was a good place to spend the night. He said it's not too far from the river."

Feeling reassured by the advice provided by Professor Katnip, they were all reenergized and carried on toward their destination of Cat Skull Rock.

The tropical sky turned to a glorious red and orange as the sun started to duck down behind the Majestic Mountains. The trio of Meow cats followed Silver along the trail through the dense forest and into an open meadow at the southernmost point of the Meow Mountains. The firebugs buzzed about in the shadows of the wide-open meadow. The bugs migrated toward the trail and flew curiously in circles around the travelers' faces, but the tiny acrobats were careful to never touch them. The firebugs flew in groups of two or more and seemed to be leading the way up the steep trail to Cat Skull Rock. Roxy Roo loved most any flying insect and was mesmerized by the way the firebugs performed their enchanted, glowing dance. The lighted bugs circled around their audience, attaching themselves to one another in perfect harmony.

Chops was seemingly annoyed at the firebugs swirling around his body as he continued to swipe at them with one paw at a time. The dancing lights seemed to be just toying with him as they swirled ever so gracefully through the colored twilight.

"How much further is this place?" asked Boo. "What did Professor Katnip say this place looks like?"

"Professor Katnip told me to look for a large rock at the southernmost point of the Meow Mountains," said Silver. "The rock looks like the skull of a cat."

"What did he just say? The rock looks like what?" asked Chops. "I know… you got it."

"That's gotta be the place," exclaimed Roxy Roo, peering up the side of the mountain at the scary-looking rock. "I see why somebody gave it that name, because that really does resemble a cat's skull."

"Whose great idea was it to stay here for the night?" asked Chops. "Sure, let's spend the night in the scariest place we can find."

The firebugs retreated back into the mountain meadows below as the cats and Silver all slowly hopped up the last few rocky steps to the base of Cat Skull Rock. Boo quietly looked around the rocks as the rest of them lay down in the shallow mouth of the cave.

"I'll take first watch," said Boo, setting the catpack down. "You all get some rest. Chops, I'll wake you in two hours."

"Two hours," replied Chops wearily.

Boo looked around at his friends as they made themselves comfortable on the hard ground inside the opening of Cat Skull Rock. Roxy Roo and Chops curled up close to one another, and Silver gathered some plants, making a bed right next to Chops.

"I don't think so," said Chops, smirking at Silver.

Chops got up and moved to the other side of Roxy Roo. He wasn't taking any chances of possibly getting poked by one of Silver's quills during the night.

The slow, rhythmic sound of metal clanking against the rocks filled the quiet atmosphere. They all opened their eyes one by one, looking over at Silver's tin-tipped tail tapping up and down on the rock.

"My apologies," said Silver as he moved his tail over the plants he had gathered.

Chapter Eight

Boo stared up at the shining lights blanketing the night sky. That night, the stars seemed as though they were putting on a brilliant, twinkling performance just for an audience of one. Their sparkles filled the heavens, and their number could not be counted. He was mesmerized by their dazzling display, and a sense of peace came over him as he gazed up at their beauty against the dark night sky. One star was especially bright, and it caught Boo's attention.

The Star of Wonder, he thought. *Could it be?*

Boo's eyes fell into a trance, bouncing back and forth in concert with the twinkling light show displayed above him throughout the heavens. He recognized the Bear and the Orion constellations and, for a few minutes, felt a sudden sense of insignificance. Looking up at the heavens, he was also reminded of the Creator and His promise that all creatures are fearfully and wonderfully made for a specific purpose. In the midst of this great adventure, he suddenly felt content, and somehow he knew everything would be alright.

Boo whispered into Chops' pointed ear and tugged on his torn scarf, hanging around Chops' neck. "Chops, wake up, big guy."

"Let go. That's my fish," mumbled Chops sleepily, pulling back on the scarf.

Chops didn't like to be woken up by anyone, but Boo knew of one way for certain that never failed to get his friend up. He gave a good hard tug on one of the long whiskers on the side of Chops' face, and the big cat jumped up to attention on all four paws and gave Boo a very disgruntled look.

"Really, was that necessary?" gurgled Chops, sounding like he had a hairball stuck in his throat.

May the whiskers on his face never fall out, thought Boo, smiling as he lay down next to Roxy Roo.

Boo quickly got comfortable in the same spot that Chops' belly had already warmed up. A couple minutes passed by, and his deep purring faded away as he dropped off into a deep dream sleep.

Boo's thoughts spiraled deeper into his mind, and then he began to hear those disturbing words from that creepy voice in his head. "Oh, I know things. Don't you worry about how," Boo heard Bones say in his very distinct, unnerving voice. "I have to go now, but we have plans for you."

Boo's whiskers vibrated from the intruder's hot breath. Instinctively, his eyes popped wide open, and he was looking at a pair of spooky yellow eyes and a set of ghost-white horns from the silhouettes standing over him. It was the creepy figure of Bones clutching the professor's catpack with his long yellow claws, and one of the hideous bullkats was standing right next to him. Boo wasn't able to move a muscle, and his lightning-fast instincts were frozen in place like he was trapped in the middle of a nightmarish dream. He watched helplessly as the frightening figures leaned in closer until both of them hovered directly over him.

tyrtle

CHAPTER NINE: RAINBOWS TO THE RAINFOREST

J ESSE BOLTED UPRIGHT IN HIS bed with sweat running down his forehead, and for a split-second an image of Bones flashed before his eyes. He was terrified for a moment, thinking about the vivid details. The familiar surroundings of his room slowly came into view as he opened his eyes and realized he'd been dreaming again. Only this time, it wasn't just his dream alone. He had no logical explanation for what he had just experienced, but somehow his recurring dream and Boo's nightmare on Cat Skull Rock had mysteriously come together. Jesse had just woken up from a double-feature island dream.

"That's not possible," he thought. "Is that possible?" he asked, questioning himself.

Jesse's room was still dark except for the moonlight peeking through the wooden shutters. He sat in bed, trying to keep the incredible adventure alive in his mind. His eyes remained open, reflecting on the animated details of last night's adventure.

"Belly birds, big-toed buggers, Bones, and bullkats," he said aloud. "That's so crazy and yet so incredibly awesome."

Jesse sensed a real fear deep down inside, but he also loved the excitement he felt from this island dream he was experiencing. It was mysterious enough, yet he had a feeling that this dream and this adventure were somehow connected. He recalled a time a few years back that he and Tinman climbed Skull Rock. Thinking back, Jesse realized that Skull Rock looked very similar to Cat Skull Rock in his dream. Could it be possible that what was happening on Tyrtle Island today could somehow be connected to the island's past? A time long before humans inhabited Tyrtle Island?

"Why were the characters in my dream so much like my friends?" he thought. "Is Boo trying to tell me something?"

Jesse's mind reflected back on the plant that he and Honey Bee had found by the professor's greenhouse.

"I wish I knew what kind of plant that is," he thought out loud.

He knew that it was time to get out of bed and get moving. He still had to finish his paper route before he could meet with Tinman to start their trip through Bow Valley to the Roundabout Rainforest. It was an easy two-hour drive over the Roundabout Mountains to the windward side of Tyrtle Island. After that, it was just a few more minutes up the winding road to reach the rainforest.

Jesse turned his head to the side, and Boo was sitting next to his pillow, staring right at him.

"Hey, why so serious?" Jesse asked Boo, pulling him closer to give him a belly rub and a warm hug.

You can never get enough belly rubs and warm hugs, thought Boo. *Especially from your best friend.*

Jesse jumped out of bed, got dressed, and peeked in at his mom, who was still sleeping. He quietly tiptoed into her room, gave her a kiss on the cheek, and whispered, "Going to meet Tinman as soon as I finish my route."

The back door opened and shut with the sound of the screen door slamming quickly after him.

Jesse pedaled down the road under the dim street lights as fast as he could toward the newspaper office. He zoomed around the street corners and zipped up and down the sidewalks with Boo riding shotgun at the front of the bike.

Mr. Smitty greeted Jesse with his usual enthusiastic reception, while wearing his Pirate cap and a big smile across his face.

"Good morning, Jesse. You're early today. Lots of inserts again today," he said.

Jesse began the familiar process of adding the inserts into the thick papers and slapping them one by one through the folding machines.

Jesse's mind was consumed with thoughts of the exciting adventure awaiting them. Before he knew it, the work of folding the papers was done. He pedaled his bicycle faster than ever, darting up and down the neighborhood streets that were glowing from the dim streetlights. For Jesse, throwing papers was a good way to make some extra money. He also viewed it as a kind of sporting competition between him and his customers' front doors. He always felt a certain pride when he managed to land the oversized newspaper precisely on the doormat. Jesse turned the corner and passed by the umbrella lady's apartment, but this morning all was dark in her doorway. He tossed the newspaper up over the railing, and after hearing the crash against the screen door, he continued down the sidewalk with his deliveries.

He pedaled down the dark trail under a canopy of exotic trees toward Tinman's farm. Honey Bee and Tinman were sitting on the porch as he raced up toward the steps, then hit his brakes and skidded slightly on the wet grass. He leaned his bike up against the wood railing. Boo jumped out of the wooden box and hopped right up onto Honey Bee's lap.

"Do me a favor?" asked Tinman. "Can you take it easy on my lawn? I have a hard enough time keeping the critters from diggin' it up."

"You're not going to become one of those old grouchy 'get off my lawn' guys, are ya?" Jesse asked Tinman, grinning.

Jesse and Honey Bee smiled at each other, their eyes lingering for a few seconds.

"By the way, Professor Katnip came by late last night," said Tinman. "He can't join us today, but he said something about his head still hurting from yesterday and that you and Honey Bee know all about it. He also gave me this leather backpack with instructions inside and asked me not to open it until we're all together. He was acting kind of strange. In fact, the whole conversation was rather odd, even for the professor."

Jesse asked Tinman, "Did Honey Bee tell you what happened last night?"

Tinman handed the backpack to Jesse and said, "Yes, she told me the whole story."

Jesse reached inside and took out the leather pouch which had a note taped to the top of it. He unfolded the note and began to read it silently to himself.

Tinman glanced curiously at Honey Bee, then looked back at Jesse and asked, "Can you read it out loud?"

Jesse read the note:

"DO NOT TOUCH THE PLANT! Go to the Roundabout Rainforest and find the RAINBOW PLANTS. They MUST look exactly like the one lying in the leather pouch. Make sure TINMAN cuts the plants using the protective gloves. This plant can be lethal to cats and harmful to humans. Cut ONLY the plants that are flowering and place them in the backpack. Take as much of the flowering plant as you can fit in the backpack. DO NOT TOUCH THE PLANT!"

Jesse looked stunned by what he had just read. He couldn't believe his eyes. He sat down on the stairs and looked back at Boo sitting in Honey Bee's lap. Boo stared back at Jesse with a weird grin on his face, which to Jesse seemed a little odd, even for a very unusual cat like Boo.

"That was exactly what Roxy Roo read from the scroll in my dream," thought Jesse. He was starting to feel a little confused and overwhelmed, wondering why his dream seemed to be coming true.

"That's exactly what Roxy Roo read," he muttered.

Honey Bee and Tinman looked at him with a bewildered expression.

"Jesse, what is it? Who's Roxy Roo and what did she read?" asked Honey Bee.

"My dream… the dreams I've been having… What I just read sounds exactly like what Roxy Roo read in my dream," replied Jesse. "How's that possible?"

"Jesse, let the cat out of the bag, would ya?" said Tinman, looking at Boo.

Honey Bee followed Tinman's lead and said, "Jesse, you're killin' the cat with curiosity over here."

Chapter Nine

Whoever came up with those old sayings, one thing's for sure, it wasn't a cat, thought Boo.

"Would you please just spell it out?" said Tinman.

"This all sounds so crazy, but the note that I just read from Professor Katnip… well… it's almost word for word the same as the note from my dream. Professor Katnip… he's a cat in my dream. Honey Bee's a cat in my dream, Caleb's a cat in my dream, and even Boo is a cat in my dream," explained Jesse excitedly.

Me? A cat? Now that's a real shocker, thought Boo.

"Are you sure about that?" said Tinman.

"Yes, I think I know a cat when I see one," said Jesse passionately, pointing his finger at Boo. "You tell him, Boo boy."

"I think he's talking about the note, Jesse. Are you sure it's the same words on the note?" asked Honey Bee.

"Positive!" snapped Jesse.

Honey Bee could tell he was getting aggravated and said, "OK… OK, we believe you."

"So, just curious… am I in your dream?" asked Tinman.

Jesse glanced back up at him, grinning, and said, "Yup."

Tinman rubbed his head, looking at Boo. He hesitated for a minute and pondered what creature he might be.

"Sooo… what am I? Since you guys are all cats, I'm probably somethin' like a big tiger?" he said proudly.

Tinman crouched down, scrunched up his face, and let out his most ferocious tiger roar with his arms lifted high in the air.

Jesse and Honey Bee laughed out loud at Tinman's dramatic performance.

"Nope, you're a porcupine," said Jesse abruptly, flipping his blond hair back off his forehead.

"OK… alright… porcupines are cool," said Tinman. "I think I would prefer being a porcupine over a cat anyways."

Hey, I'm sitting right here, and I can hear you, thought Boo, looking up at Tinman and letting out a strange-sounding purr.

"I'm just sayin'… sorry, Boo, no offense," said Tinman playfully.

"So, Jesse, now I'm buzzing with curiosity. What are you in the dream?" said Honey Bee.

"Well, actually I'm a cat also," replied Jesse, looking directly at his cat. "I'm Boo."

A few minutes earlier, Caleb had walked up on the porch and had been standing there silently while Jesse was in the middle of trying to explain his dream to Tinman and Honey Bee.

Caleb laughed out loud when he heard Jesse call himself Boo.

"Well, sprinkle me with sugar and call me a donut. Look who finally showed up," said Tinman.

Caleb pretended not to hear Tinman's wisecrack, even though donuts were without a doubt one of his favorite food groups.

"Hey, Jesse, I know you really like Boo and all... we all like him too, but I think you need some help if you think you're a cat," said Caleb jokingly. "You mean like you have dual personalities or somethin'?"

"I know it sounds crazy," said Honey Bee. "Maybe Boo's tryin' to tell us something. He's been acting a little odd lately."

Honey Bee continued to run her fingers through Boo's black and brown stripes, following them all the way down to his orange tail.

You all think I'm the one acting odd, after what I just saw and heard? thought Boo.

"I'll tell you what sounds crazy," said Tinman. "That the professor thinks we can just waltz around the rainforest and stumble upon this rare plant. I've walked all over that rainforest through the years and have never, ever seen a colorful plant like that. It's a pretty big rainforest, you know."

Jesse and Honey Bee quickly thought about it, and neither one of them could ever recall seeing that plant in the rainforest, but then they remembered something.

"I have seen that plant before!" Jesse and Honey Bee blurted out together.

Jesse held up the burlap bag that he had intended to give to the professor this morning. He opened it, turned it upside down, and gently shook it above the ground. Out fell a faded but colorful plant. The plant looked almost exactly like the one Professor Katnip had provided in the leather pouch.

"We found this last night behind the professor's house," said Jesse. "Whoever hit him on the head last night most likely dropped the plant."

Honey Bee raised her eyebrows and said, "The plot thickens."

"Bwah-hah-hah!" exclaimed Caleb, stretching his eyes and mouth with his fingers.

Everyone stopped and looked at Caleb.

"What?" asked Caleb. "This is gettin' a little weird."

"So the question is… did the perpetrator drop the plant, or did they take the plant from the professor's greenhouse?" said Tinman.

Jesse thought about the professor's note. If the rainbow plants were lethal to cats, then they couldn't be the solution for keeping Boo out of Mr. Jack's garden. Obviously, they had to be for the bullkats. He just didn't understand why the professor was still avoiding his simple question of how to keep Boo out of Mr. Jack's garden.

Jesse was more convinced than ever that, for some reason, the professor seemed to be withholding some information and that his dream was trying to tell him something.

There was silence for a few seconds as they all stood on the porch, thinking about the mystery unfolding before them.

"So, did you bring the Island Puffs?" Tinman asked Caleb.

"You never said—" Caleb paused, thinking for a minute. "Oh, OK, I got it. Havin' some fun with the big guy."

Island Puffs are without a doubt a favorite puffy pastry treat for many of the Islanders. Caleb could easily put away an entire baker's dozen all by himself. He was obsessed with these drool-worthy sweet honey donuts rolled in cinnamon sugar and stuffed with many delicious fillings. Caleb was more than confident that Tinman would stop for coffee and Island Puffs at the café along the way.

They loaded up in Tinman's Jeep with Boo riding shotgun on Jesse's lap. The ride through Bow Valley was always breathtaking. The winding road out of Tyrtle Town was protected on each side by towering cliffs and decorated with fields of flowers like a continuous, flowing rainbow.

The drive through Bow Valley took them right past the Meow Mountains which stood towering on the south side of the island. Jesse searched the mountainside to see if he could spot Skull Rock. As they drove by, it was not difficult to recognize. The unusual geological formation looked weathered and worn from years of overlooking Bow Valley, but the massive rock still clearly resembled Cat Skull Rock.

It was not unusual to see a full rainbow appear right before your eyes from one end of Bow Valley to the other. The mythical tale about the pot of gold at the end of the rainbow had a different meaning for Jesse and each one of his island friends.

Tinman was born and raised on Tyrtle Island. His pot of gold was the island itself and living within the Islander's spirit. He'd spent his entire life exploring Tyrtle Island and hoped the remainder of his days would be spent with Jesse, enjoying one adventure after another.

Jesse's pot of gold hangin' on the end of the rainbow was simply the adventure itself. Tinman had told him long ago that although his legs may grow tired, his hands may lose their grip, and his eyes may grow weary, the great adventurer always finds a way from deep within to keep the adventure going.

Honey Bee thought of her pot of gold more clearly like a pot of honey. For her, it was all about the indescribable smell of the native flowers that overwhelmed her senses and filled her lungs as she gently breathed in the sweet tropical air. She never grew tired of watching the beautiful fairy-tale waterfalls and heavenly rains that were the life's blood of the colorful island landscape. She was consumed with the life of the island. From the turtles in the oceans to the buzzing H-bees that worked tirelessly pollinating the flowers, Honey Bee knew they all worked together to make so many wonderful things possible, including her family's passion of making local honey. Honey Bee simply saw it all as a wonder of God's creation.

Caleb's pot of gold was the excitement of finding a treasure chest resting on the bottom of the ocean's floor. The treasure in the chest that he valued wasn't in the form of gold and silver, it was the miracle of the water itself that he loved. The water in any one of its dazzling displays and the life streaming through it was his personal pot of gold. After all, he knew that it was the surrounding oceans that made an island possible, and the rivers, lagoons, and rain showers flowing through that sustained life on his island.

Although each one of them had their own personal pot of gold, what they sought after most was not the elusive treasure at the end of a rainbow. It was the bond of Tyrtle love they all shared between one another and that could only be found within their hearts.

There were several clearings along the highway where the mountains separated from one another, allowing each one of them to catch a quick glimpse of the pristine beaches that gently faded into the seemingly endless blue ocean. One of those clearings was home to Tyrtle Island Coffee and Honey. It was one of Tinman's favorite places on the island and just happened to be owned and operated by Honey Bee's family.

"Are you ready for those hot Island Puffs?" asked Tinman, pulling into the crowded café and parking in his unofficial VIP parking spot.

"Is the ocean salty?" responded Caleb in a flash. "Does a cat meow?" he said, jumping out of the backseat of the Jeep.

Duh, thought Boo. "Mrrowow."

"Make sure you get two boxes. One for Caleb and one for the rest of us," said Jesse, hanging his head out of the Jeep. "I'll hang out with Boo."

Tinman followed behind Caleb and Honey Bee, disappearing through the double screen doors of the old island café. The rich aroma of the freshly brewed coffee and sweetness of the Island Puffs escaped out of the rustic doors and floated along with the breeze, enticing anyone who happened to be nearby.

"Smell that, Boo?" said Jesse, rubbing Boo's big paws. "Better than catnip."

Well, unless you're a cat, thought Boo.

Boo saw somebody he recognized approaching the Jeep, and he quickly jumped into Jesse's lap.

"Hey, boy," said a strange voice, startling Jesse. "Funny thing finding you here."

Jesse looked up, and Mr. Jack was standing right next to him with a sinister grin on his face.

"Keeping Boo out of my garden are you? Going somewhere with your friends?" asked Mr. Jack, glaring at Jesse with his cold eyes.

"Has Boo been in your garden... again?" asked Jesse uncomfortably, trying to be polite.

Mr. Jack's eyes glanced back and forth between Jesse and Boo. "Careful in the rainforest, boy. There are some dangerous creatures there."

"Are you following us? How do you know—"

"Oh, I know some things. Don't you worry about how." Mr. Jack grinned, rolling his foul-smelling cigar from one side of his mouth to the other. "I have to go now, but we have plans for all of you... Take care... Boo!"

Mr. Jack stood there motionless for a few seconds, with his eyes fixed on Boo. Jesse's stomach started to feel queasy again. He was relieved to hear Caleb's loud voice and looked over his shoulder to see his friends hopping down the wooden stairs with steaming coffee and a couple pink boxes in their hands.

"I'm not exactly sure what they're doing in that kitchen in there!" Caleb hollered, licking his fingers, "but it's pure yummy magic!"

"That guy just gives me an eerie feeling," said Jesse with his eyebrows raised and mouth open.

"Who are you talking about?" asked Honey Bee, looking around. "You look as though you just saw a ghost."

Jesse turned around and stretched his neck in every direction. "He was just right here," he said. "Where did—"

At that moment Boo wished more than anything that he could communicate through words with Jesse and his friends.

"I think he's still rattled by the professor's note," mumbled Caleb, trying to swallow a mouthful of Island Puffs.

"What's this all about?" Jesse thought, feeling more confused now than ever.

Tinman walked up to the Jeep and handed Jesse a hot box of Island Puffs.

Jesse opened the box and slowly took a bite out of the delicious pastry as he contemplated telling Tinman about his conversation with Mr. Jack.

The sweet honey dough melting in his mouth consumed his senses for the next few minutes and somehow eased a very uneasy situation. He decided just to enjoy the box of Island Puffs for the next few minutes and keep his conversation with Mr. Jack to himself.

"Bones and Mr. Jack, Mr. Jack and Bones," Jesse thought, munching on one Island Puff after another.

The Jeep continued the journey through the lush monkey-pod trees, blooming with pink powder puffs, and trekked up the winding road to Roundabout Peak.

Reaching the top of the peak, Tinman pulled off to the side of the road that overlooked the cliffs that were just below Kats Caves.

Their eyes ran up and down the stunning windward coast. This was an island view that words could never adequately describe and a scene that was painted anew every time they crested the peak. The view was stunning as they all gazed out in silence, letting the island breeze brush against their faces. The unending ocean was an ever-changing kaleidoscope of blue and green shapes which seemed to gently roll on forever. The island sky presented a brand-new horizon each day as the puffy white clouds and brilliant blues changed moment by moment with the constant breeze. The blanket of colorful tropical trees, plants, and flowers clothed the Majestic Mountains and rugged cliffs in a new wardrobe each morning and evening. It really was as good as it gets, and the Islanders knew it all too well.

"Who were you talking to back at the café?" Tinman asked Jesse, breaking the sound of silence.

Jesse hesitated for a few seconds. "That was old Mr. Jack," he said. "I'm not sure what to make of him. To be honest, he makes me kind of nervous."

Tinman looked intently at Jesse. "Why? What exactly did he say to you?"

Jesse hesitated before answering Tinman. He wasn't exactly sure how to explain the situation to his uncle.

"Jesse, what did he tell you?" Tinman asked again sternly, raising his voice.

"He knows we're going to the rainforest, and he's just plain scary," confessed Jesse. "I know he's upset that Boo keeps messing up his garden, but it's something else. Why would anyone be that upset over their garden?"

"Evidently you don't know my aunt very well," said Honey Bee. "She has a sign in her garden that says, 'IF YOU ARE NOT A BUMBLEBEE, THEN KEEP YOUR BUM OUT OF MY GARDEN.'"

"Jesse, let me know if he approaches you again. You hear me?" said Tinman. "I mean it. Make sure you let me know."

Just as the sun started to dip below the top of the trees, Tinman's Jeep started cruising down the mountain highway toward the Roundabout Rainforest.

The magnificent trees stood guard like warriors protecting the precious life below their strong branches. Tinman and the gang had camped in the rainforest many times over the years. They all knew the primitive campground very well, but Tinman knew it was always best to set up camp before it got dark.

For Jesse and his friends, this adventure would be much different from any of their previous trips. Everyone knew they were in this adventure together, but what they didn't realize was that they were all right smack in the middle of a real-life mystery. Boo sensed that their lives would be changed forever.

The seasoned campers made quick work of setting up their tents and arranging the campsite.

"Canned ham, anyone?" asked Tinman, making himself comfortable next to the campfire. "So, you're still having those dreams, huh?"

"Most every night," replied Jesse. "I'm not sure why, but somehow, I feel like these dreams... I don't know... are really important. I know this sounds strange, but I think these dreams are tied to what's goin' on with Mr. Jack and all the bullkat sightings."

"I think we all agree with you," said Tinman. "Especially after reading the professor's note and seeing the rainbow plants. You're right. Somethin' just doesn't add up."

Jesse sat quietly next to Honey Bee, staring at the glowing embers and flickering flames. He watched the burning ashes ascend into the air and then float off, disappearing into the starry night sky. His mind was quickly put to ease, feeling content with Boo on his lap and enjoying the calming spirit of the fire.

"I am blessed," thought Jesse, surrounded by his friends.

Later that evening, Jesse rested in his tent with thoughts of Boo, bullkats, Mr. Jack, and rainbow plants swirling around in his head. He was looking forward to tomorrow's adventure, even if they were only going exploring for the rainbow plants. He already knew it would be like looking for a needle in a haystack. Right now, finding the rainbow plants seemed like the only sliver of hope, and their only option for keeping the bullkats away. He pondered that for a few minutes, then closed his eyes and quickly fell asleep.

Jesse's mind was once again filled with an image of hot, flowing lava. His body began to sweat, and his mind traveled back into the imaginative world of island dreams. Jesse found himself back in Boo's nightmare, right where he had left off.

turtle

CHAPTER TEN: HOLY SMOKING CAT-ROLL

Boo INSTINCTIVELY SPRANG UP INTO the air like he was walking on hot coals. With his back arched and hair standing on end, the Meow cat cried out with a warrior's roar into the night. He slashed out into the darkness with his oversized paws and claws, intent on striking the intruders standing above him. His claws swished through the darkness without making contact with the enemy. He landed on all four paws and his eyes darted back and forth as he looked around on the ledge of Cat Skull Rock, frantically searching for Bones and the threatening bullkat. Only a split-second ago they were standing over him. Suddenly they were nowhere to be found.

Silently, he stood for a few seconds with his ears back flat against his head. His glowing cat eyes were on full alert, and his heart was beating so fast he felt like it was going to thump right out of his chest.

Boo looked back, and the catpack was still sitting exactly where he put it the night before. He quickly gazed around the shallow cave. Chops and Silver were lying down next to Roxy Roo, and all three were looking up at him with eyes wide open, as if they had just been startled out of their sleep.

"That was incredible," said Chops. "Are you sure you're not really some kind of a kanga cat? That… was one of the highest jumps I've ever seen. It's gotta be some kind of a record."

"Where are they?" shouted Boo, out of breath and frantically looking around.

"Where are—what are you talking about?" asked Roxy Roo sleepily, doing her morning stretch with her legs, paws, and claws.

"Bones and the bullkat were standing right here while you guys were sleeping," exclaimed Boo. "You didn't see them?"

"I heard you shout in some kinda crazy cat voice and opened my eyes just in time to see you striking at the air like a wildcat," said Chops. "I just want you to know that was one really incredible jump. You should've seen it."

"I did see it! I also saw Bones and his pet bullkat standing directly over me a minute ago! Didn't you see them?" Boo asked, irritated.

"I heard your roar, but I didn't see anything," said Chops, looking around as if he wasn't telling the whole story.

"Chops, were you sleeping?" asked Roxy Roo, not wanting to belabor the obvious answer to her question.

"Boo, you must have been dreaming," said Silver. "I sleep lighter than a firebug and never heard a sound. Well, except for Chops' snoring."

Boo stared at his friends looking somewhat confused and very agitated. "It wasn't a dream. They were standing right above me, and I heard Bones speak those same crazy words to me again. I felt his breath on my whiskers. I saw those glowing yellow eyes!" He paused briefly. "Well, maybe… just maybe, I was dreaming."

The sun's rays had not peeked over the Meow Mountains, and the breathtaking beauty of the plants throughout Bow Valley were still hidden in the darkness just below Cat Skull Rock.

The valley was specifically given the name "Bow" for three very special reasons. When the sun was behind them and the rain in front of them, Islanders would be graced with the most brilliant display of rainbow colors ever to be seen across the horizon. When the conditions were just right and the light passed through the raindrops, it was simply as if the Creator took a single stroke with His brush and painted a perfect arc every time. The beautiful bow was illuminated against the stormy blue sky, brilliantly displaying the promise of abiding love and faithfulness.

The island's ancient history provided the second reason for Bow Valley's darker meaning. The bows of the warriors who had fought in the valley had long been consumed by the island's blood-red dirt, but their voices could still be heard as they rose up from the depths of Bow Valley and sang out in song through the trees.

The valley was filled with a spectrum of plants and flowers so beautiful and full of fragrance that many creatures actually avoided it, including the scent-sensitive bullkats.

Silver led the way as they descended to the valley, away from the looming face of Cat Skull Rock. He meandered down the trail, and Boo was growing impatient with their slow progress. The slow-moving porcupine stopped here and there, nibbling on a few leaves and then munching on some bark from specific trees along the way. Compared to cats, porcupines are known for moving rather slowly.

"Silver, would you mind if I lead the way down? I might be able to see further down the trail in the dark than you can," said Boo, not wanting to hurt his feelings about moving rather slowly and having poor eyesight.

The path down to the valley followed along the Meow Mountains for a short distance through the thick trees and then descended sharply to the valley floor. The sun's rays had begun to penetrate the trees and light up the valley. Slowly, as if arranged by an orchestrator, the colorful array of innumerable swaying plants and trees came into full view, displaying their vibrant life.

Roxy Roo looked out over the amazing landscape in a state of wonderment. "Oh, my! Have you ever seen anything so... heavenly?"

"I didn't want to spoil it for you," said Silver, looking over at Roxy Roo. "I wanted you to be able to take in the fullness of the beauty without the slightest bit of anticipation."

"I'm... I'm so overwhelmed," she said as tears puddled up in her big brown eyes.

The friends stood at the edge of the trail and just stared out over the vast beauty that was unveiled before them. When the wind blew from the windward side of the island, flowing through the valley with the perfect pattern and proper strength, weary travelers would be delighted by the third reason for the valley's name. The sweet, flowering aroma flowing through the air, combined with the accompaniment of magical tunes, created a bouquet for the senses. The exotic psalm trees actually played songs of praise by scooping up the wind in their many tubular branches. The rushing wind was funneled upwards toward the top of the trees through the horn-shaped ends, producing a symphony of angelic songs that could be heard echoing along the cliffs of Bow Valley.

On this particular morning, the conditions for producing these songs were perfect. The scented symphony had begun. The sound of the musical bows joined in rhythm with the colorful dance of the psalm trees. The friends stood silently together looking out over the natural orchestra pit, listening to the island wind whisper a song to them in sounds of wonder.

Boo, at least for a few minutes, had forgotten all about his nightmare encounter with Bones.

The pattern of the wind changed as quickly as it had manifested itself, and the songs of the dancing psalm trees slowly faded away in the distance, replaced by the rustling of the plants and trees.

The island friends turned away from the inspirational valley and continued down the trail. Their senses continued to tingle from the natural symphony they had just experienced, and for a little while longer, that heavenly feeling continued to captivate their imaginations.

Boo's mind slowly returned to thinking about Bones. He carefully watched their surroundings, scanning the rocks, trees, and bushes along the trail.

Silver's pink nose twitched back and forth in the air. "Do I dare ask? What is that awful stench?"

"Ew! I know that foul smell," replied Roxy Roo.

Boo lifted his nose and whiskers into the air and walked over toward the mountainside from the edge of the trail. He could see some smoke lingering in the air, and it looked like it was floating out from a pile of rocks on the side of the mountain.

Roxy Roo and Boo cried out together, "Bones!"

"It smells just like his stinky cat-roll he had the night he scared us in Treetop Woods," said Boo. "I knew it. I knew I wasn't dreaming."

Boo was relieved, at least for a brief moment. He looked around at his friends' worried faces and realized that last night they had actually been visited by Bones and a dangerous bullkat.

"What does he want?" asked Roxy Roo. "I wonder why he's following us."

Chops never needed a reason to joke around, but this time he really was trying to lighten the uneasy atmosphere. "Well, I'll tell you one thing for sure. I'm seriously going to have a talk with the Meow cat elders about his littering."

Roxy Roo smiled and then looked at Boo, tilting her head from side to side. She thought back to when Chops fell asleep at Cat Skull Rock and said, "I just don't understand. Why didn't he hurt you? It's almost like he only wanted to frighten you. Since SOMEBODY fell asleep. He could've easily hurt us all."

Silver paced back and forth, thinking, and said, "I don't think he wants to hurt us. At least not yet."

"That's very comforting. I feel sooo much better now," said Chops.

Silver continued to pace back and forth, his tin tail clinking against the rocky ground with every step he took. "I think he wants us alive. That's the only explanation that makes sense. He needs us to lead him to the source of the rainbow plants. As to why, I just don't know."

The morning had passed as they reached the bottom of Bow Valley, and the dazzling display of colorful trees had turned into a protective green canopy far above their heads. Silver had taken over the lead through the dense forest. Boo carried the catpack as Roxy Roo and Chops followed closely behind.

Silver slowed his pace, pointing up at the trees. Hundreds of strange creatures could be seen hopping and swinging from limb to limb across the canopy of trees.

The creatures were so strange-looking that nobody on the island knew exactly what to call them. The "what-am-I" creature's name got changed to "what-M-I" and eventually shortened to "W-M-I" or "weemee" for short.

Silver quickly informed his friends that weemees, for the most part, were harmless creatures, although they could be very mischievous.

"Not to worry my friends, they only eat toobieworms," Silver pointed out proudly, displaying his knowledge of these peculiar creatures.

At that exact same moment, one rather large weemee had decided he was going to use Chops' head as a landing pad and Chops' back as a slide.

Chops jumped up and down, turning in circles while trying to shrug the creature off. "Get it off! Get it off!" he yelled.

The weemee leaped off Chops' back and, with one giant bounce, hopped up on the trunk of a very large tree. They all watched in amazement as the weemee knocked on the tree trunk for a couple of minutes and then, using its long boney tail, the weemee proceeded to drill a hole right through the bark. The creature dug into the hole with its small skinny fingers and pulled out several plump toobieworms, devouring them one after the other.

"Looks like the bigger the tree, the bigger the meal," said Chops with a look of disgust on his face. "No, thanks. I'll stick to fish."

"Oh, that poor ugly creature," said Roxy Roo. "It kind of looks like a boney monkey with spiked hair and super-creepy spider-like fingers. Those little eyes are almost popping out of its head."

"I just don't understand how they can eat those vile worms," said Silver.

Chops quickly glanced over at Silver and said, "And I thought your diet was disgusting."

Roxy Roo cringed and said, "Poor little creature looks like it's in pain."

"Good thing it didn't bite you," said Boo, placing his paw on Chops' shoulder.

"Oh, not to worry, they have no teeth," said Silver confidently.

"No teeth?" confirmed Boo. "Then how does it chew those chubby worms?"

Just as he asked the question, Boo graphically received his answer. The weemee turned towards them and squished one of the very plump toobieworms by wrapping his long powerful tongue around it and then popping it. Worm guts went flying everywhere.

"Oh, ewww! You had to ask," said Chops, looking like he was about to cough up a hairball.

"Oh, that's awful," said Roxy Roo, turning away.

She looked up and down on her beautiful brown fur coat to make sure no parts of the disgusting worm had splashed on her. It was no surprise that if anyone was going to get splashed by worm guts, it would have to be Chops.

Boo pointed his claw at the yellow guts hanging off the tip of Chops' ear. "Sorry, big guy, looks like you got a little on ya."

Chops was not happy as he gently picked the gooey guts off the tip of his ear.

Silver walked across a large tree that had fallen and was lying in a small pond of water. The pond was slowly being fed by a trickling waterfall coming down through some rocks on the mountainside. He stepped off the tree next to the pond onto a patch of some of the softest grass he'd ever felt. Strangely, standing right in the middle of the perfect grass there was an old moss-covered signpost.

The sign read:

"Friendly creatures and two old grouchy ones."

The very peculiar wooden sign also displayed an almost unreadable carved-out map. The map showed three different paths that travelers could take through Bow Valley, but each direction would eventually end up leading them to Walkabout Wilderness.

Silver stood on the grass looking at the three trails heading in different directions. He studied the paths for a few minutes, unsure which path would be the best one to take.

The Meow cats walked up and stood on the grass in front of the pond. Everyone laughed as they read the very unusual, but amusing, sign.

"I certainly hope we don't run into the two old grouchy ones," laughed Chops, running his paw under the words on the sign.

"Do you know which direction to take?" Boo asked Silver.

"I can't say that I know which of these three choices is the best, but it looks as though they all lead to Walkabout Wilderness," said Silver. "The first path looks like it may be the safest and hopefully would keep us from any dangerous creature encounters. Although it may be somewhat risky, since it seems you have to follow a steep, skinny trail along the ridge of the Majestic Mountains."

While Silver was talking, Chops was busy carving his name into the wooden sign.

Chapter Ten

"The second path looks relatively short, but it seems as though it will take us through a darker part of the forest, which is always risky," continued Silver. "The last path looks like it leads directly through the center of the valley and right through some more of those beautiful flowering plants and trees."

"I say that we take the road of least resistance and travel through the center of the valley with all those lovely flowers," suggested Roxy Roo eagerly.

"I like the idea of being a little safer and out of harm's way by following the ridge along the mountain trail," suggested Chops, pulling a splinter out of his paw.

"I vote for the shorter path through the forest," said Boo. "We'll get there quicker, and we have Silver's quills and our slingshots if we run into any trouble."

Silver looked around at his three friends and then gazed across the pond in deep thought. After all, he was by far the most seasoned traveler so he felt as though the decision should be his to make. He wanted to be sure to keep all his newly-found friends as safe as possible.

"What are you looking at?" barked a strange voice from across the pond. "You prickly bonehead!"

"Yeah, you knucklehead!" barked another strange voice from the same direction. "Get off of my lawn!"

"Sounds like somebody is in need of a big hug," said Roxy Roo, looking curiously across the pond.

"Oh, why don't you just go hug a prickly pear!" shouted one of the crabby voices again.

They all looked out across the dark, murky pond in the direction of the barking voices and saw there were two identical old bulldogs sitting on two identical log doghouses that were on top of two identical rocks. The bulldogs had just plain grouchy expressions on their faces.

"I think we found the grouches," said Roxy Roo.

"We certainly don't want any trouble," said Silver. "All we are trying to do is determine which direction will take us to Walkabout Wilderness and we'll be gone."

"And off your lawn," whispered Chops. "Although I love the way this grass tickles my paws."

"What do you get when you have three cats and a porcupine walking together in the middle of the forest?" shouted one bulldog, looking over at the other bulldog. "An absentminded cat'astrophe!"

The barking dogs laughed hysterically, jumping up and down on their houses.

"I'm allergic to cats!" shouted one grouchy bulldog.

"Cats have to bury their own poop!" blurted out the other bulldog.

From the top of their houses, the cantankerous bulldogs exchanged one insult after another, barking out, "Cats are a waste of perfectly good fur coats. All scaredy-cats are good-for-nothin' mouse-catchers."

The cranky bulldogs were relentless as they continued throwing insults out at their audience of Meow cats and a porky porcupine.

"What do you get when you cross a turtle with a porcupine?" growled one of the grumpy dogs.

"A slowpoke," replied the other.

Quite honestly, none of the friends had ever heard one creature insult another creature quite like this. The bad-tempered bulldogs were somewhat annoying, but they were also very funny. The canines' deep and drawn-out voices were so unusual that they easily captivated their audience.

"Who let the grouchy dogs out?" asked Boo, twitching his tail. "They're crazier than two dogs drinking a cup of catnip tea."

The bulldogs were known throughout Bow Valley as Growlin and Howlin. The dogs were not dangerous creatures, and except for the endless insults, they were pretty much harmless to Boo and his friends. The dogs were just plain old grouches with nothing but just plain mean things to say.

"I've heard enough," said Roxy Roo. "At this point, I don't care which direction we go. Let's just get away from these two dopey dogs."

The dogs were relentless. "If cats had two brains then the other one would be lonely," Growlin barked out loudly to Howlin.

"I know cats are used to losin', but you should care about which direction you're choosin'," Howlin growled loudly from across the pond.

Silver was reluctant to respond but shouted back across the pond asking, "And why would that be?"

The two bulldogs stepped down off their identical houses onto their identical rocks and began to howl out a song together.

"Three trails, three paths, three roads to unravel!
One choice is the trail taken with less babble!
You could pick the path that will certainly dazzle!
One would think the short road less of a hassle!
The right direction is almost certain the one less traveled!"

"Very clever. Very nice. Thanks for the little poem. Or was it some kind of rhyming riddle?" asked Chops. "OK, well, thanks, grumpy guys, for the entertainment and—"

Silver interrupted Chops' berating of the bulldogs. "I got it! I know which direction to take."

"We may be back in a few minutes," Chops said jokingly, watching Silver turn and waddle away.

"We will anchor ourselves to these very rocks until your triumphant return," Growlin and Howlin blurted out sarcastically as the bulldogs watched them walk off from across the pond.

The echoes from the loud barking sounds of the bulldogs grew fainter as they walked deeper into the forest.

Silver didn't walk in any one of the three directions carved into the map on the funny sign. He knew they must follow the route less traveled. One by one, the Meow cats followed behind Silver's tinkling tail as he confidently went around the edge of the mushy green pond. He led them over a moss-covered stone bridge that had partially fallen into the stream running beneath. The path Silver had chosen took them deeper into the thick tropical forest and showed little evidence of being followed by travelers before them. The trees high above them provided a protective canopy but permitted just enough sunlight to penetrate the leaves, providing a guiding light that pointed the way along the path. Large volcanic rocks were strewn about on the overgrown forest floor, covered with vegetation that weaved its way between the giant trees. The plants and twigs crunched beneath their paws as they walked along following the streams of filtered light that guided their way.

Walking in silence, they listened to the insects buzzing around and creatures scurrying about, over and under the leafy plants and rooted trees. The thick vegetation on the forest floor prevented them from seeing any critters moving along the wet ground. A lush canopy of leaves hindered them from spotting the birds and other critters gathered in the trees. Although, there was no doubt that the forest was vibrating with life as they listened to the sound of the chirping birds and chattering creatures echoing through the air.

Chops jumped up on a large lava rock and grabbed his stubby tail, rubbing the tip of it. "I sure would like a cat snack," he whined.

Silver took the opportunity to look around for some snacks of his own. He went foraging between two giant trees and found a delicious patch of tuber stems to nibble on. Chops watched Silver from the rock he was resting on as the porcupine uncovered the tasty tubers with his dirt-smudged pink nose.

"You know, I never really paid attention, but Silver eats some very strange stuff. He seems to have a healthy appetite for yummy tree bark and whatever other slimy things he's diggin' out of the ground over there," said Chops with a kind of yuck factor displayed across his face.

Boo and Roxy Roo looked up from cleaning their fur coats and made some funny faces as they glanced over at Silver, who was rummaging nose first through the dirt. The two cats smiled and then resumed cleaning their fur coats.

The sun was retreating behind the mountains and the cats and their porcupine companion were losing the stream of guiding light that was leading them through to the edge of Bow Valley Forest and into the Walkabout Wilderness.

"How much further do we have to walk tonight?" asked Roxy Roo. "We've lost most of the light, and my paws are getting sore from stepping on all the sharp rocks and twigs."

"I sure would like a cat snack," Chops said again, turning up the volume.

"Tonight, I would like to sleep in a little better shelter," said Roxy Roo.

The awful screeching sounds of the forest night creatures could be heard far off in the distance.

"Did you hear that?" said Roxy Roo.

"Yes, cat snacks and a better shelter. I heard you guys," said Boo. "I'll see what we can find."

"No! Not that! What was that awful screeching sound?"

She was not asking because she was afraid. She was more curious than anything. The loud screeching noise motivated Chops to move over to the rocks where Boo and Roxy Roo were sitting.

"Come and take a look at this. What do you make of it?" said Silver, brushing away the leaves from the top of a perfectly flat lava rock.

"I've seen those symbols before on some of the scrolls in Professor Katnip's treehouse," said Boo, concentrating on the etchings on top of the rock.

The ancient island symbols were worn, weathered, and hard to read. At the top of the rock was a carving of a single large turtle that had something hanging around its neck. Under the turtle were two rows of symbols that were also hard to decipher. They seemed to have a shape like the sun or possibly a flower with arrows or rays shooting upwards. There were hundreds of dots scattered above the symbols, but the dots stopped just below the turtle. The bottom row of symbols looked like many arrows pointing straight up and passing through the top row of symbols and dots but stopping just below the turtle.

"Hmmmm," sighed Chops. "Cat's game. Looks like somebody had too much time on their hands."

He raised his paws and hopped up on the rocks stacked in front of them. Chops leaned back and picked a white wishbone flower growing on one of the mossy rocks while his friends tried to decipher the ancient symbols. Chops picked at the dozens of white strands extending from the flower's stem and tossed the white floaties in the air.

He leaned back a little more and then, taking in a big breath, he unintentionally pressed his back hard against the rocks, trying to get as comfortable as possible. He fell slightly backwards as the rocks behind him gave way. Chops turned around and noticed a small opening behind the rocks. He tried to grip the rock with his paws while he was listening to his friends below making wild guesses as to what the symbols might mean.

"Symbol bo-bimble," mumbled Chops under his breath. "I'm having a snack attack."

He managed to get one of his paws stuck on the jagged edge of one of the rocks. Frustrated and hungry, he tugged his stuck paw and then pulled with all his feline strength. The rock flipped forward, and then he watched it roll right by him and tumble straight down, heading for the amateur archeologists just below him.

"Rocks!" shouted Chops, watching his friends dance and hop their way around the falling rock.

Boo, Roxy Roo, and Silver stood at the base of the rocks looking agitated. They all glared at Chops from down below until they noticed an opening in the rocks that Chops had just accidentally discovered.

"Why are you grinnin' like a porcupine who just ate a sweet tater?" Chops asked Silver.

Not saying a word, they all three climbed up on the rocks and walked right past Chops. He stared at them as they went by him and finally realized that the falling rocks had revealed a small opening in the mountainside.

"Who has the jar of firebugs?" asked Boo, crouching down and peering into the darkness.

Roxy Roo stepped through the small opening in the rocks and opened the jar of firebugs, releasing them into the darkness. A few firebugs quickly escaped out of the jar, revealing the walls of a small cave.

"I see some old baskets sitting next to the walls," said Silver, walking over toward them and looking inside. "I'm going to bring one outside to get a better look and see exactly what's in the basket."

Silver dragged one of the baskets out into the light while Boo, Roxy Roo, and Chops looked intently at some symbols that were carved into the cave walls.

"Looks like more of the same kind of symbols that we saw outside," said Boo. "Wish I knew what they meant. They're all pointing toward the same turtle with the same something hanging around its neck. Look at the four symbols above his head. Looks like 'W... L... K... L,'" said Boo, straining his eyes in the dim, moving light, trying to see the symbols.

"No... No, I think it's 'W... L... K... I'," said Roxy Roo. "Or maybe that's 'W... I... K... I'."

Roxy Roo let out a few more firebugs from her jar in hopes of getting a better look at the symbols on the cave walls. Firebugs only light up when they are in flight and dancing around in pairs.

"Looks like a bunch of very old, dried-up plants in this basket," shouted Silver from outside the cave opening. "I think someone was saving these for some reason. Why would they go to such lengths to conceal them in a hidden cave? It's almost like they wanted to hide them. Chops, can you bring another basket out to me?"

"I'm a little busy in here," said Chops as he used his scarf to wipe some of the dust off the symbols on the wall.

"No, no, no, don't wipe them," snipped Roxy Roo. "We don't want to touch them at all. I'm almost positive the symbols are 'wiki. I think they're 'W... I... K... I', which spells 'wiki.'"

"Wiki. I've heard that name before... I think," said Boo.

"Not busy now," said Chops, dragging a couple more baskets into the dim light.

"Did you say Wiki?" asked Silver as he waddled back into the cave. "I know what Wiki means, I know who Wiki is, and I even know where Wiki lives."

Silver looked closer at the symbols on the wall and pointed to the turtle symbol below the letters.

"I believe this symbol is referring to the legend of Wiki Tyrtle," said Silver, with a look of hope in his eyes. "The legend of the Ancient Islander claims that he is the oldest and wisest creature to ever live on Tyrtle Island. The word 'wiki' in the ancient island symbols means to quickly reveal all island knowledge, wisdom, and truth. The legend goes on to tell the story of travelers whose hearts are transformed and are able to see the Tyrtle Tunnel. They are then permitted passage to the mythical Island of Wiki."

"Do you ever listen to yourself?" Chops asked Silver. "You just said that you know what 'wiki' means, you know who Wiki is, and you know where Wiki lives. Now you're telling us that it's a legend. Not really the same things in my book."

"Let's assume that the legend is true, and Wiki Tyrtle is all those things the legend claims he is," exclaimed Boo. "There must be some truth to the legend. Why would anyone go to all the trouble to carve these symbols on the rock outside and then carve them again on the walls in a concealed cave?"

"Well, off the top of my head I can think of a couple reasons," said Chops. "Somebody could have been extremely bored, and that same somebody might just have a passion for doodling on cave walls."

Boo and Roxy Roo could not help but purr and laugh at their funny friend, but Silver was not amused.

"The carvings and the legend are somehow connected," said Silver emphatically. "I can feel it! I can see it! I just know it!"

"I think I can just sleep on it," said Chops.

He lay down near one of the old baskets and knocked over four skinny logs that were leaning against the basket.

"Timber!" said Chops, chuckling while he watched the logs fall against the cave wall.

"Now, did I come through or what?" said Boo, grinning at Roxy Roo.

Roxy Roo looked confused as she smiled graciously at Boo and said, "Or… what?"

"You don't remember? You said something about wanting a little better shelter tonight?"

At that moment, that same terrible screeching sound they heard earlier interrupted their conversation.

Her smile turned to a worried look. "Yes, I remember that awful sound."

"No need to worry about those creatures. They're far off and live up in the forest trees," replied Silver, reassuring his friends.

"OK, I feel better now. Sweet dreams, everyone!" Chops said sarcastically, cuddling up a little closer to the basket.

They all made themselves as comfortable as possible in the cave of symbols and baskets. Silver, in his customary bed-making fashion, emptied a few baskets onto the cave floor in an effort to try and make a more comfortable bed for himself.

Tomorrow they would enter Walkabout Wilderness. They were all feeling exhausted, and the quiet night inside the cave quickly passed by.

"Boo, wake up," whispered Roxy Roo. "I can't see the moonlight."

"Whaaat? Of course you can't. We're in a cave," replied Boo.

Silver and Chops were stirred out of their sleep from the voices.

"Nooo! I think the cave entrance is blocked. Look, there's no light," said Roxy Roo, no longer whispering.

They all stumbled over one another in the darkness and scrambled over to where they remembered the cave opening had been last night. Feeling around the damp cave walls, they pushed on the rocks that had been stacked in front of the opening sometime during the night.

"Chops, put your shoulder into it!" Boo yelled out as they pushed harder against the rocks. "Ouch! That's my tail!"

"It's no use. There are too many rocks," said Silver, sighing. "I can't believe we slept through all of this."

They all paused for a minute trying to catch their breath in the darkness. Roxy Roo opened her catpack and pulled out her jar of firebugs.

"Nooooo! Don't open it!" snapped Boo at the clicking of the jar opening. "We need to save the light until we figure out what we're going to do."

"It must have been the plants," said Silver. "They must be some form of catnip. I thought of that last night, but seeing that the plants were so old and dried-out, I thought they had lost their potency. Honestly, I didn't think they would have any impact on us while we slept. That's the only excuse I can think of for all of us sleeping like rocks while somebody was piling up actual rocks right in front of our noses."

Silver paused for a few seconds, thinking that he would get a chuckle out of his friends for having used the rock metaphor. There was no chuckle, but they were all smiling. He just couldn't see them in the dark.

"Well, catnip is a pretty good excuse for all the cats in here, but what's the porcupine's excuse for falling asleep?" asked Chops, smirking in the dark.

Silver smiled in the dark. "The porcupine doesn't really need an excuse," he said. "You would do well to remember that the porcupine has quills."

Silver could be heard letting out a squeaky laugh in the dark.

"I guess that would explain why the baskets were concealed in this cave in the first place," said Boo. "Looks like somebody was hiding those potent plants."

"Do you think someone was trying to hide all the symbols on the wall?" said Roxy Roo. "It looks to me like that same somebody might not believe in the legend of Wiki Tyrtle. What if the legend is true? Maybe somebody doesn't want the rest of the creatures on the island to know that the legend of Wiki Tyrtle is true."

"It looks to me like we're all trapped in this cave with dead plants and ancient symbols," said Chops. "Oh! What's that terrible odor?" He cautiously reached his paw over in the direction of the smell and felt Silver's prickly body next to him. "Silver, come on! We're trapped in this stuffy old cave!"

"I apologize," said Silver. "That's what happens when porcupines get agitated and right now I am extremely agitated. OK, what's our plan? We need a plan."

They all sat in silence in the dark for a few minutes.

"I got nothin'," said Chops.

"Chops and Boo, you two are the tallest, so would you feel along every inch of the walls that you are able to reach and let me know if any part of the wall has indentations or protrusions? Let me know if anything at all feels out of the ordinary," instructed Silver. "Roxy Roo and I will examine the floor with our paws."

They scurried about the dark cave, bumping into one another and tripping over each other's paws, claws, and tails.

"That's strange," said Silver. "This corner basket won't budge. It's stuck to the floor. Boo, can you help me out over here?"

Boo and Chops bumped into each other in the dark, trying to make their way over to where Silver's voice was coming from.

"Chops, where are you going?" asked Boo. "He said 'Boo,' not 'Chops'!"

Chapter Ten

Boo carefully felt his way in the dark to where Silver was standing and grabbed the basket with his big paws, but he couldn't budge it.

"Let's take out all the plants," said Silver.

Boo followed Silver's directions the best he could in the dark and emptied out all the plants and felt around for the bottom of the basket. He felt around with his paw for the basket's bottom, but his claws only scraped what felt like a hard rock at the bottom of the basket.

"There's no bottom of the basket. All I can feel is rock," said Boo. "Chops, quit goofing off and come over here. See if you can use those big stumps hanging on the side of your body for something useful."

"Oh, now they need the big guy," replied Chops as he felt his way around the damp cave walls to where the basket was sitting.

Chops let out a loud sound, like he was trying to move a mountain. After that, all they heard was a soft thud in the darkness.

"I can barely pick it up," said Chops, breathing heavily.

"I have an idea," said Silver. "Boo, can you try and tear apart the basket with your claws? Chops, can you find those little logs you knocked over last night?"

The dark cave was filled with sounds of ripping, tearing, and logs knocking against one another and bouncing off the ground.

Their voices could be heard shouting in the dark. "Ouch! My paw! Watch it! Get off me, Chops!"

Roxy Roo giggled in the dark as the boys all fumbled around, trying to find their way into position around the basket.

There was silence for a few seconds.

"Chops, can you lift the edge of the rock?" asked Silver. "If you can lift the edge, then Boo can slide the logs one by one under the rock, and I think we can roll it away."

Chops let out a loud grunting sound like a sumo cat wrestler.

"Success, I think!" said Silver. "I think it's time to use a few of those firebugs."

They waited patiently to hear the sound of the jar open. After a few seconds, the soft vibrations of the firebugs' wings could be heard buzzing about the cave. The firebugs joined bodies and slowly began to glow, dancing together in the darkness. The pieces of shredded basket could be seen scattered across the cave floor. They looked down and could see a hole in the cave floor where the basket had previously been sitting.

"Awesome! Boo, you go first," said Chops, peering into the dark hole.

Boo looked over at Chops and laughed out loud just before squeezing his big body through the narrow opening. After a slight hesitation, they all followed him one by one. The hole was just big enough for them to crawl through, and the ensuing tunnel was not much wider. A few firebugs followed Boo through the tunnel for several minutes until he saw a faint crack of light in front of him.

"I see some light," Boo shouted, his voice echoing through the tunnel.

Boo watched the firebugs disappear into the light in front of him. He pushed the rocks at the end of the tunnel, and to his surprise, they fell out of the opening rather easily. The sunlight rushed into the tunnel as he heard the rocks tumbling a short distance down the mountainside.

"We're out!" exclaimed Boo.

He lent a helping paw to the rest of the dirt-covered spelunkers, who couldn't wait to get out of the tunnel and onto the skinny mountain ledge outside.

"Oh, no!" said Boo. "We should've grabbed some of the plants."

"I took some," said Silver, pulling some of the plants out of his porkypack.

Boo pointed his paw toward his head and said, "As long as one of us is thinking."

They quickly wound their way down the trail to Bow Valley, chopping their way through the lush green plants and trees that almost entirely covered the short trail. They reached the valley just a short distance from where the opening of the cave of symbols was located.

"I think we should go back to the cave," said Silver.

"Back to the cave!" hollered Chops. "Like narrowly escaping a mousetrap, we were lucky to get out of that cave with the cheese."

"I agree," said Silver. "Although I would like to look around some more. I would like to see if we can find any clues that might tell us who trapped us inside."

"It has to be Bones. Who else would it be?" said Boo. "He must be following us. He seems to know every move we make."

"Maybe, but why didn't he hurt us when he had the chance back at Cat Skull Rock?" asked Silver. "I just don't understand. It just doesn't make any sense. Why wait until we're asleep and then trap us in a cave?"

Reluctantly the cats all trudged back up the trail through the forest to the big, flat lava rock with the symbols. Upon arriving, they looked up at the pile of rocks stacked in front of the cave opening.

"That's a pretty big pile of rocks," said Chops. "I have to say, somebody did a nice job."

Boo jumped up and quickly reached the pile of rocks in front of the cave. Silver and Roxy Roo were right behind him.

Chops was feeling tired and, to nobody's surprise, a little hungry. "I'm going to wait down here," he said. "What are we looking for anyway?"

"Not sure," yelled Silver from up above. "Anything that looks unusual."

Chops sat just above the rock with the symbols carved on it. He was tired and in no mood to be looking for unusual things or unknown nothings. He listened to the forest creatures making their unique sounds all around him and started daydreaming. He was skimming his foot over the rock with the symbols, and by accident, his keen feline eyes happened to zoom in on a tiny red object.

"That's an unusual something," said Chops.

He hopped down and picked up the unusual red object to play around with while his friends were playing detective in the rocks above him. Chops twirled the little red thing around with his claws, flipping it through the air. Boo jumped down to where Chops was sitting and plopped down next to him.

"Nothing up there," said Boo unenthusiastically. "Anything down here?" He glanced around, scanning the plants and rocks on the ground.

"Nope, didn't see anything. Hey, do we have anymore cat snacks?" asked Chops.

"I think so," replied Boo. "We may have to start rationing them because SOMEBODY is eating them all."

Under normal situations, Chops' eating habits didn't really bother Boo, but right now, he was slightly irritated with Chops. In Boo's mind, it was simple. He just wanted Chops to quit eating all their snacks. He glared at Chops and noticed that his good feline friend was twirling around a small red object with his claws.

"What's that?" asked Boo, slapping it out of Chops' claw and watching it fall on top of the black lava rock.

"I recognize that red thing," said Boo.

"Me too," admitted Chops. "Now that you slapped it out of my paw!"

"Professor Katnip!" Boo and Chops shouted together.

Roxy Roo and Silver heard the name Professor Katnip and quickly hopped down to the trail below.

"Where?" asked Silver, looking all around.

"Right there," said Boo, pointing at the little red claw cap resting on the black rock. "That little gem, I believe, belongs to Professor Katnip."

They all stared at the shiny red object for a few seconds.

"Are you positive?" asked Silver.

"Yes!" said all three of the feline friends together.

"Professor Katnip has some unusual wardrobe habits," said Boo. "I noticed his red cat claw caps when we went to visit him the other morning in his treehouse. The red caps really stood out to me when he handed me the catpack. We also found one inside the catpack."

"He wears them to keep from damaging his delicate and valuable plants when working in his lab," explained Roxy Roo.

"Maybe it's just a coincidence," said Silver. "There must be more than one Meow cat that wears a red claw cap. Besides, Professor Katnip's leg is hurt. Obviously he couldn't make it all the way out here."

"That's definitely true. There are some other Meow cats that wear claw caps, but not red ones," said Boo, showing them the red claw cap from the catpack. "The professor makes them in his lab. He loves to stand out from all the other Meow cats."

"Sounds like he's a bit of a Catsanova," said Chops.

"We best be moving along," said Silver, examining the red cat claw and placing it inside his porkypack.

The sunlight penetrated the treetops, providing a lighted path for them to follow. The vines stretched out from among the trees, hanging down like long limbs with spidery fingers reaching for their ears. The dangling vines caused them to walk in a crouched position most of the way along the trail.

They could hear the squeaks of the mushroom bugs under their paws as they squished along the forest floor. The strange noises of the forest creatures could be heard, but they seldom saw more than a glimpse of these unknown creatures. The snails, slugs, grubs, and other bugs moved along through hidden passageways under the thick plants and dead, decaying trees. The four adventurers were growing tired of their paws being poked by sharp twigs and of walking over squishy wet mushrooms on the forest floor.

Silver was hunting for anything edible along the way. He noticed a bright red patch just off the trail in the middle of a small field. He carefully stepped over the large tree roots and waddled over to the field that was glowing in the sunlight.

"Over here! Hurry, come over here!" shouted Silver. "We're all in for a real treat!"

Following the sound of Silver's voice and his pawprints, the cats were led into the middle of the open field. To their surprise, Silver was running around the field performing a happy dance in celebration of his delicious discovery. He had encountered one of the most wonderful treasures that a hungry and thirsty creature could hope to find in the forest. It was a beautiful patch of honey-heart melons. These amazing heart-shaped watermelons are red with seed-shaped black dots on top and green all around the underside. Best of all, the inside of the red melons is as sweet as a spoonful of honey.

Boo took his powerful sharp claws and cut the honey-heart melons in half. He handed each one of his friends a big piece of the sweetest, juiciest fruit that they would ever wet their whiskers with.

"Wow, this is the most delicious melon I've ever tasted," said Roxy Roo, scooping up some more of the red melon with her paw, dripping with juice.

"Don't eat the seeds," Boo reminded his friends, slurping on the juicy melon.

"And why not?" asked Chops nonchalantly. "Been there, done that."

"Chops, easy on the melons. You're gonna get a bellyache!" sang out Roxy Roo, spitting out the seeds.

Chops was sitting in the middle of the field surrounded by half-eaten honey-heart melons. His whiskers dripped with the melon juice as he continued slurping up the mouthwatering melons.

The honey-heart melons had quenched their hunger and thirst in the most satisfying way.

Step by step, they steadfastly moved their paws until the thick greenery of the forest slowly disappeared, and the vast wilderness came into view just beyond the last of the forest trees. Walkabout Wilderness was mostly a desolate land that extended beyond Bow Valley all the way to the Roundabout Mountains. The wilderness was known as a dangerous place where bullkat sightings and other creature encounters were not uncommon. The beautiful rainforest mountains rose high above the southern entrance to the maze inside of Kats Caves. The maze was one of the known hiding places of the dreaded bullkats.

At this moment in time, Boo and his friends were unaware that this adventure would lead them in that direction.

tyrtle

CHAPTER ELEVEN: WALKABOUT WILDERNESS

They walked out from under the last of the shade trees with a propulsive gait and into the bright sunlight as the vastness of the wilderness came into view.

Silver turned around and squeaked out a lovable laugh, noticing that his feline friends were still walking with their heads and necks still bent slightly forward.

"You can stand up straight now," he said, reminding them.

"Oh, heavens to Bugger Beach. What a relief," said Chops. "That cat crouch was gettin' old."

These felines were happier than cats fishing at Fish Flop Cove to be out of the damp forest and walking in the sunshine. Chops let out a loud groan watching Boo and Roxy Roo straighten out their backs, necks, and tails.

Silver looked out over the vast Walkabout Wilderness. His growing thirst reminded him that their food and water supply would not last long in this wide-open and desolate place.

"This looks like a great place to live. Does anyone want to move here?" said Chops, looking out over the mostly barren landscape. "Good luck building a treehouse."

Roxy Roo knew Chops was joking, but she answered his silly question anyway. "Sure. I think the landscape is lovely, and I've heard bullkats make great neighbors."

Silver stopped to look around from a higher vantage point before they descended down into the wilderness. He hoped they would be able to see some sign of water across the mostly arid land. The landscape was mostly empty, except for the patches of orange cat-a-lilies and yellow tiger lilies scattered across the desolate place. Silver noticed something that appeared to be very odd lying in the middle of one of the tiger lily patches.

"Maybe it's a large rock or some creature's abandoned house made of dried-up old sticks," thought Silver, gazing at it from a distance.

They all finished stretching their bodies back into shape and continued down the path, looking at the Roundabout Mountains far off in the distance. Silver lost sight of the unusual object in the middle of the tiger lily patch. He scanned the landscape to see if he could spot it again. He was as curious as a cat and wanted to know if the mysterious object contained anything at all that might help them through this barren land.

"Do you see that brown object in the middle of the yellow patch of tiger lilies?" Silver asked his friends, wondering if it was in the same place where he'd seen it a few minutes ago.

"Are you talking about the yellow patch by the large rocks at the base of the mountains?" inquired Boo as he swatted at a pesky bullfly buzzing around his ears.

Bullkats were usually accompanied by bullflies, which is how the nettlesome flies got their name.

"Yes… yes," confirmed Silver, still wondering if the unknown object had moved. "I was so sure that it was in the farthest patch," he murmured to himself as his curiosity grew.

"So, how are we looking on the cat-snack situation," inquired Chops, flicking a bullfly off the tip of his whiskers.

"Not so good. We're running low," replied Roxy Roo.

"Aren't tiger lilies and cat-a-lilies good for eating?" asked Chops.

"NO, ABSOLUTELY NOT!" shouted out Roxy Roo.

"OK, I was just askin'," said Chops. "I'm a fish kind of cat anyways. Big fish, little fish, smoked fish, but preferably rainbow fish. I'll wash it all down with some of the professor's catnip tea."

"Well, don't be surprised if we all have to go on a special diet for the next few days," said Boo, holding his paw over his stomach and looking over at his well-fed friend.

Silver licked his lips with his dry tongue and said, "We must find some water very soon."

They pointed their noses toward the lowest part of the trail and started walking downhill. Silver stopped to take another look out over the landscape for the mysterious brown object.

"I just don't understand it," exclaimed Silver, standing on his hind legs and straining to look out over the sparsely scattered patches of flowers. "I was so sure it was in the farthest patch, but then when I looked again, it had mysteriously moved to the second patch. Now, it looks like the thing has moved to the third patch of tiger lilies."

"As sure as a cat standing in the middle of a litter box, I'm sure it was in the second patch a few minutes ago," said Boo, confirming Silver's suspicions that the object was moving around.

The Meow cats' ears moved back against their heads, and Silver's quills stood on alert as they lost sight of the object. Walking along the trail through the wilderness they watched cautiously for the mysterious moving object.

The gently-rolling trail widened into an open area with just a few scattered low shrubs that somehow found a way to keep growing out of the dry dirt. The closer they got to the patch, the more annoying the bullflies buzzing around them became.

Suddenly, a loud screeching sound stopped them all dead in their tracks. It sounded exactly like the same sound they had heard in the forest.

Chops' heart just about thumped out of his chest as he looked over at Silver and said, "I thought you said whatever creature is making that awful sound lives in the forest? The forest is way, way back there. It sounds like whatever is making that sound lives right near here... in those there tiger lilies."

Boo looked at Silver with his eyebrows raised and said, "I think Chops is right. That sound didn't come from the forest. It sure sounded a lot closer to me."

Boo, being the tallest of the cats, stood up on his hind legs and was just tall enough to be able to see over the top of the tiger lilies. He looked out and watched as the unknown brown object slowly moved toward them through the yellow flowers.

"I think we have company, and it looks like it lives in a brown house.

Whatever lives in that house is making that annoying sound," said Boo, backing away from the patch of flowers.

Step by step they retreated, watching the brown shell-shaped house emerge out of the tiger lilies. The shell-shaped house stopped abruptly, exposing two scraggly, hairy legs protruding out of the bottom. The shell leaned forward, exposing two more scraggly hairy legs, and then the creature reared its ugly head and let out another annoying screech.

"Whatever that is," said Chops, staring at the crazy-looking creature, "it looks like it took a long dip in the ugly pond."

"Honestly, it kind of looks like a cat," said Silver without thinking. "Admittedly, a very strange-looking cat."

They gaped at the cat, waiting to see what the ugly creature's next move would be.

"If that creature looks like a cat, then you must be a porky pig," snapped Chops, feeling slighted about the unintentional cat insult coming from Silver.

"Well, it looks like this cat is coming out of his bag," shouted Boo, watching the strange and homely creature emerge from its house.

"Pigs, you see, they are one of my favorite animals to me," said the cat-like creature in a raspy voice, looking directly at Silver.

"How very rude! One more step from you and the wrath of my quills will certainly run you through!" warned Silver.

Boo stared at the bizarre cat. "Who are you and why are you bothering us? We have no intention of hurting you, but we will if we must."

"My name is Ferrel, you see," said the filthy animal, licking his lips and looking as crazy as could be. "A bird will do for a snack, yes, they are for me, but my favorite animals are really porcupines, you see."

"Well, I'll be. You're in luck then. Silver is a porky porcupine, you see," said Chops mockingly. "I know this creature is rude, but I hope by 'favorite,' he doesn't mean as in his favorite food."

Ferrel was slightly smaller than the Meow cats. In many ways, he resembled a cat, but actually he was not a Meow cat at all. The fur surrounding his face gave him the look of a masked bandit. There was no doubt that this creature was very peculiar-looking. The cat's spiked-up fur ran along his body, starting from the top of his ugly wrinkled forehead, all the way along the center of his back to the tip of his tail. His entire body was covered with black spots, and he looked like he was in desperate need of some serious grooming.

Boo and his friends had never even heard of Ferrel, and certainly had no idea that he was known as Tyrtle Island's hermit cat. He was given that name long ago. For as long as anyone could remember, Ferrel roamed Walkabout Wilderness carrying his house around on his back. As strange as it was, nobody on the island really knew why he began carrying his house on his back; he just always had.

"Cat or not, whatever you do, I'm warning you. You best move aside and let us through," warned Boo.

Ferrel looked at them crazily and said, "I'm so hungry… can't you see? I love porcupines, they are a favorite for me."

Chops grinned crazily at the curious cat. "It's plain to see that he's as crazy as crazy can be. The unkempt cat, looks like a drowned rat. The creature talks in rhyme, seems like all the time."

"It's true, I do," said Ferrel. "It's a riot. You must try it. I am so very tired of little birds, you see, and did I mention, porcupines are a favorite for me."

"How absurd. I'd be grouchy too if all I had to eat were birds," said Chops sympathetically. "I have to admit, it sounds silly, but I'm starting to feel a little sorry for him even if he does give me a case of the willies."

Roxy Roo glared at Chops and shouted, "Chops! Stop it! Here! This is all our food! Now maybe you can stop being so rude!"

Roxy Roo tossed what they had left of their smoked-fish snacks toward the hungry hermit cat. Ferrel reached down and grasped the fish with his mouth, then immediately retreated back into the hole in his shell-shaped house.

For the next few seconds it sounded like a feeding frenzy coming from the inside of the shell. This was the opportunity they had been waiting for, but the awful carnivorous slobbering sounds coming from within the walls of the hermit cat's house captivated them for those next few moments.

Ferrel sprang back out of the opening of his house and greeted them all as if it was the first time he had ever seen them.

"Good day! I'm Ferrel the hermit cat, you see! It's a good day indeed, it's a good day to be me!" he exclaimed joyfully.

They were stunned, you see. The cat was like a new creature. How could it be?

"Cat got your tongue?" he joked with a smile. "A few moments with Ferrel are the prize you have won. I'm so glad you can stay with me for a while."

He took his tongue, like a creepy mime, and ran it in a swirl around his mouth, cleaning up any crumbs of fish one last time.

"We're just passing through, so just let us be," said Boo. "That's all. We don't want any trouble, or you'll have to answer to me!"

"Oh, no worries, you see. No trouble from me," said Ferrel, smiling awkwardly.

"Oh, really? Please! Now that you've had the last of our snacks, you see," replied Chops, rolling his eyes mockingly.

"True enough, I cannot lie. I could have eaten a bird, a rat, or even a porcupine pie," confessed Ferrel. "Yes, it is a fact. I believe it's a good thing you had some leftover snacks."

Silver stood before him with a bewildered face, trying to understand the cat's unusual case. They were all moved by his personal story, but then Ferrel began to tell them a tale that was all too gory.

"This I know, I saw a couple fancy cats pass through this place a few days ago. Luckily, they were heading in the opposite direction of me. Although for one of them it did not appear to be so very lucky, as you will see," said Ferrel with no glee.

"I'm sure they were bullkats. It's their territory, I'm sure you will agree. Is this what you are trying to tell us, maybe?" said Boo impatiently.

"Bullkats… heavens, no," said Ferrel, real low. "Well, at least for one old cat, it was not a bullkat that did him in. It was his friend, who I'm sure totally surprised him.

"I was taking a nap in my shell, you see. I heard some loud voices and thought, what can it be?

"The cats didn't notice my sleek house hidden above. They were down by the creek; I could see from behind the shrubs.

"I remember they both wore fancy bow ties. One was red, the other green, and I could tell they were arguing 'bout something.

"I couldn't hear what their disagreement was about. I was listening through my shell and decided to sneak out.

"The peek I was sneaking was just in time; one cat yelled at the other, you're no friend of mine!

"They started a vicious cat fight, you see. What I have to tell you next, I certainly say with no glee.

"The cat with a red bow tie hit the cat with the green, then he threw down the jagged rock and looked around to see if he'd been seen.

"He hit the poor cat right smack in the head, and I could plainly see that the poor creature with the green bow tie was dead," Ferrel said.

They stood there stunned at what Ferrel had just said, thinking that his story had to be some kind of sick joke.

They looked at each other with shock in their eyes, like they had just lost the remaining eight of their nine lives.

Ferrel continued on to say, "The cat with the red bow tie rolled the cat with the green onto a wooden cart, and off he went, no remorse, and no heart.

"That was the last I ever saw of those cats. That's the end of my story, and that's that."

They all stood dead still in disbelief, despite the annoying bullflies buzzing about their heads, giving them no relief.

Ferrel turned around to return to his shell, but they were not all totally convinced of the truth of his tale.

"How do we know your tale is true?" said Silver. "For all we know, it could've been you."

"I don't eat cats, as you can see. I love porcupines; they are for me," said Ferrel, unashamed. "They are my first choice, you see. I'm sure, of course, you will always remember me."

Ferrel crawled backwards, crouching down through the small hole in his shell-shaped house with the swarm of bullflies following right behind him. He carried it off, disappearing back into the middle of the tiger lilies that were dancing back and forth in rhythm with the island breeze.

Boo and his friends didn't move a muscle. They were appalled as they stood, silently trying to digest the story they had just heard and understand the creature they had just seen. Not a single one of them wanted to believe a word of Ferrel's story, but as hard as it was for them to swallow, they all knew he had no reason to lie.

"A red bow tie and a green bow tie, it must be true," said Chops. "Who else could it have been, but Professor Katnip and Professor Potamus too?"

"For the last time, if I hear one more rhyme," said Boo.

Roxy Roo's pretty feline face was overcome with sadness. "Poor Professor Potamus," she said, feeling her sorrow quickly being consumed by anger. "Professor Katnip blamed it on the bullkats!"

Chops continued trying to make sense of their confusion. "Who else would wear a bow tie? Red or green, for that matter."

"Ferrel mentioned something about a creek down by the mountainside," Silver reminded them. "We really need to find some water and soon."

Chops waited until Roxy Roo was looking in his direction and then began to rub his paw over his belly with a malingering frown upon his face. He knew she was a soft touch and sometimes found himself taking advantage of that side of her.

Chops put on his best performance imitating Ferrel the hermit cat. "I believe more snacks is what we need, now that we gave that crazy hermit cat our last bits of fish, you see! Yes! Snacks are a favorite for me."

Despite the tragic news they had just learned, everyone kept their spirits high. They all chuckled at Chops and his purr-fect performance. He always kept the atmosphere lighthearted even when they really didn't want him to. Humor was Chops' way of dealing with most situations.

The sun was brightly shining directly above them. They started winding their way around the tiger lily and cat-a-lily flower patches, working their way steadily toward the mountainside.

A few of the bullflies were determined to follow them and continued buzzing around, living up to their pesky reputation. Chops and Boo swatted erratically at the annoying insects as they traveled along, and it became the main entertainment for Roxy Roo and Silver.

Smiling, Boo looked off to the northern sky and said, "I have some good news and some bad news. The good news is… we may get some rain. Bad news is… we may be standing out in it when it comes."

Boo understood that Meow cats and porcupines really didn't mind getting wet, but given a choice, they would rather not be caught out in the wet weather.

The crooked creek was running along the base of the mountainside just as Ferrel said it would be. The flowing water followed the natural landscape just below the wilderness plains and continued toward the southernmost part of Kats Caves.

Silver, Boo, and Roxy Roo found a pool of fresh water and filled up their waterskins while Chops was still battling with the bullflies. His yelling and screaming, while jumping up and down and flailing his limbs, never failed to entertain his friends.

Boo chuckled and shouted, "Chops, quit playing with the bullflies and fill up your waterskin!"

Ignoring Boo, Chops continued to swat spastically at the pesky insects. Roxy Roo walked over by Chops and started to sing out a song with her sweet, gentle voice.

"Bullfly, stop buggin' me, bullfly, stop buggin' me
Don't wait, hurry up and pollinate, all for you and me
Bullfly, stop buggin' me, bullfly, stop buggin' me
Use your eyes and antennae, all for you and me
Bullfly, stop buggin' me, bullfly, stop buggin' me
Steer your wings to sticky things, all for you and me."

By the time Roxy Roo had finished her enchanted song, all the bullflies had miraculously retreated to the patches of orange and yellow flowers. The awe and fascination could not be contained on the smiling faces of her friends. They didn't understand the magical power that Roxy Roo held over insects, but they could feel the wonderment of it all. Chops' face still had a look of disbelief at what had just happened. "That was amazing," said Chops. "I only wish you would've sang that beautiful bug tune a little while ago."

Roxy Roo picked up a pawful of dirt and chased Chops down the side of the creek bed toward the opening of Kats Caves. Her chase stopped just short of the cave opening, allowing them to catch their breath. She looked back along the creek to see if Silver and Boo were following behind them.

The mountainside was growing darker, being consumed by its own shadow as the sun started to take refuge on the other side. The gathering of the clouds made it seem later than it actually was, and the rain that Boo had predicted earlier looked as though it was on its way.

Roxy Roo looked up at the darkening sky and then peered into the dark cave, saying to Chops, "I think we can spend the night in here."

Chops gave her a crazy look and said, "I think—maybe not!"

"And… why not?"

Chops looked over at the side of the cave opening and replied, "I see bones!"

Roxy Roo looked around, frantically shouting, "Bones! You see Bones?"

"Yes!" shouted Chops. "I see bones and lots of them! Look! Look! They're all over the place!"

The worried look on her face quickly turned to a smile as she let out a sigh of relief. "Oh, those kinds of bones. Not the creepy-cat-Bones kind of bones."

"Well, if you ask me, both kinds of bones are a little creepy," said Chops, chasing his tail in circles.

Roxy Roo watched Chops for a few seconds as he ran in circles try to "kill" his stubby tail. She smiled and then jumped up on some rocks as she cautiously moved closer to the mouth of the cave. The sun-bleached bones were scattered about like a graveyard in front of the cave and throughout the rocks.

Boo and Silver walked up behind Roxy Roo where she was standing in front of the cave.

"What's he doing?" asked Silver, looking curiously at Chops running in circles.

"Chasing his tail," said Boo nonchalantly.

"I can see that," said Silver. "Why is he doing that?"

"It's his hunter instinct," said Boo. "He's been doing that since he was a kitten. He hasn't caught his tail yet." Boo laughed and swished his long tail through the air.

"Hmmm. So, just like his food, he'll probably never catch it," said Silver.

"I heard that," said Chops. "Practice makes perfect. Besides, it's not my fault that I have a stubby tail… just like somebody else I know."

Boo looked up at the darkening sky and peeked into the dark cave saying, "I think we can spend the night here."

"Oh, now don't start that again. I think… maybe not?" said Chops emphatically, again.

"And why not?" asked Boo bluntly.

Chops looked at Roxy Roo smiling and then pointed over at all the bones lying around and replied once more, "The bones!"

"Oh, don't worry about them there bones," said Boo. "Whoever or whatever ate them was probably on the outside of the cave. We're spending the night on the inside of the cave."

Chops knew that Boo was just having some fun with him but decided to play along and replied, "Or maybe, whoever or whatever ate all of them there creatures—that are now only them there dry bones—was on the inside of the cave and threw all of them there bones outside when it was finished with its meal!" said Chops, finishing his long statement very enthusiastically and imagining it was somewhat of a great comeback.

The island weather decided it would settle their differences for them. Huge raindrops started to fall from the darkening island sky. Bones or not, Kats Caves was the only shelter anywhere near them. They all knew it was risky to stay in a cave where bullkats were known to roam at night, but tonight the choice had been made for them.

"Looks like it's going to be a toad-floater," said Chops, wrapping his scarf around his neck. "Well, we better get in the cave. Go ahead, Boo, you go first."

Chops stood behind his friend and gave him a gentle push toward the cave opening. Boo smiled, looking back at Chops while flicking his tail like a whip, just missing him.

"Do we have any firebugs left?" said Boo.

Roxy Roo handed Boo the jar and grinned at him. "OK, I'll go with you."

"Thanks, Roxy Roo," said Boo, flicking Chops on the ear. "But… I think Silver and his deadly quills should go in with me."

Boo and Silver slowly crept into the large opening of the cave. Their paws stopped abruptly after only a couple steps. Boo could see the silhouette of something moving toward them, and it looked to be about the same size as a Meow cat. They slowly retreated out of the cave to where Roxy Roo and Chops were standing in the rain.

"That was quick," said Chops. "Looks like you did a pretty thorough—"

Chops was interrupted by a cat-like creature that emerged out of the darkness and into the gloomy daylight, right behind Boo and Silver. The unknown creature's face and body seemed to change before their very eyes. At first, they thought their minds were playing tricks on them. They were sure that the mostly-normal-looking cat standing in the light before them had looked much more like a dreaded bullkat only a few seconds ago as it came out of the cave. They could only see the outline of the grotesque details of the cursed creature while it was walking toward them in the dark, but, unexplainably, the cat had been transfigured as it came out into the light.

They could feel a sense of uneasiness from the creature as it just stood on all four paws in front of the cave and gazed at the four of them. Boo and Silver were not sure what to make of this cat and were ready to defend themselves and their friends.

"So, are you a good cat or a bad cat?" asked Roxy Roo, breaking the silence. "Maybe you're not a cat at all?"

There was no response from the cat. He just continued to stare at them and in the process was making them all feel much more on edge. Their ears pointed straight up, and Silver's quills instinctively moved into their protective position.

"Do you live in this cave?" asked Silver. "Any other cats or creatures inside?"

"Not very talkative are you?" said Chops. "Do... you... understand?"

Boo's patience was growing thin with this "cat got your tongue" creature. Especially since he was soaked to the bone and felt wetter than a fish swimming through the ocean.

The cat had a haunted look in his eyes, but the expression on his face was one of sadness. The feline was somewhat smaller than the Meow cats, especially now that he was soaking wet in the rain. Boo saw a kindness behind the cat's downcast eyes. He was determined to get out of the rain, one way or another.

"We're getting out of this nasty weather. The cave is dry, so we're coming into the cave with or without you," Boo said, walking forward toward the cave opening while keeping his eyes on the unknown cat and his long claws in attack position.

"I'm a bullkat," confessed the cat shamefully. "I have to warn you... there will be others... sooner or later. Probably sooner, and they hate getting wet."

Boo walked cautiously around the self-professing bullkat and stood just inside the cave opening. Silver and Roxy Roo were guarded as they followed right behind Boo and out of the stormy weather. The rainwater was quickly filling up the creek and starting to overflow close to where Chops was still standing out in the rain. He was starting to resemble a wet gray rug while he kept his eyes fixed on the unnamed bullkat.

"Are you just going to stand out there?" shouted Boo.

"It will stop raining... eventually," said Chops, gurgling. "Not going in there with a bullkat."

"In case you haven't noticed, the bullkat is still standing out there with you," said Boo. "Have it your way."

Boo turned and walked deeper into the dark cave but still kept a watchful eye on his good friend.

Buckets of rain continued to pour down on Chops and the small bullkat. They were still standing across from one another and still in the middle of a staring contest. Chops finally found the courage to make his move. He glared at the cat and shouted, "YOU STAY THERE!"

Chops slowly walked sideways through the cave opening, making sure to steer clear of the bullkat while trying to look as fierce as possible in the process. He fuzzed up his fur and stood tall on the tips of his paws, stumbling over a couple of small rocks as he walked backwards into the cave. He quickly moved further inside the cave and out of sight of the bullkat. His friends were busy looking around on the inside of the cave.

Surprisingly, and for reasons unknown to Chops, everyone else didn't seem to be afraid of this particular bullkat, who was still standing in front of what appeared to be their only escape route.

"Helloooo?" said Chops, his voice echoing loudly through the cave.

He took his eyes off the bullkat and focused on his friends for a few seconds as they continued to wander through the dimly-lit cave.

Chops was growing impatient and finally blurted out, "Hello? There's a bullkat outside! Remember? The grotesque-looking evil creature!"

Turning around, they stopped what they were doing and looked over at Chops, who was standing just inside the cave opening. Boo held his paw up in the air, pointing toward the cave opening.

Chops stared straight ahead, gasped, and said, "He's standing right behind me, isn't he?"

Not waiting for his friends to answer his question, he leaped over to the other side of the wall, landing on all four paws. Sliding sideways on the slippery cave floor, Chops smashed through a big pile of bones, crashing into the cave wall. Seemingly ignoring Chops' acrobatic stunt, they all looked back at the bullkat standing in what was left of the low light at the cave's entrance.

"Why are you telling us that you're a bullkat?" asked Roxy Roo. "You don't really look like a bullkat. You certainly don't smell like a bullkat, and you are not acting like a bullkat. So are you really sure you're a bullkat?"

Silver was not happy. In fact, he was boiling mad inside thinking about the destruction of his home and the unknown whereabouts of his family, caused by a bullkat just like this one. He hid his emotions well and, without saying a word, he boldly walked over to the cat. Silver stood up on his two back legs and slipped one of his curved claws into the cat's pointed ear.

Chops watched in disbelief while the heroic porcupine stepped right in front of the unconfirmed bullkat and actually stuck his claw inside the bullkat's ear.

"He is either really brave or not playing with a full set of quills," whispered Chops.

Silver kept constant eye contact with the cat, and the cat didn't move a muscle. Silver felt the tip of his sharp claw scrape against the tiny horn hidden down inside the bullkat's ear.

He calmly lowered himself back down on all four paws, then walked back toward his friends and pronounced, "There is no doubt about it: this cat is a bullkat!"

"OK, thanks for checking that out for us!" declared Chops, taking a step back and positioning his paws in a fighting stance. "Great news! So should we now prepare to defend ourselves from being shredded to bits or just start running?"

Roxy Roo ignored Chops' comments and theatrics. Although she did notice that his sarcastic comments were becoming more and more frequent.

"Let's start again, now that we're positive you're a bullkat," said Roxy Roo. "So, what's your name?"

"Calico. Well, that's what all the other bullkats call me," he said. "They gave me that name because I live in this cold cave all by myself."

"Sooo… is your name Cold or Calico?" said Chops.

"Chops, stop it!" shouted Roxy Roo, glaring. "You know, sometimes you're just not as funny as you think."

Chops grinned and said, "What? That was a serious question."

"Where are all the other bullkats?" asked Boo.

Calico noticed the sun was almost down and the opening of the cave was growing darker. He moved back to make sure he was still exposed to the fading sunlight that was quickly being consumed behind the mountains.

"I have to go now," Calico said quickly. "The other bullkats might find you here if they come by looking for me tonight or just to get out of the rain. There's an escape tunnel through the back of the cave under the pool of water. I have to go before it's too late."

The sunlight had almost given way to the darkness throughout Walkabout Wilderness, and they watched in amazement as bullkat horns began to grow out of Calico's pointed ears. His eyes took on an eerie yellow glow, and his body began to transform, showing the hideous signs of a bullkat. He turned and vanished out of the cave and into the night. The creature's hideous sounds could be heard as he ran off shrieking through the dark, dead landscape.

Roxy Roo gave Boo a perplexed look, listening to the sound of the awful screeches fading away in the distance. "I don't understand. Calico's a bullkat? Why didn't he attack us? He had us cornered in this cave."

"I'm not sure. I know he didn't really act like a bullkat. It all has something to do with the bullkats being cursed; at least, that's how the legend was passed down," explained Boo. "I've heard Professor Katnip and some of the Meow Cat elders telling stories about the legend of Wiki Tyrtle and the curse of the bullkats."

"Silver, what do you know about these legends and curses?" asked Boo.

Boo's words bounced off the cave walls as he walked to the back of the cave looking for the pool of water that Calico mentioned just before he disappeared into the darkness. Boo wanted to make sure they were ready if they needed to escape quickly.

"After our home in the Land of Wig Waggle was attacked and destroyed—" Silver lamented, walking in circles in the dark.

"Take your time," said Roxy Roo compassionately.

"Well, since that day of terror," Silver continued, "I've talked to some friendly creatures on the island, and they have confirmed that some bullkats are good and really have no desire to do any harm. They say it's their cursed nature that takes control, and it happens when they are absent of light and covered in darkness. The curse is at its worst when there is no visible light from the moon."

Roxy Roo sighed deeply, whispering, "Poor Calico."

Chops looked at her with sympathy, saying, "I love you, Roxy Roo, but seriously? Now we're feeling sorry for bullkats… after all the awful things they've done over the years?"

Boo yelled from the back of the cave. "I found it! I hope we don't need to use it to escape because I've already taken one bath tonight!"

Roxy Roo tried to capture most of the firebugs back into the jar, hoping to conserve some of their light for later. The cave was now without even a flicker of light. They picked out a spot to bed down for the night. It was as close to the pool of water as they could possibly get and still keep dry.

Roxy Roo curled up on the damp ground and purred sweetly, "'Night, all."

One by one, the boys gave their goodnight wishes. The sound of the water trickling through the hollow walls seemed to grow louder as they all settled down for the night. They hoped it would be a night with no interruptions, especially from unwanted visitors.

Silver took the first watch and quickly discovered that the night was not destined to be a peaceful one. He positioned himself just outside the cave opening, making himself comfortable among the dead bones. Fortunately for Silver and his creature companions, a porcupine's hearing is much better than its eyesight. His strong sense of hearing began to detect noises far off in the distance. Not just any creature noises, though: these were the unmistakable sounds of bullkats echoing across the desolate Walkabout Wilderness. The horrid sounds continued to get louder and closer to Calico's Cave. The number of screeches and growls could no longer be counted as they constantly echoed through the night.

"Wake up!" shouted Silver, alarming his sleeping friends. "They're here! Hurry! Time to get wet!"

He felt it was necessary to give Chops a good old poke with one of his quills.

Chops jumped up and snapped angrily, "Ouch! Stop that! Why are you always picking on the big cat?"

"Bullkats are almost at our front door!" shouted Silver. "I don't think they will be so kind as to only give you a poke."

They all frantically gathered their catpacks and belongings in the dark.

Roxy Roo took out her jar of firebugs and set a couple free so they could at least see the pool of water they would be jumping into.

The dreadful sounds could now be heard loud and clear. The unwanted and uninvited snarling guests crouched at the cave opening looking for the occupants of Calico's Cave. The evil bullkats only paused for a few seconds, and without further warning, their yellow eyes and glowing horns crept deeper into the cave.

"NOW!" Boo shouted at the top of his lungs, tossing the deadly plants they had gathered toward the oncoming bullkats. He slashed his claws through the air with lightning speed at the fiery eyes darting all around them.

Silver attacked with his deadly quills into the darkness, and they could all hear the hideous shrieks of pain as the quills pierced the bullkats' bodies.

Roxy Roo leaped into the pool of dark water without knowing where it would lead, nor how long it would be before she would catch her next breath. Chops jumped into the water whiskers first and frantically followed behind her, trying to catch her tail that was like a snake moving along through the water.

"Go, Silver! Into the water!" commanded Boo with a great shout.

Silver ignored Boo's command and stayed back, hoping that the potent plants and his piercing quills would slow down the attacking bullkats. Boo could see the sparks fly off the ground as Silver's deadly tin-tipped tail whipped around like a cat-o-nine tails in the dark. Each strike of his tail was matched by the bullkats' hideous screeches that pierced their ears as the shrieks bounced off the cave walls.

The growling bullkats retreated for a few seconds, giving Boo and Silver the chance they needed to dive into the pool of water and make their escape into the unknown.

"Water! Now!" shouted Boo, looking back at the bullkats.

Boo caught the silhouette of a tall cat figure standing just beyond the cave opening. In the middle of the chaos, his keen night vision observed the eerie green glow of the mysterious cat standing calmly just beyond the attacking bullkats. In that split-second, Boo was sure of one thing, the unknown figure was not a bullkat. Bullkats only have yellow eyes.

Chapter Eleven

Boo turned back just in time to witness Silver's poor jumping performance. It's well known that porcupines are not especially good jumpers, and once again, that proved to be true with Silver.

The flickering light provided a movement-by-movement, slow-motion picture as Silver attempted to leap from where he was standing to the pool of water, and he landed terribly short. Silver sprang back up and jumped into the water with his tail clinking against the rocky edge just before he sank into the darkness.

Boo reached the water in one giant leap. He felt the pain of one of the bullkats' claws tearing at his tail just as he cleared the edge of the pool of water and ducked out of sight. He moved his paws as fast as he could, scratching his way along the narrow water tunnel and into the utter darkness beyond Calico's Cave. For those few moments Boo knew what it was like to be totally alone, trapped in an unknown water world.

tyrtle

CHAPTER TWELVE: HIDDEN PARADISE

Jᴇssᴇ's ʜᴇᴀʀᴛ ʀᴀᴄᴇᴅ ᴀs ʜɪs lungs struggled to gasp for a single breath of air. His mind was murky. He was in the middle of his island dream, trapped in a watery tunnel world. He tried desperately to move his arms and legs, but it was not possible. It was like they were made of stone. His mind told him his eyes were open, yet all he could see before him was total darkness. He was sure that he had died, but then instantly, the life that had been sucked out of him quickly flowed back into his body.

The darkness faded away, and slowly his world came into view. Sweat dripped profusely off his head. His body struggled to catch a breath of air, and then he instinctively took a deep breath and sat straight up in his tent.

"That was insane," Jesse thought as he sat up, breathing heavily and leaning against the walls of the tent.

He stared out into the night through the window of his tent, gathering his thoughts and waiting for the beating of his heart to calm down. Boo rubbed his soft fur up against him, purring gently. The light of the moon shined through the window as Jesse looked into Boo's glowing eyes that were staring right back at him.

"I wonder if you're dreaming too," Jesse thought, looking at Boo.

He sat quietly in his tent listening to the concert of sounds throughout the rainforest. The creatures were going about their nightly business of searching for food and the perfect mate. The damp night air was filled with the deafening mating cries coming from the giant rainforest bullfrogs that were calling out from a nearby pond.

Jesse heard some commotion coming from a nearby tent.

Chapter Twelve

"Alright already! Don't they ever sleep? Anyone got ear plugs?" yelled a voice in the dark that sounded very much like Caleb.

It appeared he was not pleased with the ruckus being raised by the lonely-heart amphibians. Unknown to Caleb, he was in for a long night, because bullfrogs don't really ever sleep in warm weather, and they would most likely be serenading all through the night.

Jesse rested his head back down on his pillow and tried to clear his mind, which was running away with thoughts of Boo, bullkats, and his never-ending island dream. He leaned over and wiped the sweat off his forehead with the sleeve of his shirt. He collapsed back down on his pillow, allowing his mind and body to be quickly overcome with sleep. Once again, he sailed off into the island dream tunnel and his mind melded with the mind of Boo. Jesse's eyes fluttered uncontrollably, unaware that Boo was still staring at him in the darkness.

Boo's mind was lost in between unknown worlds as his heart raced and his lungs struggled to gasp for a single breath of air. He felt like he'd been swimming for an eternity. His mind was trapped in a mysterious world between the water tunnel and the unknown. He opened his eyes, hoping to see any trace of light, and yet all he could see before him was total darkness.

At that exact moment he popped up through a blowhole, and his body instinctively gasped for a breath of air. His body uncontrollably shot straight up into the air and then flopped like a dead cat onto what felt like a slippery rock waterslide. Through the blackness Boo slid uncontrollably down the waterslide. He attempted to slow himself down, but the rush of the water kept his claws from being able to grasp the sides of the smooth rock. A moment later the tunnel spit him out into a lagoon filled with dazzling blue water. His eyes opened slowly, and he struggled to process the vivid details of one of the most enchanted places he'd ever seen.

Roxy Roo and Chops watched as Boo shot out of the water.

They shouted out together with joy, "Boo!"

Words could not describe their elation when their longtime friend popped out of the water tunnel. Boo forgot all about the bullkats and his badly hurt tail, at least for the moment.

"Oh, heaven's helpers! I am so thankful!" said Silver gleefully. "I was afraid, albeit just for a moment, they might have damaged you."

Boo was so completely overcome by his surroundings that he unintentionally ignored everyone.

He gazed around, and after a few minutes, he slowly responded to Silver, "Yeah, seems… they did… get my tail… pretty good."

Boo was suddenly bombarded by Roxy Roo and Chops. They smothered their friend by wrapping their paws all around him and rubbing their furry faces on his cheeks. They were so excited to see Boo that they pulled him under the water again. It was a moment of hot-lava happiness.

Boo hugged his friends awkwardly while gurgling and spitting water out of his mouth. "Easy, I don't want to drown again."

"What took you so long?" said Chops, dog-paddling to the shore.

"Oh, very funny… a cat comedian," said Boo, smiling.

Standing on the shore of the lagoon, they all slowly looked up and down, left and right, and forwards and backwards. They gazed at the natural rock walls that extended high above and encircled the hidden lagoon like the petals of a flower protecting its sweet nectar.

The lagoon and surrounding rainforest made an incredible pristine sight. The walls were draped with the most colorful spectacle of flowers and plants to ever fill a painter's palette. There was an unfathomable diversity of plants and giant banyan trees encompassing the shimmering lagoon, just below a thin layer of marshmallow clouds. The clouds provided a protective covering that concealed this paradise from the outside island world.

One of the plants attached to the towering walls released a kaleidoscope of colorful flowers that twirled in unison along with their vibrant dangling tails. The amazing flowers looked like jellyfish dancing out of the water high above the lagoon. The flowers swirled around at the mercy of the island breeze and after a few minutes were lifted up and over the walls. One by one, the unique flowers sailed away and disappeared over the never-ending ocean.

The mist of the tall and picturesque waterfall tumbling quietly down from the towering walls provided just the right amount of water for these celestial jellyfish flowers to flourish.

Roxy Roo marveled at the unspeakable beauty that surrounded her. "Wow, and I thought Bow Valley was the most amazing place I had ever seen."

"Look! In the lagoon!" shouted Silver. "Turtles are such strange and funny-looking creatures."

They were all astonished to witness dozens and dozens of magnificent sea turtles of various colors, shapes, and sizes gracefully swimming around on the bottom of the crystal-clear lagoon. The lagoon was filled with an underwater garden teeming with marine life, creating a feast for their eyes.

"Where did they come from?" cried Roxy Roo rapturously. "I just adore them!"

The sea turtles, who were sometimes referred to as the ancient ones of Tyrtle Island, entered the lagoon through the Coral Way Cave. The turtles paddled through the kaleidoscope of vibrant colors, swimming in and out of the coral reef encircling the lagoon. The natural cave was the perfect size to allow sea turtles to swim into the hidden waters, circle the lagoon, and then disappear into the ocean once again.

"I like turtles, but I really love rainbow fish," said Chops.

His eyes glazed over watching the abundance of rainbow fish swimming in and out of the coral reef in the center of the lagoon.

Chops stepped closer to get a better look at the yummy fish. "I'm in heaven!" he sang out loudly in a deep, melodramatic voice.

"No, Chops! Not here!" said Boo abruptly and loudly.

"What?" whined Chops, focusing on the delicious fish. "I'm so hungry. Not even a little one?" He continued to smack his lips and run his tongue around the outside of his whiskers.

Before any of his friends could answer him, a loud, goofy voice coming from the middle of the lagoon surprised them all by saying, "Not even a little one!"

A really large and goofy-looking Tyrtle , with a giant bump protruding from its throat, called out in a goofy voice from the top of the reef, "I better not catch you with even one!"

"What are you gawping at? Who are you to tell us that we can't eat any fish?" said Chops.

"You're welcome to the seaweed. It grows along the lagoon shores in abundance. Its salty sweetness is especially delicious," explained the Tyrtle.

"Do I look like a turtle?" asked Chops. "Cats don't eat stinkin' seaweed."

"Nothing compares to a delicious seaweed-and-jellies sandwich," said the Tyrtle, assuming it was a well-known fact among all the creatures of Tyrtle Island.

"Although a macadamia butter and fish sandwich can be pretty tasty. I'm just sayin'," said Chops, licking his whiskers.

"We're not going to argue with a turtle," Roxy Roo blurted out in her most gentle voice. "No fish from this lagoon! No fish! End of story," she said, looking at Chops.

Chops had to fight the urge to pout about the fish, so he quickly started looking around the lagoon for the so-called delicious seaweed.

"Mr. Turtle, I don't know your name," said Roxy Roo. "I'm sure it's a very nice name, whatever it is. I wasn't expecting to talk to a turtle today, but I assure you there is no need to worry about our friend. I promise he will not be eating any fish from this lagoon. Chops, tell the nice turtle thank you for the seaweed and—"

"You're welcome!" he gurgled, interrupting her and looking over at Chops. "By the way, my name is Wacky Tyrtle."

"Did I just hear him say his name is Wacky?" Chops could not contain himself any longer as he fell over on his back, rolling around and laughing hysterically. "What a perfect name! Wacky! I can't believe it… but I love it!"

Boo and Roxy Roo stared at each other, doing their best to keep from laughing out loud.

They both looked over at Chops and at the same time said, "Chops! Don't be rude!"

Wacky Tyrtle was appalled and said, "Well! My brother Wiki and I have been swimming these oceans for well over a hundred years, and I've been swimming in and out of this lagoon for just as long." The Tyrtle was so flustered that he had to pause for a moment to choose his next words very carefully. He rubbed the slipper on his foot up against his chin as he continued to think. "Well, being a Tyrtle … I'm not going to tell you what

I think of your feline friend's island etiquette. Yup! I'm sure that's the right word ... etiquette."

"What? What'd I say?" appealed Chops. He turned around, holding some seaweed in his paw, and looked at his friends. "What can I say? Beauty doesn't just happen, ya know."

"Did you say your brother is Wiki Tyrtle?" inquired Silver. "The Wiki Tyrtle of whom the legend speaks of? The Wiki Tyrtle of the mythical Wiki Island and the Tyrtle Tunnel?" Silver continued enthusiastically, running out of breath.

"That's the one! Tyrtle Island's finest since forever!" he proclaimed proudly.

Wacky Tyrtle ducked into the water, and with his slippers attached to his feet, he swam ever so gracefully toward the lagoon tunnel and vanished.

Boo and Roxy Roo stared at each other cat-faced, with their ears pointing straight up. They were clearly a little upset at Chops even though they would both agree that he was pretty hilarious.

Silver stood alongside Boo and Roxy Roo, and collectively they all stared at Chops. It was clear they were all disappointed. Chops had ruined their opportunity to learn more about the mythical Wiki Tyrtle from his wacky brother.

Chops was preoccupied with satisfying the grumbling of his stomach and oblivious to the consequences of his unintentional rude behavior. He was down by the lagoon shore, nibbling on some of the seaweed that he'd scooped up with his claws.

"Ew! Just can't do it," said Chops, grumbling, spitting the slimy green plants out of his mouth. "Guess you gotta be a turtle."

Silver had been looking around at the towering walls surrounding Calico's Lagoon as he had begun to wonder about something. In the middle of all the excitement, he was pretty sure that none of them had thought about how to get out of the hidden lagoon. One thing was for sure: they couldn't go back the same way they had arrived.

Calico told them about the pool of water in the cave but didn't even mention the lagoon, much less any other clues about how to get out of this incredible place.

Silver looked through his porkypack to see how much bark he had left to nibble on, and then asked everyone, "I don't want to spoil the atmosphere of enjoying this hidden gem, but did anyone consider a way out of here?"

Roxy Roo raised her paw in the air and shouted, "I have an idea! We can try and swim out the same way as Wacky Tyrtle, and go through the lagoon tunnel. On second thought, maybe we should try and look for another way out so that we don't get swept out to sea. This time of the year I think the rip current is really strong, which is dangerous, of course, unless you're a turtle or a fish."

Chops was snacking on some seaweed, still trying to convince himself that it wasn't so bad. He pointed up at the towering walls and said, "So, what about the spiraling staircase? Wonder where that goes?"

"What staircase?" inquired Boo.

"The one hiding in back of the falls," Chops blurted out.

Chops had a disgusted look on his face while munching on some more seaweed.

He sat down by the lagoon and pointed nonchalantly over to the falls. Boo, Roxy Roo, and Silver all looked up at the towering waterfall and were amazed at what they saw behind it.

The spiraling rocky staircase was almost invisible to the naked eye. The waterfall stirred up a curtain of mist, camouflaging the staircase behind it. The crystal-clear water tumbled down the length of the wall until it coalesced once again with the lagoon far below.

Silver was busy munching on a tender piece of bark as he gazed up at the staircase, then said, "Chops, time to go. I think we'll find some tastier treats up top more suitable to your finicky taste buds."

Chops looked up with a slimy green piece of seaweed hanging out of his mouth. He shook his head in disgust, watching Silver gnaw on a piece of bark with his big orange incisors.

After staring at him for a few seconds, Chops refocused on the fish swimming in the lagoon and said with a loud voice, "No seaweed or bitter bark for me! Real cats eat fish!"

They searched for the best path leading to the staircase. Silver and Roxy

Chapter Twelve

Roo became distracted by all the amazingly rare plants and flowers they encountered while walking the trails. For Roxy Roo, the fragrant flowers and flourishing plants growing around the lagoon were all new and exciting. The exotic flora surrounding her could not be found in Treetop Woods.

Boo's paws came to a quick stop when a particularly colorful flowering plant caught his attention.

"This plant looks familiar," said Boo. "Hey, Silver, take a look at this. Do you know what this is?"

Silver walked up the dark red dirt trail, stopping just short of the plant Boo was referring to.

Chops looked at Boo and chimed in, saying, "Pretty sure it's a plant."

"Thanks so much, I didn't know that!"

"Apparently not."

Silver was careful not to get too close or touch the plant until he was sure what kind it was. Without saying a word, Boo took off his catpack and reached inside, carefully pulling out the leather pouch.

"Careful there, little buddy," cautioned Chops, remembering that Professor Katnip had warned them about the harmful plant.

Boo chuckled at Chops' "little buddy" expression. It was true that Chops was a much bigger and thicker Meow cat, but Boo had always thought of him like a little brother.

Boo handed the pouch to Silver. Porcupine paws are much thicker than a cat's paw, which is why it was safer for Silver to handle the potentially toxic plants than for one of the cats. This was precisely the reason Professor Katnip had instructed them that a porcupine should be the only creature to handle the rainbow plants.

Silver cautiously opened the leather pouch. Although the plant in the pouch was mostly dried out, he was almost certain that Professor Katnip's plant and the plants they had just found were one and the same. They all realized that this toxic and potentially deadly plant was one of the most valuable commodities on Tyrtle Island.

"It's a match," said Silver confidently. "I'm sure this is the rare rainbow plant."

"It looks exactly like it," said Boo, "but the professor said the plant is in the rainforest. He never mentioned anything about finding the plant in this lagoon. Who knows, maybe he doesn't even know about Calico's Lagoon. After all, it is hidden."

Boo scouted around and could see that deeper into the exotic plants and closer to the rocky lagoon walls, the area was blanketed with more rainbow plants than he could possibly count.

"It looks to me like these plants were all planted in perfect rows in this area," said Silver. "It does look a bit suspicious. Obviously, they're not naturally growing this way."

"Calico's Lagoon is full of them," said Boo. "You know… things don't look good for the professor right now. First, we found the red claw cap by the cave. Then Ferrel said he saw a cat in a red bow tie knock Professor Potamus over the head, and now we're seeing all these rainbow plants planted in perfect rows."

Boo walked around the rows of plants, being careful to keep his distance while collecting his thoughts, and finally said, "These rainbow plants were planted purposely by somebody. If it's the professor, then I wonder what he's up to."

"I doubt that Professor Katnip ever expected us to find these rainbow plants," said Silver. "I believe he intentionally wanted to mislead us by letting us get close enough to keep us from becoming suspicious. I'm not sure why, but for some reason he wants this lagoon and the rainbow plants to remain a secret or, shall I say, his secret."

"He's trying to make sure we believe he is exactly who he says he is, but it's starting to look like the professor is pretending to be someone he's not," said Roxy Roo.

"We have absolutely been cat-fished!" shouted Chops. "I just call a cat as I see a cat!" Chops paused, thinking for a few seconds. "Although I could be wrong."

Silver carefully cut as many of the flowering rainbow plants as he could fit in the protective catpack. They walked along the bottom of the towering rock walls until they came upon the amazingly high and fragile-looking stairway spiraling up to heaven, or so it seemed, looking up from the ground.

Chapter Twelve

Boo came to an abrupt stop, surprising everyone following closely behind him and causing a creature pileup in front of the first step. A spider web blanketed the entry to the staircase, and hanging right in the middle of the beautiful silk creation was a big, bright yellow spider that looked like it was actually smiling.

"Is that spider smiling at me?" said Roxy Roo, gently pulling the amazing web to one side with the tip of her claw and laying it softly against the rocks. One by one, they shuffled past the colorful eight-legged creature. The expression painted on the happy-face spider was so contagious that it caused each one of them to grin from ear to ear as they passed by the fascinating arachnid. Their grins quickly turned to frowns as they pondered the stairs stacked up before them.

"That's an incredible number of steep stairs, and that staircase looks very fragile," said Chops nervously. "Sure you guys wouldn't rather swim through the wacky cave?" He didn't really like either option but continued, trying to sound confident, "If a turtle can do it, then so can we."

"How long can you hold your breath under water?" asked Roxy Roo. Before Chops could answer her question, she blurted out, "The answer is: not long enough."

Chops stepped back out of the way and said, "OK, then you go first."

"I'll go first," said Boo, placing his paw on the first step cautiously. He nervously watched as part of the first rocky step started to crumble under his weight.

Silver waddled past Boo and up to the second step. "Let me go first. I have the deadly quills. Remember? Just in case we—" He continued to waddle up a couple more rocky steps.

Boo watched nervously as the stones crumbled beneath Silver's paws after each step. "It's the stairs themselves that have me worried."

Chops watched Silver from the bottom as he crawled up a few more steps and shouted jokingly, "You're almost there! One!… Two!… Three!" He quickly counted the number of steps. "You only have a couple hundred more to go," he said under his breath.

"You never know what we will run into at the top," said Silver, bending his short neck in an attempt to see all the way to the top and flexing his mighty quills.

Chops was still holding a grudge against Silver. He never really got over the painful way they first met by Silver bumping into him and poking him with all those needles. Well, that's Chops' version of the story.

Chops whispered under his breath, "You can bet I'll never forget that you have sharp needles."

Up the stairs they all trudged, step by step, placing one paw in front of the other with Chops in the rear. Up and around they went, following the spiraling staircase until everyone but Chops had reached the end of the stairs and the top of the towering wall stood before them. At the top of the stairs stood the biggest banyan tree on the island. The ancient tree's humongous branches extended over the top of the rock wall and reached out over the lagoon, with its aerial roots hanging above the treetops below.

Chops paused for a moment, trying to catch his breath. He looked toward the top of the stairs and sighed heavily, realizing he still had a ways to go.

"I… gotta take… a break," he said, breathing heavily.

Boo looked down. Chops was leaning up against the rock wall. "Hey, big guy, you gonna make it?" he yelled, tossing some tiny stones that hit Chops on his furry head. Roxy Roo gave him a look of disapproval.

"I got this," said Chops, huffing and puffing. "Am I there yet?"

Chops scooped up a pawful of tiny stones and threw them upwards toward where Boo was standing at the top of the stairs. Chops not realizing his own strength, the tiny stones flew past Boo and scattered as they hit the overhanging branches of the banyan tree.

"Nice try, big guy!" hollered Boo.

Silver heard a faint buzzing sound coming from the banyan tree branches. He stopped moving for a few seconds, concentrating on the buzzing sound as it got louder and closer. "I believe that was a very bad idea!" proclaimed Silver. "Down! Go back down!

Everyone looked up toward the deafening buzzing sound coming from the banyan tree. It was too late. Chops had stirred up a swarm of insects, and they sounded like they were preparing for war and heading right toward them.

Silver, Boo, and Roxy Roo leaped down from the top of the stairs, unable to keep their balance. They slid down, bumping against each step on their backsides. Round and round they went in an uncontrolled spiraling slide until they crashed into Chops. He was still standing frozen in place, looking shocked, as the swarm of wasps headed straight toward them.

"Peppermint plants!" yelled Silver. "Get the peppermint plants!" he screamed once more as the wasps darted all around their furry faces.

"I thought you said this place was pure paradise! What happened to pure paradise?" meowed Chops loudly, his legs flailing as he tried to fight the aggressive wasps off his head and ears. "They're meat-eaters! Meow yeow!"

In the middle of all the chaos of flailing limbs, swinging tails, and swatting paws, Roxy Roo started singing in her purr-fectly amazing voice:

"Don't come buzzin' round me! Don't come buzzin' round me!
Gee I sing and gee I wish, gee I hope you stop this bizzness.
Gee I love and gee I free, gee I hope you stop buzzin' me.
Gee I hear and gee I see, gee I wish the buzzin' was bees.
Gee I smell and gee I repent, gee I have some peppermint.
Gee I rainbow and gee I treasure, gee I have a bunch of nectar.
Gee I nice and gee I naughty, gee I hope you won't be haughty.
Don't come buzzin' round me! Don't come buzzin' round me!"

By the time she sang out the last verse of her made-up buzzin' song, the buzzing had stopped, and the wasps returned to their nest somewhere up in the big banyan tree. Once again, they were in awe of this unexplainable gift she had over the insects.

Chops almost always had some kind of wisecrack to say, but there was no doubt that he was amazed at the singing miracles that Roxy Roo could perform in the face of danger, especially when it came to insects. Chops was well aware of Roxy Roo's love of bees. He looked at her with a big cat grin on his face and asked, "Not bad, but how would bees have been any better?"

She grinned, saying, "Bees are always better. Besides, I'm made out of honey, and bees love honey. Now quit your scratchin' and rub some catmint on your stings." She handed each of them a piece of the catmint plant out of her catpack. "Not too much though, we still have to make it back up the stairs again. We certainly don't want anyone falling off… do we?"

Roxy Roo didn't pretend to understand why the insects seemed to respond to her singing, but in situations like this, she was just happy they did. She had always loved insects, especially pollinators, and bees were defiantly her favorite pollinator. Since she was a kitten she could recall playing with the creepy, crawly things with her paws and being amazed by the miracle of the flying bumblebee and the magical flight of a butterfly. She knew her love for these magnificent creatures had started to blossom when she and Boo were kittens and they began running around Treetop Woods chasing H-bees and any other flying insects that came across their path.

Chops' bee comment buzzed around in Roxy Roo's mind for the next few minutes. She thought back to those days of catching H-bees and swatting at butterflies. "I haven't seen many H-bees lately," she said to herself, feeling a sense of sadness come over her.

Silver glared at Chops and shouted, "Do you realize that you nearly got us all killed? No more rocks or stones… or sand, for that matter!"

Once again, up they went, step by step. Up and around they trudged until everyone was lined up in back of Silver, who was stopped at the last step. Together they looked up. They looked to the right of the tree and then to the left of the tree, and were perplexed as to where they should go. Looks of disappointment were drawn across their faces as they realized the stairway dead-ended right into the massive trunk of the banyan tree. It appeared that their only available option was to, once again, climb back down the stairs. The trunk of the banyan, along with all of its roots shooting upwards, grew in such a manner that it provided a perfect natural barrier between the rock walls on either side of the tree. The massive branches hanging over their heads were bigger than most other tree trunks on the island.

"It's a stairway to nowhere," said Chops, looking back down at the beautiful lagoon far below them.

"Somewhere there has got to be a way through," said Silver. "It certainly makes no sense that somebody built all these stairs that go nowhere."

"Maybe somebody was a little overzealous and decided to build a really amazing lookout point," said Roxy Roo.

Silver and Boo scrounged around, pushing and pulling on the tree roots that protected the front of the trunk and extended from the ground all the way up to the top of the tree. Silver pushed, pulled, and tugged at every root in front of the massive trunk.

Chops was very amused watching Boo and Silver push, pull, and tug at everything around the tree.

"Maybe there's a secret passage," Chops blurted out. "Hey, you never know. Remember the cave?"

Chops bent his neck back, gazing up at the huge branches above him. "Maybe we could just climb up and over the branches?" he said, slowly walking up the last couple of stairs.

Boo smiled at him. "I don't think we want to go there."

They all looked curiously over at Boo, waiting for him to continue.

After a few seconds of silence, he finally blurted out, "Wasps, remember? I'm not sure if Roxy Roo has another song to woo them."

Chops walked toward the banyan tree and banged his big cat head in aggravation between two big thick roots connecting the top of the tree to the bottom of the tree. His head slipped in between the roots, causing the roots to fall sideways, exposing the massive old trunk of the banyan.

"Hey, big guy, that's using your head," said Boo, laughing loudly at his own corny joke.

Boo looked closer at the trunk and noticed something very peculiar about this tree trunk. With the roots moved out of the way, he could see what looked like two thin cuts going across the width of the enormous trunk. He pushed on the side of the trunk with all his feline strength, and the small section of the trunk slowly began to spin around, exposing a tunnel that opened up and shot right through the middle of the trunk. They all stood staring in amazement at the tunnel.

Silver looked gleefully at everyone and said, "Hey, what do you know? Chops was right after all. There is a secret passageway."

Chops gave him a displeased look and said, "I'm right here, standing right next to you."

Boo slowly finished turning the trunk, exposing the entire tunnel. He peeked inside the tunnel and shouted, "Unbelievable! I can see straight through to the rainforest!" They heard his voice echo through the shadowy tunnel and out into the rainforest.

Boo walked into the tunnel and, one by one, they all followed him through the hollow tree, being careful to duck under the spider webs, until they reached the roots barring them from exiting the other side. Chops moved quickly around Boo, catching his black and white checkered scarf on one of the roots inside the trunk. A small piece of the scarf tore off and was left hanging on the inside of the trunk. He tightened his torn scarf back around his thick neck and used his strong skull to push the log-sized roots out of the way.

"Show-off," said Boo. "By the way, you owe me a new scarf when we get back home."

They squeezed past the roots and popped out into the lush rainforest. The tropical forest was vibrating with life and filled with gigantic ferns, colorful orchids, dense bamboo groves, and vines draped across the magnificent trees.

"Welcome to the Roundabout Rainforest!" exclaimed Chops triumphantly.

His friends looked at him and wondered what that was all about, but it was Chops, so they just took it in stride.

Instinctively they all jumped backwards as an unknown creature leaped down from one of the tall trees and landed right in front of them. Shocked, they backed up to the banyan-tree tunnel, and each of them took on a fighting posture.

Boo and Roxy Roo had their ears back, paws up, and sharp claws ready to strike. Silver's deadly quills were extended out all along his body. Chops had his paws positioned in a type of ancient fighting style, looking as though he was prepared to chop wood with his paws. They all turned and looked at Chops standing in a rather awkward position. Their current situation was certainly a serious one, so they tried as hard as they could to keep their smiles from turning into laughter and quickly refocused on the creature approaching them.

Calico was happy to see their smiling faces. He awkwardly smiled back at them as he got closer.

"It's about time you got here. I've been waiting for hours and hours up in that tree!" said Calico, hoping they were just as happy to see him.

"Good grief, Calico!" shouted Boo. "You could've warned us before jumping right down on top of us!"

"What in the spirit of all that is good and true are you doing here?" demanded Silver.

Chops, still maintaining his fighting position, said, "He's still a bullkat, right?"

Looking at Chops, Boo chuckled and said, "I think you can relax now."

"We have to get you out of here before it gets dark. The professor is on his way with his bullkats," said Calico, looking anxious.

"The professor?" they all shouted together.

"Professor Katnip?" asked Roxy Roo perplexed.

"What do you mean by 'his' bullkats?" asked Boo.

"They all call him 'the professor,'" said Calico. "I also know he will do anything to make sure the location of the rainbow plants is kept a secret."

Chops burst into laughter and said, "Cat's out of the bag on that one."

Boo was sure that he already knew the answer, but he asked Calico anyway, "Does he wear a red bow tie?"

Professor Katnip was one of the most respected Meow cats on the island and famous for his catnip and herbal teas. Boo and Roxy Roo had always looked up to Professor Katnip. Calico's disappointing news confirmed all of their suspicions, but it still hit them like a shovelful of dirt in the face. They already knew the evidence was mounting against the professor but, still, they didn't want to believe he could be involved in something terrible.

Meanwhile, beyond the tranquility of the giant banyan tree, the rainforest was being trampled by the dozens of bullkats clawing their way through the unsuspecting green flora. They were like a plague, destroying everything they touched along the way.

Calico was right. The friends had better move quickly.

"I know a way around them, but you're probably not going to like it," said Calico.

He led the way through the dense rainforest plants and trees, down toward the shore of the Loud Ocean. Along the way they passed by many ancient rock formations that were used in olden times for landmarks and shelters. Most of these old structures were constructed out of flat lava rocks, tree branches, and bamboo poles that were abandoned long ago.

One awe-inspiring monument in particular sat on a pillar and was carved out of pure black lava rock in the shape of a giant turtle. The turtle's head was pointing toward the northeast side of the island. Silver wanted to explore some of the rock formations that were piled high and other structures that might hold some hidden island secrets inside their cold, damp walls. He knew they had to keep moving. The bullkats were on their way, and it was a matter of life or death that they get out of the rainforest and down to the jagged cliffs before dark.

Warm raindrops, the size of wild blueberries, fell against their heads. Their paws sloshed through the muddy stream zig-zagging its way toward becoming a short-lived waterfall, pouring out over the cliffs into the ocean.

Roxy Roo wiped the rain from her wet, furry face with her paws. She wanted to ask Calico some questions but wanted to choose her words carefully.

"I don't want to seem ungrateful," she said. "I appreciate all the help you have given us, but I'm really curious and just have to ask. You're a bullkat. So, why are you helping us? Most bullkats only want to—"

"To hurt, kill, and destroy!" shouted out Silver passionately. He was distraught thinking about his lost family of porky porcupines.

Calico's countenance fell, and his heart felt like it was crushed. "It's true," he said. He wanted desperately to explain that he felt like he was different than other bullkats but just wasn't sure where to start. "We're not all like that. Whether we have been born to be good or bad cats... well, I can't say for sure… right now, I just want to help, and to do that, I have to get you outta here before dark."

Roxy Roo looked at Calico with an encouraging smile and said, "I believe the Creator of all creatures provides a path for change if we look for it."

"Even for bullkats?" asked Chops, looking sympathetically at Silver.

"They may have been born cursed creatures, but I believe there's hope for every creature on Tyrtle Island. Otherwise, what's the point of it all?" said Boo.

Calico didn't say another word and continued to lead them toward the shore.

The rain turned to a sprinkle. They stopped briefly so Chops could get something prickly out of his paw. Instantly they were all bombarded with green, blue, and yellow frogs leaping from the trees onto their heads and backs. Chops, who was busy picking at his paw, didn't see the slimy frogs landing one by one on Calico and his feline friends. Instinctively, they avoided Silver and his sharp quills.

Chops sprang up as one of the slimy green frogs pounced on his back. "Hey, get it off! Get it off!" he squealed, trying to reach the unknown creature sitting in the middle of his back. He jumped around in circles, trying to shake off whatever was clinging to his fur.

"Chops, stop it! You're going to hurt yourself!" cried Roxy Roo, walking over to him and gently brushing the frog off his back.

Chops watched as the vibrant-red-eyed amphibian took a single giant hop and vanished under the lush tropical ferns. He turned and looked over at Roxy Roo who, to his amazement, had a bright-yellow frog sitting right on her forehead between her eyes. She had a big smile on her face, looking back at Chops. They all laughed together, including Calico, who was hoping that he had finally found some friends.

Roxy Roo scooped the smooth creature off her forehead and placed the colorful frog safely on the damp ground, watching him bounce away. "They're harmless," she said.

"Good thing he didn't pee on ya," said Chops.

Now, Chops was not a fan of touching even the gentlest of God's creatures, even if it was impossible for that creature to hurt him. In his mind, getting peed on was definitely one way of getting hurt.

The Ricochet River bounced through the dense rainforest, guiding them to the cascading waterfall pouring its precious cargo over the island cliffs. The cliffs stood like a fortress around the outer edge of the tropical rainforest, protecting its precious interior.

Standing near the edge of the cliffs, they watched the perfect rhythm of aqua-blue waves rolling in one by one, drenching the shore. The ocean left a whipped-cream layer of foam with each wave it delivered on the small golden beach.

"That's where your cat-a-canoe will be in the morning," revealed Calico, pointing down to the sandy beach below.

"In the morning?" asked Silver, looking doubtfully at the bullkat. "What about the other bullkats? They will find us tonight."

"I gotta agree with Silver," said Boo. "I don't think it's a great idea to be sitting on the shore like a bunch of polecats with no escape route." He looked out over the cliffs and then up and down the beautiful shoreline. "We would be trapped."

"The professor thinks you're in the rainforest looking for the rainbow plants. He has no idea you made it to the ocean shore," said Calico, grinning at them oddly with a bullkat smile. "Right now, this is the safest hiding place for you."

Silver was still bothered by the presence of the bullkat, and his facial expression didn't hide it very well. "Why should we trust you?" he asked.

Calico frowned at Silver and said, "I showed you the way out of my cave and I warned you that the professor is looking for you. If I really wanted to hurt you, don't you think I would have already? I'm a bullkat!"

"Point well taken," said Chops swiftly. "Can I touch your little horn?"

Boo looked over at Chops, shook his furry face, and tried to hold back his laughter, saying, "We have to trust Calico. I don't think we really have any other choice." Boo was trying to convince himself as much as everyone else, but they could all tell, Calico included, that he had a hint of skepticism in his voice.

Calico looked anxious, watching the sun sink deeper into the ocean.

"Good, it's settled then. The cat-a-canoe will be on the beach in the morning." He turned and quickly disappeared back into the rainforest.

Following the switchbacks down the side of the cliffs, they passed a solitary mangrove tree that was growing out from the side of the cliff. The tree looked like it was clinging for life with its root-like arms hanging onto the jagged rocks. The long seashore came into view as they worked their way back to the golden sandy beach. Walking along, they splashed through the water with their paws, watching as the curled-up waves gracefully rolled on top of the salty water and then gave way against the shoreline.

"My mittens are as tired as a kitten after playing hide-and-seek," said Roxy Roo as they approached the sandy meeting place.

"Yes, that salt water is a miracle worker for my cat claws," said Chops, laughing and picking up one paw and raising it up to his face.

"Soooo," purred Boo calmly, "I guess we can spend the night up under that rocky overhang. That will keep us out of the wind and out of sight from the shore."

There was another mangrove tree growing off to the side of the rocky covering that was just above the golden beach.

Inside a hole within the giant tree lived a beautiful blue-and-green-feathered macaw. This colorful parrot was a very chatty bird who loved to gossip and was easily offended. Boo and his band of friends had never met a creature quite like this one before.

A voice squawked loudly from above, "Hi ya!"

Startled, they all looked up, searching for the source of the mysterious voice.

"Hello?" said Roxy Roo. "Where are you?"

The voice squawked even louder, "Hi ya!"

"Hi ya, you too!" shouted Chops, trying his best to imitate the sound of the voice.

The parrot popped his head out of the hole in the mangrove tree, looked in both directions, and hopped down to one of the lower branches. The parrot's piercing white eyes were now focused right on Chops, who apparently had successfully ruffled the colorful creature's feathers.

The parrot hopped down to the lowest branch on the tree. He let out a long whistle and then squawked, "Oh boy. It's my side of the island. Don't come over here—pew, pew, pew—and mock me."

The macaw was not so much irritated at being awakened out of his sleep as he was offended at being mocked, especially by a cat. He was very aware that, from time to time, cats had been known to make a meal out of a bird.

"Pretty, pretty, pretty, pretty bird… old bird, old bird," said the parrot. "Oh boy, I've been living on this side of the island for—" The feathered creature paused for a few seconds, looking confused, and then let out a loud whistle. "Oh boy, it doesn't matter, long time, long time. I've a strong sharp beak and big claws, big claws."

Roxy Roo tried to calm down the perturbed parrot, who was looking like he was ready to do battle. "You're the most beautiful macaw I've ever seen. In fact, I don't believe I've ever seen such brilliant colors on any creature on the island."

Everyone watched the macaw just melt away as Roxy Roo walked up a little closer to the parrot and held out her big soft paw.

"So, beautiful bird, what's your name?"

Magically, the macaw descended from the tree branch and gracefully floated onto her shoulder.

"Hiya," the parrot said softly, as if he had just fallen in love with his new feline friend.

"Hi ya, Hiya," said Chops.

None of them were sure what to make of this unique situation with their newly-acquainted feathered friend. Not wanting to be seen from the beach, they all jumped up and quickly entered the cave.

Hiya the macaw, as he was known on the island, followed them into the shallow cave. The blabbering bird chatted endlessly in his squawky voice, or so it seemed to everyone trapped with him on the side of the cliff. He whistled, squawked, and talked nonstop about the turtles, fish, birds, cats, and just about every other creature in the rainforest. The talking continued well after the sun had set below the horizon and the light of the full moon could be seen reflecting off the ripples of the ocean.

Chops had long since plugged his pointed ears with the ends of his scarf. Boo and Silver walked outside to get as far away from the cave as they could while still keeping out of sight from the shoreline below and rainforest above. Roxy Roo patiently listened to Hiya as he continued to complain about everything. Then, with no warning at all, he just stopped talking and flew back up to his hole in the tree.

Chops removed his scarf from around his ears and said, "You hear that?"

"Hear what?" asked Roxy Roo.

He breathed out a sigh of relief. "Exactly. I hear nothing."

They all went through their bed-making routine as best they could with the few plants and sticks available on the side of the cliff.

Boo could see the eyes of his friends growing weary. He listened to their soft purring sounds and funny kazoo noises, and thought to himself, "Best friends ever. Best day ever."

turtle

CHAPTER THIRTEEN: BLAST FROM THE PAST

Jesse slowly opened his eyes to the sound of voices outside his tent. He thought about last night's dream and the crazy way he woke up with his heart racing, gasping for breath. It was a dreadful feeling, not being able to move his arms and legs, thinking he was actually going to die.

"I wonder if you can actually die in a dream," thought Jesse.

He sat up in his tent and glanced around among the scattered clothes, looking for Boo. He peered through the screen door and could see Honey Bee standing in front of her tent, holding Boo in her arms. She was talking to Tinman, but Jesse couldn't hear exactly what they were saying.

He sat still for a few minutes as he listened to the creatures of the rainforest chirping, humming, and buzzing, going about their busy lives. He heard the rustling of leaves from an unknown critter scurrying around the outside of his tent, and he wondered what type of creature it might be.

The scent of wet soil, decaying plants, and wood filtered through his tent. Jesse didn't think it was necessarily a bad smell. It was the familiar smell of life in the rainforest. The decaying plant smell reminded him of the bullkats and the events of his ongoing dream. He hoped that the mystery of his dream would start to unravel and begin to reveal its purpose.

Jesse emerged from his tent rubbing his eyes.

"Hey, it's about time you returned to the land of the living," said Tinman.

Boo jumped out of Honey Bee's arms and ran toward Jesse. He purred softly and rubbed his body against Jesse's bare legs, almost tripping him in the process.

Chapter Thirteen

"Hey, Boo, I dreamed about you last night... again," said Jesse. He laughed quietly, rubbing Boo's back. "Well, actually, I dreamed I was you."

Jesse reached down, picked up Boo, and walked over to join Honey Bee and Tinman sitting at the picnic table.

Tinman popped open a can of ham for breakfast and said to Jesse, "Sounds like your dreams are still happening."

Tinman did not totally understand what Jesse was dreaming about but knew something unusual was happening. He was concerned for his nephew, who also happened to be his best friend.

"Yeah, almost every night. They just seem to pick up right where I left off the night before," said Jesse.

He felt his stomach quiver as he watched Tinman scoop the so-called meat from the can.

Boo knew that Jesse was no fan of canned ham and never understood why. He once heard Tinman say that three cans of canned ham are eaten every minute and thought to himself, *Why am I the only cat on the island whose best friend doesn't like ham in a can?*

"Is the big guy up yet?" asked Jesse just as Caleb stuck his head out from inside his tent. "It's about time you rise and shine."

Coughing loudly, Caleb shuffled over and sat down by Jesse. "Somebody was in the camp last night," he said, coughing again and rubbing the sleep out of his eyes.

"Somebody needs a tic-tac," said Jesse, waving his hand in front of Caleb's mouth.

"I thought I heard someone or something walking around last night also," confessed Honey Bee.

"I wish you guys would wake me up," said Tinman, glancing around the camp. "Although I don't see anything missing."

"We have a full day ahead of us trying to find Professor Katnip's rainbow plants. Especially since none of us have any idea where they are. It's a really big rainforest," said Tinman anxiously. "We better get cleaned up and get to it."

"I think I have an idea where they might be," Jesse said abruptly.

Honey Bee looked surprised. "You do? Where?"

"Well, I'm not sure exactly, but I have an idea it's somewhere between the rainforest and the mountains, next to a huge banyan tree," said Jesse enthusiastically. "I was there last night."

Caleb laughed and said, "That's a long way to sleepwalk. I'm no expert, but I don't think that narrows it down very much."

Caleb looked around pointing at all the banyan trees in the rainforest and said, "This place is full of banyan trees."

"No, you don't understand," said Jesse. "This is a really humongous banyan tree somewhere over by the mountains."

Over the years, Tinman had walked many miles through the rainforest, and he had an idea of where this humongous tree just might be. He also had a feeling that somehow Jesse's dream was tied to something happening on the island, and it probably involved bullkats.

Honey Bee always trusted Jesse and could tell that something strange and wonderful was going on with this dream he was having. With that in mind, she asked, "Jesse, was that banyan in your dream?"

"Yes," Jesse replied, "and a whole lot more."

The sun shined through the dense vegetation, lighting up the rainforest as they began to gather their backpacks. Jesse and Boo led the way down the lighted trail with his dream and Tinman's experience as their guides. Jesse hoped the path they followed would lead straight to the giant banyan and Calico's Lagoon. The red clay clung to their shoes as they sloshed through the bamboo forest, jumping on and off the giant lava rocks hiding under the canopy of trees.

Crossing over a shallow river, Boo noticed a bright green lizard that had just jumped into the water. His curiosity got the best of him as he hopped off the trail and ran over to check out the unusual creature.

"Boo, come back here!" Jesse yelled.

Jesse followed behind Boo. He carefully watched the green dragon-like lizard hop right in front of Boo and move slowly through the water.

"Jesse, don't let Boo look that lizard in the eye!" shouted Caleb to his friends "He'll die!"

Jesse looked back at Caleb, yelling, "What are you talking about?"

Jesse knew perfectly well that Boo would not die but wanted to hear Caleb's amusing story anyway.

"It's an ancient island legend. You know, if any animal looks the dragon lizard in the eye, then they'll surely die," said Caleb, sounding as though it was absolutely true.

Standing by the river, they all watched in amazement as the long dragon lizard slapped its webbed feet and appeared to be zipping along the top of the water.

"It's walkin' on water!" exclaimed Honey Bee.

Caleb tried to look away, but the creature put on quite a show. Its bright green webbed feet with long green toes moved miraculously on the surface of the river for a few seconds, and then slowly the creature's body sank down into the water up to the crest on its head. Eventually, the light-footed lizard ducked its bright green body into the smooth-flowing water and disappeared.

Boo was totally entertained watching the crazy dragon lizard dance, skip, and swim down the river. *It's a good thing there's no truth to that particular island legend*, he thought to himself.

Along the way they passed by many ancient rock formations that began to look very familiar to Jesse. He saw one in particular that was made out of pure black lava rock, shaped like a giant turtle with its head pointing to the northeast side of the island.

"Are we there yet?" asked Caleb jokingly, not expecting an answer from anyone.

"I think we're close," said Jesse. "That lava rock turtle was in my dream."

"Seriously, did you really see that turtle in your dream?" asked Honey Bee.

Jesse nodded his head, looking at Honey Bee and said, "Sure did."

"That is so awesome!" shouted Caleb, scooping Boo up in his arms and jumping up, holding him high in the air. "Wow wee, Boo is getting heavier all the time. How much canned ham have you been feedin' him?" He smiled as he looked over at Tinman and then back at Jesse, who playfully showed him his mean eyes.

Jesse looked as far as he could across the rainforest, through the lush trees and plants, and caught a glimpse of the massive banyan that looked just like the one in his dream. He stopped walking for a few minutes as he thought about his dream.

The others walked on ahead and then stopped, seeing the massive banyan tree in front of them.

Caleb looked back at his friend and shouted, "Jesse, this one is a biggie!"

Jesse's heart started to beat faster as he approached the humongous tree. He thought it looked even bigger than he remembered in his dream. That strange déjà-vu feeling came over him and he sensed that he had just stepped back in time.

Suddenly Jesse remembered the aggressive wasps in the dream and shouted out to his friends, "Stay back from the tree and, for goodness sakes, don't throw anything at it. Caleb, that means you too!"

Jesse jogged up to where they were standing and heard them talking about the monstrous banyan tree and the amazing rock fortress surrounding it.

"This tree is definitely the one in my dream," confirmed Jesse. "Although I think it's even bigger than it was in the dream."

Jesse approached the tree cautiously like he was approaching an ancient enemy who had now become a friend. He looked up, then to the right and then to the left.

"Wasps," he said. "There are… or at least there were, wasps protecting the entrance."

"Up in the tree somewhere?" asked Tinman, looking at the massive branches above him and the huge roots in front of the tree. "I don't really see an entrance."

The tree trunk was surrounded by numerous thick roots. Jesse walked up to the two biggest roots shooting straight up in front of the tremendous tree trunk and said, "Caleb, Tinman, push back and then sideways on these two roots at the same time. No need to use your head like Chops did." Jesse laughed to himself thinking about his dream.

"Chops?" said Tinman. "Who's Chops?"

"I'll tell ya later," said Jesse. "Let's see if this still works."

Tinman and Caleb set their backpacks down in the dirt and pushed with all their might. Amazingly, the roots gave way, moving slightly outward, exposing the bark on the trunk.

"Not sure how that works," said Tinman, thinking through the mechanical process with his best engineering mind. "We'll take it, though."

Jesse stepped over and through the roots and, standing in front of the ancient tree trunk exclaimed, "You think that's amazing, wait until you see the tree's next trick!"

Everyone was so preoccupied watching Jesse unveil the tree's secrets that they didn't hear the rustling of the plants and the crunching of the dead twigs in the rainforest behind them.

Jesse saw the same lines above and below the trunk and placed both his hands on the bark, pushing as hard as he could. To his surprise, the trunk didn't budge. His hands slipped off the side of the tree, and then he fell face first into the tangled roots.

"Pretty impressive," said Caleb, stepping in and helping Jesse up again. "Medic!"

Honey Bee doctored up Jesse's bleeding forehead and gave him a quick kiss on the top of his head. Jesse sat down on some roots and wondered why the tree trunk wouldn't budge.

Tinman's engineering skills went to work again, thinking out loud. "Maybe it only moves in one direction?"

Jesse took his hand off his forehead and started to get back up, wobbling a bit. Tinman steadied him and said, "You rest and let me give it a try."

He pushed on the opposite side of the trunk in the opposite direction and magically, the trunk slowly began to move, and the tree tunnel came into full view.

Tinman was astonished as he watched it move. He still didn't understand how a tree could possibly move like this, but without further ado, he entered the tunnel.

Jesse wobbled to his feet and followed right behind him. Caleb entered the tunnel holding Jesse steady, with Honey Bee right behind him, holding Boo in her arms.

Boo's sharp vision detected an old piece of torn material hanging on the side of the tunnel. He recalled it was a piece of Chops' torn scarf that was left behind in the dream. He jerked toward the side of the tunnel wall and almost fell out of Honey Bee's arms.

Honey Bee looked at Boo curiously and then noticed the old piece of checkered cloth attached to the trunk. She carefully pulled the material off the side of the trunk, looking at it curiously.

They emerged out of the tunnel and into the sunlight, standing on the towering rocky stairway that was hidden behind the falls. Calico's Lagoon looked just as fantastical as it did in Jesse's dream.

"Look what I found!" announced Honey Bee, stepping out of the tunnel.

She maneuvered through the roots and walked onto the ledge of the ancient stairway. Her attention was quickly diverted to the wondrous place surrounding her.

"Heavenly," she said, looking out over the blue lagoon and the impressive rock walls protecting the paradise.

"Look, it's a super old piece of cloth," said Honey Bee, holding it up in the breezy air.

Jesse looked at the torn piece of checkered cloth and couldn't believe what he saw. He snatched the material out of her hand to examine it closer.

She glared at him and said, "All you had to do was ask."

"Sorry, lost my head. I think that's Chops' scarf. How can that possibly be?"

"Chops again?" said Tinman. "I've heard of lamb chops, pork chops, chopsticks… you know you're making me hungry. By the way, when are you going to tell us about Chops?"

"Hmmm… it's kind of hard to explain. He's—well, he's like Caleb, but like I said back on your front porch, he's a cat… in the dream."

Disappointed, Caleb looked at Jesse and reminded him, "Yep, I already got the news that I'm a cat in your dream."

Caleb glanced over at Honey Bee, who was holding Boo in her arms. Caleb knew that Boo was a very smart cat, but he still wondered how much Boo really understood.

"So you're saying that's a piece of his scarf... that was torn in the dream?" asked Tinman.

"No way, Jesse," said Caleb. "Cut it out."

"Yes, way! I'm not making any of this up!" Jesse shot back loudly. "I know... I get it... I know it sounds unbelievable."

"You think? I believe the part about the scarf," said Caleb. "I just can't get over the fact that I'm a stinkin' cat."

"Hey, that hurt," purred Boo, looking over at Caleb from Honey Bee's arms.

At that moment, Caleb knew that Boo understood much more than he realized. He wasn't sure if it was because of the sound of his voice, the scent of his body, or his facial expression but, somehow, Boo understood.

"Sorry, Boo," said Caleb. "No offense."

Sticks and stones, thought Boo.

Boo looked back toward the tunnel and let out an alarming cat sound: "MeowROWW!"

They all turned together, looking back through the tree tunnel, and could see someone from the waist down, standing out in the rainforest just beyond the tunnel.

Tinman leaned down into the tunnel and could hear the unmistakable low, whiny sounds of several bullkats. He could see their chilling faces peering into the tunnel as they crowded next to the body of the unknown figure.

"Go down the stairs, now," whispered Jesse, quickly moving the roots back in their protective position and wedging them in place. He knew this would not hold the intruders out for long. Honey Bee carried Boo, with Caleb right behind her as they jumped down the fragile stairs.

Tinman stood at the top of the stairs holding his pistol. He glanced over at Jesse and could see the worried expression on his face.

"It's only if we have no other way," said Tinman.

"I have another idea. Quick, get some stones," said Jesse, picking up the first small stones he saw. "Here goes." Jesse threw the stones up into the branches of the banyan tree.

Tinman wasn't exactly sure why they were tossing stones into the tree, but he quickly followed Jesse's lead. They instantly heard the buzzing of the wasps above. Now Tinman understood the risky plan.

Jesse knew it was a gamble as to who the wasps would attack, so he put the second part of his plan into action. He grabbed the peppermint oil from the side pouch of his backpack and quickly sprayed it on himself and Tinman.

Before departing the campground, Jesse had anticipated they might have a problem with the aggressive wasps. He wanted to be prepared just in case one of Honey Bee's amazing songs was not enough to chase them off. Honey Bee had taught him many things about insects over the years, and he found out long ago that bees and wasps don't like peppermint oil.

They both started down the steps, stopping to look back at the swarm of wasps. The agitated insects buzzed over their heads, darting around the huge tree branches. After a few seconds, the wasps whizzed over the rock wall and disappeared to the other side of the tree.

Jesse belted out a very loud "Yeah!" Tinman reached up to give him a high five.

"You smell so fresh and pepperminty," said Tinman, laughing and then stopping for a second to listen.

Tinman and Jesse faintly heard the painful screeches from the other side of the banyan tree. The shrieking bullkats could be heard running away from the stinging wasps into the protective covering of the rainforest. Even in the daylight, an encounter with a bullkat was always a very scary and dangerous situation. It was only with total darkness that bullkats transformed into their most hideous form. It was the unnatural sounds they made that were the most unnerving thing about bullkats.

Jesse's shoulders quivered, listening to the shrieking in the distance.

"That noise gives me the willies," he said.

Turning around, they could finally concentrate on the breathtaking surroundings of Calico's Lagoon as they walked down the spiraling staircase far above Honey Bee, Boo, and Caleb.

Jesse shouted out from above, "WELCOME TO CALICO'S LAGOON!" introducing the tropical paradise like a Tyrtle Island tourist guide.

"Calico's Lagoon, hmmm… for some reason, the name Calico sounds more like it should be in front of the word 'saloon,'" said Tinman, chuckling.

Honey Bee was almost in tears as she watched the beauty in motion before her. She gazed at the jellyfish flowers twirling in the air as they slowly disappeared over the towering walls. She was overjoyed watching the sea turtles swimming gracefully around the lagoon, then quietly vanishing through Coral Way Cave, out to the ocean.

"This place is so incredibly amazing," said Caleb.

"Incredibly and amazing are not big enough words for this place," said Honey Bee. "It's like saying the sky is big and blue."

Caleb looked at her, slightly confused. "But the sky is big… and blue."

Jesse interrupted their philosophical conversation to say, "I have some good news and some bad news. Which do you want to hear first?"

Tinman looked anxiously at Jesse. "Given a choice, I always like to hear the good news first."

Jesse rolled up his sleeves and pointed with one hand toward the rock wall, saying, "Rainbow plants are over by the wall. There's plenty of 'em. More than we can carry back."

"Great, that is good news. That part of our problem's solved," said Tinman. "Now all we have to do is figure out who's trying to kill us and why."

"So… is that the bad news?" asked Honey Bee. "Do you know who's tryin' to hurt us?"

"Well, if that's the bad news, then it sounds like good news to me," said Caleb.

Jesse figured it was time to let everyone know about the encounter with Mr. Jack back at Honey Bee's family café.

"Maybe it's good news, maybe it's bad news. I'm really not sure, but one thing I do know is it's really bizarre," said Jesse. "Mr. Jack … well … back at the café, it seemed like he was threatening me and Boo. Do you think it's him who's out to get us? It can't just be about his stupid garden. There has to be more to it than that."

"I'm not so sure," said Caleb. "Everyone knows that he REALLY likes his garden. If you ask me, Mr. Jack and Professor Katnip are both a combination of a crazy gardener mixed with a mad scientist. I think—"

Honey Bee interrupted, "Oh, I think Professor Katnip has Mr. Jack beat hands down when it comes to who loves their garden more. Mr. Jack may be very creepy and all, but the professor is crazy obsessed with his garden, not to mention his catnip and tea recipes."

She paused, thinking for a few seconds, and then continued, "I understand because I love insects and flowers too, but I really believe that he would go to almost any length or do almost anything to protect what he loves."

"So, was that the bad news?" asked Tinman.

"Well, yes and no… but it wasn't my bad news," said Jesse. "Obviously, we can't go back that way."

Jesse pointed up at the magnificent waterfall cascading down the rock wall in front of the steep stairs.

"I think we're going to have to swim through Coral Way Cave," said Jesse. "It leads out to the ocean."

Jesse walked closer to the shore of the lagoon to get a better look at the tunnel.

"What about Boo?" said Honey Bee, following behind Jesse. "Cats can't hold their breath at all, much less through that tunnel. Come to think of it, depending on how long the tunnel is, I'm not even sure if I can."

"What about the Jeep and all our camping gear in the rainforest?" asked Caleb.

"Right now, that's the least of my worries," said Tinman. "Our safety is first, and someone—I don't know who—maybe Mr. Jack, but someone is definitely trying to hurt us, and it appears they're using bullkats to do it. We can always get the Jeep and gear later. Well, assuming it's still there when we get back."

Honey Bee stayed with Caleb by the lagoon shore watching the sea turtles as Tinman and Jesse walked back toward the mountainous wall. The boys quickly found their way to where the flowering rainbow plants were growing and carefully opened the protective backpack. They put their gloves on, careful not to touch the plants.

Tinman cut the valuable plants one by one, placing them gently into the backpack until they filled it to the top. While they were gathering the plants in silence, Tinman started to think like a private investigator. He went over the scenario in his mind and started to question Professor Katnip's motives.

"Mission accomplished," said Tinman. "You know, I've been thinkin', and I'm pretty sure the professor never intended for us to find the rainbow plants. He never even told us about Calico's Lagoon. He just said the plants were somewhere in the Roundabout Rainforest. We could've been looking forever, and chances are, we would've never found them if it wasn't for your amazing dream. I'm beginning to think he was just trying to distract us."

Tinman grunted, lifting up the heavy backpack.

"Old guys rule!" he shouted, trying to give himself a boost of confidence. "Little heavier than I thought it would be. Guess I'm just gettin' old."

Jesse laughed at Tinman, helping him hoist the heavy backpack around his shoulders, and then said, "I agree."

"Oh, thanks a lot!" said Tinman.

"Nooo, not that you're getting old. I agree with you… I agree that the professor sent us chasing after the pot of gold at the end of the rainbow. We just have to figure out why."

Tinman and Jesse walked back toward the lagoon where Boo was waiting at a safe distance, just to make sure he didn't get his nose into the rainbow plants.

Tinman set the heavy backpack down, pointed towards the tunnel, and said, "Here's the plan. Jesse and I will go check out the passageway. I want to make sure we can all make it through to the ocean… including Boo, of course."

Including Boo, of course… What am I? Kitty litter? thought Boo.

They stepped into the clear blue water, swimming over toward the tunnel. The sea turtles slowly paddled out of the way to the other side of the lagoon.

Honey Bee watched Jesse and Tinman as she rubbed Boo's head. She tried to reassure him, saying, "We got this."

Easy for you to say, thought Boo. *You're not a cat about to be dunked under the water.*

After a few minutes Jesse and Tinman emerged out of the glassy blue tunnel, and Jesse yelled, "So easy even Caleb can do it!"

It was a rare occurrence when either one of them passed up a chance to poke fun at the other. Jesse knew very well that Caleb was a pretty good swimmer.

"Boo will get wet, but we shouldn't have any problems because there're plenty of air pockets and resting spots along the way," said Tinman.

"Hey, Boo, in my dreams you're an awesome swimmer," said Jesse, dripping all over his best friend as he rubbed his soft head.

Not sure if that was a compliment or not, but one thing I do know… this is no dream. It sounds like a nightmare, thought Boo.

It wasn't that Boo actually hated getting wet, it just wasn't his favorite activity. Jesse knew Boo very well. He had an idea that he hoped would keep Boo somewhat dry through Coral Way Cave.

Jesse pumped up a small life raft that was perfect for a situation like this and placed Boo in the middle of it.

"This ought to keep you from scaring the rainbow fish along the way," he said, smiling at Boo.

Optimistically, they all entered the water and floated through the lagoon, watching the fish scatter and jump in and out of the water. They entered the rocky opening and moved along through the tunnel ducking and dunking their heads. The atmosphere was quiet as they watched several sea turtles move past them, heading toward the lagoon. Boo could hear the echo of the ocean water as it softly slapped against the tunnel walls. The tunnel put on a light show of its own with cloudy blue and green shadows reflecting off its walls.

As always, they were fascinated by the sea turtles, gracefully paddling by them, with scattered barnacle patterns across their colorful shells.

This too seemed like a short-lived dream. Before they realized it, they had quickly reached the end of the tunnel and floated out into the Loud Ocean, which on this day happened to be very calm and quiet.

Boo exited the tunnel with a rather grumpy-looking, wet face.

"You never cease to amaze me," said Jesse, wiping the water off the top of Boo's head.

"We have company," said Tinman, floating over toward the hidden shoreline.

Coral Way Cave exited out to Coral Way Bay through a natural waterway that was concealed from the rest of the shoreline by large piles of lava rocks. A tall, thin man was standing by the shore waiting for them to arrive. From a distance, the eerie figure looked like Mr. Jack.

"What's he doing here?" asked Jesse nervously, paddling his feet as they bobbed closer to the island's sandy beach.

"Don't worry, Jesse," Tinman said in a stern voice. "We're going to find out once and for all what this guy is really up to."

They walked out of the salty water and felt the soft sand under their feet as Mr. Jack hobbled toward them.

"Ah, good. I see you're keeping Boo out of my garden," said Mr. Jack, gazing at Jesse with his cold eyes. "Yes, very good. Coming from somewhere in particular, are you?"

Tinman took a step toward Mr. Jack and asked, "What do you want?"

"Yes, very good indeed. I see you were careful in the rainforest. Some dangerous creatures roam through there," said Mr. Jack in his unnerving voice.

Tinman wiped the salt water dripping off his brow and said to Mr. Jack, "I asked you once already. What do you want and why are you following us?"

Mr. Jack grinned with his cigar hanging from his lips, and the foul scent lingered in the air. It was like he was purposely stalling before answering their questions.

"I told you before, I know some things," continued Mr. Jack in his unusual way. "I know secret things. After giving it much thought, I have decided to tell you about some of those things. I've had a change of my mind."

Mr. Jack stared at them with his empty eyes. His creepy personality and drawn-out voice made him uniquely unsettling, even when it appeared he was trying to be helpful. His appearance was chilling. He had beady eyes and a skinny, wrinkled face. His weathered body, along with a hunched back, didn't help his frightening figure.

There was one more thing that made Jesse uneasy around him: the fact that he always had a foul-smelling cigar hanging between his pale lips.

"What would you know that could possibly help us?" asked Tinman, glaring at Mr. Jack.

"I must say, I'm so glad you asked," said Mr. Jack. "I know where the rainbow plants are, and I also know that you already found them. Yes, very good indeed. I also know the professor has a dark secret, and that secret is hidden in Kats Caves. I know he's using the bullkats to protect his secret. I told you, I know some things."

"So why tell us all of this now?" asked Tinman angrily.

Mr. Jack took two steps backwards and said, "I told you already. I've had a change of my mind."

"Sounds like he's out of his mind," Caleb whispered to Honey Bee.

"How do we know you're telling us the truth?" asked Honey Bee.

Mr. Jack grinned and said, "You don't." He slowly turned and stepped awkwardly through the sand, disappearing into the rainforest.

Jesse stared at the back of Mr. Jack's unique island shirt with black and gold fern leaves on it as he watched him walk out of sight and into the trees. Jesse was absolutely sure he had seen that shirt somewhere before. He tried to remember, but at that moment, he just couldn't recall.

"He's one very unusual man," said Tinman. "And I guess that's putting it mildly."

"He gives me the creeps," said Caleb, shaking his shoulders and head.

Honey Bee continued to think about Mr. Jack, gazing in the direction he had gone.

"How long has Mr. Jack lived on the island?" asked Honey Bee. "For some reason, I feel kinda sad for him."

"He's an Islander, born and raised here," said Tinman. "He's older than I am, but I remember him. When I was a kid hobbling around on my braces, I would see him around the island." Tinman paused for a few seconds, reflecting back. "I understand his wife died a few years ago, and he has since fallen on hard times. I think he has a daughter living somewhere on the island."

"How did she die?" asked Honey Bee, watching the waves roll gently onto the beach.

"Mysteriously," said Tinman, taking a sip of water from his canteen. "I heard it was some kind of accident. Whatever happened—I'm not exactly sure—seems like it was very sudden."

Tinman paused to collect his thoughts. "I do remember, though, he once helped me out when some boys were messin' with me down by the lighthouse." He chuckled, taking a trip down memory lane for a few seconds more, and then continued, "Even then, I remember being more scared of Mr. Jack than I was of those boys."

There was silence for a few minutes as they thought about Mr. Jack and his news about Professor Katnip's dark secret.

"I'm not sure if we should go back to our campground or stay on the beach tonight," said Tinman, looking out over the ocean as the sun was starting to set.

Caleb was still nervous from the odd conversation with Mr. Jack and said, "So, I wonder what this big dark secret is that Mr. Jack mentioned."

"It just doesn't make any sense to me," said Jesse. "Somehow, Mr. Jack, the bullkats, and whatever this deep, dark secret is that the professor is hiding are all tied together."

"Yeah, and we're assuming Mr. Jack is telling us the truth," said Honey Bee.

"Won't Professor Katnip be waiting for us with his pretty pets?" asked Caleb.

"I don't think so," said Tinman. "Professor Katnip is probably wondering where we are. He doesn't even know for sure if we found the rainbow plants. He never told us about the lagoon, so he probably thinks we never found the plants."

"Unless Mr. Jack goes and tells him everything!" blurted out Caleb, waving his arms.

Tinman thought for a few more minutes and then continued, "It seems to me like his plan was just for us to wander aimlessly through the rainforest until we got too tired looking for the plants… or scared off by the bullkats. I think that he thought we would just eventually give up and head back home. I don't believe he ever imagined we would find the plants… and truth be told, we never would've found them, but he didn't count on one thing that happened."

"What's that?" asked Caleb, looking around at everyone.

Tinman smiled, pointing at Jesse, and said, "Jesse's dream."

"Well, we better decide what we're going to do," said Honey Bee. "Either way, I don't think it's smart to get caught after dark in the rainforest."

"I think we should play it safe and stay out of the rainforest tonight," said Jesse. "I think I know a place up along the shore that we can spend the night."

"Is it far?" asked Caleb, following the coastline with his eyes.

Jesse looked northwest and pointed toward the cliffs lined up along the island shore and said, "Right over there… somewhere."

"Let's do it," said Tinman, turning around and almost tripping over a huge crab that had snuck up behind him. He jumped out of the way, yelling, "That… is one big robber crab!"

"Wow, I haven't seen one of those guys in quite a while," said Jesse.

The monstrous creature with bone-crushing red claws stopped for a second, quickly glancing around at them, and then scurried away toward the coconut palms.

The grains of sand tickled their feet as they trudged up the beach toward the cliffs. The breaking of each new wave delivered an amazing collection of seashells that tumbled around with the rhythm of the waves before finally coming to rest on the foamy shoreline.

"I really love the way the sand massages between my toes," said Honey Bee as they approached the hidden sandy beach by the cliffs.

Tinman's stomach was starting to feel pretty empty. He thought about his next meal and licked his lips, saying, "I'm gonna love the way that canned ham is going to taste."

"I know you love that stuff, but I just don't get it," said Jesse, cringing and shaking his head as he looked over at Honey Bee for some kind of confirmation.

Honey Bee smiled and nodded politely but didn't say anything.

Jesse looked surprised and said, "Don't tell me you like that stuff too."

"It's really pretty tasty, but it's even better if you wrap it in seaweed," she said.

The expression on Jesse's face showed he was beyond disgusted. Just thinking about adding seaweed to the recipe made his stomach feel queasy.

Honey Bee put Boo down gently on the soft sand, and he ran over toward Tinman, rubbing up against his legs and putting on his best purring performance. He was hoping that Tinman was willing to share his favorite snack.

"Just like in my dream, there should be a nice comfy cave right up on that cliff," said Jesse. "I'll check it out. If so, we can spend the night up there."

Jesse was blown away when he saw the same giant mangrove tree growing off to the side of the rocky cliff covering. He looked around to see if he could spot the hole in the tree that was home to the beautiful blue-and-green-feathered macaw. He recalled that this colorful creature was very friendly but also incredibly annoying. He hoped that Hiya only existed in his dream, or that the colorful creature had moved to a new home on the island.

"Hi ya!" squawked a voice loudly from above.

Jesse cringed when he heard that same familiar voice from his dream. His friends looked up from the beach below and searched for the source of the mysterious squawking voice.

A second later the macaw poked his head out of the hole in the tree.

Jesse held his finger over his lips and waved his other arm, trying to warn his friends below him not to say a word.

"What? What is it?" yelled out Caleb at the top of his lungs.

Jesse, somewhat agitated, looked at Caleb and said, "Too late… I was trying to tell you not to say anything."

"Peekaboo," the voice squeaked quickly as the creature poked his head in and out of the hole. "Hi ya!" the voice squawked louder.

"That was the cutest peekaboo I've ever heard," said Honey Bee.

"Hi ya, you too!" Caleb squawked, trying to imitate the sound of the voice.

"Oh, no, you didn't!" Jesse yelled at Caleb, thinking about this amazing déjà-vu moment. "I can't believe how much you act like Chops in my dream."

The macaw popped his beautiful head out of his home in the mangrove tree, looked back and forth, and then hopped down to one of the lower branches, focusing his piercing white eyes on the visitors standing on the beach.

"Hi ya!" squawked the macaw loudly as he hopped down onto the lowest branch of the tree.

"My island, my island!" screeched the feathered creature, pausing for a few seconds. "Got yum-yum grubs?"

They all just stood there looking back up at the incredibly colorful and comical macaw.

"I've seen a lot of birds," said Caleb. "You are without a doubt the most—"

"Most beautiful macaw I've ever seen," piped in Honey Bee. "I also believe you're the friendliest bird I've ever met on the island. And what a strong squawk you have." She spared no effort trying to win the parrot's approval with her sweet voice and beautiful smile.

"Sorry, fresh out of yummy grubs, though," said Caleb, laughing. "Although we do have plenty of canned ham."

Honey Bee's magic was not lost on any of the island creatures, and the macaw was no exception. Honey Bee walked up closer to the parrot and held out her arm as Hiya descended instantly. He sailed through the air, landing gracefully on her shoulder.

"Hi ya," the parrot said softly, as if he had just fallen in love with his new-found friend.

Honey Bee's first love was with her Creator and every amazing creature on the island. Somehow, the creatures instinctively felt that same love and were content with the influential gift she had over them.

"OK, don't say I didn't warn you," chuckled Jesse. "He'll talk you to death."

His friends, along with Hiya riding on Honey Bee's shoulder, walked up the steep trail and joined him under the shallow cave opening.

Hiya wasted no time beginning his incessant talking. The bird was very fond of repeating a few things over and over, such as "I'm Hiya!", "It's my island!" and "Got yum-yum grubs?" The bird went on nonstop for hours.

Jesse's mind was preoccupied with trying to unravel the cobweb of thoughts concerning his dream about the bullkats and the strange events surrounding Professor Katnip and Mr. Jack. To his surprise, it was not that difficult to totally block out Hiya's squawking and talking. Honey Bee's imagination was consumed by the wondrous cloud formations and the radiant blue, red, and orange colors painted by the sun as it settled down into the ocean. She smiled at Hiya as he continued his unrelenting parroting, but her mind was somewhere else. On the other hand, Hiya was driving Tinman and Caleb out of their minds.

"That's enough!" shouted Tinman, pulling his hat down over his ears. "I'm not sure if I can take one more, 'Got yum-yum grubs?'"

Tinman gathered his backpack and headed down the short rocky trail to the sandy beach below the cliffs with Caleb following right behind him. They had both decided to spend the night somewhere quieter. Tinman hoped that being below the cliff, with the help of the soothing sound of the ocean waves, there would be enough distance between his ears and the blabbering bird.

The ocean provided a natural breeze that felt refreshing blowing across their skin. The mounds of soft sand massaged their backs as Tinman and Caleb positioned themselves for a good night's rest under the stars. They quickly fell asleep. It was not long after that they began to regret their decision to spend the night on the beach.

Awakened by the clinking and clanking of camping equipment, Tinman opened his eyes and yelled, "Caleb, cut it out!"

The clinking and clanking continued. Tinman lifted his head up and started to yell at Caleb again, but he saw something completely unexpected. Caleb was kneeling on the sand, watching as several red, white, and blue robber crabs scurried around him. The ten-legged bandits were about to run off across the sand with his smelly sandal and some of his shiny camping gear.

"Give it back!" shouted Caleb, playing tug-of-war with the giant robber crab attempting to run off with his sandal clenched in its massive claw.

Tinman jumped up and danced his way around and over the giant crabs.

Meanwhile, up in the cave on the side of the cliff, Jesse and Honey Bee heard all the noise below them and ran to the edge of the cliff to see what the commotion was all about. To their surprise and amusement, Caleb was still in a tug-of-war with one of the gigantic fighting crabs, and Tinman was hopping around across the sand like his feet were on fire. He was attempting to pick up the shiny objects that the crabs had scattered across the beach.

Both of them burst out laughing as they watched their friends clash with the crustaceans on the sandy beach below. Caleb didn't appear like he was going to give up the fight with his husky opponent as he continued his back-and-forth contest.

Jesse shouted from above, "Let it go!"

Caleb reluctantly relinquished one of his favorite sandals to the crusty creature and watched him scurry across the sand, disappearing behind the palm trees.

He grabbed his other sandal and hurled it at one of the other crabs, shouting, "Take this one too, you crusty pirate!"

The curious crab looked up at him with its eyes atop their stalks, then quickly picked up the other sandal and ran off in the same direction as the rest of the cast of thieves. Caleb watched him run along the bottom of the cliffs and then disappear into the darkness.

"Small wonder they left anything," grumbled Tinman.

Tinman looked around at the gear scattered all over the beach and burst out laughing uncontrollably as he reflected on the campground chaos over the last few minutes.

"It's not that funny!" exclaimed Caleb. "My papa gave me those sandals."

"Sorry about your loss, Caleb, but that was insanely funny," said Honey Bee from above.

"You can't imagine how hilarious you guys looked from up here!" yelled Jesse.

A few minutes later, Tinman and Caleb were back up in the cozy cave on the side of the cliff and settled down for the night. Hiya had gone back into the hole in his tree and, despite Tinman's snoring, they were finally able to enjoy a few hours of sleep.

Boo woke up to the sound of crashing waves and singing birds. He rubbed his head against Jesse's blond hair and stretched out his paws and claws. Boo was ready for another adventurous day in paradise with Jesse and his friends. He also knew there was a good chance they would encounter Professor Katnip and the bullkats on their way back through the Roundabout Rainforest.

Jesse picked Boo up in his arms and sleepily walked toward the edge of the cliff. He looked out over the ocean just in time to see a gray humpback whale spray salt water out of his blowhole. Jesse and Boo stood watching as the pod of whales gracefully breached the water. The gentle giants continued their voyage, gliding along the island's coast through Coral Way Bay, toward the coastal town of Yogi Falls. Along the way, the whales sang a magical underwater song, sending mysterious sound waves across the ocean. Jesse looked at Boo and somehow knew that his best friend understood that watching these beautiful creatures was something very special.

"Let's just keep this one to ourselves," said Jesse, whispering.

"We better get movin'," said Tinman. "It'll take the better part of the day to get through the rainforest and back to the campground. I know it takes longer, but it'll be safer if we take the trails that go through the densest part of the rainforest."

They all headed down the trail leading back to the beach with Hiya starting a new day squawking away. The bird was not shy about reminding Jesse and his friends that Tyrtle Island was still "his island."

"Hey, anyone recognize these?" asked Tinman, picking up Caleb's worn-out sandals, slapping the sand off them.

"Looks like they were even a little too stinky for the robber crabs," said Jesse, watching as Tinman tossed Caleb his sandals.

"Awesome. I love these sandals," said Caleb, slipping them on his feet.

The rainforest never failed to reward Jesse and his friends with sightings of some incredible creatures and fascinating flowers. Body and soul, they took it all in as they promenaded along through the tropical landscape, heading toward the campground.

Jesse took the lead as they walked past the tropical ferns, yellow hibiscus flowers, and red ginger plants. He caught sight of a rare red-eyed tree frog sleeping on a tree branch that was stretched above the edge of the trail. Further up the trail, the prehistoric-looking vines produced huge leaves that provided a launching pad for a coqui frog to jump onto Jesse's shoulder as if just to say hello for a brief moment. The tiny green frog then leaped to the ground and hopped across the clear stream meandering its way through the rainforest. The stream eventually found its way to the rocky cliffs and poured out its life, tumbling down into the ocean.

Honey Bee watched in wonder as butterflies fluttered, bees buzzed, and bugs of all shapes and sizes flew about, busily performing their daily pollinating duties.

Honey Bee's eyes tried to keep up with the lightning-fast moves of the giant hummingbird moths. She watched the moths dart from flower to flower sipping on the sweet nectar, and said, "Look at how fast their wings move. I wonder how they move that quickly."

The unnatural sound of Tinman opening a can echoed through the trees. He devoured the salty ham like he was feasting on a filet mignon. While chewing on his last bite, Tinman was entertained by an army of ants carrying leaves the size of ant tables on their backs. They marched downward toward the rainforest floor through the dead leaves, scurrying over and under the tree roots with their new-found treasures.

Tinman marveled at the ridiculously strong creatures, thinking, "Good thing they're tiny."

An old tree had fallen next to the river, providing the right place for everyone to rest for a few moments.

They watched in delight as several members of a giant otter family played a game of tag in the gurgling river. Other not-so-playful family members attempted to sunbathe as the blue morpho butterflies fluttered around their adorable faces, trying to steal away salty tears from the squirming otters' eyes.

Honey Bee marveled as she watched this rare performance of nature play out before them.

"Have you ever seen such a thing… cute little otters' eyes and beautiful annoying butterflies!" she sang out.

Caleb watched a charm of finches playing and singing while they darted in and out of the trees. The birds' soft chirping soothed Caleb's mind for those few minutes. The rainbow-colored lories glided from branch to branch, feeding on the never-ending supply of sweet tropical fruits. They bounced up and down, dancing together, kissing each other on the cheek.

Jesse could see that Caleb was enchanted by the dancing birds.

"His moves are better than yours," said Jesse.

Jesse laughed as Caleb gave him a crazy look and said, "Right… and you're a bird of paradise."

The pair of parrots swooped down over their heads, and the words that Jesse heard come out of their beaks took him by total surprise. "Chop! Chop!" they called out, before soaring off to explore the island paradise beyond.

Boo loved the rainforest creatures, and to him the rainforest was by far the most entertaining place on the island. He never really felt the natural tendency to attack birds or any other creature on the island. Everyone that knew Boo also knew he was a very special kind of cat. Whatever the reason, Boo loved to watch and listen to the birds of the rainforest. They chirped, tweeted, and chattered while going about their business of gathering twigs and leaves to finish making their perfect nests. Their songs could be heard echoing throughout the rainforest. He took in the wonder of it all as he walked along with Jesse and his friends. He was always content to be with his best friend, no matter where the day's adventure would take them.

Tinman peered through the trees and saw they were approaching the campground.

"Keep an eye out as we get closer to the campground," he said, glancing back over his shoulder.

Everyone crept quietly down the last part of the trail, watching to make sure they didn't crunch any branches or rustle any leaves. Jesse stopped just short of entering the campground. He turned back toward his friends with a look of frustration and said calmly, "I guess we shouldn't be totally shocked."

Their gear was thrown all over the campground and their shredded tents scattered everywhere. It was as if their camp had been attacked by a legendary bigfoot creature, but they all knew it was no mysterious legend that had ransacked this campground.

The bullkat tracks in the surrounding mud provided all the evidence they needed. They also knew that, at any moment, Professor Katnip and his bullkats could return to the campground.

"We have to put a stop to this," said Tinman as he salvaged what was left of their camping gear scattered throughout the campground. "I'm going to get the Jeep. Can you guys clean up the rest of this stuff so we can get out of here?"

Tinman had parked the Jeep away from the campground in a hidden location they had known about for years.

He returned to the campground a few minutes later with good news. "Well, they didn't find the Jeep," said Tinman. "I think we should hoof it down to Kats Caves. If we take the Jeep closer to the caves then they'll find it for sure."

"Yep, I agree. Let's go," said Jesse. "We have to stop this before anyone else on the island gets hurt."

"Well, we don't have to go," replied Caleb.

"Tinman and Jesse are right," said Honey Bee. "If we don't stop the professor, then who will?"

"Uh, hello. They call them the police," said Caleb. "People that are actually trained to do this sort of thing. Police officers like my Uncle Kai."

Tinman looked seriously at Caleb and said, "Most of the time I would agree with you, but this time the police may not believe us. Think about it. We have no proof at this point, and Professor Katnip is well known and well respected throughout the island. Honestly, we don't even know what the professor is really up to. We have to go to Kats Caves and find out what's going on. Whatever this dark secret is that Mr. Jack told us about, well, anyways… I'm not sure why, but I think I believe him."

Meanwhile, Professor Katnip was waiting for Jesse and his friends down by Kats Caves. The professor was confident that Tinman and Jesse would be heading to Kats Caves. He was bound and determined to keep them from discovering what was going on in the caves beneath Tyrtle Island.

"We can spend the night at the old rock house on this side of the rainforest. It's just past the Roundabout Point lookout," declared Tinman. "With the rainbow plants, rocks, and my tranquilizer gun, it will provide us some protection should we get attacked. It's our best bet at this point." He looked around at his friends. "Everyone OK?"

Jesse believed in his friends and said, "Keep calm and Tyrtle on!"

Caleb said, "You guys are my friends, and if you're good with this, then I'm good with this." He smiled as he extended his arm to his friends, initiating their form of a secret handshake.

Jesse returned the gesture by extending his arm out to his friend. They crossed arms at the elbow and folded their arms slowly together. This gesture was an old Tyrtle tradition and something very special between Islanders. It was similar to making the sign for friendship with your index finger, but by locking arms at the elbow and then gently pulling the person toward you, it was demonstrated in a much bigger way.

The rock house was an ancient fortress mostly forgotten by the Islanders, but Tinman and Jesse knew of its treasured past. The old ruins had been the gathering place of past island kings and warriors. The entry tunnel was covered by thick bamboo stalks which concealed the age-old treasure from most tourists hiking through the rainforest. Although there were those exceptional few who had the courage to venture deeper into the unknown or the fortunate ones who already knew of its isolated location.

A stone pathway marked the way to an old rock wall that encompassed the ruins. The enduring stone walls were built with precision by fitting and stacking each rock carefully together like an ancient puzzle. Tinman always felt the presence of past kings, warriors, and Islanders within these ancient walls, and he knew their spirits would provide the inspiration and strength against anyone who wished to do them harm.

Boo had visited the rock house on previous adventures with Tinman and Jesse. He thought about the strong connection to his feline ancestors that he always sensed when he trotted through the bamboo tunnel and into the ancient stronghold. He could almost see his much larger ancestors protecting the sacred place as they stood atop the giant stone walls.

Tyrtle Island is well known for its treasured sea turtles, but the island also has a rich history of ancient cats and other extinct creatures that roamed the island long before the first humans arrived on the shores of this paradise.

"How about a song?" Caleb asked Honey Bee as they sat down inside the damp stone walls. "My favorite is the 'Island Wonders' song."

Caleb started to play his ukulele as Honey Bee started to sing out softly:

"My mind begins to wander as I think of island wonders!
My heart skips a beat as I think of life so sweet!
My spirit starts to soar around this island I adore!
My being in awe as I see what you saw!
Colors of the rainbow explode as the beauty overflows!
I see the island wonders! I see the island wonders!
And I have no reason to be afraid,
We have no reason to be afraid.

My hands reach out as I give out a shout!
My arms embrace as I see each creature's face!
My feet explore as I walk the rainforest floor!
My eyes glow as I gaze at the show!
Colors of the rainbow explode as the beauty overflows!
I see the island wonders! I see the island wonders!
And I have no reason to be afraid,
We have no reason to be afraid."

Honey Bee's voice was just as sweet as the honey made by her family for generations, and her songs were just as comforting as the aroma of the coffee they had brewed for ages.

"I'm in love with that song," said Caleb, smiling at Honey Bee and his friends. At that moment there was no place he would rather be. When Caleb said he loved her song, everyone knew it was Honey Bee that he really loved. Everyone on the island loved her beautiful smile, and the love that flowed out of her was poured out to every living creature. She had a gift from God, and she freely shared it with everyone she encountered.

Tinman gathered some soft palm fronds and laid them down on the inside of the rock house, hoping that they would help make their night of sleep a little more comfortable.

He looked at Jesse, all snuggled up in the corner with Boo curled up on his lap, and said, "OK, guess I'll take the first watch."

"Sweet dreams," said Honey Bee, giving Boo a gentle pet on his head and Jesse a kiss on his cheek.

A kiss from Honey Bee was all that Jesse needed to send him into la-la land. He dozed off with a smile on his face. Boo looked around the rock house, watching intently as the ancient ones stood prepared for battle atop the black and gray stone walls.

The imaginations of Jesse and Boo melded together as Jesse entered the mysterious world between island dreams and reality. An image of hot, flowing lava flashed through his mind. Jesse's heart was racing as his mind tumbled deeper into the dream tunnel.

tyrtle

CHAPTER FOURTEEN: THE RIDE OF YOUR LIFE!

Upon opening his eyes Boo welcomed the sunlight peeking into the shallow cave on the side of the cliff. He was relieved to see they had made it through the night without being attacked by the bullkats.

He stretched out his paws and sleepily walked toward the edge of the cliff, glancing over toward Hiya's mangrove tree. He looked out over the horizon, daydreaming for a moment as he thought about how small and insignificant the ocean can make you feel.

His daydream was short-lived when he noticed a rare monk seal and her pup lounging on the sand below. Inch by inch, the blubbery seal and her pup scooted closer to the water. Every movement of the mama seal's body revealed the scars from past shark attacks. He watched as the playful pair continued to edge closer to the calm waves, then together, they glided along the shore and into deeper water. As he watched them swim away and disappear, Boo thought about how amazing it would be to swim as gracefully as a monk seal.

"I'm just glad I'm a cat," said Chops, propping his furry chin on Boo's shoulder. "I hope that's not our boat."

There was an old wooden cat-a-canoe tied up by the shoreline, bobbing up and down with the movement of the gentle waves.

Boo smiled with his blue tongue hanging halfway out of his mouth and then reminded Chops, "Calico said that the cat-a-canoe would be on the beach in the morning, and like magic, there it is. I know I sound like a crazy cat, but I'm really beginning to like that bullkat."

"Better not let Silver hear you say that," said Chops. "I'm not sure he'll ever forgive a bullkat for what they did to his family in Wig Waggle."

Chops and Boo looked with sympathy at Silver, who was in the cave talking to Roxy Roo and gathering their packs. They knew that Silver was one of the bravest creatures on the island, and a more loyal friend could not be found. Although he had a cheerful disposition, his friends could see that the immense heartache of being separated from his family was hidden somewhere deep within and masked under his cute prickly face.

Chops looked out over the water, trying to get a better look at the cat-a-canoe, and asked, "You think that old thing will make it to the other side of the island?"

Boo glanced at him quickly. "Well, we're about to find out."

"Good morning!" shouted Roxy Roo. "Look at that magical—"

Boo interrupted her quickly by covering her mouth with his big paw and said, "Shhhh! We don't want to wake that wacky bird."

They both stretched their necks and tilted their heads, looking up toward Hiya's treehouse.

With their packs on their backs, they tiptoed down the trail. The ancient cat-a-canoe was more than big enough to fit Boo and his three friends inside. The craft had a strong wooden hull and an outrigger float attached between two booms that would help stabilize the craft should they encounter rough weather as they navigated around the northern point of the island.

"Cat-a-canoe!" squawked Hiya, loud and clear.

The macaw was not shy as he announced his desire to go along on the canoe ride to the other side of the island.

"Ummm, unfortunately, we really don't have enough room on this rickety old cat-a-canoe," said Boo unconvincingly.

Thinking he could somehow talk the persistent bird out of it, Chops chimed in and said, "Are you sure you really want to get on a boat with three big cats?"

"Hiya, cat-a-canoe surfin'!" squawked Hiya louder.

The bird would not take no for an answer and immediately flew down from his hole in the tree, landing softly on the tip of the stern. The cat-a-canoe was a primitive-looking structure except for the stern, which had a carved image that curiously resembled a macaw. Hiya quickly made himself at home on the cat-a-canoe with his island friends.

"Did he say he wanted to go surfing on the cat-a-canoe?" said Chops, looking at Hiya sitting like the king of macaws, just above his own likeness on the stern. "He's the nuttiest bird I've ever seen. There's not even any waves this morning. Crazy canary!"

"Uh oh! Here we go again! Oh no!" Hiya screeched excitedly.

"Here you go again," said Chops. "Now don't start all that crazy bird yappin' again."

Hiya saw something that the others did not. Professor Katnip and his gang of bullkats were headed up the beach, quickly moving in and out of the mangrove trees. The bullkats were steadily moving along the shore and had not been noticed by the canoeing creatures, who were preoccupied with Hiya's unusual, but entertaining, comments.

Boo and Silver were already inside the cat-a-canoe, consumed with the task of preparing the craft for its short trip around the tip of the island.

"Bullkat! Danger! Bullkat!" screeched Hiya in a panic.

This time he caught everyone's attention.

"QUICK! EVERYONE IN THE CANOE! NOW! NOW!" commanded Silver.

Now, it's a well-known island fact that most Meow cats don't mind the water. Especially when it involves fish, fun, or avoiding dangerous situations. Attacking bullkats running up the beach definitely fit into the "avoiding dangerous situations" category.

"Chops!" yelled Roxy Roo. "Push the canoe!"

Chops was frozen in place standing on a lava rock as he watched the gang of bullkats leaping from rock to rock and getting closer to them.

Boo and Silver pushed with all their strength at the back of the cat-a-canoe as Roxy Roo paddled frantically, steering through the maze of lava rocks. She flinched as a school of fish darted out of the way and the sea creatures below the cat-a-canoe scurried past her into the shallow water. The bullkats hopped like frenzied frogs from one jagged rock to the next, leaping ever closer to their prey.

Hiya might have been a blabbermouth, but he was certainly no bird-brain and knew he had to act quickly. He flew from the safety of his perch and pecked Chops on the tip of his ear, hoping it would snap him out of his trance.

"Ouch! Watch it, you crazy bird. What's that for?" cried Chops, shaking his ear.

Chops looked behind him and was stunned to realize how dangerously close the bullkats were. He rushed up behind the cat-a-canoe, pushing it with all his Meow cat strength, and the old wooden boat floated out into the oncoming waves.

"What took you so long?" shouted Silver, spitting water out of his mouth.

The cat-a-canoe floated away from the rocks into deeper water and out of reach of the claws of the vicious bullkats. Boo, Silver, and Chops clung to the sides of the canoe like wet rats, bobbing up and down with the waves as they drifted away from the evil creatures. They looked back toward the shoreline and could see that the crazy bullkats were disappointed as they jumped from rock to rock, turning in circles. The crazed creatures were frustrated, realizing once again that their vicious attack had failed miserably.

"That was way too close!" shouted Roxy Roo, out of breath.

She pulled her friends' wet furry bodies up and over the top railing, watching them flop into the cat-a-canoe like wet fish.

"I'm so glad bullkats don't like to get wet," she said, splashing some more water on Boo.

"Hiya saved our furry behinds," said Boo, looking at Chops. "How's your ear?"

Chops glared at Hiya and said, "How do you think it is? My poor little soft ear just got pecked by that huge hard beak."

The bullkats continued jumping from rock to rock, following the cat-a-canoe along the rocky shoreline.

The faint screeches of the bullkats being carried out into the open ocean by the offshore winds could still be heard by Boo and his friends. The salt-water mist from the paddles sprayed into their whiskers as they rowed the cat-a-canoe slowly toward the island's northern point.

"Hiya, cat-a-canoe surfin'," squawked Hiya, repeating his earlier demands.

Chops looked at Hiya, who was still sitting like the king of macaws on the stern, and said, "There he goes again, talking about going surfin' on the cat-a-canoe. He really is one crazy bird."

"I'm just guessing, but I don't think he likes it when you call him crazy," said Roxy Roo, examining Chops' ear. "It's kind of like calling an alligator a lizard. Maybe if you didn't call him names, he wouldn't have pecked your ear so hard. We're going to have to find some cat's claw plant to put on that ear when we get ashore."

The ocean waves swelled, growing larger by the hour. Hiya somehow seemed to know from the very beginning of their canoe trip that surfing the ocean waves was in their immediate future.

A very powerful wave splashed against the cat-a-canoe, and Hiya excitedly squawked, "Akaw! Akaw! Hiya, cat-a-canoe surfin'."

Unknown to surfers everywhere, this is why they shout out "Akaw" when catching a big perfect wave.

Roxy Roo looked out into the water as dozens of green sea turtles gracefully followed the ocean currents. She thought about her home in Treetop Woods and for a moment she felt homesick. The turtles powerful flippers moved through the water and she was reminded of how far each one of these incredible creatures had traveled through the aquatic jungle to reach its home again.

Chops watched the turtles slip along through the water and noticed one very familiar-looking face. He jumped up on the side of the cat-a-canoe and turned to Roxy Roo, shouting, "I can't believe it! That looks like the same goofy-lookin' turtle we saw in Calico's Lagoon. No way, can't be!"

"Chops! Get off there!" yelled Boo. "You're too big to try and pull back in."

"Hey, it's Wacky Tyrtle!" shouted Roxy Roo.

She gazed into the water, watching his slippers, attached to his feet, propel his golden shell through the ocean.

"How about a delicious seaweed-and-jellies sandwich?" suggested Chops, laughing out loud. "Yum! Yum!"

Roxy Roo looked curiously at Chops and said, "I hope you're not going to start an argument with a Tyrtle again."

"It's the ruuude ones from the lagoooon," gurgled Wacky Tyrtle, skimming by the cat-a-canoe. "Since I like the prickly creature on board, I will warn you: a giant swell is coming soon. Best to get ashore unless, of course… you're a turtle."

"Hiya, cat-a-canoe surfin'," squawked Hiya as another big wave splashed against the cat-a-canoe.

Roxy Roo didn't like Wacky Tyrtle's comment. "You know, my friend has already apologized for his bad behavior," she said emphatically. "I hope you can forgive him."

Chops looked at the goofy expression on the Tyrtle's face and couldn't hold his tongue. "What a perfect face for a perfect name like Wacky! Prettiest shell I've ever seen," he said, letting out a roar of laughter.

Boo smiled at him, chuckling, and said under his breath, "I got nothin'."

Roxy Roo tried her hardest to keep from smiling but couldn't help herself.

"Well, my brother Wiki and I have been swimming these oceans for well over a hundred and fifty years. I'll let him know you're on the way," said Wacky Tyrtle. "One more thing… this pretty shell I carry around is much more than a dazzling display of floating art. Its incredible design helps to keep me safe, makes me an awesome swimmer, and even helps me soak up the sun. So let that amazing information soak in awhile."

Wacky Tyrtle's slippers quickly turned him away from the cat-a-canoe, and he disappeared into the deep water.

"Bless his little wrinkled heart," said Chops, watching Wacky Tyrtle swim away. "I just love that Tyrtle, but ya know somethin', it was only a hundred years back in the lagoon."

"How does he know if we're going to see Wiki Tyrtle?" asked Silver.

"Who knows? But one thing I do know… we have to get to shore quickly," said Boo. "Hiya's right. If we wait too long, then we'll be surfing the big one right into the cliffs."

Looking out at the horizon, they could see the ocean swell and the storm clouds gathering above. Looking at the shore, the bullkats were steadily moving north along the bottom edge of the cliffs in pursuit of the cat-a-canoe. It was just a matter of time before the cat-a-canoe would get caught up in one of the powerful waves and launched toward the shore, crashing into the cliffs and the bullkats.

The clear tropical skies quickly gave way to the darkening thunderclouds. The wind started to whip across the ocean, and the swells began to curl up like aqua monsters ready to devour them with their salty lips. The dark green water sloshed around the cat-a-canoe and crashed against the rocks. In only a few minutes, the calm ocean had turned violent and began to pound the cliffs surrounding the northern point of the Roundabout Rainforest.

Everyone ducked as a monster wave crashed over them, almost capsizing the cat-a-canoe.

The cats and porcupine were holding on tightly to anything they could, but the macaw seemed to be enjoying the excitement and squawked, "Akaw! Akaw! Hiya, cat-a-canoe surfin'!"

Hiya was ready for a surfing adventure, but Boo and his friends knew they had to get ashore quickly before a monstrous wave capsized their cat-a-canoe.

Boo and Chops' hearts pounded as they paddled to try and catch the next big wave. They hoped the swell would carry them past the rocky point and land them closer to the sandy beach on the other side.

Hiya let out a squawk each time he flew off his perch and up in the air. He would flutter back down, landing on the stern of the cat-a-canoe as it slapped down, hitting the raging ocean below them.

Roxy Roo and Silver let out a loud wailing sound as they sailed up off their wooden seats into the air while the cat-a-canoe went in the opposite direction. The wind whipped the salt water into their eyes, and the stinging raindrops hit their faces as the cat-a-canoe returned to meet the ocean, pounding the dark, turbulent waves below them.

"Hang on for the ride of your life!" yelled Boo, crouching down into the cat-a canoe with his tail lowered and watching with big eyes as the huge wave engulfed them.

The monster wave wrapped the cat-a-canoe into its curly lips, and they zoomed through the monster's dark green throat. The outside world disappeared as the aqua green curtain closed in front of them, and the powerful wave wrapped its watery arms around them.

The ocean evaporated, the sky vanished, and the shoreline dropped out of sight. They were swallowed up in a moment of unspeakable beauty in an unforgiving water world that cannot be explained by the imagination but, once experienced, will never be forgotten. The raging storm outside of the wave fell deathly quiet as the cat-a-canoe streamed along inside the barrel. It was surreal. The fear of being captured by this ominous wave dissolved as they were overcome by the wonder of it all. Their eyes radiated with amazement, and their whiskers dripped from the salt-water spray as the cat-a-canoe zipped along inside the green barrel. In an instant, the barrel formed a small peephole and slowly opened back up until the outside world came back into full view. The monstrous wave released them from its powerful grip, shooting the cat-a-canoe out into the white water, and the swell disappeared behind them. It was the end of an epic ride.

"Akaw! Akaw!" Hiya squawked, flapping his wings wildly.

"I couldn't have said it better myself!" exclaimed Boo, exhilarated by the rush they had just experienced.

Silver looked at the shoreline to see if he could still spot the ruthless bullkats pursuing them. He spoke loudly into the wind. "Good news, my friends! I think they got cut off by the considerable waves crashing against the cliffs, and they had no choice but to take to the high ground! That should give us some time to make it back on shore and give us a head start to Kats Caves!"

Chops was seated at the back of the cat-a-canoe and sang out loudly, "I can't hear you!"

To everyone's relief, Silver was right about Professor Katnip and his gang of bullkats. The relentless crashing of the breaking waves against the lava rocks prevented the bullkats from taking the rocky path around the northern point. The professor was forced to backtrack along the shore and take the winding trail back up to the Roundabout Rainforest.

Boo and his friends hoped that Calico really was an ally and that he would figure out a way to stall the professor.

Meanwhile, Calico was doing all he could to slow down Professor Katnip and give Boo and his friends a little more time to reach Kats Caves first.

"Calico, where are you going? Is that the shortest way up to the rainforest?" Professor Katnip questioned Calico as he tried to lead them further down the beach away from the rainforest.

"That trail goes right through the pencil-plant forest," Calico said to Professor Katnip. "If we try and maneuver through those plants—"

Professor Katnip quickly cut him off, looking suspiciously at him. "I know all about pencil plants. Sometimes I think you forget that you're a bullkat."

All the bullkats gathered impatiently around Calico. They snarled and snapped at each other as they listened to him and the professor debate which direction they should travel.

Skin was known as the "biting cat" and, therefore, the leader of the bullkats. He was the biggest and strongest bullkat and without a doubt, the most dreadful-looking bullkat. His body was mostly hairless, and the skin around his face was bald like sun-bleached leather.

Skin walked through the clowder of bullkats, pushing Calico aside, and said, "I'm growing tired of chasing these pathetic Meow cats and their pink-nosed little porcupine companion. We're taking this trail and we're going to make up some lost time."

Skin walked in circles in the middle of the other bullkats as they nervously moved back, giving him more room. Calico stood his ground as Skin bumped up against him. Skin licked his lips and squinted his red eyes, making even Professor Katnip feel uneasy.

"I'm getting very, very hungry," said Skin, glaring at Calico.

"Skin, lead the way to Kats Caves!" ordered Professor Katnip.

Skin turned around slowly, scowling at the other bullkats, and said, "We must find these Meeeow cats and their tittle-tattling little friend… and destroy them."

The bullkats were whipped up into a frenzy, and their hideous screeching could be heard by every creature as the piercing sound echoed throughout the rainforest. They raced through the rainforest decimating the plants and scattering the creatures along the way as they became more determined than ever to hunt down and capture their elusive prey.

Outside of the rainforest and beneath the cliffs, the waves gently scooted the cat-a-canoe through the white water and up onto the beach. Boo jumped out, scanning up and down the beach.

"I think we better hide the cat-a-canoe," said Boo.

"That's kinda like sayin' let's hide a baby whale," said Chops.

Everyone pitched in to help push the long cat-a-canoe over the sandy beach and closer to the rock-face cliffs.

Keeping an eye out for the bullkats, Silver looked back toward the cliffs jetting out into the white water while everyone else searched for a spot to hide the cat-a canoe.

Boo found a long shallow cave that was higher up on the beach and out of reach from the waves. The cave opening was partially hidden by a group of coconut palms and mangrove trees.

The friends managed to wedge some thick palm fronds between the jagged rocks and the cat-a-canoe to make sure it wouldn't be noticed from the beach.

Silver used some of his strong quills to secure a few palm fronds to the front of the cat-a-canoe, explaining, "I have no doubt that the professor is either on his way to this beach or will be waiting for us in Kats Caves. We certainly don't want to get trapped on this beach, and right now our only way out is this cat-a-canoe. Although, I think our best chances are to beat the professor and his bullkats to Kats Caves."

Bouncing down the narrow beach, their paws kicked up wet sand each time they jumped from one lava rock down to the sand and from the sand back up to another lava rock. This exercise of hopping up and down the rocks went on for most of the way.

With every jump, Chops kicked the sand up in the air, trying to see how far back he could fling it.

"Chops, stop it!" shouted Boo. "This isn't your litter box."

Chops grinned and said, "Ahh, but the whole island is my litter box."

Roxy Roo had a displeased look on her face. "That is disgusting," she said.

Chops looked at Silver and said, "Well, at least cats bury theirs."

"I like to think of it as fertilizing the trees," said Silver.

"Would somebody please change the subject!" hollered Roxy Roo.

Using their acute senses, they continued to keep a watchful eye on the beach in front of them and listened for any unusual sounds coming from the rainforest above. Hiya flew above them awhile, quietly circling the shoreline as they progressed toward Kats Caves. Chops watched as Hiya's shadow moved across the sand and along the shoreline, and then, without saying anything, the macaw quickly disappeared back into the rainforest.

"We just surfed the most awesome wave of our lives, and he didn't even say goodbye. I suppose that's not very odd for a very odd creature," said Chops. He thought for a minute and then chuckled, saying, "That crazy bird talked non-stop for the last two days."

Chops glanced around for Hiya in the cloudy skies above him, but at this very moment his mind was really focused on the bullkats. He carefully scanned the cliffs for any signs of movement. To his relief, there was no sign of the bullkats, but he did see something very colorful perched on one of the branches of the biggest trees along the rainforest ridge. The colorful creature began to make loud squawking noises.

Chops pointed upward, shouting, "There he is! That macaw is one loud bird!"

Boo looked up and could hear Hiya squawking from high above. "I can't quite make it out. What's he squawking about?"

"Oh, I'm sure it's just some more senseless noise," said Chops, scanning the cliffs one more time for the bullkats.

Boo looked curiously at Chops. "Did I hear him say 'zippity Boo'? Is that what he just said?"

Boo wasn't exactly sure why, but when he heard what he thought he heard from Hiya, once again he sensed that déjà-vu feeling.

Roxy Roo turned Boo's thoughts and the conversation back to the bullkats. They talked about bullkat tales and debated reasons why Professor Katnip would do something against his own Meow cat family. Each one of them had their own opinion about the creepy cat Bones and how he might fit into this mystery. The general consensus was that, over the years, the professor had sipped too much of his own catnip tea. As to Bones and how he fit into this mystery, they concluded that he was actually an undercover bullkat who was now working for the professor. That's the only reason they could come up with to explain why he was so creepy.

Silver was getting agitated listening to their bullkat conversations, and he finally interrupted them. "We better pick up our pace, and can you please talk about something else?"

Roxy Roo understood why the bullkat stories didn't sit well with Silver. She knew that they only made him think of his lost family and the pain he felt.

"I believe your family is still alive," said Roxy Roo, looking at Silver with her big green eyes. "We'll find them, and you will all be together again. I really believe that with all my heart."

Roxy Roo's kind and encouraging words floated through the air and were caught up with the island breeze and carried away into Kats Caves. The caves are known for being the home of Tyrtle Island's most feared creatures. These same caves are shared by one of the island's most beautiful and legendary creatures.

Out from the midst of the cavern sailed a pair of giant unicorn butterflies. Like an answered prayer, they were a sign from heaven. Soaring above the beach, they gently fluttered their colorful wings and floated right past Silver. The butterflies glided around in circles, dancing above their heads.

Many of the island's creatures had the power to take your breath away. Roxy Roo's eyes followed the flight pattern of these heavenly creatures, and they not only took her breath away but also melted her heart.

The unicorn butterflies floated through the sky showcasing their oversized rainbow-colored 'unicorn spit' wings and their long, spiraling, pearly-white horns. They zipped through the air at super-speeds and captivated their audience as they fluttered and glided through the sky. The phenomenal butterflies performed a jousting dance, piercing the air with their deadly horns as they passed dangerously close to one another. It was unthinkable for the captivated audience to even imagine that a spectacle like this one could get any better. Suddenly, a flurry of unicorn butterflies sailed out of their cave and joined the first pair of performers, flying wing-tip to wing-tip.

"Heads up and tails down!" cried Chops, ducking as the unicorn butterfly's lethal horn zipped past the tips of his furry ears.

Now if anyone was going to be a target for these angelic creatures, it was most likely going to be Chops. Why unusual things always seemed to happen to Chops was a mystery to his friends. Boo and Roxy Roo had plenty of stories to tell about Chops and trouble's ability to find him.

Boo and Silver tried their hardest not to laugh as they watched Chops duck and run for cover, trying to avoid the butterflies' sharp unicorn horns. Chops was the biggest of the Meow cats and much larger than his porcupine friend. For some unknown reason, it seemed that if one of them was going to get stung, stabbed, sliced, scraped, or suffer in any way, it was almost certainly going to be Chops.

Although unicorn butterflies do possess a lethal dagger-like horn, they truly are angelic creatures and have no intention of hurting anyone unless they feel threatened.

"What a fascinating creature!" said Roxy Roo, pondering the butterflies' brilliant design.

"I know a few facts about these amazing creatures," said Silver, capturing everyone's attention. "Unicorn butterflies are a symbol of life after death. Their miraculous lives start out very humbly as crawling cave caterpillars. The caterpillars hibernate in a cocoon attached to a cave wall, but not just any cave wall will do for these unique butterflies. Only one of the caverns in Kats Caves has the perfect environment to allow the giant caterpillar to attach itself to the cave wall and form a rainbow-colored cocoon. Finally, these one-of-a-kind creatures are miraculously transformed to become the beautiful unicorn butterflies you see flying all around you."

Roxy Roo didn't think it was possible these butterflies could amaze her any more than they already had, but she was wrong.

The unicorn butterflies flew once more over the heads of her friends and then darted down the beach, swooping down and skimming over the ears of the two cats marching toward them. Their audience was gobsmacked and goggle-eyed, and didn't notice the two cats coming toward them.

Chapter Fourteen

The multitude of wings circled around one more time performing their encore and then vanished over the cliffs and into the rainforest.

The thrill of seeing the unicorn butterflies was short-lived. Boo became alarmed at the two familiar, but suspicious, feline figures walking up the beach toward them.

"We have company!" he shouted. "Quickly, get over to the cave!"

They jumped up on the rocks in front of the unicorn butterfly cave, prepared to make their escape from the approaching cats.

"I recognize that hat and creepy walk," said Boo, stepping out from the cave opening.

"Boo!" yelled Calico. "Roxy Roo, wait! Don't run!"

Calico slowly approached the cave entrance with Bones right behind him.

The appearance of Bones was more than enough to alarm the Meow cats and the porcupine, but Bones tried to smile and soften his creepy mannerisms, saying "Don't be afraid. I told you that I know some things. I know secret things, and now is the time to reveal those secrets to you."

Bones knew that he had a lot to explain and only a very short time to do it.

He stared at everyone with an unintentional glare and said, "First, let's talk about what is most important. Silver, I know where your family is, and trust me when I say that they're safe… at least for now."

Bones stunned Silver and the Meow cats with this astonishing news.

Silver's tail repeatedly tapped the ground as he took a couple steps forward and loudly demanded, "Where are they? I insist that you take me to them now!"

He looked at the shocked faces of his friends and shouted, "Now!" He took another step forward, and the quills on his back rose straight up and rattled against each other.

Bones took his tall black hat off his head. "I'm so sorry. I couldn't tell you before," he said, apologizing in his most sincere, frightening voice. "If I had told you where the professor was hiding them and he found out that you knew, then he would've hurt them or might have even killed them.

I couldn't let that happen. They are held captive in Kats Caves. There's more—"

"We're out of time," shouted Boo. He jumped forward, pounding his paw in the sand.

Bones raised his voice. "Please listen! We don't have much time!"

"Why should we trust you at all?" Chops blurted out.

Bones didn't answer but began to tell them his story. "Professor Katnip and Professor Potamus thought they were the only ones who knew the location of the rainbow plants, and they were right, up until a few days ago. With Calico's help, you all found the lagoon, and now you also know the secret location of the most powerful plants on the island. That knowledge makes you enemy number one to Professor Katnip."

Bones paused for a few seconds, collecting his thoughts. It was unintentional, but those few seconds were long enough to allow the suspense to build up in the minds of his listeners, and they all felt like their heads were going to explode.

"Go on! Go on!" said Silver anxiously.

And Bones did. "Boo, you weren't dreaming that night at Cat Skull rock."

"I know," said Boo confidently, like he had never really doubted himself.

"Calico was the bullkat that was with me that night. I told you I know some things, and because I know some things, I also knew that you would not be hurt that night."

"But Professor Potamus is dead!" shrieked Roxy Roo. "He's not hurt, he's dead!"

Bones' scary nature transformed to a mournful look as he said, "Professor Potamus was my very good friend. He found out that Professor Katnip was after more than just being the catnip king of the island. Professor Katnip killed Professor Potamus that day in the wilderness. He thought that blaming it on the bullkats would be easy enough, but what he didn't know was that there were two witnesses in the wilderness that day."

Roxy Roo shouted, interrupting Bones, "Ferrel! That's exactly what Ferrel the hermit cat told us!"

Chapter Fourteen

They all looked at Roxy Roo, and everyone knew they were all wondering the same thing. Who was the other witness?

"Go on! Go on!" Silver said again anxiously. "Please hurry! Finish telling us what you know!"

Bones continued with the rest of the story. "We all know the professor made the most potent catnip on the island, and because of that, he became the most prominent and wealthy Meow cat. Professor Potamus was shocked when he found out that Professor Katnip also believed that he should control all creatures on Tyrtle Island. The only way he could achieve that was to make himself the master over an army of bullkats and use them to force all the island creatures to… well, I'll put it like this… drink the catnip tea."

Silver's quills instinctively rose again as he looked at Bones and said, "Are you saying it was Professor Katnip that attacked Wig Waggle and killed the porky porcupines?"

"Yes, well, he sent the gang of bullkats. He has concocted an irresistible catnip formula in his secret lab, deep down in Kats Caves. The formula makes a bullkat extremely aggressive and, combined with their cursed nature, it will make them more evil than ever before. They became addicted to the professor's catnip formula, and now he has the bullkats under his control."

"I've heard enough about the professor! What about my family?" Silver demanded, rattling his silver quills along his back.

"Who is the other witness?" Roxy Roo asked, almost demanding an answer.

Calico and Bones started to turn and walk away, but Calico hesitated for a second to answer her question. "I'm the other witness. Come on, let's go rescue Silver's family."

"Those poor little porkies," said Roxy Roo, following behind them. "They must be very frightened and confused."

Silver ran faster than he had ever run. Well, as fast as a porcupine can possibly run. He was determined to stay up with the two frenemies leading the way down the beach toward the entrance into Kats Caves.

In the beginning, the mythical lava monster was formed far beneath

Tyrtle Island. The molten blood of the monster flowed freely, carving out a labyrinth of lava tubes spreading like veins underneath the island. The lava rock that was frozen in time created a maze of passageways leading to innumerable secret caves and undiscovered caverns. The fear of the lava monster itself had been the guardian of the treasures hidden in those underground chambers. From the mouths of these unknown chambers were the beginnings of a puzzle of pathways and underground tunnels that twisted and turned their ways to the windows of Kats Caves. These windows were the eyes through which the monster observed the world outside.

There was tremendous anticipation as they approached the eyes of Kats Caves that looked out over the shoreline.

Boo looked puzzled, asking, "How do you know which one to take? There are so many cave entrances to choose from."

"Oh, don't you worry about how I know. I told you. I know some things," said Bones, smiling like a sunbird.

"Now don't start that again!" said Chops, glancing around at all the cave openings.

The truth was that Calico knew just about every twist and turn through the tunnels and every secret cavern in Kats Caves. Bones also knew the caves as well as any bullkat and much better than any Meow cat, including the professor.

Bones had a deep, dark secret that was unknown to Boo and his friends. In fact, nobody knew Bones' history except for Professor Potamus, Professor Katnip, and a few others of the Meow cat elders.

"What if it's a trap?" said Chops, whispering to Boo and Roxy Roo, a worried look on his face.

Following a few steps behind Silver, Boo contemplated Chops' question for a few seconds and said, "The way I see it, Bones and Calico didn't hurt us when they had the chance. I think we can trust them." He paused, thinking about what he had just said.

Raindrops started to fall as storm clouds quickly gathered in the tropical skies above.

Boo raised his paw in the air and said, "Chop-chop."

"What?" said Chops, looking at Boo, confused.

"What, what?" replied Boo, wiping the raindrops off his furry forehead.

"You asked me a question," said Chops. "You said, 'Chops, Chops.'"

"I said, 'Chop-chop.' As in… hurry up! Step on it! Get a move on!" shouted Boo, slapping Chops across his pointed ears, flicking water droplets into the air.

A brilliant double rainbow extended across the dark blue ocean, touching the tip of the Land of No End. The rocky cliffs of the peninsula glowed with all the colors of the rainbow as if the artist had taken one quick stroke with his brush.

"The Tyrtle Tunnel," said Boo, thinking about the island legend.

Calico and Bones led the way for the rescuers through one of the many cave openings leading into the body of the island's old lava monster, also known as Kats Caves. They jumped up through the rocky opening and hopped into a dimly-lit cavern. The light flickering off the walls came from a burning torch hanging inside. They walked through, watching their shadows dancing along the walls.

The cave had several dark passageways, quietly inviting those who dared to enter down into its steep, unknown paths. Calico did not waver and continued his quick pace along beside the damp tunnel walls, weaving in and out of passageways.

Calico pointed to the slippery, thin edge of the natural bridge and said, "Be careful. Only walk where I walk."

The walls of the cavern were riddled with holes that were filled with steam rising from the pools of lava and water gurgling far below in the lava monster's bowels.

Calico carefully led them over a thin, arched natural bridge that was partially eroded away from the constant beating of a small waterfall that splashed on one side of the lava rocks. He paused for a moment to make sure the trail of troopers was keeping up in the maze of tunnels and bridges. They stopped in a grand cavern with natural chimneys extending up into the blackness. Their torch lights were swallowed up into the darkness.

"Are we there yet?" asked Chops, trying to break the awkward silence that seemed to be magnified as they stood between the cold, dark walls of the massive cavern.

They could hear each other's breathing, standing quietly in the flickering light, while their eyes glanced around at the monstrous black walls of the cavern. The long stalactites dangled down from the shadows of the towering ceiling above their heads like spears waiting to drop at the lava monster's command.

Silver, being a porcupine, was not able to move as fast as a cat. Despite his eager anticipation of seeing his family again, he was the last to enter the cavern. Upon entering the cavern he stopped and listened closely to the sounds he heard off in the distance.

"What's that sound?" he said excitedly. "I know that sound!"

Everyone heard the echo of the rainwater trickling through the cracks in the lava monster's rocky skin, and flowing into the underground rivers running deep below. Silver's ears were tuned into a more precious sound.

"It's the water from the—" said Bones.

Silver quickly interrupted him, shouting, "No, I hear voices! I hear porky voices!" He took a few steps inside the tunnel, concentrating on the sounds echoing through the dark passage. He scooted as fast as he could through the cavern until his back full of silver quills disappeared into the dark tunnel.

Boo, Roxy Roo, and Chops hesitated for a minute, listening for the sound of the voices before following Silver into the black tunnel. At the same time, but from a different tunnel, they began to hear the faint screeching of the bullkats heading toward the cavern they were all standing in.

Bones looked intensely at Calico and said, "Calico, take everyone and follow Silver. I will do my best to slow down the bullkats. I'm certain they've picked up on the porcupine's scent. Go to Sparkling Caverns. They'll be safe there." Bones paused briefly before saying, "For a little while anyway."

Bones stepped away from them and stumbled forward before regaining his posture. He continued walking in his usual disturbing manner toward the tunnel which would lead him in the direction of the oncoming bullkats.

"Smell ya later," said Chops. "I'm going to try and catch the stinky porcupine."

Calico laughed and said, "Follow me."

Everyone fell in line behind Calico and followed his pouncing pawprints through the tiny tunnels, deeper into the lava monster's abyss. The sound of the rushing water became louder as the passageway descended and curved around until it finally opened into a spectacular cavern.

Their paws came to a skidding stop at the end of the pathway, sending the crumbling black lava rock over the edge to drop straight down into a fast-moving underground river.

Silver was pacing back and forth along the edge of the divide, waiting anxiously for his friends to join him. The river flowed through the center of the cavern, creating a massive gap between the two sides. Silver and his companions were on one side of the chamber, seemingly trapped in the land of the cursed bullkats, who were rapidly approaching right behind them.

On the other side of the great divide, in the land of the living, were Silver's family awaiting their rescue. The cavern itself was filled with rock formations that looked like golden candles that were melting. As they scooted along the crumbling edge with their torches, the rocky wonderland and the river flowing below were brought to life. The flickering light showed off the splendor of the stalactites as the light reflected off the swiftly-moving water, casting a spectrum of natural colors dancing across the cavern walls.

Silver looked longingly across at the sweet faces of his porky-mate and precious little ones standing in the dark on the other side of the divide. He was so close to them, yet still felt worlds apart.

The little porkies' voices echoed off the walls, calling out from just beyond the divide, "Poppi! Poppi!"

Roxy Roo heard their squeaky little voices crying out from across the darkness and shouted, "Hold on, little ones! We're coming to get you!"

Chops looked at the river flowing far below the sharp drop-off and the great expanse between them and the little porcupines.

"We're coming to get you!" shouted Chops. "All we have to do… is figure out how," he mumbled quietly and then sighed as he looked at the great divide.

Calico darted into a small dead-end tunnel and called out to Silver and the others, "Hurry! Grab the logs along the wall!"

They knew the raging bullkats were getting closer every second. There was no time to waste if they were going to get across to the other side of the cavern before the bullkats reached them.

Calico and Roxy Roo each picked up one end of a long log and raised it up on its end. Calico placed one end between two rocks near the edge of the drop-off, being careful not to stumble and fall into the fast-moving water below.

Calico looked at Roxy Roo and shouted, "Let it go on three. One! Two! Three!" The log fell across the ominous gap above the river. The log hit the other side with a thud, bouncing up and down until it finally settled in between the rocks on the opposite side.

Boo and Silver grabbed the other long log and raised it high into the air. They tipped it over the expanse between the cavern, and it quickly fell into place right next to the first one.

"Calico, you can go first," said Chops, always ready to volunteer somebody else.

Silver was not debating or waiting for anyone to decide who would cross first. The porcupine had already started his balancing act, walking slowly across the twin logs to the other side. He could see the movement of the spooky water below his feet as his toes gripped the logs with each step. Looking across the divide, he saw three little figures standing at the other end of the logs with their paws stretched out toward him.

"Keep calm and Tyrtle on!" yelled Chops, holding the ends of the logs steady with his powerful paws.

Silver's strong curved claws dug into the wood as he inched his way over the life-saving bridge and closer to his family with each movement of his prickly paws. The excited squeals of his little ones grew louder with each step he took. His friends, with paws pumping in the air, rooted him on from the other side of the cavern.

"Chops, you're next," said Calico. "But wait until Silver's safely across."

Silver's tail tapped on one log and then the other as he took his last step, stumbling forward and tumbling onto the ledge.

Roxy Roo gasped as she watched Silver and yelled, "Oh, no! Silver!" She was relieved when she saw his silhouette embrace his family and said, "Oh, don't do that. You scared me to death."

"I hear 'em. The bullkats are coming!" exclaimed Calico in his raspy bullkat voice.

Everyone exchanged nervous looks in the dim light and hesitated for a second, wondering who should be the next one to cross.

"Chops! Go now!" shouted Boo. "And don't look down!" Boo steadied the logs as Chops took his first step with his big paw. "Dig in with your claws! You're a Meow cat. You can do this!"

"Once Chops is across, you and Roxy Roo go," said Calico to Boo, glancing back over his shoulder into the dark passageway. "When you get to the other side, ride the river until you see a cavern that has sparkling walls. You can't miss it. Make sure you get out of the river there, because it's only a short distance from there to the waterfall. If you don't get out there, then it's a long way down the falls."

"Waterfall?" said Boo. "What do you mean—"

"Go!" interrupted Calico as Roxy Roo pulled Boo by the arm.

Silver watched the dramatic scene from the other side of the river. His family was wrapped around him as they watched Chops take his last clumsy steps across the logs. Boo and Roxy Roo walked across sure-footed and almost had to push Chops from behind as they took their last steps.

Once they were safely across, Calico pushed the logs off the edge of the cavern. With eyes wide, they all watched as the logs tumbled into the swift-moving water below. The life-saving bridge was quickly swept away into the darkness.

"Calico!" yelled Boo, his voice bouncing off the cavern walls.

Boo, Roxy Roo, and Chops stood motionless at the cliff's edge, gazing out over the chasm, wishing they could help Calico, but he was now beyond their reach.

The squeaks of Silver's family could be heard as they huddled together next to the Meow cats. They watched the friendly bullkat disappear back into the tunnel, heading for a straight-on collision with the angry bullkats.

With Calico now out of sight, their eyes slowly refocused, trying to absorb the natural beauty of the gold, black, and copper formations surrounding them. Their shadows danced off the cavern walls, and the watery ribbon patterns bounced off the jagged ceiling above them like the colors of a stormy tropical sky.

"Why didn't Calico come with us?" Boo asked Roxy Roo, perplexed.

Before responding to his question, she was briefly hypnotized by the patterns of light reflecting off his blue eyes.

"Are you OK?" asked Boo.

"I don't know," she said, frowning.

"You don't know if you're OK… or are you just now answering my first question?" asked Boo, looking concerned but smiling at her.

"Oh, sorry. I'm not sure. Bones told him to show us the way to Sparkling Caverns, and next thing I knew, he was tossing the logs into the river," she said.

Roxy Roo turned around to see Silver and his family together again. Her frown quickly turned to a smile, and she was overcome with joy looking at all their cheerful faces. With his family gathered around, Silver's two big front teeth were fully exposed as he smiled joyfully. He was so excited to show off his little porkies to his island friends.

"Everyone, I would like you to meet Briar Bee and Briar Bud," said Silver, with his paws placed on his little ones' shoulders. "And this, my dear friends, this is my beautiful porky-mate, Briar Bow," he said, sighing heavily and puffing up his quills on his back.

Roxy Roo touched Briar Bee and Briar Bud gently on their adorable little pink noses. "You are the cutest little creatures I've ever seen," she said, extending her paw to their adorable mother, Briar Bow.

"Hi ya, porcupettes!" said Chops enthusiastically, running his paw over Briar Bud's head.

"I wouldn't do… that," said Roxy Roo, watching Chops yank his paw back with several quills sticking out.

"MeOuchy! MeOuch!" yelled Chops, jumping around in the dark cavern while holding his paw up in the air.

Briar Bee and Briar Bud squeaked and kazooed with laughter as they watched Chops' theatrical antics.

After Chops stopped jumping around, Briar Bud looked at him, exposing his two little orange teeth, and said shyly, "Sorry, Mr. Chops."

"Briar, Briar, pants on fire," said Chops painfully.

Roxy Roo smiled and gently touched Briar Bud on his nose. She then glared at Chops, saying, "Chops, don't be so mean… it was an accident."

"I hate to break this up, but we have to stop lollygagging around. We must get going," said Silver, looking back at the other side of the cavern.

The chattering stopped for a few minutes as they all looked around for a way down to the river's shore. The sound of the roaring water below them could be heard as it flowed deeper into Kats Caves.

Across the cavern was a much scarier sound. The screeching of the bullkats and the scraping of their sharp claws coming through the tunnel were getting much closer. Then, in a flash, a bullkat came flying out of the dark tunnel, scraping his claws against the hard lava rocks on the edge of the cavern. Without breaking his stride, the hideous cat leaped into the air and soared high above the deadly chasm.

Boo couldn't believe his eyes. He was mesmerized, watching in horror as the bullkat's legs climbed through the darkness. The creature snarled, lashing out at the air with its claws extended. With every evil bone in its body, the bullkat tried to reach the opposite edge of the expanse.

"Get back! Everyone back!" screamed Boo, pushing them all toward the back of the cavern.

Boo watched in shock as the bullkat came flying toward him with its legs stretched out, grasping for life. The bullkat's forward motion stopped like he was frozen in mid-air, inches short of the edge of the cliff.

Boo's eyes followed the hideous creature's every move as the bullkat fell below the ledge and vanished into the dark, moving water below. By this time, all the other raging bullkats were lined up across the cavern, pacing back and forth, lashing out at one another. They screeched and clawed in aggravation at once again missing out on their feeding frenzy. Their next meal would have to wait awhile longer as there was no way for them to cross over to the other side.

"That was a little terrifying, but totally amazing," said Chops, stunned by what they had all just witnessed.

"'That was totally terrifying' is more like it!" said Roxy Roo loudly, following right behind Boo and the others as they climbed their way down the rocks toward the river.

"Well, no easy way about it," said Boo, surprising everyone by just jumping into the water tail first. He was immediately swept away by the current and disappeared out of sight.

"How rude! He didn't even say goodbye!" shouted Chops loudly above the sound of the water. "See you at the Sparkling Caverns… I hope!"

Chops hesitated a moment, poking his paw into the frigid, moving water in front of him. He jumped in and was swept away, following Boo down the river. Chops could be heard screaming and yelling something about fish in the water as he floated down the underground river.

Roxy Roo jumped in the water with Silver and Briar Bow right behind. Silver and Briar Bow held their little porcupines tightly in their grasp while riding down the river leading to the Sparkling Caverns.

One by one, the force of the river sloshed them around in circles as they flowed through the dark cavern. The rapid current of the water pulled them up and down like they were riding through the ocean on the back of a spy-hopping whale. Suddenly, the movement of the water slowed enough to allow Boo to fish them out of the river and onto the rocky bank.

"What a ride!" shouted Chops, shaking the water off his big furry body.

Water flew everywhere as the cats vigorously shook their heads and poked their tongues out of the sides of their mouths, trying to expel every drop from their furry faces.

When all the wiggling and jiggling finally stopped, they were astonished once again. With eyes wide and mouths gaping, they looked around at the spectacle of sparkling rocks. None of them had ever seen anything quite like this. The walls twinkled with as many diamonds, gemstones, and gold veins as there were stars twinkling in the heavenly sky.

Roxy Roo jumped up onto the cavern floor in awe of the twinkling display illuminating the cavern walls.

"I don't know how much more I can take," said Roxy Roo, looking straight up.

Although Sparkling Caverns were a spectacular sight, diamonds, gemstones, and gold were not often worn by the Meow cats or any other island creatures. The natural minerals provided no use to the creatures and therefore held no real value.

Catnip was the real treasure. The exotic herb was by far the most valuable and precious commodity to the Meow cats and many other creatures on Tyrtle Island.

"Now, this is the cat's meow," said Chops, helping himself to a few rainbow-less rainbow fish that were flopping around in a clear pool of water.

Chops liked catnip, but without a doubt, his number-one commodity on the island was any kind of fish. He loved fish and especially fish that happened to be flopping around right in front of him.

"We can't stay here too long. We have to find the secret lab where the professor is making the dangerous catnip formula," said Boo, watching Chops munch on the cave fish.

"Let's wait here for Calico. He'll show us the way there," said Silver, helping his family out of the river and up the rocky shore.

Gathering in the center of the beautiful cavern, they all rested, gazing up like they were sitting outside under the starry night sky.

Roxy Roo smiled and said, "Enchanting."

"Unbelievable," said Boo, beaming.

"I'm tickled to bits," said Silver, content to hold his family close again under the brilliant cave stars.

"Scrumptious," said Chops, moaning, rubbing his belly and feeling like it was time for a short catnap.

The little porkies' two orange front teeth stuck out in front of their faces as they smiled and watched Chops. The big Meow cat flicked a cave cricket through the air just before making himself comfortable against a hard rock. Their eyes grew heavy as they rested securely between Silver and Briar Bow.

Everyone agreed that Chops had the right idea.

"I'll keep watch," said Silver.

Boo smiled at Silver. Exhausted, he was ready for a catnap and quickly fell asleep.

turtle

CHAPTER FIFTEEN: ZOOMING AND ZIPLINES

Boo woke up in the dark to the soothing sound of crickets rubbing their wings together. He had the most wonderful feeling inside. Waking up happy was not unusual for Boo. He was usually sleeping next to Jesse, which was where he found his happy place, and that's exactly where he was at this moment. He wasn't sure why, but he had the feeling that he had just been somewhere spectacular. His eyes peered past the dark stone walls and followed the silhouettes of the tall trees toward the night sky where he could still see a few twinkling stars above.

Boo purred softly and thought, *Purr-fect*. He knew that this wonderful feeling and the twinkling stars were somehow connected together.

Instinctively his ears twitched and stood straight up. The chorus of crickets was now silent and replaced by the far-off sound of creatures trampling through the rainforest.

It must be the bullkats, he thought.

He jumped up, pouncing back and forth on Jesse and Tinman. Jesse shrugged Boo off and rolled over, mumbling some unknown words. Boo's pouncing around was nothing unusual. Jesse was used to getting pounced on early in the morning, especially when Boo was hungry.

"Everybody up!" shouted Tinman, giving Jesse and Caleb swift kicks on their backsides. "Come on, get up. Gotta get movin'!"

Tinman scrambled to quickly gather their gear. Having known Boo since he was a kitten, Tinman knew that this amazing cat would only pounce on them for a couple of reasons: when he was hungry or when he sensed danger. This time, Tinman was pretty sure it wasn't because Boo was hungry. Tinman was well aware that Boo's hearing was much better than theirs, and if Boo was hearing strange sounds coming from the rainforest, it just might be the bullkats.

He gave Boo a cat snack and rubbed his furry head, saying, "You're a life-saver."

Tinman didn't hear anything unusual, but he wasn't going to take any chances and wait around to find out if the sounds were bullkats or not.

"Hurry up!" shouted Tinman, rushing past the ancient black and gray stone walls.

Jesse was half asleep as he picked up Boo and tucked him down into his backpack. Boo looked like a grumpy cat after being shoved down inside the large backpack with only his head sticking out the top.

Jesse grinned and said, "Sorry, big guy. I know you don't like this."

You think? thought Boo, meowing loudly as he stared at the back of Jesse's neck.

"Look how cute he looks," said Honey Bee, rubbing the top of Boo's head.

With a scrunched-up frown on Boo's face, Jesse followed Honey Bee and Caleb out of the old stone structure and into the wet rainforest. They followed closely behind Tinman, who was headed north toward the cliffs.

"Our best chance is to get to the cliffs. We can't outrun the bullkats through the rainforest, but we can through the trees," said Tinman, picking up the pace.

Caleb ran to catch up with his friends as they moved swiftly under the canopy of trees, dodging the exotic ferns and the heart-shaped leaves of the taro plants.

"What if… they catch us?" asked Caleb, breathing heavily.

"Well, we have the rainbow plants and that should slow them down a little. I brought this just in case," said Tinman, pulling out his tranquilizer gun. "It's only a last resort since there are so many of them. You know, only if they leave me no other choice."

"I feel a little better now," said Caleb, pulling his ancient war club and slingshot out of his backpack. "I brought these along also… just in case."

Jesse knew his uncle's heart and had no doubt that Tinman cherished all of God's creatures. Even the creatures that could possibly hurt them. He knew the only reason Tinman would ever hurt an island creature would be in self-defense or to protect someone else from getting hurt.

Jesse smiled at Caleb and shouted, "Remember, only if we need it! Keep calm and Tyrtle on!"

Tinman and Jesse had been down this trail before and knew there was a tree-top zipline trek through this part of the rainforest. They remembered the zipline ended at a huge banyan tree that grew at the edge of the cliffs overlooking the ocean. The banyan tree had a long rope that could be used to escape to the shore.

"Caleb, slow down a minute," said Honey Bee, trying not to alarm him as she scooted a red-spotted spider off the middle of his backpack.

Caleb stopped in his tracks to look at the impressive spider as it crawled along the ground. "Look at the size of that thing," he said, backing up a step.

"Don't worry. It's not poisonous," said Honey Bee, looking back over her shoulder.

The unnatural sounds of the bullkats could now be heard in the distance, and they knew the cursed cats were getting closer every minute. Tinman and Jesse continued up the trail while Honey Bee and Caleb were being entertained by the big red-spotted spider crawling into the rainforest.

The thrashing of the rainforest plants and crunching of twigs startled Honey Bee and Caleb. They looked around, peering into the trees and plants. They were surprised when they saw two heads sticking out through the giant leaves of the taro plants.

"Did you see those scary-looking wild cats?" asked a young man, cautiously stepping out from the middle of the plants and into the clearing. An anxious young girl with a backpack followed closely behind him.

"What are you guys doing in this part of the rainforest?" asked Honey Bee. "You guys need to get out of here. Those scary-looking cats are called bullkats, and they're headed in our direction. You can follow us if you want."

The girl looked at them frantically and said, "Thanks, but our car is just down the trail."

She ran across the trail, tripping over a huge tree root.

"I thought those creatures were just an old island legend," said the young man. "We gotta get to our car."

They both ran off down the trail with Honey Bee and Caleb shouting at them to come back. The hikers didn't even bother to turn around, just vanished into the rainforest.

"I hope they make it," said Honey Bee, pausing for a moment to listen for the sound of the bullkats.

"Jesse!" shouted Honey Bee through the trees. "Jesse, sounds like they're gaining on us!"

Tinman and Jesse waited next to a huge tree trunk at the bottom of the first zipline tower. Honey Bee and Caleb ran quickly to catch up with them.

Honey Bee stretched her neck back, looking straight up at the towering tree, and said, "I think they're right behind us!"

She stopped for a moment and leaned over with her hands on her knees, trying to catch her breath. "We saw a couple people hiking out there—tried to warn them."

"Where'd they go?" asked Tinman, taking a couple steps away from the tree, looking down the trail.

Caleb wheezed, trying to catch his breath.

"Said they were headed back to the parking lot to find their car," said Caleb, with a funny look on his face, feeling nauseous. "Hope they make it."

"It's Tarzan time," said Jesse, climbing up the tree toward the top of the canopy. "Two at a time, and make sure you hold on tight."

Two at a time? What about me? thought Boo, bouncing up and down with each big step that Jesse took as he climbed upward toward the top of the towering tree.

Several minutes later and far below them, the bullkats rushed up violently, crashing heads-first into the bottom of the huge tree trunk. The wild cats hesitated for just a few seconds before starting their climb upwards, scrambling through the tangled tree limbs and bunched-up branches. The snarling of the evil cats pierced the air as they climbed and clawed their way up the tall tree trunk closer to Jesse and his friends.

"Looks to me like they're pretty good tree climbers," said Caleb, glancing down at the oncoming bullkats.

Jesse held the zipline handles steady and yelled, "Bee and Caleb, GO! GO! GO!"

He gave them a hard shove off the platform, catapulting them over the canopy of rainforest trees.

"Good thing the bullkats don't know how to zipline!" cried out Caleb. "Wahoooo!"

He zipped off with his feet raised in the air, zooming through the trees, hollering at the top of his lungs.

Honey Bee catapulted forward through the air, feeling a shiver of excitement come over her. The beauty of the island once again completely captured her imagination as she zipped along like she was on a magic carpet ride. The fear of the bullkats was quickly forgotten as she flew high above the top of the rainforest, taking in every natural detail with the eyes of a hawk. The bird's-eye view provided a panoramic scene of the rugged northern cliffs. She watched the crystal-clear waters of the Roundabout Waterfall cascade down and disappear over the cliffs into the turquoise waters embracing the coast of the island.

"Tag, you're it!" hollered Caleb, zipping by Honey Bee on his way to the next zipline platform.

Caleb was moving fast and furiously, smashing hard into the next platform. Honey Bee was only a few seconds behind him.

"Incoming!" yelled Honey Bee, streaking past Caleb and crashing into the tree trunk.

"Thanks a lot," said Honey Bee, picking herself up off the platform.

"You're welcome," said Caleb. "But I don't think I did anything."

"Exactly! You're supposed to keep me from crashing into the tree!" said Honey Bee loudly, catching Tinman and Jesse who came flying in not far behind.

Jesse and Tinman looked down through the trees and saw the trail of bullkats thrashing through the rainforest plants. They were beating a path of destruction and quickly heading toward the next zipline platform.

"Game on!" shouted Jesse, grabbing the next set of zipline handles. He steadied them for Honey Bee and Caleb.

"Ladies first!" said Caleb, holding the zipline handles tightly and sailing off through the open air high above the ground. "Woo-hoo!"

Honey Bee held on tight, coasting along over the exotic landscape next to Caleb, with Jesse and Tinman following right behind them.

The tropical air brushed against their faces. The island wind moved through the towering bamboo forest as the giant stalks below them swayed back and forth against the green landscape. The dancing bamboo was accompanied by a symphony of sound as the strong wind blew through the mighty stalks.

This amazing world would only last for a few more seconds before they were reminded that the race was still on. They were only seconds ahead of the bullkats, who were racing to reach the last zipline stand. Jesse and his friends knew they were not out of danger yet.

All this excitement was a little much for Boo. *Now I understand why cats don't have wings*, he thought, relieved that the ride was over as they reached the last platform. He had never experienced anything quite like this before. He wasn't prepared for what was coming next.

"Quickly, get the rope from behind the tree!" called out Tinman, landing with his feet squarely on the last platform.

The last stop of the zipline was built around the massive trunk of one of the tallest trees in the rainforest. The tree had grown upward, towering over the side of the cliff, and had a wide platform built around it. The structure provided the zipliners with a complete and unobstructed view of the coastline.

Honey Bee swiftly walked around the back side of the tree and, just before she disappeared, she yelled, "I got it!"

There was silence for a few seconds which seemed like an eternity to Jesse.

"Bee, did you find it? The rope should be anchored to the back of the trunk," said Jesse, setting down his backpack and wondering why it was taking her so long.

"Be right back," said Jesse, rubbing Boo's head.

There were some rustling sounds coming from behind the tree and, all of a sudden, Honey Bee screamed loudly. Jesse rushed toward the tree and then stopped dead in his tracks. He was shocked to see Professor Katnip step out from behind the tree with Honey Bee right in front of him.

"My dear, sweet friends," said Professor Katnip, smirking and holding his arm around Honey Bee's neck, pressing a gun hard against her back. "Are you having a bee-utiful day?"

Jesse, Tinman, and Caleb stood in front of the professor, in disbelief at the situation unfolding before them.

"Let her go!" shouted Tinman, realizing his worst fears had come true.

"I want those lovely plants you have," demanded Professor Katnip, glancing down at the bullkats gathering below and gnawing at the bottom of the tree.

"What if I say no?" said Tinman, looking into Honey Bee's worried eyes.

"Let me explain this to you… shall I say… in scientific terms," said Professor Katnip. "Either you can give me the plants, or I can let you experiment with the nice little kittens."

By this time, a number of bullkats had clawed their way up the tree and through the giant limbs. Some of the creatures bounced around like cats on hot coals. The bullkats scowled at their prey, waiting for Professor Katnip's next command.

"The plants!" shouted the professor, glaring at them.

"OK! OK!" shouted Tinman. He slowly took off his backpack and set it down on the platform. He started to open the flap.

"Throw me the pack!" snapped Professor Katnip.

At that exact moment, the loud buzzing sound of a bee filled the air. A big black bumblebee buzzed in front of the professor's face, and he quickly removed his arm from around Honey Bee's neck, slapping at the buzzing bee.

Honey Bee could not help but smile, if only for a fraction of a second. It was amusing to her that at this exact moment it was a bee that was antagonizing the professor.

In a flash, a stone whipped through the air off of Caleb's slingshot, hitting the professor in the middle of his forehead. The impact brought him down to his knees on the platform. The professor's gun fell out of his hand, slid across the platform, and vanished over the side. Everyone listened as the weapon went bouncing down the tree, hitting one limb after another until it finally made a thud on the ground. The professor leaned over the edge of the platform, watching his gun sink into the soft mud and disappear.

Honey Bee ducked as Jesse whipped around, flinging rainbow plants at the surrounding bullkats. The cats jumped and scattered instinctively down to the lower limbs of the tree, out of range of the toxic plants. Jesse leaped forward and tackled the professor to the ground.

"Call them off! Now!" shouted Jesse, struggling to hold the professor down against the platform.

"Let him up, Jesse," said Tinman, pointing his tranquilizer gun toward the professor. "Honey Bee, take Boo. Everyone get down to the beach."

Jesse looked at Boo, who had a very unusual look on his face. Jesse moved a few steps away, letting Honey Bee pass with Boo in her arms. He wanted to keep his distance from Boo since he still had a handful of the toxic rainbow plants in his hand. He was hoping the potent plants would hold off the bullkats just long enough to allow them to climb down the rope and safely escape to the ocean below.

"You best hurry. They're starting to lick their lips," said Professor Katnip. His forced smile quickly turned into an irritated look. "The scent of the plants will only hold them off for so long. I promise you: this is far from over."

Tinman glared at the professor and said, "This gun is intended for the bullkats. Don't make the mistake of thinking I won't use it on you."

Jesse leaned out over the edge of the cliff and could see that Honey Bee and Caleb had just about reached the bottom. They were almost down the dangling rope that was sloshing about in the white water below. It was high tide, and he could see the waves crashing over the rugged rocks, smashing into the cliffs.

"Boy Scout skills are coming in handy now," said Jesse, watching Tinman tie the professor's hands to the zipline stand as he kept his eyes on the bullkats.

Tinman knew the bullkats had no way down to the ocean floor, and the professor would make no attempt to go down the rope without his evil pets. They would be forced to go back through the rainforest and down the trail to the ocean side of Kats Caves.

"They're down! Let's go!" yelled Jesse, waving Tinman toward the cliff.

Professor Katnip grinned as he watched one of his larger bullkats quietly sneaking back up the tree, hopping from limb to limb. The bullkat crept slowly, step by step across the back side of the platform, inching closer toward Jesse and his uncle. With each passing minute, the rainbow plants grew weaker, losing their effect on the bullkats.

"Good kitty," whispered the professor, anticipating the cat's every move.

From the corner of his eye, Jesse saw the ugly creature sneaking toward them and crouching, ready to attack. He grabbed the rope tightly and yanked Tinman by the shirt just as the charging bullkat took a giant leap forward.

Jesse and Tinman let out their best Tarzan yells as they leaped out into the sky, high above the crashing waves. Tinman reached out for the rope, wrapping his fingers around it as they were both propelled out over the cliff and away from the striking bullkat. They felt the adrenaline rush through them as the forward motion of the rope carried them out and away from the edge of the cliff.

Suspended in the air for a brief moment, time stood still for Jesse and Tinman as they dangled on the rope high above the rippling blue waves. The two daredevils released their hands at the same time, and their howling screams could be heard in unison all the way down to the ocean below. Honey Bee and Caleb felt their stomachs drop. The rhythm of their hearts beat faster and pounded louder inside their ears as they looked up in horror from the rocks below. Jesse and Tinman splashed feet first into the water and disappeared under the waves.

"Jesse!" Honey Bee cried, standing on her tiptoes, bracing herself against the face of the cliff. She looked frantically through the blown-out waves, searching for any sign of Jesse and his uncle.

"Come on, you guys! Quit playing around!" shouted Caleb, scanning the white water for any sign of their friends.

"On the rocks!" yelled Honey Bee, covering her mouth with her hand and pointing to the jagged rocks.

"Ahhhh!" screamed Caleb, looking at the body lying on the rocks.

The attacking bullkat had found his final resting place atop a bed of saw-toothed black lava rocks anchored to the ocean floor. Honey Bee and Caleb watched as the powerful waves swept the bullkat's mangled body off the deadly rocks and buried the creature in a watery grave.

Honey Bee looked at Caleb with hope in her eyes. With all her strength, she called out once again across the waves, "Jesse! Tinman!"

"Look!" said Caleb, spotting a giant leatherback sea turtle as it paddled magnificently through the rippling water.

Their spirits were lifted watching the amazing creature glide in and out of the waves as the turtle followed the coastline around Tyrtle Island.

"Oh, thank You, Lord," sighed Honey Bee, relieved to see the sea turtle passing in front of them. She knew it was a sign of a blessing from above whenever one saw a sea turtle, and this blessing could not have come at a better time.

All of a sudden, Honey Bee and Caleb heard faint voices calling out to them from over on the shore. Jesse and Tinman were shouting and waving their arms from atop the rocks piled up in front of the beach.

Honey Bee and Caleb grinned from ear to ear as they stepped carefully from rock to rock along the cliffs. They braced themselves against the splashing white water of the crashing waves. Step by step they carefully hopped over the scurrying rock crabs who were going about their daily duties of scavenging for a tiny morsel wherever they could find it.

Boo scanned the water, looking for some tasty treats, but the unusual sea creatures that he spotted from the safety of Honey Bee's arms did not look tasty at all. The friends tiptoed through the tide pools, placing their shoes carefully around prickly sea urchins and soft sea cucumbers who were resting on the ocean floor.

After reaching the shore, they quickly walked up to a grove of coconut trees where Jesse and Tinman were sitting, resting in the shade.

Honey Bee ran up to Jesse and Tinman and gave them each a big hug, squishing Boo in the process. She then punched Jesse in the arm and said, "You guys really scared us."

"Sorry, but there wasn't anything else we could do," said Jesse, rubbing his arm. "Before we could get to the beach, the current carried us around the cliffs."

"That was probably a little bit out of my comfort zone," said Caleb, trudging through the sand and plopping down under the shade trees.

"This should help get you back into your comfort zone," replied Tinman, handing Caleb one of the fallen coconuts he had quickly and skillfully opened.

Over the years, Tinman and Jesse had learned the art of conquering the coconut quickly and easily. Their years of exploring Tyrtle Island together had turned this island pastime into a competitive game of who could crack open the delicious treat the fastest. The winner was rewarded by being the first one to taste the refreshing water and sweet white meat.

"Who won?" asked Honey Bee, about to drink some of the sweet water from the coconut that Jesse handed her.

"I think Boo did. He didn't have to open any of them," said Tinman, still trying to catch his breath from the exhausting swim around the north point.

Jesse walked back into the grove of coconut palms, hunting for another coconut to crack open. Wandering through the grove he noticed something sticking out from the rocks at the bottom of the cliff. He became curious and pulled away some of the debris wedged between the rocks, exposing a very old-looking wooden structure.

"It can't be," he thought to himself, quickly clearing out some more of the dried-up fronds.

"Hey, come over here!" yelled Jesse to his friends as he continued to clear away more of the debris and throwing it aside. "Impossible!"

"Looks like you stumbled upon a very, very old canoe," said Honey Bee, helping him clear out the opening.

Jesse goggled at them in total disbelief and said, "Unbelievable... Do you know what this is?"

"Ummm, I'm no genius, but looks to me like an old moldy, dilapi-
dated, crusty boat?" said Caleb. "Just a guess, though. Why? What do you
think it is?"

Jesse was quiet for a few seconds staring at the ancient canoe. Everyone
stared at Jesse and then looked back at the canoe, wondering what this was
all about.

"Jesse, what is it?" asked Honey Bee, pulling on the side of the canoe
and sliding it out of its resting place behind the rocks.

Tinman walked up through the palms, munching on his signature can
of ham. "Hey, found us a new boat?" he asked, laughing out loud. "Looks
like it's going to need a little TLC before we can make that one seaworthy."

"It's the cat-a-canoe!" said Jesse, still looking at the crumbling wooden
structure in disbelief. "Boo and his friends. You know… the porcupine and
the cats. They hid their canoe right here."

They all gave Jesse a crazy confused look.

"From my dream," said Jesse, looking around at everyone like they
should understand what he was talking about.

I did? thought Boo, sniffing the old structure and rubbing his damp
orange fur up against it.

"Are you telling us that this canoe is in the same place that you left it in
your dream?" asked Tinman, looking at Jesse somewhat confused.

"Well, yes… I mean, not where I left it. Where Boo left it," said Jesse,
feeling frustrated. "You know what I mean. I told you already, I'm Boo in
my dream."

"This just keeps getting weirder and weirder," said Caleb, walking back
toward the beach throwing his arms up.

"It's really hard to explain it," said Jesse, frustrated and breathing heavily. "It's kind of confusing… even for me… and it's my dream."

He walked over and softly pressed his fingers over the detailed edges of
the wooden image carved on the stern of the cat-a-canoe. The worn and
weathered bird image still resembled Hiya, the macaw. Miraculously, it was
just like the macaw that had talked their ears off yesterday and the macaw
he remembered from his dream.

Jesse was perplexed at the new revelation before him. There was no doubt that the cat-a-canoe, unveiled from its rocky grave, was something much more than just a dream boat. He was sure that the cat-a-canoe in his dream and this ancient canoe were one and the same, and that, somehow, it had played a crucial part in the history of Tyrtle Island.

"Impossible," he thought out loud, still mesmerized by the cat-a-canoe before him.

It was getting late in the afternoon, and the sun was resting atop the peaks of the Majestic Mountains. Tinman thought it would be a good opportunity for them to catch up on a little rest. He realized that by this time Professor Katnip and the bullkats were probably just a little agitated with having to backtrack through the rainforest toward Kats Caves. Tinman had a pretty good idea of how long it would take the professor to get down to the south side of the caves. It was just about the same amount of time they needed for a catnap. Everyone settled in under the shade of the coconut palms and quickly dozed off.

"Could my dream be taking me back to a time before humans even arrived on Tyrtle Island?" Jesse thought, pulling Boo closer to him and rubbing his belly.

"You know, don't you, Boo?" he said, looking into Boo's wild blue eyes.

Jesse's eyes slowly closed, and he thought to himself, "Only for a few minutes."

A flash of hot, flowing lava flowed through his mind, and drops of sweat formed on his forehead. Jesse's eyes moved back and forth, and his nose twitched as a vision of beautiful precious stones danced in his head. He quickly drifted deeper into his island dream world. Sparkling Caverns slowly came back into view, filling up Jesse's imagination with visions of diamonds, gems, and veins of gold.

turtle

CHAPTER SIXTEEN: UP IN SMOKE

A STRANGE, RECURRING NOISE CAME FROM inside the cavern walls, interrupting Boo's daydream. Slowly raising himself up on all four paws, he walked closer toward the Sparkling Cavern wall. He listened intently, searching high and low for the source of the peculiar noise that was steadily growing louder. Boo cautiously poked his whiskers around the rocky corner then instinctively jumped back in a flash.

Out popped Calico, sliding tail first. The bullkat rushed out from one of the hidden tunnels, hollering, "Bullkat-crush! Bullkat-crush!"

The bullkat flew out of the tunnel, bounced on his backside, and then flipped through the air, landing on all four paws, just like cats always do.

By this time, all the creatures in the cavern were fully awake and wondering what all the commotion was about. After watching the bullkat fly through the air and perform a perfect landing, everyone stood wide-eyed looking at the acrobatic bullkat. The little porkies hugged Silver and Briar Bow's legs as they stared at the alarming creature.

"You gotta be careful, Boo. You almost got bullkat-crushed," said Calico, a big smile across his scary bullkat face.

They all stood motionless in shock, gazing at the bullkat standing before them.

"What's up, you courageous creatures?" shouted Calico, moving a little closer to them as he pounced like a kangaroo-cat into the middle of the cavern. "Paw-some! I knew you would all make it! Got the whole family of porcupines with you now!"

Boo smiled at him trying not to stare at Calico's spooky bullkat features. "You really know how to make an entrance, don't you? Just about clobbered me, though. By the way, I'm just curious. Where'd you disappear to?"

"Oh, yeah, sorry about that," Calico said nonchalantly. "I wanted to make sure that Bones was able to distract the other bullkats."

Meanwhile, Chops was looking at the terrified faces of Briar Bee and Briar Bud and said, "Oh, don't worry, little porkies. I know he looks pretty ugly in the dark, but Calico is really a very friendly bullkat. There is absolutely nothing to be afraid of. Here, let me show you."

Chops gulped and slowly walked up to Calico, placing his paw on the sharp point of one of his glowing white horns. He then cautiously walked around Calico and looked into his eyes as he slowly pulled on his long skinny tail. Out of nowhere, Chops suddenly yanked hard on the end of the bullkat's tail.

Calico jumped high into the air with claws out, bellowing out a hideous sound with his raspy bullkat voice: "RRRrrrrryum-yum-yum."

Chops leaped backwards and landed in his Meow-cat fighting position with all four paws spread out on the ground.

Calico landed back on the ground, smiling curiously, and yelled, "Got ya! Just kidding."

Breathing a sigh of relief, Chops regained his composure. He looked over at the little porkies and said, "See, little porkies? I told ya he's friendly."

Everyone looked at Chops and then back at Calico, who was still smiling after Chops' insulting comment and ridiculous stunts.

"What's wrong?" asked Chops. "Well, Calico doesn't look near as hideous as all the other bullkats I've seen. I mean—"

"Chops!" yelled Boo. "Just stop! Sorry, Calico. It's Chops… not much else I can say."

Roxy Roo looked at Calico anxiously and asked, "Where is he?"

"Who?" asked Calico, still thinking about Chops' hurtful comments and pranks. "Oh, yeah, Bones. He told me that he would meet us in the amphitheater."

They looked at each other and knew that, by now, Professor Katnip was most certainly waiting for them in the amphitheater, along with his gang of bullkats.

"Silver, I just want you to know that we'll do everything we can to protect your family," said Boo, looking at their little pink noses. "When we get in there, stay back toward the entrance. Chops will protect the little ones."

Chops did a double-take looking at Boo, then smiled confidently looking back at Silver's family.

Silver had his doubts. At this particular moment he was not overflowing with confidence in Chops.

"All I have to say to those creepy cats is… SCAT!… LITTLE BULLKAT!… and they'll run like a big rat!" said Chops, standing up on two paws, bellowing out a Meow-cat roar.

Silver's little ones squeaked out lovable laughs, but Boo, Roxy Roo, and Calico just smiled and rolled their eyes.

Silver looked directly at Chops and said, "I do believe you got this!"

Calico led the way through the lava tube surrounding them. The colorful geological formation seemed endless as it rolled along, twisting and turning like water rolling through a wave that was frozen in time. Then the massive lava tube began to crisscross with smaller tubes that wormed their way deeper under the island.

They crawled through tree root tips, dangling down by the thousands from the rainforest trees above. Over time and inch by inch, the long roots fought their way through the lava tubes' cracks and crevices, linking the environment below to the world above. The lava monster's rooted hairs dangled in front of them like a red curtain providing a grand entryway into the ominous amphitheater.

One by one they passed through the root curtain and entered a geological wonder known to Professor Katnip and Bones as the amphitheater.

"Welcome to the creepy creature show!" shouted a loud voice from the other side of the monstrous room.

They all recognized the voice of Professor Katnip as they cautiously entered the cavernous room which was lined with gloomy prison cells along the back black walls. Under the towering rocky ceiling at the center of the amphitheater were tables filled with a variety of exotic plants and smoking lab equipment. Between each of the tables sat gigantic black pots boiling over with concoctions that appeared to be in the process of making another batch of the professor's secret oils. Scattered across the cavern floor were holes filled with hot, bubbling minerals that steadily released puffs of steam from the lava monster's breath from far below. The professor had learned how to harness these rare and valuable resources to make his secret formulas.

Bones was standing at the back of the amphitheater in front of the professor. Boo and his friends slowly stepped forward, stopping just inside the entrance. Everywhere they looked, along the damp walls and within the dark cells, they saw nothing but hideous and hungry-looking bullkats.

"I knew we couldn't trust Bones," said Chops angrily, watching some of the bullkats step toward them.

"Stay back!" shouted Boo, opening the top flap of the catpack. "I've got a catpack filled with deadly rainbow plants!"

"What pretty colorful plants you have," said Professor Katnip, laughing like a mad scientist. "What do you think those are going to do? Those plants have very little effect on these cursed cats. They're addicted to the recoil oil now!"

Recoil oil was the professor's most powerful and toxic catnip potion.

Bewildered, Roxy Roo looked at the professor. "Why? Why would you do it? You have everything. You control almost everything in Treetop Woods and all the catnip for the Meow cats. What more could you want?"

The professor laughed out loud then said calmly, "It's very simple. I want the island... the whole island."

Roxy Roo had never before seen the coldness that she saw displayed in the eyes of the professor as he stood before her. She could not fathom the evil pride of a mind like Professor Katnip's. She wanted to cry, but at this moment she was much too angry to let her emotions get in the way.

She looked at the professor angrily, the hair on her tail standing straight up, and shouted, "That's crazy cat talk!"

"It's my island!" exclaimed Professor Katnip, straightening his red bow tie with a crazed look in his eyes.

"Your island?" shouted Boo. "Nobody owns the island! Tyrtle Island was created for all creatures!"

"You may be the 'King of Catnip,' but I think you've been drinking too much of it lately. You sound like a real wackadoo cat," said Chops. "I told you we couldn't trust Bones."

"I really thought we could trust you," said Boo angrily, looking at Bones. "I wanted to trust you."

Professor Katnip pushed Bones forward, knocking his tall black hat off his head and onto one of the lab tables. The hat rested against the bottles filled with recoil oil lined up on the table.

Bones hobbled closer to the lab table and stopped, standing motionless. At the same time, the biting bullkat named Skin stepped out from behind a large lava rock and crept slowly forward to stand next to the professor.

"Oh, you poor kitty-cats," said Professor Katnip, laughing heartlessly. "You thought you could trust old Bones? Don't you know that he's really a bullkat? He will always be a disgusting bullkat no matter how much he wants to be... one of us."

"A stinkin' bullkat! You're not a Meow Cat?" shouted Boo. "You deceived us!"

Realizing what he had just said, Boo glanced over at Calico and saw the painful expression on his bullkat face. "Calico, I'm—"

Skin interrupted him, leaping forward. "I'm the bullkat that bites back hard!"

Skin moved his head from side to side, pridefully showing off his large, pointed horns growing out from the inside of his ears. He took a swipe at Bones' hind leg with his sharp claws. Bones flinched, flattening the ears on his head. The fur on his crooked back puffed out, but the old cat did not make a sound.

Bones cringed and continued to look down for a few seconds. He then took another step forward, slowly picking up his hat off the long wooden table. He took his paw and, in a flash, slapped at the bottles filled with the toxic oil, launching the bottles in the direction of Professor Katnip and Skin. The bottles hit the ground in front of the evil cats, exploding into a ball of flames. Skin's fur ignited in a fiery blaze, and the amphitheater quickly became a frenzy of chaos, with bullkats racing in every direction.

"Boo! Look out behind you!" shouted Silver, watching in terror at the oncoming bullkat.

Silver's quills stood straight up in attack position as he moved about in a circle, performing his amazing porcupine fighting dance. He was like a dancing whirlwind, piercing the charging bullkats with his mighty quills as he moved across the room.

"Hi ho, Silver!" cried out Chops, marveling at Silver's fighting technique.

Boo, Roxy Roo, and Chops quickly hurled bottles of the deadly explosive oil at the attacking bullkats, causing them to stop dead in their tracks and turn back toward the rear of the amphitheater.

Deadly stones from the slingshots of Boo and Roxy Roo zoomed across the room, picking off the bullkats one by one as they streaked around the chaotic room.

Chops stood in front of Briar Bow, Briar Bee, and Briar Bud, guarding them with his life while shooting his stones with deadly accuracy at the bullkats across the cavern.

"Chops! Behind you!" screamed Roxy Roo.

Briar Bow and her two little porcupines turned around and instinctively their quills leaped to attention, persuading the oncoming bullkat to stop dead in his tracks. Chops' powerful cat claws swooshed through the air above the little porcupines' heads, knocking the bullkat away from them.

"Ouch!" bellowed Chops, falling into Briar Bud's sharp quills... again. "Good grief, like poppi, like little porky."

"Sorry, Mr. Chops," squeaked Briar Bud, squirming as he moved closer to his mom.

The amphitheater was ablaze as the smoking laboratory tables went up in flames one by one, and the boiling concoctions exploded into fireballs throughout the room.

Boo glanced quickly toward Silver and saw Skin charging directly at him from behind. Boo jumped like a roaring tiger onto a burning lab table and leaped across the flames, landing on Skin's smoking back so they both went tumbling to the ground. The courageous Meow cat and the hideous bullkat rolled on the ground through the flames, fighting for life or death. Their sharp claws slashed through the air, striking at one another. Boo's strong paws flipped Skin into the air, and the bullkat tumbled into one of the bubbling holes. The evil bullkat disappeared into the monster's abyss with gaseous flames spewing out behind him.

"Boo, are you OK?" shouted Silver, relieved to see his friend still alive.

"Follow me!" shouted Calico. "I know a way out of this inferno!"

"Wait! We can't leave Bones here!" shouted Roxy Roo, dodging the flames and bubbling holes as she ran in the opposite direction.

Bones was lying down in the middle of the burning amphitheater. The deadly wounds inflicted by Skin rendered the courageous cat unable to move.

Boo peered through the flames whipping around the smoke-filled room and saw Professor Katnip's burnt body limping toward one of the lava tunnels. Suddenly he disappeared from sight as a puff of smoke erupted from one of the deep caverns. Boo wanted desperately to go after Professor Katnip, but he knew he had to get his friends safely out of the burning amphitheater before it was too late. Boo watched in horror as the professor's evil lab, scattered with the bodies of burnt bullkats, was quickly becoming totally consumed by the raging fire.

Briar Bow and her little ones stayed close to Chops, holding on tightly to his strong legs. Silver and Boo continued fighting the last of the bullkats, who wouldn't give up until they had finally chased them off through the burning lava tunnels.

With singed whiskers and burnt tails, Silver and Boo emerged through the clouds of black smoke to meet their friends in the only safe place left, the middle of the amphitheater.

"Are you hurt?" asked Roxy Roo, looking at them both, limping with singed fur and quills.

"I'll be OK," said Boo, licking the wounds on his clawed-up leg.

Silver looked at the tip of his burnt tail that now resembled a chunk of black lava rock. Letting it go out of his paw, he could still hear it clink as his tail hit the ground.

Bones' old feline body was sprawled out on the cold, damp floor. Roxy Roo crouched over him, hoping there was something she could do to help the fearless old cat.

"Go," said Bones, groaning and purring in pain. He looked up at her with his weary cat eyes. "I may have been born a bullkat, but in my heart I was always a Meow cat."

Bones closed his eyes as his old frail body lay still on the cold black rocks. Standing in the middle of the frenzied room, with flames all around them, everyone looked compassionately at Bones' lifeless body.

"We gotta go… now," said Calico, placing Bones' black hat gently next to his body.

Tears welled up in Roxy Roo's green eyes. "We just can't leave him here," she said, pleading with Boo and waiting for him to answer.

Boo looked at Bones' dead body and then back up at her. "Bones is gone, Roxy… his Tyrtle spirit will always be with us," said Boo. "We'll make sure Tyrtle Island knows the truth. They will know that Bones is the one who saved us from the bullkats, and even though he was born a bullkat, in the end… he became a new creature in his heart."

The smoke concealed the sadness in Calico's eyes as he listened to Boo's heartfelt words. At that moment Calico's heart was filled with heartache and with hope for change to come.

The amphitheater was now totally consumed with fire and smoke. The screeching of the bullkats who were left alive and trapped in their cells was unbearable for Boo and his friends to hear and see. The fate of the imprisoned cats was already sealed, for the flames and smoke had already overcome their locked cells. Boo felt helpless, watching as the smoky flames consumed the cells and the bullkats, one by one.

"Roxy Roo, we have to leave now," said Boo, coughing, placing his paw on her back.

Everyone quickly followed Calico through the thick smoke toward the back of the amphitheater. They could hear each other's wheezing and coughing as they felt their way past the iron bars leading into one of the only empty dark prison cells.

Calico waited at the back corner of the cell for his friends to catch up with him. The rock wall that was their escape route had already been slid open, and the burning oil lamp revealed the secret opening of a small lava tube leading upwards. The stench of bat guano filled the stagnant air as they started to climb up through the dark narrow passageway.

"Stanky!" said Chops, coughing and trying to hold his breath. "Gross, I think I got some on me!"

They followed Calico, slipping and sliding blindly through the darkness. Up they crawled along the wavy walls of the twisted tube leading them toward the rainforest floor.

"Do we have any cat snacks left?" asked Chops, running his tongue across his whiskers in the dark.

"Chops! Gross!" exclaimed Roxy Roo. "How can you think about food at a time like this? Especially when that awful smell just takes your breath away."

"The little porkies are hungry. We're just preparing mentally for when we get out of this stinky tube," said Chops. "Right, little porkies?"

They could all hear the echo of Briar Bee's and Briar Bud's chuckles and squeaks through the lava tube.

Calico led them upwards, toward the opening of the long lava tube. Boo, Silver, Briar Bow, Briar Bee, Briar Bud, Roxy Roo, and Chops followed behind, bumping into one another along the way in the dark.

"Everyone OK?" asked Boo, crawling along.

"Keep calm and Tyrtle on!" cried out Silver.

"Boo yeah!" shouted Chops.

Briar Bee and Briar Bud squeaked loudly again.

The smoke from the burning amphitheater started to float through the narrow lava tube and crept its way dangerously close to Chops.

"We got smoke!" cried Chops, coughing and crawling behind the rest of them. "Can we pick up the pace a little?"

"Almost there!" shouted Calico, his words reverberating throughout the tube. "I see a glimmer of light."

"I hope so," said Chops, whispering in a low voice, "because I have to go number one."

The laughing and squeaking coming from the little porcupines above him in the lava tube made him break out into a big smile.

Calico popped his head out of the hole and into the sunlight, shouting, "Hello paradise!"

"Yahoo!" hollered Boo, his big blue eyes taking in the beautiful surroundings of Calico's Lagoon.

One by one, they emerged out of the smelly lava tube into the sunlight and breathed in the sweet, flowering aroma of the magical lagoon.

Roxy Roo emerged from the lava tube taking in a deep breath of air and said, "That's the most wonderful scent on the island."

"Oh, thank you very much," said Chops, hoping for a few more squeaks and giggles from the little porkies.

Briar Bud and Briar Bee did not disappoint him. This crazy and amusing cat was quickly becoming one of their favorite creatures on the island.

Just as they had made themselves comfortable under one of the magnificent shade trees surrounding the lagoon, they heard a big splash coming from the edge of the water. They scurried down to the lagoon's shore and saw a familiar, goofy-looking face.

"Oh, no, it's the ruuude ones," said the goofy voice from the middle of the lagoon.

"Hey, it's Wacky Tyrtle!" cried out Chops, wearing a big grin. "I love that name, and I love that face! Wacky Tyrtle... just can't make this stuff up, ya know."

"You know... you know I can hear you?" said Wacky Tyrtle, swimming closer to the shore. "By the way, since I happened to see you ruuude cats again, I just want to let you know that my brother knows you're on the way to see him."

"He does?" asked Boo. "How does your brother know that?"

Wacky Tyrtle watched the smoke billowing out of the top of the lava tube. The Tyrtle looked at everyone staring at him. He then refocused on the thick smoke that was rising up and over the towering walls.

Boo watched the smoke billowing out of the underground hole and floating through the air. He then looked back at the goofy Tyrtle again.

"Oh, I suppose you're wondering about the smoke... Well, we just left the amphitheater in a hurry. Just in case you haven't heard, the professor's lab is destroyed, and the bullkats are, well... dead," said Boo.

Boo waited for a few minutes, staring at Wacky Tyrtle, waiting for him to respond.

"Is he just thinking?" asked Chops, looking curiously at the Tyrtle. "I can't tell… maybe he fell asleep?"

Boo stared at Wacky Tyrtle and finally said, "I don't think we have a need to see your brother any longer."

"I still do," said Calico. "I don't want to be a bullkat anymore."

"What do you mean you don't want to be a bullkat anymore?" asked Chops. "That's what you are. That's what you were born to be."

"Bones told me that with the help of Wiki Tyrtle, I can become a different creature … a new creature," said Calico. "I want to change… like Bones changed."

"Boo, we have to help Calico," pleaded Roxy Roo. "After all, it was two bullkats that helped save our lives and… defeat the bullkats."

Boo looked at them earnestly and said, "OK then, I think we need to go visit a Tyrtle."

Wacky Tyrtle had slipped away under the water without answering Boo's question. Boo figured it really didn't matter anyhow. Somehow, Wiki Tyrtle knew they were on their way. Once they got to the Land of No End, all they had to do was figure out how to find the legendary Tyrtle Tunnel.

The night sky closed in over the lagoon, and the stars lit up the heavens above them like the sparkling stones in the cavern below them. The panorama was breathtaking, looking up from the shore of the lagoon. Peacefully, they all drifted off to enjoy a restful night's sleep.

tyrtle

CHAPTER SEVENTEEN: HIDDEN SECRETS

Jesse was awakened by the twitching of his nose. He opened his eyes expecting to see Caleb or Honey Bee tickling the tip of it. Instead, he was looking cross-eyed at a golden ladybug that was happily resting on the tip of his nose. He slid his finger up under the end of his nose, and the beautiful ladybug, known as the golden tortoise beetle, gently walked onto his finger.

The happy-go-lucky bugs have always been a symbol of living a joyful and full life, and that's why he loved this particular insect so much. Jesse watched the beautiful bug fly across the sand and gently land on a fern next to the old cat-a-canoe.

Jesse recollected for a moment and then shouted out, "I got it!"

Caleb rolled over in the sand and sleepily mumbled, "Got yum-yum puffs." He sat up against the coconut tree and wiped off the sand stuck to his cheek.

Tinman and Honey Bee quickly opened their eyes from their afternoon nap and wondered what Jesse's yelling was about.

Jesse jumped up and said, "Yes, I got it. I remember now. Mr. Jack's ugly fern-leaf shirt. I knew I'd seen that shirt before. That shirt is way too ugly to ever forget."

"He's right. That was a really ugly shirt," said Honey Bee, dusting the sand off her legs.

"Remember the evening we went to the professor's house and he'd been attacked in his greenhouse?" asked Jesse. "The person I chased to the edge of the jungle was wearing that same ugly shirt. It must have been Mr. Jack that was with the professor that evening."

"Must've been, because there's no way there could be two of those awful shirts on the island," said Honey Bee, flipping her long brown hair back over her shoulders.

"So he's lying to us?" said Caleb, throwing a handful of sand up into the air. "I knew we couldn't trust him."

Jesse gave Caleb a dirty look, wiping the windblown sand off his face. "I'm not so sure."

Jesse pondered the details of what happened that night in the professor's greenhouse, but before he was able to get the words out of his mouth, Honey Bee had beat him to it.

"By the time we saw Professor Katnip in his greenhouse, he was already hurt, but we didn't actually see Mr. Jack with the professor or how the professor got hurt," said Honey Bee, drawing butterflies in the sand with her finger.

Jesse chimed in, interrupting Honey Bee, "Mr. Jack certainly looks like he could hurt someone, but I guess that doesn't necessarily mean he did. No doubt about the professor, though… now that we know what we know about him, maybe the professor tried to hurt Mr. Jack. Maybe the professor hurt himself to try and make it look like somebody else hurt him."

Honey Bee gave Jesse an aggravated look and interrupted him again. "Mr. Jack told us the professor has a secret, and the secret is in Kats Caves. Is it possible that he told us that just to lure us into the caves?"

"I wonder, though, why would he do that?" asked Jesse, rubbing his fingers in circles on his forehead.

"Not every question gets an answer," proclaimed Tinman, raising a finger in the air to make his point of wisdom.

Caleb smiled at everyone and said, "Stop using your brains so much."

Tinman gathered his gear and strolled down toward the water's edge. For a moment, he was lost in his thoughts, staring out into the big blue. From the shore of Tyrtle Island it looked as though the ocean went on and on, until it stopped and dropped off the face of the earth. He reflected on how much he loved exploring the island with all of its incredible beauty. Standing there, he could almost hear the ocean once again inviting him to come and explore its vastness.

"Home is where the Tyrtles are, and I think it's time that we join them for another adventure very soon," he thought out loud.

Jesse had snuck up behind Tinman and tickled his ear with Boo's big paw. "I hope when you say 'we,' you mean me, you, and a cat named Boo," he said.

"You know better than to say that. Wherever an adventure takes me, you and Boo are always welcome to come along," said Tinman, rubbing Boo's big paw.

The vastness of the ocean can calm our souls, but when it's angry, the power of the mysterious waters can stir up our greatest fears.

Jesse, Tinman, and Boo stood along the shore, captivated by the water as they gazed out at the brilliant blue. A giant green sea creature with what appeared to be a long, spiked green tail breached the water and then quickly disappeared.

Jesse and Tinman thought they were seeing things as it came up out of the water again and quickly disappeared.

"What was that?" asked Tinman.

"I think that was a whale," said Jesse.

"That wasn't like any whale I've ever seen," said Tinman. "I've never seen a whale with a spiked green tail."

Jesse's emotions swelled, and he felt a lump form in his throat. He picked up a small lava rock and threw it with all his might into the crashing waves.

He cleared his throat and said, "I remember my dad telling me that he saw a creature like that once. If I remember right, I think he saw that creature when he was fishing with you."

Tinman smiled, staring out at the ocean, and said, "Your dad and I used to go fishing all the time. Not only was he my brother, but he was my best friend."

"Do you think he'll ever make it back someday?" asked Jesse.

Tinman put his arm around Jesse's neck and said, "I hope so… I really hope so."

Honey Bee and Caleb brushed the sand off each other's dirty clothes and started walking along the seashore, just out of the reach of the white foamy water. They all started marching down the golden beach toward the bullkats' hiding place. It was getting late in the evening, and the sun was slipping below the stormy horizon as they reached their point of no return. They all stood facing the jagged entrances, looming up against the treacherous mountains, to the caves known as Kats Caves.

Jesse and Tinman had been through many of these caves before, but this time their adventure would be very different. This adventure somehow involved Tyrtle Island's ancient history and the fate of Tyrtle Island's future. They all knew that once they entered the lava monster's mouth, there was no turning back until the battle ensued and was won.

Shadows covered the front of the caves as they cautiously stepped up and crawled through one of the entrances leading into the abyss under the island.

"Everyone stick together and be careful," said Tinman, glancing around at the familiar, dark surroundings of the cavern. "Caleb, that means you too."

"You don't need to worry about that," said Caleb, cautiously stepping further into the spooky cavern, with Honey Bee and Jesse following right behind him.

"Many of these caverns and tunnels connect together, and we don't know where the professor and the bullkats are right now," said Tinman.

"Hello, Jesse. I see you're keeping Boo out of my garden," said a familiar but unnerving voice from a dark corner of the cavern.

Mr. Jack's unmistakable, strange voice startled everyone and stopped them dead in their tracks. Jesse stared straight ahead, struggling to focus on the dark figure standing against the black wall.

"OK, I gotta ask. What's with all the sneaking around and boogeyman stuff?" said Caleb. He did his best to sound brave by lowering the pitch of his voice, but his voice cracked, and he impulsively took a couple steps backward.

Mr. Jack stared straight ahead, peering past Jesse and into the darkness. In the dim light of the cavern, they could see that his worn and weary face was overcome with sadness. His disposition changed almost instantly, and it was like he had become a different man. His heart of stone had finally crumbled and filled with the love and spirit of Tyrtle Island.

"I'm tired," lamented Mr. Jack, slowly stepping forward into the dim light. "I was born on Tyrtle Island, and although it was so long ago, it seems like it was just yesterday. This island is my home. It's the only home I've ever known."

Mr. Jack cackled oddly, as oddly as he did everything else. He stood in silence, staring at the sparkling stone he was holding in his open hand. Mr. Jack moved his hand into the dim light, and a spectrum of colors shot out from the stone, catching everyone by surprise.

"Follow me and I will show you something that I'm certain you will be amazed to see," he said, turning and walking toward one of the many tunnel openings.

Tinman followed behind Mr. Jack at a distance while still keeping an open ear and a watchful eye out for the bullkats. They hiked through the maze of tunnels, ducking their heads under the jagged ceiling and stepping around pools of water until they reached a great open cavern. This ominous chamber was divided by a deep canyon running through the center, which continued into the darkness. The massive geological marvel was one of the most beautiful caverns they had ever set their eyes on.

Jesse danced around in a circle, exploding with excitement. "I know this place! I've been here before!"

Tinman looked at Jesse like he was crazy and said, "I hate to lock the lid on your treasure chest, but we've never been to this part of the caves before."

Smiling, Jesse glanced over at Tinman and said, "It's just as phenomenal as I remember."

Tinman realized that Jesse really had been here before and whispered to himself, "Ah yes, the dream."

Together, Tinman and Jesse had never explored this part of Kats Caves. In Jesse's mind, though, he had walked along the edge of this chasm before and even crossed over to the other side. Only the last time he was here, he had walked on four paws and had a furry tail. Each of the golden candle rock formations had grown much larger than they were then. Just as he recalled, each amazing geological shape was a stunning masterpiece. He looked longingly across the canyon and could still see the sweet faces of Silver's little ones standing close to the edge on the other side. It was only a short dream ago, but somehow it felt like millennia and worlds apart.

Long after the time period of Jesse's dream, and prior to the river running dry, a footbridge was constructed of logs, with a handrail on one side. The rickety old bridge was used to cross over the dry river canyon below.

One by one they followed Mr. Jack across the bridge, holding onto the worn-out wooden rail and gently tiptoeing over to the other side of the divide. They stepped down the makeshift rocky stairway that wound its way around and down to the damp trail that was once a powerful underground river. Following the riverbed that was scattered with old bones, they descended into the core of the caves and into a new world far below Tyrtle Island.

Jesse wondered if any of these whitewashed bones were from the flying bullkat that had leaped to his death right in front of him and Silver in the dream.

"I got a bone to pick with you!" said Caleb, roaring with laughter.

Caleb began to sing:

"Them bones, them bones, them dry bones!
The toe bone's connected to the foot bone!
The foot bone's connected to the ankle—"

"OUCH!" yelled Caleb, rubbing his backside.

Jesse had interrupted Caleb's one-man party by throwing a small rock and hitting him squarely on the backside.

Caleb glared at Jesse but was determined to finish the last word of his song as he sang out, "Bone… head!"

Jesse stepped over two logs that were now wedged into the side of the river rocks. The long logs had been polished smooth by years of water rushing over them. He wondered if these were the same two logs that Boo and his friends had used so long ago to cross over and rescue Silver's family. They all walked along the riverbed with Jesse feeling confident that he knew exactly where Mr. Jack was headed. He decided to keep those thoughts to himself, wanting his friends to feel for themselves the fascinating experience of seeing that special cavern for the very first time.

Tinman was perplexed with Mr. Jack and asked him, "You never answered our question. Why the change of heart now?"

"It was just about a year ago that my wife and I walked through these same caves," said Mr. Jack, sighing heavily. "She insisted that I bring her here so she could see this place for herself. I told her it was a dangerous place and I refused, but she wouldn't take no for an answer."

"Is it just me or does he talk in circles?" whispered Caleb, a few steps in back of everyone.

Jesse gave Caleb a glancing smile as he reached back over his shoulder and scratched Boo on his head. Boo responded with a loving, motoring purr.

"I've worked for Professor Katnip for many years now—in secret—for two reasons," divulged Mr. Jack. He stopped abruptly, shone his bright light up into the cavern, and said, "This is the first reason."

They all stood silently before the most amazing display of diamonds, gemstones, and gold veins. The Sparkling Cavern's walls were decorated from one end to the other with the precious stones. The twinkling stars and shiny metallic surfaces sprinkled around the cavern had been formed with the same hands that created the brilliant stars and placed them perfectly across the island night sky. The old mine had buckets and barrels full of brassy yellow gold rocks and raw colorful gemstones cluttering the cavern floor.

"Wonders never cease," said Honey Bee, stepping out of the dry riverbed in absolute awe of the dazzling display illuminated across the cavern walls.

"As I live and breathe!" exclaimed Tinman, looking up at the twinkling geological stars on the cavern ceiling above.

"More amazing than a pocket full of jelly beans," said Caleb, touching his fingertip on one of the many bright red gemstones shining on the cavern wall.

Jesse stood in silence. "I never dreamed. Well, actually I did," he thought, amusing himself.

"All that shines might not be so divine," said Mr. Jack in his very peculiar way. He lifted a mining pickaxe from the ground and bumbled over to the center of the cavern. "Professor would say to me, 'You're a crackerjack of a miner you are,' and after a while... I was simply known as Mr. Jack."

Jesse and Tinman moved closer to Honey Bee, sensing that everyone was beginning to get very nervous with Mr. Jack stumbling around the poorly-lit cavern carrying a pickaxe in his hand.

"Jesse, do you recognize this cavern?" whispered Tinman. "Look. It's the same cavern."

Jesse glanced around and gave Tinman a puzzled look.

"When we got chased by the bullkat," said Tinman. "I know you didn't forget that. We were just over there on the other side."

Jesse's eyes lit up when he finally put two and two together and realized that this time they added up to a cavern full of diamonds, gems, and gold.

"I suppose I got caught up in it all," interrupted Mr. Jack, waving the pickaxe erratically through the earthy-smelling air. "I forgot what was most important to me... I forgot what was most important in this life."

The brilliance of the diamonds, gems, and veins of gold painted on the cavern walls slowly faded into obscurity with every word of truth that Mr. Jack spoke. He laughed out loud and then paused to glare around the room. He was like a crazy man, consumed by his own desperation.

"I failed to recognize that my most precious jewel was standing right in front of me, and I was blinded by all this so-called treasure surrounding me," he said, hanging his head down in anguish and bumping his head against the pickaxe.

"How... how did she die?" asked Honey Bee, cautiously walking closer to Mr. Jack.

"I will show you," he said. "Follow me."

turtle

CHAPTER EIGHTEEN: RECOIL OIL

Mr. Jack held the chipped wooden handle of the old pickaxe tightly as he walked back down to the riverbed trail, leaving the grandeur of Sparkling Caverns behind. He navigated through the cave system with everyone following behind him, ducking under the icicle-shaped stalactites and maneuvering around the tall stalagmites pointing upwards. Each one looked as though it had been sculpted individually by the master artist's hand. The golden-brown hues of the ribbon formations and the translucent turquoise colors of the tunnels and caverns changed as they descended deeper into the lava monster's maze.

"Hey, big guy, I bet you're ready for a break," said Jesse, stopping for a minute to take Boo out of his backpack. "Only for a few minutes though."

Cat's out of the bag now, thought Boo, amusing himself while stretching out his paws on the damp ground.

Mr. Jack stopped, took his old pipe out of his worn-out shirt pocket and lit it with a wooden match. The soft glow of his pipe reflected off the cavern walls. He took a couple quick puffs from the stem of the wooden pipe and, like magic, blew out a couple of perfectly round smoke rings from his crooked old mouth. He watched them float through the air and circle around until they broke apart against one of the most spectacular stalactites hanging down from the ceiling above. There was something mysteriously fascinating about Mr. Jack. Whatever it was, it was slowly unfolding before everyone's eyes.

Caleb raised his hand in the air and said, "I got a question. Is it even safe to smoke in here?" He forced out a fake cough and waved his hands frantically to fan away the vapors billowing past his face.

"I think we'll be OK," said Tinman, his eyes watching Mr. Jack curiously.

Mr. Jack watched the smoke rings float around the cavern and said, "Life is like these smoke rings. They kind of just float around, almost invisible for a short time, going wherever they will, rising up for an instant, and the next moment… they're gone."

"I'm getting the feeling that Mr. Jack is not very optimistic, is he?" whispered Honey Bee to Jesse, following behind him.

The path before them led through a black lava-rock corridor that opened into a rocky chamber. The steamy chamber was filled with bubbling pools of rich mineral water that came from the large raindrops dripping from the tips of the stalactites above. Puffs of ghostly vapors escaped from the gurgling pools of water back into the air. The vapors continued to float up into the chamber and then disappeared against the flesh-colored jagged rocks above.

"Is the water safe?" asked Caleb, looking at the colorful bubbles slowly rising out of the gurgling pools.

Tinman watched the bubbles burst open and splattered on the ground like boiling pots of thick soup.

"Not sure if you're talking about safe to drink or safe to touch, but I'd say no," said Tinman. "That really doesn't look like the kind of water you want to drink."

"My wife would relax here, soaking her feet in the pools," said Mr. Jack. He gazed at the bubbling pools for a few minutes, letting his mind get lost in the memories of the time spent relaxing in the natural hot springs.

In the meantime, on the other side of the cavern Caleb was taking off his shoes, preparing to dip his toes into one of the relaxing bubbling spas.

"Caleb, what are you doing?" asked Jesse, grinning. "This isn't a day at the spa. Remember Professor Katnip and the bullkats?"

"Although that doesn't sound too bad," said Honey Bee, sliding her shoe back on her foot.

I know my precious paws could certainly use some pampering right about now, thought Boo, looking down at his dirty paws.

Mr. Jack's old hand was trembling as he waved and signaled for them to follow him. "We best keep moving. We really don't have much time."

Honey Bee and Caleb watched the cave geckos scatter across a pile of lava rocks and disappear between the shadowy cracks. A black and yellow striped cave gecko sat on the rock like a statue and stared at Honey Bee and Caleb. The relaxed reptile looked up at her with its blood-red eyes and nodded his head back and forth, as if to say, "Take me with you."

Honey Bee was always willing to help creatures of any size and kind. She reached down slowly, laying her hand wide open on the black lava rock. To her surprise, the little creature didn't move a muscle. She scooted her hand a little closer toward the red-eyed reptile and scooped him up in the palm of her hand.

"Hmm, what should we call you?" said Honey Bee, staring at the amazingly colorful creature and running her finger along the gecko's long black tail. "I think... I'll call you... Lava!" She reached up with her hand and placed Lava directly on her shoulder.

Boo looked curiously at the little gecko, who looked nervously back at him. "No worries, I prefer fish," Boo meowed.

Somehow Lava seemed to understand that he was in good hands and was content resting upon Honey Bee's shoulder.

"OK, we've all been patient. We keep going deeper into the caves, and I need to know exactly where we're going before we take another step," said Tinman to Mr. Jack. Tinman stopped in the middle of the lava tunnel and, looking at Mr. Jack eye to eye, he said, "You helped me long ago. Let me help you now."

Mr. Jack turned around and pointed down the tunnel. "We're headed in the direction of the amphitheater. It's just a little deeper under the island," he said.

The mystery unfolding before them and the lava tubes deep under the island were two separate worlds that Tinman and Jesse had never explored. They knew about the countless caves, caverns, and lava tunnels that crisscrossed deep under Tyrtle Island, but they had never explored to this depth beneath the island nor to this depth in their minds.

The secrets hidden within Tyrtle Island continued to amaze everyone as they entered the largest lava tube they had ever seen. The upper surface of this spectacularly wide and long tube was protected by thousands of clear lava-icicles that were formed when the last blast of volcanic heat flowed through ages ago.

"Why the amphitheater? What's there?" asked Tinman, tempted to touch one of the thousands of transparent icicle stalactites hanging from the curved lava-tube ceiling.

"You need to see for yourself," said Mr. Jack, with a look of shame as he glanced at Tinman.

The light from their headlamps revealed the never-ending lava tubes' colorful, mineral-rich walls and the unbelievable natural shapes of the seemingly endless passageway. They twisted their bodies and turned their heads as they were consumed by each and every dripping icicle. The once-liquid river of lava flowing through this island wonder created a solid lava cave. The artistic wave pattern on the walls of the lava cave were frozen in time and left as a natural wonder for the Islanders to enjoy forever.

"I had no idea these lava caves were so massive and they extended so far under the island," said Tinman, surprised at the width and height of the fantastic tube.

"How far do they go? Does anybody know?" asked Jesse, turning in circles as he walked along.

"Like Swiss cheese, these tunnels are," said Mr. Jack, slowing down his pace. "All I know is far below and under the rainforest they go."

Water dripped down through the porous lava rocks, following the path of the cauliflower-shaped walls, and gathered in a perfectly shaped lava-rock bowl ready to serve a thirsty caver. Mr. Jack stopped at one of the watering pools, took his stainless-steel cup out, and filled it with some of the cool, clean water filtered by the many layers of lava rock above. He walked over and looked Jesse in the eyes as he placed his cup down on the damp ground in front of Boo's long whiskers.

Boo looked at the peace offering before him. *What's this?* he thought.

Boo loved ice water in a glass, but the next best thing was drinking cool water from a cold metal cup. He looked up at Jesse and back at Mr. Jack's sorrowful face.

"Go ahead, big guy," said Jesse, leaning down and rubbing Boo's tiger-like head.

On the surface, this may have looked like a small gesture, but everyone present in the lava tube knew this was Mr. Jack's way of telling Jesse and Boo that he was sorry. This was the first time that any of them had seen anything close to a smile on Mr. Jack's face. His crinkled eyes and unorthodox grin brought a sense of ease to Jesse and his friends.

Honey Bee walked slowly up to Mr. Jack without saying a word and gently hugged his neck. She watched as a single tear welled up in the corner of his tired, bloodshot eyes. The teardrop slowly rolled down his wrinkled old cheek and dripped into the pool of water below. The splash of that single teardrop quietly echoed the sound of forgiveness through the ancient lava tube and out to the island above.

Boo walked without hesitation over to Mr. Jack and rubbed up against his jeans.

"Does this mean I get a little of that catnip growing in his garden?" purred Boo.

"Looks like you and Boo have finally become friends," said Tinman, placing his hand on Mr. Jack's shoulder. "Professor Katnip has got to be close now, so we better keep moving along."

The massive lava tube just kept on rolling before them with many smaller tubes crisscrossing in front of them.

"Careful not to break any of the roots," cautioned Mr. Jack.

Everyone understood the importance of navigating carefully around these dangling fingers that looked like they belonged to a creature from another world. The cavers also understood that these massive roots were the life blood of the rainforest trees above. Everyone ducked as they walked around the hundreds of roots dangling from above. The roots of the monstrous rainforest trees reached deep down below the rich soil and wiggled like fingertips into the lava monster's tubes, providing a source of food for the insects and microorganisms that called this volcanic wonderland home.

Caleb, who knew better, was tempted to reach up and slap at the roots. "This is a first. It's a curtain of roots hanging from the ceiling," he said. "How much further?"

"Pack your patience," said Mr. Jack, looking back at Caleb.

"'Pack your patience'?" asked Caleb, mumbling quietly. "Pack your patience. That's another new one. I don't even think I know what that means."

Honey Bee looked over at Caleb and laughed at the aggravated look on his face.

They wiggled their way around the root curtains, row after row, and finally the amphitheater opened up before them.

"Ta-da!" sang out Caleb.

"This is where the professor makes his most potent catnip formulas to control the bullkats," said Mr. Jack, scanning the dark room with a look of shame.

The back walls of the cavernous room were lined with dark rock prison cells that were used to hold bullkats that needed a new dose of the professor's special recipe. The center of the room was filled with an assembly line of smoking catnip recipes and other herbal oil experiments in the process of being perfected.

"This is where we make the recoil oil," said Mr. Jack. "This is the oil made from the rainbow plants that is used to control the bullkats but also makes them much more aggressive."

Jesse and Caleb walked up to one of the dark cells along the back of the amphitheater. They peered through the iron bars into the deep prison cave carved out of the black lava rocks. The cell was puddled with pools of water seeping through from the rainforest high above. There was a foul smell lingering inside the cage. Jesse took off his headlamp and slipped his hand through the iron bars, pointing the light toward the dark corner of the cell.

"Shine your light on it," said Jesse, holding his headlamp.

"Pretty sure I know what's back there and really don't wanna see it," said Caleb, his hand shaking as he held his light out.

The yellowish eyes stared from the dark corner of the cell. The grotesque cat's white horns glowed from each ear. The bullkat's low growl rumbled through the cell as the creature crept slowly away from the back wall and paced back and forth like a caged white tiger. The cell became silent, and like a ghost, the disfigured feline floated silently closer to them. The bullkat slowly revealed its face, which was full of silent pain and rage. The animal's mangy body came into view as it moved closer to the iron bars. With each calculated step they could hear the scraping of its long claws against the jagged rocks lining the bottom of the cell.

"Get back!" cried out Mr. Jack, approaching the dark cell. "Get away from there!"

Jesse and Caleb screamed as they were yanked back by their shirts. They fell backwards onto the cold, wet ground not a split-second before the long, powerful claws of the bullkat crashed violently through the iron bars. They watched in horror as the creature came into full view, crashing repeatedly against the hard cell.

"What is that thing?" asked Caleb, terrified. "It almost doesn't even look like a bullkat."

"It's an experiment gone bad," said Mr. Jack, watching the poor creature pace back and forth in its cell. "This one's name is Skin. He's what you might call the lead bullkat. Professor Katnip calls him the biting bullkat. He had to lock him up. Let's just say that, lately, Skin and the professor have not been getting along so well."

"I know bullkats are mean and nasty creatures," said Tinman, peering into the cage. "But not like this. These cats look like monsters, not bullkats."

"Cats? They're not cats! They're a-paw-ling creatures!" meowed Boo, his head sticking out from the safety of Jesse's backpack.

Jesse could feel Boo squirming around inside the backpack. He reached back over his shoulder just to make sure he wasn't trying to climb out. "Hang in there, Boo," he said, rubbing his furry friend's head.

"It's the oils from the rainbow plants," said Mr. Jack, walking away from them.

He walked over toward the toxic assembly line and picked up a couple bottles of the potent concoction off the metal rack. Jesse and Tinman followed closely behind Mr. Jack looking at the rows of clear, colorful bottles lined up in the racks.

"He's been testing the formula for years now, and I'm afraid… what you're looking at is the pitiful end result," confessed Mr. Jack. "I would suggest carefully picking up a few bottles. We have some very agitated company coming our way, and we will probably need all the help we can get."

"Why? Why would the professor do this?" asked Honey Bee, her eyes painfully looking back at the miserable creature roaming around in circles in the cage.

"I told you... I know some things," said Mr. Jack, holding the bottle up in the air against the dim light.

"Yeah, you keep repeating that," said Caleb in a quiet voice, rolling his eyes.

"Professor Katnip used the rainbow plants to make the recoil oil," Mr. Jack continued. "The potent oil affects every bullkat a little different, but most of them are turned into these rather ravenous creatures that he's able to control... most of the time anyways. He wants the bullkats to keep scaring away the Islanders from Kats Caves. That's the only way he can be sure and keep his secret mine... well, a secret."

Caleb walked over and picked up a bottle of the recoil oil, tossing it like a soda bottle in the air.

"Caleb, careful with that. Haven't you been listening?" said Tinman as he picked up a couple bottles.

Mr. Jack laughed. "Recoil oil... he gave it that name not because of the effect that the oil has on the bullkats, but because of the effect it has on the bullkats' victims. They are so terrified it causes them to suddenly spring back in horror and disgust. You have no idea. He's a very, very sick man."

"Is this where... well, where your wife died?" asked Honey Bee. "What happened?"

"It was an accident," said Mr. Jack. "I refused to bring her this far into the tunnels, but again, she insisted."

Mr. Jack looked back at the grotesque bullkat named Skin and said, "She did exactly what you just did a few minutes ago. She took one look at that hideous creature, and she was so terrified that she fell backwards and hit her head on the lava rocks."

They all stood still in silence for a couple of seconds.

"We're so sorry," said Tinman.

"I'm sorry, I just don't understand," said Honey Bee passionately. "Why would you help the professor do such terrible things? Especially after your wife died in this very cavern. This island is your home! You're an Islander! You're a Tyrtle!"

"I think I know why," said Tinman, looking at Mr. Jack compassionately.

Jesse, Caleb, and Honey Bee all waited for Tinman to reveal the reason why, but the conversation was interrupted by loud noises coming through one of the lava tubes funneling through into the amphitheater. All eyes went from watching Mr. Jack and Tinman to the location of the approaching sounds coming from the front of the amphitheater.

A dark figure clapped loudly. "Glad you could all join us again!" shouted a voice coming out of the shadows of the lava tube and echoing into the dimly-lit amphitheater.

Professor Katnip entered the cavern holding his walking stick in one hand and walked directly toward everyone standing at the back of the massive room.

Tinman and Jesse quickly looked around for an escape route, but it was too late.

"How nice and convenient that you're all finally gathered in one place, and that place happens to be my... well, not so secret anymore... lab," said Professor Katnip, waving his arm and snapping his fingers, signaling the bullkats into the smoky room.

The multitude of claws scraping against the rocky floor and the low, grumbling growls of the bullkats could be heard as they slowly crawled into the room one by one, lining up along the walls in front of the smoking lab equipment. Their unnerving growls rumbled off the amphitheater's glowing black walls as the cats aggressively pushed against one another, moving closer to their prey. The cats' yellow eyes came alive as they snarled at the sight of their victims trapped in the amphitheater. The cats grinned hideously exposing their razor-sharp teeth, knowing that their long wait was almost over, and they would only have to restrain themselves for a few moments longer.

"Good ol' Crackerjack. How are your wife and daughter?" said Professor Katnip, smirking. "Oh, I'm so sorry... how cruel of me... my apologies.

I'd almost forgotten about your poor, sweet wife. I do hope your daughter is doing much better."

"Professor, you ought to be ashamed of yourself!" shouted Honey Bee, stepping toward the professor. "I thought you were our friend. How can you be so cruel?"

"What makes you think you'll get away with any of this?" said Jesse, watching the bullkats push their way toward the front of the room and along the walls surrounding them.

"SILENCE!" snapped the professor, his words ricocheting off the walls. "I'm not really a betting man, but if you look around the room, I would say that... strictly scientifically speaking... the odds are slightly in my favor."

"Scientifically speaking, this is just an experiment gone bad!" shouted Tinman, pointing his tranquilizer gun at the professor. "CALL THEM OFF!"

"There is no escape for you," said Professor Katnip, calmly looking around the room. "Once I'm gone, they will attack. You may get me, but you can't get all of these nice kitties."

Mr. Jack moved back toward the prison cell that held the large, ravenous bullkat named Skin. Tinman moved back following Mr. Jack's lead and motioned for the rest of them to follow.

"All for what? Treasure? Money? Look around at what you've done... this will all be for nothing," said Tinman, carefully stepping backwards. "This is not the Tyrtle way."

"It's over, professor!" shouted Mr. Jack, standing in front of the iron bars. "This experiment has gone too far!"

Mr. Jack took a couple bottles of recoil oil out of his pocket and heaved them across the room. The bottles shattered and splattered against the sharp rocks, showering the backs and heads of the horned bullkats. The burners from the labs instantly exploded into flames, splattering the fire onto the backs of the bullkats. The flames engulfed the cats' dry, mangy fur as the fire instantly spread along the entire length of the amphitheater wall.

Jesse and Tinman threw the bottles high into the air and watched as they sailed over to the other side of the amphitheater. The rows of laboratory tables in the center of the room exploded in one gigantic ball of flame, sending a wave of heat across the cavern.

"Get back!" shouted Mr. Jack, pulling them behind him.

He quickly opened the cell door, releasing Skin into the chaotic flaming amphitheater. Skin clawed his way past the iron bars of the cell door, and like a caged animal that was released into the wild, he never looked back. The bullkat headed straight toward the professor, who was standing in the middle of the burning room.

"Quickly! Into the cell!" called out Mr. Jack, holding the heavy iron door open for Jesse and his friends. "No time to argue!"

All the smoking tables along the walls exploded in succession around the monstrous room. The bullkats crashed into one another and frantically slashed around the room with their bodies ablaze. Tinman stood in the entryway of the cell watching the mayhem across the room. He waved Jesse, Honey Bee, and Caleb into the dark cell.

"There's an exit at the back of the cell on the left-hand side," said Mr. Jack, pushing Tinman into the cell. "Just push hard on the white rock. You can't miss it."

Mr. Jack handed Tinman a bottle of recoil oil. He looked Jesse in the eye, placed one hand on Jesse's shoulder, and pulled him close, saying, "Remember, everyone makes mistakes, but life has fewer heartaches if we choose to do the right thing in the first place."

Mr. Jack closed the cell door with Jesse staring back at him through the iron bars, wondering what that was all about.

"Where're you going? Aren't you coming with us?" Tinman said tersely, looking unconvinced at Mr. Jack.

"I have some unfinished business with the professor," said Mr. Jack, looking through the iron door.

They all watched from the inside of the dark cell at the fiery destruction taking place inside the amphitheater. The painful screeching of the burning bullkats was deafening. Professor Katnip was in a standoff with Skin. He splattered the vicious bullkat with the toxic oil. The billowing dark smoke filled the room, and after a few seconds, everyone lost sight of Mr. Jack and Professor Katnip. They watched from inside the prison cell as the professor's catnip lab and the frenzied bullkats were swallowed up in the ferocious flames.

"We gotta get out of here!" cried Tinman, choking on some of the toxic fumes. "Mr. Jack said there's an escape route in the left corner of this cell."

The dark prison cell started to fill with smoke from the anarchy in the amphitheater beyond the iron bars. The dirty, stinky cell had many rocks protruding out from the jagged wall, but if any of the rocks were white, the color was now camouflaged in dirt and filth.

"Push 'em all," yelled Jesse, shoving hard against the rocks.

Scrambling out of Jesse's backpack, Boo placed his front paws on Jesse's shoulder and leaped toward the dark wall. He pounced on one of the filthy rocks sticking out of the wall and then, like a spring, bounced back. Instinctively, his reflexes kicked in, and he landed on all four paws on the gritty ground.

"Boo, I think you did it! That rock moved!" shouted Jesse, pushing it with all his might toward the wall.

"Boo, you really are a magical cat," said Honey Bee, picking him up off the cell floor and holding him close.

Aw, stop… Go on, thought Boo. *Yeah, I know… all that and a box of kitty litter too.*

Caleb smiled at Boo saying, "Show-off."

Boo purred loudly and rubbed his head on Honey Bee's shoulder, thinking, *I just may be the purr-fect cat.*

The wall magically popped open a few inches. Tinman and Caleb breathed heavily, preparing to push open the rock wall, but to their amazement it slid open like it was greased with bat guano. Little did they know, it actually was. They both fell forward, crashing into each other and against the wall.

"Oh, that stinks," said Honey Bee, holding her nose and trying to keep from laughing at Tinman and Caleb as they untangled themselves from one another.

"Let's get out of here," said Tinman. "I'm pretty sure that nasty smell is bat poop, and it can be harmful. Don't touch your face."

Jesse's headlamp revealed rocky stairs spiraling upwards through the dark cavity. The dark stairs turned into a narrow lava tube tunnel. Jesse continued to climb, circling upwards into the darkness with his friends following quietly behind. A glimmer of light could be seen far above their heads, streaming in from the side of the wet tunnel.

"Something just hit my shoulder," said Caleb.

"Don't touch it," said Tinman, flicking a cockroach off his shoulder.

Honey Bee turned her light on the wall and saw that it was crawling with countless cockroaches.

"Now that's… a whole lotta-buncha of roaches," she said, grimacing at the wall plastered with the crawling creatures.

Not too far above him Jesse could see that the tunnel opened up, revealing a very old rocky cathedral. The stone structure permitted the sunlight to stream into the tunnel, and the rainforest came into view just above its walls.

They watched a cauldron of bats fly out from the tunnel and quickly scatter into the morning mist. Jesse popped his head out of the tunnel, and at the same time Boo popped his head out of Jesse's backpack.

"Yahoo!" hollered Jesse, his eyes bulging. "Wahoo! I can't believe it!"

Jesse was thrilled to see they were right smack back in the most stunning place on the island, and that place was Calico's Lagoon.

Honey Bee was the next one to pop her head out of the tunnel. She was relieved to get a breath of fresh air and reinvigorated when she saw the huge vines crawling all over the cathedral walls, adorning it with their colorful fragrant blossoms.

"Oh, what a relief! That smells so good," she said, taking in the fresh flower scent.

Caleb crawled out behind her and was glad to be out of the tube for another reason. He could not hold it any longer and had to let it go.

"Oh, my stomach feels so much better now," said Caleb, sighing.

Tinman was the last to exit the lava tunnel and took in a huge breath of what he thought was going to be fresh air, but he was sorely disappointed.

"Ew! Oh, Caleb! Seriously, couldn't you wait a little longer?" cried Tinman, fanning the air.

Their bodies felt exhausted and their minds emotionally drained from the events they had all just experienced. After escaping the fire in the amphitheater, fighting off the bullkats, and battling the professor, they were ecstatic and relieved to see that their escape route led them to Calico's Lagoon.

Everyone ambled down to the edge of the water and plopped down for a much-needed rest. The sun was still shining brightly, highlighting the magnificence of the flora surrounding the lagoon. The plumeria trees, covered with red, white, and purple flowers, provided the perfect atmosphere for some long-awaited relaxation. The fullness of the tropical trees furnished an abundance of shade. The fragrant blossoms swirled around the lagoon, lingering in the air, and then eventually were carried up and away by the island breeze. This added up to the perfect recipe for the island's unsung heroes to slow down and enjoy some heaven-sent rest.

Jesse leaned back against a smooth rock beneath one of the blossoming trees. Boo crawled up in his lap and watched as his best friend drifted off to sleep surrounded by the dreamiest landscape on the island. The fragrant smell of the blossoms turned to visions of plumerias dancing around in Jesse's head.

tyrtle

CHAPTER NINETEEN: TYRTLE TUNNEL

Jᴇssᴇ ᴏᴘᴇɴᴇᴅ ʜɪs ᴇʏᴇs ᴀɴᴅ found himself in that same magical place. Once again, he was dreaming through those same blue cat eyes.

The first beams of sunlight streaked across the top of the wall far above the lagoon. Boo woke up to the realization that his first real island adventure with his friends was coming to an end. He knew it would be forever etched in his memory. What he didn't realize was that it would also be forever etched in Jesse's memory. The Meow cat and his friends had brought an end to Professor Katnip's evil lab and his reign over the bullkats. They were all exhausted, and their countenances did not hide the sadness they felt from Professor Katnip's betrayal.

The next day they all rested and enjoyed the splendors of Calico's Lagoon. Silver and his family would soon return to their home in The Land of Wig Waggle. The Meow cats would return to Treetop Woods to await their next adventure. For now, though, they were content knowing they had brought an end to Professor Katnip's diabolical plan to control Tyrtle Island. The loss of Bones was a great price to pay. The sadness they felt was overwhelming, having learned the truth about who Bones really was and where he originally came from. Calico was happy to be with his new Meow cat friends, but the bullkat still felt like there was something missing, and he still had a sense of emptiness inside.

"This was one amazing adventure that you can be sure I will never forget," said Silver, looking at Boo and his friends. "My family and I will always be thankful to all of you for how you've helped bring us back together again."

The splendor of Calico's Lagoon filled their senses with inspiration and wonder. Chops floated on his back in the magical lagoon, and everyone watched from the shore as Briar Bee and Briar Bud sprang off of Chops' belly like it was a diving board. They leaped high into the air and splashed into the water, playing with the big Meow cat, who, all of a sudden, didn't seem to mind the water.

Chops launched them high into the air with his powerful paws. "Ouch! Hey, watch out for those needles!" he hollered.

"They're quills!" cried the little porkies, making squeaking and kazo-oing noises just before they splashed into the water.

Everyone wanted to seize the day and enjoy the gift of Calico's Lagoon because they knew the time had come to say goodbye.

Silver and Briar Bow gathered their little porkies from the lagoon and reluctantly said their goodbyes. The exotic birds chirped, whistled, and tweeted their songs and melodies, performing a symphony within the towering walls. The scents of the plumeria trees dazzled their senses of smell, and the stunning colors of the flowers lit up their bright eyes.

Briar Bud and Briar Bee each handed Chops one of their quills as a reminder of their friendship. Everyone was quiet as the prickle of porcupines started their long climb up the stairway toward the top of the wall.

"You know, I think I'm going to miss those little prickly creatures," said Chops, holding the quill in his paw. Using his scarf that was dirty, torn, burnt, and just plain disgusting, he wiped away a tear from the corner of his eye.

"Are you crying?" asked Boo, smiling.

"No, I just have watery eyes," said Chops. "Must be the jellyfish plants."

Boo grinned as he recalled all the funny things that had happened between Silver and Chops. He knew one day they would see Silver and his family again.

Roxy Roo laughed. She looked over at Chops and said, "I don't think I'll ever forget how you and Silver first met… and that yodeling sound was hysterical."

The clowder of cats quietly watched Silver and his family waddle up the last few steps of the spiraling staircase. They could hear the clinking of Silver's tin-tipped tail as it tapped the top of each step and slowly faded away. The lovable creatures disappeared through the magnificent banyan tree leading to the Roundabout Rainforest.

"I'm going to miss those pudgy pink noses," said Roxy Roo, looking at Calico's sad face.

Calico gazed at his bullkat reflection that rippled across the water in the crystal-clear lagoon. His once-unnerving bullkat looks had become quite ordinary to his friends. They saw Calico almost as if he was just an ordinary Meow cat. They knew in their hearts he was still a bullkat, but, somehow, they saw him much differently now.

"I know I'm just a bullkat," said Calico, purring heavily. "I just don't understand why bullkats are cursed."

"Oh, you're not cursed," said Chops. "Don't listen to all that silly stuff that Silver said about legends, curses, and Wiki Tyrtle. If you want my opinion, I think he's been nibbling on some funny bark."

"Why? What's the matter?" asked Roxy Roo.

"We are going to find Wiki Tyrtle," said Boo. "I promised Calico."

"You mean the legend?" said Chops sarcastically.

"We met his brother Wacky right here in this spot, and we all saw the writing in the cave," said Boo. "I want to help Calico, and I think we should all help him. The only way we can do that is to find out if there's any truth to this legend. The only way that will happen is if we go to the Land of No End and find the Tyrtle Tunnel."

"Wacky Tyrtle!" shouted Chops. "His name is Wacky. Doesn't that tell you everything you need to know?"

"We have to try," said Boo. "It's the least we can do for Calico after all he's done for us. Besides, we already agreed we would take him there, and Meow cats always keep their promises."

They watched as the dancing jellyfish flowers swirled around and around until they were caught up in the air and lifted over the lagoon walls. Usually, the flowers floated in the direction of Coral Way Bay, but this time they were swept toward the Land of No End and the mythical Wiki Island.

"I think the jellyfish flowers are trying to tell us something," declared Roxy Roo.

Chapter Nineteen

Boo led everyone up the stairs and through the banyan tree leading out to the rainforest and beyond.

Calico informed them of an old big-toed bugger that had a raft on the Roundabout River. He had no doubt that the creature could take them down the river safely to the Land of No End.

When they arrived at the river, the sight of the gigantic big-toed bugger was not as shocking as the first time they crossed paths with one of these creatures at the Rainbow River.

This big-toed bugger was much larger but no stranger-looking than the first one they encountered. He moved ridiculously slow just like the other one and looked as though he was just as miserable. Amazingly, the big-toed buggers' reputation for making sure that island creatures made it safely up, down, or across the river was a well-known fact.

There was no point in greeting a big-toed bugger by saying hello or goodbye. One way or another, they didn't seem to take notice of anything much at all. For reasons unknown to the island creatures, big-toed buggers were only concerned with accomplishing the task at hand. They were only interested in making sure that island creatures got safely to wherever they were going. For a big-toed bugger, that meant getting across the river, down the river, or up the river. They seemed oblivious to anything else going on around them.

"They all look the same," said Chops, looking curiously over at the oversized hairy creature.

"How would you know?" asked Boo. "You've only seen two big-toed buggers in your entire life."

"True, but both of them looked like they could be twins," replied Chops. "Maybe they're brothers... or... maybe sisters? How can you tell?"

Boo grinned at Chops and asked, "Seriously?"

One by one they hopped up on the big river-raft and scurried over toward the bow of the raft, quickly lining up along the railing. Without speaking a word, they all watched intently as the slow-moving big-toed bugger painfully moved into position at the stern of the raft.

After what seemed like an eternity, the raft started to float slowly down the long river. They floated past the lush green slopes of the Roundabout

Mountains on their starboard side and watched the steep, treacherous slopes of Kats Caves disappear behind them on their port side.

Calico was noticeably quiet as he thought about the legendary Tyrtle Tunnel and Wiki Tyrtle.

"I miss Silver and his little pink nose," said Roxy Roo. "Porcupines have the cutest little noses."

"Oh, yeah, I miss him too," said Chops. "Especially all those cute little sharp needles."

Roxy Roo and Boo burst out in laughter. They knew Chops really did miss Silver, even if he would never admit it.

The raft started to pick up speed, moving swiftly down the river.

The big-toed bugger was almost motionless, sitting at the stern of the raft as he moved the keel handle ever so slightly with his giant claws. He somehow managed to steer the raft just enough to miraculously miss the huge boulders poking out of the bubbling white water of the Roundabout River. The friends held on tightly, digging their claws into the weathered railing and deck made of logs. Their big eyes watched the skilled navigator as he seemed to maneuver effortlessly around each and every giant rock with absolute precision. Before they knew it, the fast-moving river slowed, and the raft floated into an emerald-green lagoon. Boo watched through the trees as the water from the middle fork of the river tumbled over the rocky cliffs and into Bullkat Bay below. The main fork of the Roundabout River continued to wander off in a winding course toward the Three Peaks.

"I'm not really sure how he did it, and to be honest, I don't think I really want to know," said Chops, prying his claws out of the wooden railing.

Calico looked at the water cascading rapidly over the cliffs. "I'm just happy the big-toed bugger didn't miss his turn."

The big-toed bugger never looked over in the direction of his grateful passengers. The creature just gazed toward the swiftly-moving river as Boo and his friends jumped off the raft onto dry land.

Boo looked back at the raft and wondered how the incredible creature would manage to get it back upstream. He quickly shrugged off the thought and focused on the massive lava-rock trail before them. The barren volcanic rock was covered with scars created long ago by the toxic gases released, leaving only a landscape covered in bubble-like holes that were known as vesicles.

The playful cats jumped over and pounced around the large holes. Roxy Roo leaped and bounced off of Boo while Calico leaped and bounced off of Chops along the way. They planned on playing the whole way to the mythical Tyrtle Tunnel through the Land of No End.

Chops looked at Calico sternly. "I'm not sure how I feel about a bullkat jumping on me."

Calico's face was overcome with worry as he looked back at Chops.

"Got ya!" blurted out Chops, jumping on Calico and knocking him to the ground.

"Strange name, 'Land of No End,'" said Calico, picking himself back up off the rock. "Wonder what it means."

"It's because of the Tyrtle Tunnel," said Boo. "The legend tells of a mythical passageway at the end of the peninsula called the Tyrtle Tunnel. Once you find the tunnel, then there's no end to the places you can go."

Boo continued, "I was also told the same thing by Harriet, who is one of the elder Meow cats. She said that the Tyrtle Tunnel can lead to many places, including Wiki Island."

"Really?" said Chops, looking skeptically at Boo. "It must be true if that's what the legend says, or Harry or Harriet or whoever. I wonder how they would know anyway."

"I also heard that even if by chance you do find the Tyrtle Tunnel, some creatures may not be able to pass through. Whether you can pass through or not depends on the condition of your heart," said Roxy Roo.

"Oh, I see," said Calico, sounding concerned. "I wonder if I have a good heart."

"Yeah, right… and cats have nine lives," said Chops.

Boo and Roxy Roo gave Chops the look of death. He then realized what he had just implied to Calico.

"Oh, wow… Sorry, little bullkat buddy," said Chops apologetically. "That 'nine lives' comment was for Roxy Roo. I'm not really sure I can tell you the condition of your heart, but I do know this much: I think I can speak for everyone when I say that you have left your pawprints on all of our hearts."

Calico's face lit up like the sun. He began to run around and pounce all over the bumpy lava rock like a kangaroo. Not that any of these Tyrtle Island cats had ever actually seen a kangaroo.

Roxy Roo grinned from ear to ear as she looked at Chops. She felt the most wonderful feeling flow through her bones, and she was so happy to have a friend like Chops. She rubbed her furry cheeks up against his face and purred softly.

Boo smiled from ear to ear looking at the big Meow cat and said, "Sometimes you really surprise me."

Chops actually looked a little embarrassed from all the heartfelt attention he was suddenly getting, but that look was short-lived.

Boo grinned at Chops and said, "Reminds me of the time I found out that you're afraid of cucumbers."

"Hey, they really do look like snakes," said Chops.

Boo quickly changed the atmosphere back to normal by slapping Chops across the head, and they both went pouncing down the plateau, chasing after one another.

The Land of No End's long lava plateau was unlike any landscape or terrain they had seen before. The plateau continued to rise in elevation as they climbed closer to the tip of the peninsula.

The closer they got to the end of the plateau, the more centipedes and crabs they encountered crawling in and out of the holes and crevices.

Roxy Roo was careful where she placed her paws. "Watch out for the centipedes."

"Ouch!" Chops yelled painfully. "Centipedes… I hate centipedes."

She had warned him a couple seconds too late.

"Tried… to… tell… you," said Roxy Roo, looking at Chops' painful expression.

Chops was hopping around holding his paw, looking madder than a barefoot centipede standing on a pile of hot lava rocks.

"Oh, wow," said Roxy Roo. "Boo, come and look at the size of this thing before he disappears."

"That's a big one!" said Boo, in awe of the insect's massive claws.

"Hello? I'm in some serious pain over here," said Chops, wiggling around in agony as he sat on the lava rock.

"Chops, are you alright?" asked Calico, showing off the size of the centipede dangling from his claws. "You're right, this is a big one. Bet that bite really hurt."

Chops tried to open his mouth, but it was clenched closed from the stinging pain. He picked up a loose lava rock from the ground and threw it at a crab scurrying sideways across the plateau, missing it completely before the creature disappeared into a hole.

"You'll be OK, big guy," said Boo, slapping his friend on the back. "Let's get going."

Boo helped Chops up off the hard ground and pointed in front of him to another centipede that was crawling out of one crevice and into another.

Calico watched Boo and his friends closely and wanted more than anything to be as close to another creature as they were to one another. He knew that kind of friendship would never be possible with another bullkat. He felt like something was missing from deep inside. He hoped that Wiki Tyrtle would provide the answer he was looking for.

The sun setting behind them stretched out their shadows across the plateau as the cats walked along on the barren, pockmarked landscape. Their eyes watched intently as they placed each paw in front of the other, carefully dodging the crawling creatures, bubble holes, and crevices along the way.

The anticipation of reaching the end of the plateau and seeing the Tyrtle Tunnel made the journey through the Land of No End seem like... well... it would never end.

Boo looked over at Chops, and seeing the expression on his face, he knew what was on his mind.

"Here it comes," he said, whispering to Roxy Roo.

"Are there any cat snacks left?" asked Chops, glancing curiously at Boo and Roxy Roo, who were smiling.

Without saying a word, Roxy Roo took out the last of the fish snacks and divided them equally among everyone.

The end of the plateau had finally come into view as Chops gulped down the last bits of his cat snack. They threw down their catpacks and walked over to the edge of the plateau. There were rugged black rocks following the shoreline around the tip of the peninsula. The scent of the salt water and the roar of the waves crashing against the lava rocks far below them in Bullkat Bay filled their senses, but everywhere they looked there was no sign of the Tyrtle Tunnel.

The built-up anticipation inside each of them came to a crashing halt, and the disappointment was written plainly across their faces. Looking around the plateau, they saw no obvious signs or helpful clues pointing to the mystical Tyrtle Tunnel. All they could see before them was millennia of erosion caused by the unrelenting salt water and tropical storms that had continually splashed and sprayed the barren landscape.

"Calico, is everything alright?" asked Roxy Roo.

Calico didn't answer her right away. She already knew what was on his mind, but this time she didn't have any answers for him.

"There's no Tyrtle Tunnel," said Calico sorrowfully.

One more time, walking in different directions, they searched up and down the edge of the plateau that was high above the water. Boo looked over the length of the plateau and peered out over the edge of the cliffs, trying to spot anything unusual at all, but he saw nothing other than the barren landscape, the rugged rocks resting in Bullkat Bay, and the vast ocean surrounding him.

Chops was disenchanted and worn out. He meandered in the opposite direction and sat down to rest next to a large open hole nestled between some large lava rocks. He peered down into the deep dark hole and could feel the rocks rumbling beneath his paws.

"I think there's something down here!" yelled Chops, his voice echoing down the hole.

Calico leaped over the rocks to where Chops was sitting and yanked Chops' head back from above the hole. Unknown to Chops, if Calico had waited another second, he would have been blasted with water gushing up through the giant hole. A second later, a powerful blast of ocean water jetted out from the blowhole, spraying high into the air. The salty water returned to the top of the plateau like a tropical rain shower pouring down on them.

Roxy Roo ran over to Boo and swished her paw quickly back and forth over his wet head. "I know what they mean!" she cried out.

"What who means?" asked Chops, wiping the water off his face.

"The ancient island symbols," said Boo, looking at Chops. "Inside the cave of symbols, remember?"

"It's the blowhole," said Roxy Roo. "The symbol of the turtle and the lines that we thought were sunrays. The arrows shooting upward and dots scattered above. They symbolize the water spraying out of the blowhole. It's the blowhole! The way to the Tyrtle Tunnel is through the blowhole!"

"The blowhole leads to Wiki Tyrtle and to Wiki Island," said Boo. "Yes, of course. That's why the symbols of lines, arrows, and dots stopped just below the turtle symbol."

"OK, I love you cats, but this time, I think you're crazy-cats," said Chops. "That blowhole will suck you in and then crush you like a firebug."

"I don't think so. Not if we time it right," said Calico. "Excuses are like litter boxes: they all stink. I'm in!"

"What do you mean 'I'm in'? I think you're in for it if you go down that blowhole," said Chops. "By the way, what kind of symbol was that hanging around the turtle's neck?"

"Don't know the answer to that one," said Roxy Roo. "But I gotta believe we'll find out after we go down that hole."

The cats watched patiently as the waves continued to grow in size with each passing swell. They waited for what seemed to be the precise moment when, finally, a huge swell of water pushed up under the plateau and, after a couple of seconds, the water came blasting out of the top of the blowhole, showering them once again.

"I say we go now," said Calico. "That seemed like it was forever and ever between blasts."

"Let's roll!" said Boo, peering into the blowhole.

Just as the water stopped and started to suck back down into the hole, Boo abruptly jumped in, tail first, and disappeared below the rocks.

Calico and Roxy Roo jumped in, following Boo into the unknown.

Chops stood on the flat lava rocks, peering into the hole as his friends slid down and disappeared from his sight.

"I must be a ditzy cat," he thought to himself, plugging his nose with his big paws before jumping in tail first.

This leap of faith would change each one of these incredible creatures forever, but for Calico, it was a life-changing event. Calico's life, as he knew it, vanished the instant he leaped out of the sunlight and into the dark blowhole. Whether he was flying or floating on a cushion of air he could not be sure, but there was no doubt he was in a state of freefall and headed toward an unknown destination. The bullkat could feel the intense sensation of the violent water spraying against his face. The scent of the salt water rushed up his nostrils, stealing his breath away. The adrenaline rush he felt falling through the blowhole instantly changed from an exhilarating fear into something he could've never imagined. He was in the middle of a slow-motion, supernatural journey. This unexplainable phenomenon allowed him to see his Meow cat friends slowly floating and rolling through a kaleidoscope of rainbow waves, but he could also see himself with his own eyes. It was like he was looking into a magical mirror.

Looking into each other's big, colorful cat eyes, they were swept away into an incredible unknown world. Not a word was spoken as they rolled around in the kaleidoscope wave. At that moment, there was not a doubt in any one of their minds that the legend was true. These cats were on the ultimate catwalk; they were passing through the legendary Tyrtle Tunnel.

The kaleidoscope of rainbow colors continued to rotate slowly around them. It looked and felt like they were swimming in the ocean, but amazingly, their fur was dry, as if they were somehow waterproof. With eyes bulging and cheeks puffed out, the cats held their breath for as long as possible, until they could hold it no longer. To their surprise and relief, they could breathe perfectly. When they finally stopped moving, the cats landed like cats always do, with all four paws. This time they landed on the shore of a mystical island somewhere under the ocean.

The island's sandy shores glistened with flakes of gold, and the fantastical palm trees swayed along with the ocean currents. The palms that lined the glittering shore continued along both sides of a river that flowed with crystal-clear water. The pristine water cascading down the unending falls into the river illuminated the rainbow fish that jumped in and out as they worked their way upstream. The source of the magical underwater falls flowed out of the powerful ocean currents above. The lush island trees abounded with every kind of edible fruit imaginable. The island landscape was carpeted with glowing seaweed grass that moved around as the current swept over the ground. The fields of seaweed were teeming with sea turtles chomping on the life-giving grass just before they ventured across the ocean. Three brilliant rainbows arched across Wiki Island in a zigzag pattern, touching end-to-end against the watery sky.

"Are we dead or are we dreaming?" asked Chops. "I'm hoping we're dreamin'."

"I'm going with dreamin' and I think he's doin' the same thing," said Boo.

Wiki Tyrtle gracefully moved through the kaleidoscope waves, gliding toward Wiki Island like he was swimming in a magical ocean of flowing rainbows.

"I know why you're here," said Wiki Tyrtle, speaking in a calming voice.

"It's our friend, Calico," said Boo. "He wants—"

"I know what he wants," said Wiki Tyrtle, looking at Calico directly with his big wise eyes. "In your heart, you have asked to become a new creature, and you took a leap of faith. Follow the Creator of all creatures and, today, you will be made into a new creature."

Wiki Tyrtle slowly took the ring of glowing seaweed from around his wrinkled neck and placed it over Calico's head.

A sense of peacefulness came over Calico as he looked into Wiki Tyrtle's calming eyes. Calico tilted his head side to side as he watched the colors of the ocean flow through the Tyrtle's eyes.

The wise old Tyrtle then turned his wondrous shell around, and with his colorful slippers covering his feet, he paddled silently away. The legendary Tyrtle moved gently through the water and quietly disappeared back into the maze of kaleidoscopic rainbow colors.

Chops peered out into the watery vapors and couldn't believe his eyes. He saw Wacky Tyrtle waving at him with one of his slippered feet.

Tyrtle Tunnel

"Well, I'll be a skunk's armpit. It's Wacky Tyrtle!" cried Chops.

In the next moment they could feel themselves being pulled off the shore of Wiki Island and back into the kaleidoscope of rolling rainbow waves. Just as quickly as they had entered the Tyrtle Tunnel, an unknown force pulled them back up through the blowhole and spat them out into the air above the peninsula.

The cats all landed on all four paws, just like cats always do, except this time they were soaking wet. Stunned by the unimaginable events they had just experienced, they stood frozen in place. The cats looked into each other's eyes and then slowly realized what had just taken place. Everyone started to jump up and down with incredible joy.

"That was cat-tacular!" shouted Chops.

"That was the most unbelievable thing that I could have never imagined," said Roxy Roo.

"That was beyond unbelievable," said Boo.

"That was a new beginning for me," said Calico, a big grin across his face.

At that very moment of celebration, a kaleidoscope of unicorn butterflies sailed over the top of the cats, sprinkling the sky with rainbow-colored confetti. The unicorn butterflies dazzled them with the biggest extravaganza of acrobatic flight they had ever seen.

"The unicorn butterflies!" cried out Roxy Roo, looking upwards and holding onto her full and fluffy tail as she danced around in circles on the lava rock plateau.

Chops brushed the butterfly confetti off his head and looked up, gazing at the colorful acrobats in the sky. "I hope that's confetti," he said, sniffing some of the colorful particles that landed on his paw.

Together the friends celebrated the spectacular performance by singing and dancing along the edge of the Land of No End.

They sang out together, a song something like this:

Rivers of rainbows and unicorns above!
All made possible out of love!
Oceans of creatures, heart to heart!

It's our Creator from the start!
Friendship and freedom, we stand upon!
Keep calm and Tyrtle on! Keep calm and Tyrtle on!

They danced, sang, and purred until their paws grew tired and their bellies started to growl, reminding them that the time had come to start back toward the Roundabout River. They were all sad that this magical time was coming to an end, but everyone knew it was time to start the journey back home to Treetop Woods.

"I can't wait to take Calico fishing at Fish Flop Cove," said Chops, slapping Calico on the back.

Boo smiled and looked at Chops. "Yeah, that will be awesome, and I hope you actually let him have some of the fish."

"Any kind of fish sounds good right now," said Roxy Roo and Calico at the same time.

"Even a macadamia nut and jellyfish sandwich," cried out Chops, making a goofy cat-face as he pulled on his whiskers.

The journey back across the plateau went by quickly as they listened to each other's stories and laughed about their adventures along the way.

They all missed their treehouse homes in Treetop Woods and all the cat comforts that a feline could hope for. Most of all, they were excited that they would now be able to share their home with Calico.

Arriving back at the emerald lagoon, they quickly filled their bellies on the multitude of delicious fish. Then, as usual, a long catnap seemed like a great idea. Each one of the cats quickly found their own comfy place next to one another under the island night sky.

"Today is the best day ever," said Boo.

Calico smiled at his friends and said, "It's much friendlier with friends."

"Just makes me wish I could eat more fish," said Chops, rubbing his full belly.

"I can't wait to see what happens tomorrow," said Roxy Roo.

Before long, the tropical breeze whisked them off to sleep. The sound of the water falling over the cliffs into Bullkat Bay was like a soothing lullaby, and everyone slept soundly through the night.

The sun was bright the next morning when they started to stir. To no one's surprise, there was a big-toed bugger waiting patiently on his raft ready to take them down the river. Nobody had a clue as to how the big-toed bugger actually knew they needed a ride on that particular morning, but nonetheless, there he was.

Chops stretched out his furry body and looked over at the big hairy creature waiting on the raft. "Well, fry me in butter and call me a catfish. I don't really understand it, but I'm glad he's here."

"Let's go, all you courageous cats," said Boo, jumping up on the raft. "We still have a long way to go, and I'm looking forward to getting back to my favorite scratching post."

The big-toed bugger navigated quietly down the river, floating smoothly between the Rainbow Roads. The island creatures scurried through the fields and gathered along the side of the roads. The colorful native flowers swayed along in the island breeze, dancing with the creatures in celebration of the return of the Meow cats and their defeat of the bullkats. Unknown to Boo and his friends, their heroic story had already spread throughout all of Tyrtle Island.

The island creatures gathered together, eagerly sharing the adventurous tales of the Meow cats. Birds from all over the island soared high above the raft, squawking and chirping in song. The macaws, finches, and red-crested cardinals flew in colorful patterns, encircling the raft, while the ducks, geese, and swans paddled alongside, flapping their wings. Each songbird greeted the passing heroes by whistling its own unique song of celebration.

The courageous cats looked out over the side of the raft toward the Three Peaks and watched the wild island hogs, dogs, cats, and rats scurry down from their hiding places. Merrily, merrily, the raft meandered gently down the river as the creatures celebrated together and life was but a dream.

Chops observed all that was going on around him and said, "This is crazy… look at all these strange creatures. Looks like the cat's outta the bag."

"Tyrtle Island is amazing," said Roxy Roo, walking to the other side of the floating raft and gazing at the beautiful creatures and landscape surrounding her.

Chapter Nineteen

"I wonder if there are other Tyrtle Islands out there somewhere," said Chops.

"Some of the turtles and birds returning from their long journeys across the ocean tell tales of faraway places with many strange and incredible creatures," said Boo.

"Do you know why Tyrtle Island is so wonderful?" asked Roxy Roo.

"Don't know what you're thinkin', but it's gotta be the fish," said Chops, running his tongue over his whiskers.

Roxy Roo smiled and said, "It's because of you and every other creature that lives on Tyrtle Island."

Roxy Roo thought about each and every one of those incredibly designed creatures and knew they had a story to tell. Their invisible lives were full of struggles, ambitions, families, and even foes. She knew that each creature lived a life as complex as her own. In many ways, all of the creatures were miraculously connected together.

"How do they already know about the professor and the bullkats?" asked Chops.

"Gotta be Silver and his family," said Boo. "I'm sure they wasted no time in spreading the good news."

The Roundabout River turned sharply, flowing west past the Three Peaks, and then gently emptied into the Quiet Ocean. The natural monument of the Three Peaks symbolized the spirit of Tyrtle Island. The three giant peaks stood towering above the southeast side of the island as a symbolic reminder of the Creator of all things. The island itself and the amazing creatures living on it were all the proof the creatures needed to understand they were all wonderfully made. The spirit of Tyrtle Island taught all of the creatures that each of them have an inherent worth and value, and they are all connected to one another. Most importantly, they all had to stick together and live according to the Tyrtle spirit.

The raft slowed and almost came to a stop as they slipped into the blue water of the Quiet Ocean. They floated along smoothly across the bay until something unknown bumped hard against the bottom of the raft. The big-toed bugger didn't even flinch as he continued heading straight for Fish Flop Cove.

"What was that?" asked Chops, sticking his head through the railing and peering into the water. "Where'd everyone go?"

The thriving sea life swimming through the water quickly vanished, and large ripples could be seen flowing across the bay. The Land of Meow Cats and their home in Treetop Woods came into view across the other side of the bay.

"I can see the treetops!" shouted Roxy Roo. "First thing I'm going to do is have a nice cup of—"

Roxy Roo stopped short of finishing her sentence as she realized that any mention of catnip tea was a sad reminder of Professor Katnip.

Boo quickly changed the subject and said, "I can't wait to see Silver and his family again."

Chops' eyes were fixed on something very large and green slithering slowly through the calm waters. "Yeah, well, speaking of funny-looking creatures, what in the world is that thing?" he asked, pointing his paw toward the creature.

The green sea creature flicked its massive spiked tail and quickly vanished under the water, leaving a trail of large ripples rolling through the water behind it.

"What thing?" asked Boo, looking at Chops. "I missed it. Are you sure it wasn't just a big fish?"

"If that was a fish, then I'm a saber-toothed tiger," said Chops. "I hope I'm never in the water with a monstrous creature like that."

None of the Meow cats had ever seen a saber-toothed tiger. They had heard about the ferocious cats from the Golden Plover birds who had encountered the cats when visiting faraway lands. The only thing Chops really knew about saber-toothed tigers was they were very big cats with big scary teeth. Best of all, he knew they didn't live on Tyrtle Island.

As quickly as the mysterious creature vanished, the waters surrounding the raft filled up again with every kind of sea life imaginable. The broad spectrum of fish jumping in and out of the water was indescribable. The green sea turtles paddled around the raft while the dolphins performed their aquatic dance over and over. The happy dolphins jumped for joy, high into the air, returning nose-first into the water with a giant splash.

The good news had also been spread throughout the ocean by Wacky Tyrtle and his Tyrtle friends. The humpback whales could be seen offshore performing their aerial antics. Air sprayed out of their powerful blowholes, creating a giant fountain in the sky above them.

"Look how beautiful! It's a rainbow above the whale!" shouted Roxy Roo.

"That's a first," said Chops. "That's what I would call a whale of a rainbow."

The stream of warm air from the whale's lungs sprayed out through the spout in the top of the creature's head. The cloud of mist, created by the whale's breath and a mixture of salty water, streamed high above the giant mammal's black and white body, forming a perfect little rainbow against the silky blue sky.

Roxy Roo looked around at her friends' happy faces. She looked back with empathy at the old big-toed bugger, who was seated at the stern of the raft, leaning against the tiller. Big-toed buggers were known to be very solemn creatures and almost never displayed any emotions at all. Her heart swelled as the creature's countenance changed from his usual expression of sadness and a smile formed across his coconut-shaped face. She was happy to see the gigantic creature enjoying the celebration taking place all around him.

Earless monk seals relaxed on the sandy shores of the beach, revealing their land and sea battle-scars, tattooed across their beautiful brown and black bodies. The robber crabs climbed out of their underground homes and quickly scurried down the beach, heading for the closest of the coconut palms lined up along the shoreline.

The familiar inlet between Fish Flop Cove and the Pouncing Place came into view as the raft rounded the corner. A few minutes later, the craft gently bumped up against the marshy shore.

"I can smell those good ol' mint-n-fish cookies from here," said Chops, running his tongue across his long whiskers.

Calico was the first cat to jump off the raft onto the rickety wooden dock. He was so excited he could hardly keep from bouncing around as he turned back toward his friends and said, "Let's go, you guys. We gotta go fishing."

"Where is everyone?" asked Boo, surprised that they were not greeted by a single Meow cat, or any other creature, for that matter.

The sunbeams filtered through the tall trees as the sun started to set. At that moment, one of the Meow cat elders came into view from out of the shadows of the trees. The elderly cat walked up slowly to Boo and his friends, who were still standing up on the dock.

"Hello, Harry," said Boo. "It's a good day to be back home in Treetop Woods."

"What? Oh… yes… indeed. Welcome home! Everyone is gathered at the Pouncing Place," said Harry. "We've all been anxiously awaiting your arrival."

"Sorry, Calico, looks like we have to wait a little longer to partake of some of those delicious fish snacks," said Boo apologetically.

"What did you say?" asked Harry, straining his ears and pointing the way down the well-worn path toward the Pouncing Place.

"I said… we're so excited to be home!" said Boo, raising his voice.

"We're all shocked to hear the sad news about Professor Katnip," said Harry. "Some Meow cats, and many other creatures, doubt your—well—everyone wants to hear your side of the story. I hate to say this, but there are those who doubt the truthfulness of it all."

They walked slowly behind Harry, listening to what he had to say as everyone continued along the path toward the gathering place.

"Some even say that you have befriended a bullkat," said Harry, looking back at Calico suspiciously.

It was just about dark as they arrived at the old fortress walls. Climbing up through the opening, they could see a very large crowd of Meow cats and other island creatures gathered together. Some of the curious crowd were waiting to greet the island heroes and hear firsthand about their exciting adventure. Others were angry about what happened to Bones and Professor Katnip. In fact, they doubted the cats were heroes at all.

Boo walked into the center of the old fortress walls and waited for the creatures to quiet down. Roxy Roo, Chops, and Calico followed him into the middle of the crowd that had now closed in around them.

Harry raised his old, quivering paw in the air and said, "Please, everyone calm down."

Boo's heart began to beat faster as he looked out into the crowd and started to speak. "I know you have all come together in this special place anxiously awaiting to hear about our adventure. More importantly, I know you want to hear about what actually happened to Professor Katnip, Bones, and the bullkats. It has been a very long road for all of us. Today, this adventure has come to an end. Without further ado, I would like to introduce our good friend Calico to the Meow cat family."

The voices of the crowd grew louder and could be heard murmuring about Bones, Calico, Professor Katnip, and the bullkats.

"First, I know how sad we all are at the loss of Bones. His Tyrtle spirit will always be with us. All of the Meow cats and creatures on Tyrtle Island must know that it was Bones and Calico who saved our lives, and they did this more than once," Boo said loudly, feeling quite uncomfortable and aware of all the creatures glaring at him. "They are the real heroes of this story."

Boo tried to continue, but the voices of the crowd erupted at the very thought that any bullkat could possibly be considered a hero.

"QUIET!... QUIET!" Chops shouted thunderously, easily drowning out the voices of the overzealous crowd.

"Some of you may or may not know that Bones was born a bullkat, but along the way... he became a new creature... in his heart he showed us that he truly was a Meow cat and lived by the Tyrtle Spirit," said Boo, placing his paw on Calico's shoulder.

The crowd closed in on the cats, and some of them glared at Calico.

Chops stepped in front of Calico and whispered, "If they want to get to you, they'll have to go through me first."

"What about Professor Katnip? What really happened to him?" asked a voice shouting out from the crowd.

"We're all shocked to hear the sad news about Professor Katnip," said Boo. "I don't believe he made it out of the amphitheater alive."

The crowd went crazy, accusing Boo and his friends of lying about Professor Katnip. After all, he was the most famous and respected Meow cat on the island.

Boo nervously looked around at the cast of creatures surrounding them and said, "I know you have your doubts, but there are witnesses who will testify to the truth of our story. I'll write down all the details of our adventure, starting with our very first steps in Treetop Woods, all the way through to the bittersweet ending."

At this time, Boo had no way of knowing that this adventure would be the first of many for him and his companions. He listened to the whispers and murmurings of the crowd as he walked out from amidst them.

He and his friends were quiet as they walked back through Treetop Woods in the moonlight.

Finally Boo broke the silence and said, "It's funny how things can change so quickly."

All of the island creatures had celebrated them as heroes on their return trip home. That feeling of complete euphoria had now turned to disappointment and confusion after the greeting and accusations they had received from their very own family of Meow cats.

"Just remember, lies are like a litter box: if you don't come clean, then you'll eventually start to stink," said Chops, trying his best to make everyone feel better.

Boo smiled at his good buddy and said, "Chops, I don't know where you come up with this stuff, but I love it."

The warmth of being able to sleep in their own cozy cat beds and the creature comforts inside their treehouses, along with Chops' humor, brought some solace to the cats as they went to bed that night.

Early the next morning Boo and Calico met Roxy Roo and Chops at their familiar meeting place by the old coquina wall in the midst of the giant trees. Boo was sporting a brand new black and white scarf around his neck.

"Oh, no, I forgot my scarf," said Chops, looking over at Boo.

"I don't think so… not this time, big guy," said Boo, glancing at Roxy Roo.

Chapter Nineteen

Their hearts raced with excitement, and their paws moved with exhilaration down the trail, knowing the day had finally come to take Calico fishing at Fish Flop Cove.

They were happy to be home in Treetop Woods, but at the same time their minds overflowed with thoughts of their journey and the desire to continue to explore their island. Everyone was excited as they hurried along the path that led around the inlet to one of their favorite places in the Land of Meow cats.

"I'll bet you can't put more fish away than Chops," said Boo, lying down next to Calico at the edge of the water.

"I know I saw it with my own eyes, but I still have to scratch myself every time I realize that the legends of Wiki Tyrtle and the Tyrtle Tunnel are true," said Roxy Roo, catching the first fish flopping up out of the water.

"We all rode it, and we all stood on that unbelievable beach on Wiki Island," said Chops, gulping down a rainbow fish.

Boo tossed Chops another fish and said, "Wow, Tyrtle Tunnel and Wiki Island... and now it seems like it was just a dream."

Calico smiled at his friends, saying, "You know, these fish are almost as tasty as the ones swimming in my lagoon."

"Oh, OK, I see how it's going to be. A little friendly competition. May the best cat win," said Chops, grinning with a mouthful of fish.

Boo was content as he looked around at the beautiful surroundings of his island home and the smiling faces of his friends. They were as happy as a cat... well... a cat fishing at Fish Flop Cove. They all knew this really was as good as it gets, as each one of them filled their bellies with an abundance of rainbow fish.

Boo grinned from ear to ear, handing Chops another fish, and said, "Today really is the best day ever."

turtle

CHAPTER TWENTY: THE JOURNEY HOME

Jesse woke up with a feeling of contentment, and as far as he could tell, he was as blessed as anyone could possibly be. The flowering plumeria trees above him filled his world with a rainbow of colors from the moment he opened his eyes. He didn't have to look around for Boo. He could feel Boo's soft fur snuggled up against his bare feet, and as far as he was concerned, that was one of the greatest feelings in the world. He sat up and pulled Boo close to him, looking out over the lagoon.

Jesse noticed that the magical water had changed from an incredible emerald green to a crystal-clear blue. His stomach rumbled with hunger. He reached into his pocket, hoping to find something to eat, but he was almost certain that his pockets were empty. Deep down in the corner of his pocket, his fingertips rubbed against something that didn't feel anything like food. Curious, he quickly pulled out the object, which happened to be a beautiful stone. Jesse gazed at the alluring stone as he held it in the palm of his hand. He had absolutely no idea how one of the precious jewels from Sparkling Caverns had found its way into his pocket.

"Look what I found!" announced Jesse, holding the radiant stone up above his head.

A spectrum of colors shot out from the jewel as the sunlight penetrated it, casting colorful beams across the water.

"Jesse, what are you doing with that?" asked Tinman. "Why did you take that?"

"I didn't… well, not on purpose anyway," said Jesse. "I just found it in my pocket, honest."

Tinman, Honey Bee, and Caleb stared at Jesse for a few seconds.

"What?" asked Jesse, defensively. "Honest... I'm not a thief!"

"Nobody's calling you a thief," said Tinman. "Here's the problem. If anyone were to see you with that stone and the word got out that you know where Sparkling Caverns is located, then you and I will have more trouble at our doorsteps than we know what to do with. Not to mention what would happen to the island. It would become overrun with treasure hunters."

Jesse knew that Tinman was right. If people found out about Sparkling Caverns, then Tyrtle Island would be flooded with treasure-seekers from around the world. They had just destroyed the professor's evil lab, and his threat to the island had come to an end, but as to the survival of Professor Katnip, none of them were completely sure. They really had no idea if he or any of the bullkats had escaped the fiery inferno.

They knew the odds were against Mr. Jack making it out of the amphitheater alive, but they all hoped that he had. Everyone understood they didn't need to invite more trouble to the island by making the riches of Sparkling Caverns known to the outside world. They had no choice; it had to be kept a secret.

Jesse felt uncomfortable keeping the stone in his pocket, but for some reason he could not simply toss the amazing stone away.

Sitting close to the edge of the clear blue water, they rested for a few more hours. The turtles swimming in the lagoon, along with the rest of the sea creatures, easily entertained them. They were mesmerized by the twirling jellyfish plants with their long colorful tails floating up and over the top of the lagoon walls. The plants floated around the towering waterfall, and everyone gazed in wonder, watching them spin around until they disappeared into the tropical blue sky.

"Well, as much as I hate to say it, I think we better get going," said Tinman. "We need to let the authorities know that Mr. Jack and the professor are missing."

Honey Bee sighed. "I love this place and feel like I could stay here forever," she said, knowing it was time to leave.

"I can promise you this much: we will be back," said Tinman.

"I hate to leave too, but I'm gettin' hungry, and we're just about out of food," said Caleb, munching on the last of their snacks.

Tinman smiled at Caleb. "That's what I love most about Caleb: he's always thinking about what's most important."

Lava was resting contently on Honey Bee's shoulder. The big gecko glanced back with his blood-red eyes, looking at Boo.

"OK, last chance, Lava," said Honey Bee. "It doesn't get any better than Calico's Lagoon."

She set Lava down by the shore and waited for him to scurry away, but he didn't appear anxious to go anywhere. Lava just sat there, looking back and forth, before running up onto her shoe.

"I'm no Dr. Dolittle, but I'm pretty sure he's saying, 'take me with you,'" said Jesse.

And so Honey Bee gladly did. Honey Bee knew this wouldn't be the last time she would see Calico's Lagoon. She could already feel a sadness coming over her, knowing that she would miss this unmatched beauty until the day they returned. Honey Bee saw something that she thought was extremely odd. One of the sea turtles looked very unusual. She wasn't completely sure, but upon glancing at the turtle, she thought the creature had slippers on its feet and a seaweed necklace around its head.

"How oddly funny," she thought, wondering if her imagination was playing tricks on her.

Everyone followed Tinman up the spiraling staircase, leaving the splendor of Calico's Lagoon behind, at least for now. The return hike back through the rainforest went by quickly. By now, they were all feeling a little anxious to get back home.

Along the way they passed by the old ruins where they had stayed the night and steered clear of the bullkats. They followed the Ricochet River past many other places and landmarks familiar to and revered by them. The hike, for the most part, was uneventful. Well, as uneventful as the Roundabout Rainforest could possibly be.

Tinman's Jeep was still hidden away in the same spot where they had left it. Everyone, especially Tinman, was happy to see that it was unharmed.

Jesse and Boo rode shotgun as they drove out of the rainforest, heading toward their home in Tyrtle Town.

"How about we stop by the café on the way home?" said Tinman. "I could sure use something else to eat besides breakfast bars and canned ham."

Jesse smiled and said, "I can't believe I just heard you say that."

I could eat canned ham every meal. I don't see what's wrong with that, thought Boo.

The Jeep pulled into the large parking lot of the café. Honey Bee saw her papi and Caleb's Uncle Kai standing on the steps in front of the café doors.

"My mouth is watering just thinking about munching on a few of those Island Puffs," said Caleb, licking his lips.

He jumped out of the Jeep before it came to a full stop and waved as he ran right past his uncle. He crashed through the café doors, flinging them wide open.

"My thoughts exactly," said Tinman. "Let's go, Jesse."

"Give me a minute. Gotta feed Boo," said Jesse, rubbing Boo's belly.

Jesse watched as Honey Bee ran across the parking lot, gave her Papi and Uncle Kai big hugs, and then headed inside the café through the wooden doors carved with swimming sea turtles.

"Keeping Boo out of my garden?" asked a familiar voice behind them.

Shocked, Jesse turned around and said, "Mr. Jack, we thought you—"

Tinman quickly interrupted, saying, "We thought you made it out."

Mr. Jack had a smile on his face. "This is my daughter Natia," said Mr. Jack, giving her a kiss on the forehead. "Natia, why don't you go and order us some of those delicious chocolate Island Puffs?"

She smiled at Tinman and Jesse, then quickly ran up the café stairs.

Mr. Jack had a worried expression on his face as he said, "I need to ask a favor of you both. I would appreciate it if nobody mentioned that I was in the amphitheater."

With a look of grave concern, Jesse glanced over at Tinman.

"You see, I have my daughter to think of," said Mr. Jack. "I'm all she has, and she is all I have left."

Mr. Jack walked away from the Jeep toward the café.

Tinman and Jesse walked into the café and over to the table where Honey Bee and Caleb were sitting with Uncle Kai.

"Hey, isn't that Mr. Jack?" asked Uncle Kai. "Been awhile since I've seen him around. Who's that with him?"

"It's his daughter. His only daughter," said Tinman, looking at Honey Bee and Caleb's shocked faces.

"Hey, lucky I happen' to run into you guys," said Uncle Kai. "Jesse, I almost forgot. Professor Katnip asked me to give this to you." He reached into his pocket and handed Jesse a small dark bottle full of liquid. "He said you would know what it is. Looks like one of his special oils."

"What?" said Tinman, looking perplexed. "Professor Katnip?"

Caleb blurted out, "Professor Katnip is—"

Tinman stomped on Caleb's foot under the table and quickly interrupted, "Is a very generous man."

"Yes, yes, he is. In fact, he was just in here gettin' a cup of coffee," explained Uncle Kai. "As a matter of fact, he bought me a cup. He's a little odd. He kind of reminds me of a mad scientist, but he seems like a great guy."

"You have no idea," said Jesse, nervously looking at the bottle in his hand.

Uncle Kai had a look of uncertainty on his face and said, "Hey, well, gotta go. Duty calls."

Uncle Kai got up from the table and headed toward the exit, stopping just below the vintage tin coffee sign hanging above the doors.

The sign read: "Wake up and smell the coffee."

"Oh, by the way… I almost forgot," said Uncle Kai, turning around with a puzzled look on his face. "He also wanted me to let you all know that he was going sailing for a while, but to assure you he would be back soon."

The café doors creaked as they slowly closed behind Uncle Kai.

Jesse, Tinman, Honey Bee, and Caleb all sat around the wooden table in silence for a few seconds, stunned by the news of Professor Katnip.

"We have to let everyone know about the amphitheater," said Honey Bee.

"We can't," said Tinman. "If we tell them about the amphitheater and the professor's lab then they will find out about Mr. Jack. I can't do that to his daughter. Her life has already been difficult enough."

"The lab is gone," said Jesse. "We know that for certain. We saw it go up in flames."

"How about the bullkats?" asked Caleb nervously. "I saw some of them go up in flames."

Everyone knew there was no way of knowing how many, or if any, of the bullkats had survived the massive amphitheater fire, but they realized it certainly was a possibility.

The drive out of Tortoise Hills and through Bow Valley was a quiet one. Deep in thought, everyone reflected on the incredible island adventure they had just experienced. As they entered Tyrtle Town, Jesse looked out over the ocean along the west coast of the island and wondered if they had made the right decision concerning Mr. Jack and his daughter.

Jesse's mom was excited to see him walking through the grass with Boo at his side as she held open the screen door. She gave him a big hug and a kiss on the cheek, and said, "Jesse, I'm so glad you're home. I've missed you... and Boo too, of course. Another exciting adventure with Tinman?"

"This one was a little more exciting than usual," said Jesse. "Don't you agree, Boo?"

Boo let out a very strange, loud burbling sound. Smiling, Jesse and his mom quickly looked at Boo, but his mom's smile quickly turned to a frown.

"Boo seems to agree with you. What exactly did happen that was so exciting?" she inquired.

Jesse looked at her lovingly and said, "Oh, we just found some really cool caves."

"I think I'm going to have a talk with your uncle," she said. "By the way, Mr. Smitty, your boss, remember him? He wanted to check and make sure you would be at the paper route office in the morning. I told him you would."

After finishing his delicious fish dinner, Jesse gave his mom a good-night kiss and headed off to bed with Boo right behind him. Boo settled into his usual place at the foot of the bed. Jesse was exhausted from their adventure, and he easily fell asleep.

The next thing he heard was the goofy sound of his alarm going off, and he sat straight up in bed. He rubbed his eyes and sat there for a few minutes with a feeling that something was very different this morning. He felt Boo crawling up along his body and then plopping down on his pillow. He then realized why he had a strange feeling and what was missing. He remembered that for the first time in many nights, he didn't dream.

"Does this mean it's over?" he thought out loud, overcome by a feeling of sadness. He pictured the faces of his island dream friends and thought about how much he would miss them. If this was the end of his dream, did that also mean this was the end of the bullkats? Jesse looked into Boo's eyes and rubbed his cat's soft belly. He wished more than ever that he knew what Boo was thinking.

His mom cooked up his favorite breakfast of hummingbird pancakes smothered in island honey. Of course, the honey was made locally by Honey Bee's family. Jesse loved the taste of honey. What he loved the most about honey was that every time he tasted it, he was reminded of Honey Bee.

His morning routine of Boo's belly rubs, breakfast, and biking through the dark to the paper route office went by quickly.

Mr. Smitty wanted to talk to Jesse about the last few days, but Jesse was in a hurry and just thanked him for covering his route while he was gone. Jesse distracted Mr. Smitty by offering him another tempting Island Puff from the half-empty box sitting on the dusty table.

After finishing his route, Jesse pedaled past Mr. Jack's house and saw Mr. Jack in the garden with his daughter. Mr. Jack and Natia looked up when they heard the rattling of the bicycle coming down the street. Boo was sitting in the wooden box enjoying the view, and as they peddled by, Jesse waved at Mr. Jack and his smiling daughter. He knew at that moment they had made the right decision. He was glad they hadn't said anything to Uncle Kai about what happened in Kats Caves.

The rest of the morning and early afternoon couldn't pass by quickly enough for Jesse. He had already made plans to meet Honey Bee and Caleb at the cove later that afternoon. Fishing at the cove late in the afternoon was one of their favorite things to do together. The sun had begun to set behind the mountains to the west, casting a long shadow over the cove, turning the clear turquoise color of the water into a dark blue.

Jesse arrived at the cove shortly before his friends and sat down on his favorite rock with the least number of jagged edges poking at his backside. He stared out at the ocean, thinking about everything that happened during their last crazy adventure. He realized his incredible journey through his island dream helped them bring the professor's crazy plan to an end, and Tyrtle Island was safe, at least for now.

"Amazing," Jesse thought out loud.

"I know I am," giggled Honey Bee, sneaking up behind him.

She sat down next to Jesse, picked up Boo, plopping him onto her lap, and said, "Hey, big guy. And look at how amazingly big he is."

"He's a biggin alright!" said Jesse loudly and proudly.

"Better get the poles in the water. Sun's settin' quickly," said Caleb, arriving just after Honey Bee. "I don't want to go home empty-handed."

"Not a chance of that happening here," said Jesse, throwing his line in the water.

"Do you think we did the right thing?" asked Honey Bee, double-checking her conscience, which seemed to be getting the best of her.

"You know, I saw Mr. Jack with his daughter this morning, and they both looked very happy," said Jesse.

He reeled in his first fish of the afternoon and placed it in the cooler while Honey Bee watched him.

"I know how terrible this sounds, but I can't believe the professor made it out of there," she said.

"We should turn him in," said Caleb, grunting as he reached to pull his fish off his line. "I feel kind of bad. That's just the way I feel."

"Yes, you guys should feel bad," said Tinman, surprising them all as he walked up behind them. "You're all fishing and you didn't even invite me. I'm hurt."

Tinman smiled and slapped Jesse across the top of the head as he sat down on the other side of him.

Jesse smiled, glad to see his uncle. "I was pretty sure you would be here," he said.

"We can't turn him in," said Tinman.

"Who? Jesse for not inviting you fishing?" said Caleb, casting his line out again.

"That would only hurt Mr. Jack and his daughter. They need each other now more than ever," said Tinman.

Jesse thought about his island dream and said, "In my dream, Calico had a change of heart and was given a chance to change. He had the faith to go through the Tyrtle Tunnel and start a new life. Boo, Roxy Roo, and Chops accepted Calico into their family. I know in my heart that Mr. Jack should be given that same opportunity and we should accept him into the Tyrtle Island family."

They were all quiet for the next few minutes, thinking about Jesse's words as they reeled in one fish after another. Tinman prepared some of the fish with his secret island sauce recipe that he had borrowed from Jesse's mom. Boo watched, licking his lips as the delicious meal hanging in the middle of the fire pit cooked over the flames.

Jesse gazed out at the ocean, watching as the blue water sparkled across the waves. It reminded him of the amazing stone from Sparkling Caverns that had somehow found its way into his pocket.

Tinman's next words of wisdom really took Jesse by surprise. It was not so much what he said, but the timing of it. Jesse felt like this "Tinman's Tip" was either an incredible coincidence, or at this very moment, his uncle was actually reading his mind.

Tinman crouched next to the flames, stirring up the fire. "Just remember, your treasure is where your heart is," said Tinman. "Family, friends, and fresh fish. On this earth, that's the real treasure, and I hope none of you ever forget that."

I think it's fish, family, and friends. Yep, that's gotta be the correct order, thought Boo, his cat motor purring loudly as he gently rubbed against Jesse.

The red sparks from the fire were caught up in the island breeze and floated out over Fish Flop Cove. The glow disappeared as the sparks softly landed on the rippling water, glittering by the light of the moon.

"Now the million-dollar question," said Caleb. "Mr. Jack survived the fire, and it sounds like the professor survived the fire too. Do you think any bullkats made it out alive?"

"I doubt it. They were trapped at the back of the amphitheater by the massive fire," said Honey Bee. "I just don't see how they could've survived it."

"Last night, for the first time in many nights, I didn't dream," said Jesse. "Do you think that's a sign that the bullkats are all gone?"

"Honestly, I just don't know," said Tinman, handing Caleb the first cooked fish.

Boo's whiskers twitched as he concentrated on the fish cooking above the flames. His nostrils were filled with the savory scent, and his eyes watched as the shadows created by the flickering light cast an ever-changing wave of colors across the tropical terrain surrounding the cove. His eyes darted back and forth until he stopped and stared at a pair of eyes glowing in the darkness. Boo arched his back and flattened his ears as he peered into the eerie pair of yellow eyes staring back at him.

Boo hissed and then growled. *Bullkat!* he thought, leaping through the air.

tyrtle

TYRTLE ISLAND: LAND DESCRIPTIONS

Tyrtle Town: Home of Jesse Quinn, his cat Boo, and their island friends.

Land of the Meow Cats, also known as Treetop Woods: Island dream home of the Meow family of cats, along with many other curious creatures.

Bow Valley: Beautiful valley full of radiant rainbows and singing psalm trees, but beware of belly birds and strange-looking weemees.

Walkabout Wilderness: Desolate place where the feared bullkats can be encountered and Ferrel, the island's hermit cat, can be seen wandering around.

Land of Roundabout Rainforest: Land where Calico's amazing lagoon can be found and Hiya the "friendly" macaw talks away the day.

Land of To Fiddle About: Home of the pee-wee poppers and place where Meow cats will find some irresistible rainbow wobbler catnip plants.

Land of Three Peaks: The Three Peaks stand tall on the southeast side of Tyrtle Island as a symbol of the island's spirit.

Land of No End: Land where the natural lava-resembling landscape leads to the legendary Tyrtle Tunnel and Wiki Island.

Land of Wig Waggle: A place where you can find a monk seal lounging on the beach or dream about visiting the home of Silver and his family of Porky Porcupines.

tyrtle

TYRTLE ISLAND: CHARACTERS

Jesse Quinn: Jesse was born and raised on Tyrtle Island. He lives in Tyrtle Town with his mom, Kay Quinn. Jesse is a courageous teenage boy with a very active imagination. He has blondish-brown hair. Just like his cat Boo, Jesse loves any kind of adventure. Although, he never imagined that his island dreams would somehow allow him to experience these adventures as a cat. Not just any ordinary cat, though: Jesse sees everything in his Island dreams through the eyes of Boo.

Honey Bee or Bee: Honey Bee is Jesse Quinn's best friend. She lives with her parents on their farm in Tyrtle Town. This kind-hearted girl with brown eyes and long brown hair has a "Tomboy" personality. Honey Bee, just like Jesse, is always ready for the next adventure. Honey Bee, or Bee for short, is like her island dream creature Roxy Roo in personality, character and spirit.

Caleb: Very loyal friend of Jesse and Honey Bee. Caleb grew up with Jesse and Honey Bee in Tyrtle Town. Caleb has green eyes, wavy brown hair, and a thick, muscular build. Caleb's personality is just like his island dream creature Chops. He's big-hearted with a funny personality and an inclination to be a little clumsy.

Uncle Tinman: Tinman is Jesse's uncle and adventure buddy. To Jesse, Tinman is as close to a real-life superhero as you can get. Tinman was born and raised on Tyrtle Island, and lives by the spirit of Tyrtle Island. This laid-back uncle has hazel-colored eyes and a slender, muscular build. Tinman is also known for offering unsolicited advice and his love for canned ham.

Professor Katnip: The professor is a well-known science teacher, botanist and avid gardener. He is also well known for his love of creating catnip and herbal tea recipes, along with some rare essential oils. Professor Katnip the science teacher and Professor Katnip the Meow cat are two peas in a pod.

Mr. Jack, also known as "Crackerjack": This old islander has an unnerving physical presence and nasty disposition. Mr. Jack is similar to his dream creature, Bones the Meow cat. They both have creepy looks and scary dispositions. Mr. Jack, just like Bones, has a mysterious past and holds some island secrets close. Old Crackerjack has a daughter named Natia.

Kay Quinn: Jesse Quinn's warmhearted mom, who is known around the island for her famous recipes, including her hummingbird pancakes.

Axle Quinn: Jesse Quinn's dad, who is a renowned archeologist. Axle Quinn left Tyrtle Island several years ago to join a group of notable scientists and archeologists on a dig in an undisclosed location. Jesse and his family still have faith that one day his dad will return to Tyrtle Island.

Mr. Smitty: Jesse's friendly boss at the paper route office. Mr. Smitty has a love for baseball and any kind of island pastries.

Uncle Kai: Caleb's uncle who is also a police officer on Tyrtle Island.

Natia: Mr. Jack's daughter, who is hoping this time her father makes the right decision.

tyrtle

TYRTLE ISLAND: CREATURES

Boo the Cat: Boo is a very large domesticated cat and Jesse Quinn's best furry friend. He has long whiskers, big orange paws, and a muscular orange body with black and brown stripes and a white underbelly. This amazing cat looks similar to a baby Bengal tiger. Although Boo is larger than the average-sized domesticated cat, he is smaller in size than the dreamy Meow cats. Boo's character tends to be confident, calm, and friendly.

Boo the Meow Cat: Boo the Meow cat lives in Treetop Woods, along with his friends Roxy Roo and Chops. Boo's wild looks can be described as a cross between a Bengal tiger and a striped domestic shorthair cat. Meow cats are larger than domesticated cats, and all Meow cats have very large, colorful eyes. Boo the Meow cat's appearance and character is similar to Boo the domesticated cat. This Meow cat also has a collection of signature scarfs he likes to wear.

Roxy Roo the Meow Cat: Roxy Roo is Boo's best friend. They have known each other since they were kittens. Roxy Roo is a beautiful Meow cat with white whiskers and brown eyes. Her fur is light brown with dark brown stripes and a white underbelly, followed by a long brown tail. Roxy Roo has a beautiful-sounding singing meow and a magical way with all the island creatures.

Chops the Meow cat: Loyal feline friend of Boo and Roxy Roo. This big gray cat has white stripes and a short, stubby tail. Chops is a big-hearted cat with a funny personality and an inclination to be a little clumsy. He also has a big appetite that's been known to get him in trouble.

Silver the Porky Porcupine: Silver is a very proud porky porcupine. This unusual porcupine has a porcupine mate and two little porkies. Silver and his family live in the Land of Wig Waggle. Similar to Tinman's leg braces, Silver has a tin-tipped tail. Silver is very articulate and also has a love for any kind of delicious tree bark. The porky porcupines struggle to protect their homeland from invading bullkats has long been documented throughout Tyrtle Island history.

Professor Katnip the Meow Cat: Professor Katnip lives in Treetop Woods inside one of the most exotic treehouses in the Land of the Meow cats. The professor is the creator of many famous catnip recipes, catnip teas, and other exotic island oils. To many cats and creatures on the island, the variety of catnip plants are by far the most valuable commodity. Some island creatures will do anything to keep the source of these valuable and rare plants a secret.

Bullkats: Once thought to be extinct, these creatures have been seen roaming around Tyrtle Island and in Jesse's dreams. Bullkats are scary creatures with eerie yellow eyes and bone-white horns that glow. Their sharp horns are concealed inside their ears and can only be revealed in the dark. These hideous creatures have disfigured bodies and mangy-looking fur coats covered with battle scars. They have pointy tails that can be used like whips to inflict pain on their victims. Most bullkats are smaller than the average Meow cats and about the same size as a domesticated cat.

Bones the Meow Cat: Like Mr. Jack, this scary-looking Meow cat has an unnerving appearance and nasty disposition. Bones has a mysterious past and knows some closely held island secrets. Some island creatures say that, long ago, Bones was the creature that led the bullkat rebellion across Tyrtle Island.

Calico the Bullkat: Calico is a different kind of bullkat in appearance and personality. This good-natured bullkat has orange and black patches across his white fur coat. He hopes that one day he can find a way to break the bullkat curse. Calico hopes to discover the truth about the legend of the Tyrtle Tunnel and Wiki Tyrtle.

Skin the Bullkat: The most feared and ferocious bullkat. Skin is notoriously known for leading the bullkats into many island battles. His name alone can make island creatures tremble.

Hiya the Macaw: Very talkative macaw that lives in a giant mangrove tree growing on the side of a cliff on the northwest side of the Roundabout Rainforest. It's very strange that this macaw or one very similar to him has been living in the same treehouse for a very, very long time.

Wiki Tyrtle: Very cool and wise old Tyrtle. Some islanders claim the island's name originated with Wiki Tyrtle. The word wiki means to quickly reveal all island knowledge, wisdom, and truth. The legend of Wiki Tyrtle speaks of the mythical Tyrtle Tunnel and the Island of Wiki.

Wacky Tyrtle: Wiki Tyrtle's goofy-looking brother. He may sound and look goofy, but he's a Tyrtle and therefore very wise.

Ferrel the Hermit Cat: Ferrel wanders around the island carrying his shell-shaped home on his back. He's similar to a Meow cat with the exception that he loves to talk in rhyme and lives in dirt and grime. He's sort of a legend on Tyrtle Island, and according to some, he has been around since the beginning of island time.

Growlin and Howlin the Bulldogs: Two grouchy bulldogs that live deep in the forest of Bow Valley. The bulldogs are identical in almost every way, especially when it comes to throwing out non-stop insults and bad jokes.

Big-toed Bugger: A big-toed bugger resembles a sloth. Big-toed buggers are large in size, covered in very stinky matted hair, and of course have two very big toes on each foot with two large claws. They have very large, long noses and little tiny eyes popping out of their coconut-shaped heads. The island legend speaks of good and bad big-toed buggers. This is bad news for big-toed buggers and sad news for Jesse and his friends, because today on Tyrtle Island, these creatures only exist in Jesse's island dreams. But like many legends, some islanders claim to have spotted big-toed buggers.

Belly birds: These birds once flourished on Tyrtle Island and are now thought to be extinct, but very much alive in Jesse's dream. These lovable-looking birds have no legs and no feet. Belly Birds appear to be harmless with their cute and colorful faces, but they do possess very sharp beaks.

Rarely do these birds land on the ground, but when they do, all they are able to do is wobble back and forth until they can flap their tiny wings fast enough to take off again. If an islander happens to see a flock of birds resembling Belly Birds they are advised to take cover.

Briar Bow, Briar Bee and Briar Bud - Porky Porcupines: Silver's family of porky porcupines. Briar Bow is Silver's porky-mate. Briar Bee and Briar Bud are their little porcupine porkies.

Unicorn Butterflies: Gigantic rainbow-colored butterflies that live in Kats Caves. These fantastic creatures have pearl-white spiral horns protruding from the center of their heads. These unbelievable butterflies have over-sized wings splattered with the colors of the rainbow.

Pee-Wee Poppers: These little green geckos make their home in the Land of To Fiddle About. Poppers spend their day popping up and down from one rainbow wobbler plant to another, nibbling on the sweet nectar. Their popping from plant to plant causes the colorful plants to wobble back and forth, which is how the plant got its name.

Weemees: Weemee creatures can be seen hopping from limb to limb across the canopy of trees throughout Bow Valley. In the beginning, these creatures were so strange-looking that nobody on the island knew what to call them. Eventually, the creatures' name became known as "weemee." Weemees look scary, but for the most part, they are harmless creatures. These creepy-looking creatures have no teeth and live on a diet of yummy tubbieworms.

Harry, Harriet and Henry: Meow cat elders and friends of Bones and Professor Katnip.

Firebugs: Glowing black bugs that fly around, dancing in pairs. These incredible insects can be found flying throughout Bow Valley.

Bullflies: Black annoying flies that can usually be found buzzing around bullkats, which is how the pesky insects got their name.

Giant Bullfrogs: Very large bullfrogs that live in the Roundabout Rainforest. These lovable amphibians have a very, very loud croak, especially during mating season when they are serenading after dark.

Hummingbird Moths: These magnificent moths move their wings at incredible speeds as they zip from flower to flower. They beat their wings over a thousand times per second as they hover over a flower, sucking on the sweet nectar.

Lava the Cave Gecko: Lava is a very large gecko, measuring about ten inches long. This lovable lizard is black with yellow stripes and blood-red eyes.

H-Bees: H-bees look very similar to honey bees, although they do have a perfect H-shaped marking on their backs. However, H-bees are not really a bee at all. They're actually a drone fly.

Green Sea Creature: The legend of the green sea creature has been passed down through the ages by islanders who claim to have seen the prehistoric sea animal surfacing around the island. Some islanders believe the creature is protecting something hidden deep below the island in the underwater caverns.

Lava Monster: The lava monster might be a creature that only lives in Jesse's imagination, but one can only know for sure if they dare to explore the maze of lava tubes far below Tyrtle Island.

tyrtle

TYRTLE ISLAND: PLACES AND POINTS OF INTEREST

Amphitheater: A massive cavern far below Kats Caves and only accessible through a maze of lava tubes.

Bullkat Bay: Rocky bay on the east side of the island situated between Land of No End and Land of Three Peaks.

Cat Skull Rock: Huge rock located in Bow Valley that is used by the Meow cats for shelter on their adventure.

Calico's Cave: A cave located in Walkabout Wilderness that is home to Calico the bullkat.

Calico's Lagoon: A hidden lagoon in the Roundabout Rainforest that is full of sea turtles and other amazing sea creatures. The lagoon has a passageway through Coral Way Cave that leads out to Coral Way Bay. The lagoon is hidden by towering rock walls shaped like the petals of a flower.

Coral Way Cave: Passageway under the massive rock wall surrounding Calico's Lagoon. This tunnel allows sea turtles to swim from Coral Way Bay to the underwater coral reef gardens in Calico's Lagoon.

Fish Flop Cove: In real life and in the island dream, this paradise is the favorite fishing spot of Boo and his friends.

Island Café: Coffee house and café owned by Honey Bee's parents that's nestled in the town of Tortoise Hills. The family makes and sells local honey and homegrown fresh brewed coffee. Her parents love honey and honey bees so much that they could not imagine naming their daughter any other name but Honey Bee.

Kats Caves: Located on the east side of the island, this maze of caves, caverns and lava tubes runs deep down below the island into the lava monster's abyss. This gloomy place is the home of the feared bullkats, and in Jesse's imaginative mind, it's also the home of the lava monster.

Marshmallow Lighthouse & Trail: Lilac-covered trail that's home to the H-Bees and leads to the Marshmallow Lighthouse.

Majestic Mountains: Located along the northern coast, the Majestic Mountains are the highest on the island. This majestic range is also the home of the lovable-looking but carnivorous belly birds.

Meow Mountains: Mountain range along the southern coast of the island where Cat Skull Rock is located.

Old Fort: Jesse and his friends meet at the old fort which some islanders believe long ago was called the Pouncing Place.

Ricochet River: A river that zigzags through the rainforest and flows south toward the cliffs, emptying into the Loud Ocean.

Sparkling Caverns: Located deep within Kats Caves, these caverns are filled with surprises.

The Pouncing Place, also known as the PP: Located in the Land of the Meow Cats, the Pouncing Place is the long-time gathering place of the Meow cats.

Tyrtle Town: A small town on the southwest side of Tyrtle Island and the home of Jesse Quinn, Boo, Uncle Tinman, Honey Bee, and Caleb. Tyrtle Town is known for its large cat population. Some islanders claim that Tyrtle Town is located in the same area as the ancient place that was once known as the Land of the Meow Cats and that many of the cats are descendants of the Meow family of cats.

Tortoise Hills: Located between the Meow Mountains and Bow Valley, this quaint town is home to many of Tyrtle Island's butterfly and botanical gardens. One of the Islander's favorite destinations, the Island Café, can also be found in this old-fashioned island town.

Tyrtle Tunnel: The mythical passageway that leads to Wiki Island and the legendary Wiki Tyrtle. According to the island legend, the first tales of creatures traveling through the Tyrtle Tunnel began long ago during the great battle that took place in the Land of No End.

Wiki Island: The legendary Wiki Island is the home of Wiki and Wacky Tyrtle along with many other island dream sea creatures.

Yogi Falls: This little town is located along the north central coast at the base of the Majestic Mountains. A short drive up from Coral Way Bay road will take you to the edge of a lush jungle. Yogi Trail will lead you through a tropical landscape until you reach a clear pool of water at the base of the falls. Standing atop the huge boulders, you can gaze at the towering waterfall cascading down from the mountain ridge.

tyrtle

TYRTLE ISLAND: PLANTS AND FOOD

Catnip Plants: Catnip is an herb that is a member of the mint family and has a "go crazy" effect on most cats. Catnip is nonaddictive and completely harmless to cats.

Honey-heart Melons: A sweet-tasting, heart-shaped watermelon that grows in the forests of Bow Valley. The melons are red with black dots that look like seeds on top and green around the sides and underneath. When found, this refreshing treat will satisfy any creature's thirst and hunger.

Island Puffs: Sweet donut pastries made at the Island Café.

Jellyfish Plants: Colorful twirling plants with long colorful tails. These amazing plants come to life in Calico's Lagoon. When the island breeze is just right, they are caught up in the air and lifted up over the top of the lagoon walls, eventually sailing across the island and over the Loud Ocean.

Psalm Trees: Exotic trees that actually play songs of praise by scooping up the wind with their many tubular branches and funneling the air toward the top of the trees through the horned-shaped ends. This process produces a symphony of angelic songs that can be heard echoing along the mountain walls of Bow Valley.

Recoil Oil: Rainbow plants can be processed into an essential oil called recoil oil. Recoil oil, depending on how potent the blend of the oil is, can be deadly to all cats, including bullkats. This deadly oil was given the name "recoil" because it causes any person or creature that has an encounter with a bullkat that has been given the potent oil to suddenly spring back or "recoil" in fear.

Rainbow Plants: These are the most potent and rarest of all catnip plants found on Tyrtle Island. They can only be found somewhere in the Round-about Rainforest. When made into a special oil, the rainbow plants can be deadly to most creatures, including bullkats.

Rainbow Wobblers: A colorful and delicious plant located in The Land of To Fiddle About. Rainbow wobblers were named with the help of little green geckos called poppers. Poppers jump up and down on the flowering plants, causing them to wobble back and forth.

Scaredy-cat Plants: Scaredy-cat plants are lavender plants disliked by most cats, including bullkats. Tinman had an encounter with bullkats when he was young and used lavender plants to scare away the bullkats. It's for that reason he gave lavender plants the nickname "scaredy-cat plants."

tyrtle

TYRTLE ISLAND: WORDS AND PHRASES

A few jellies in your bellies always makes the day a little less smelly: The magic of jelly beans and a small act of kindness are sure to brighten up anyone's day.

Akaw Akaw: Unknown to modern day surfers, this stoked surfing term was originated by Hiya the macaw.

Bullkat-Crush: When a bullkat comes rushing out of a lava tube, crushing a creature.

Cats always do what they want to do, when they want to do it, always: This is a simple phrase to describe all cats and how they behave.

Excuses are like litter boxes, they all stink: Conquer your fears and excuses, and see your dreams come to life.

Home is where the Tyrtles are: The sound of water is calming, the feel of water is relaxing, and when we gaze out at the water, just like Tyrtles, we feel like we're home.

Hot-Lava Happiness: That feeling of excitement that is so strong it runs through your veins like hot lava pouring into the ocean.

Just remember, lies are like a litter box: If you don't come clean, then you'll eventually start to stink: Be honest with yourself and others. It's the right thing to do and it just makes life easier.

Keep Calm and Tyrtle on: This is the Tyrtle Island mantra.

Think Happy Thoughts, get a belly free of knots: Like most creatures on Tyrtle Island, try and think about happy things and your whole body will start to sing.

Tinman's Tips: Simple advice from someone that cares about you.

Tyrtles: Since the first inhabitants of Tyrtle Island arrived, the turtle symbolized "the spirit of love in motion" for the Islanders. They wanted to emulate that same spirit and have referred to themselves as Tyrtles ever since.

Made in the USA
Columbia, SC
09 July 2021

41496655R00176